Solomon's Thieves

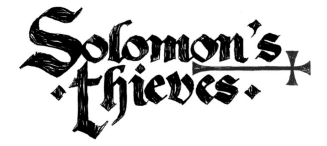

First Second

New York & London

Solomon's Thieves

Book One

Jordan Mechner

Artwork by LeUyen Pham

& Alex Puvilland

Color by Hilary Sycamore

From humble beginnings the Knights Templar rose to become the most powerful military monastic order of the medieval world.

Pledged to protect pilgrims during the Crusades, the Templars became heroes to Christians everywhere. Their fighting prowess was legendary. The sight of their white cloaks and red crosses inspired the faithful and struck terror into their enemies. Young men rushed to join the Order, taking vows of poverty, chastity, and obedience to fight for God.

By the thirteenth century the Order commanded thousands of men, ships, and castles in every country in Europe. Considered untouchable, the Templars owed allegiance to no king—only to the Pope himself.

But the Crusades were an expensive, blood-soaked failure. In 1291, after two centuries of warfare, the Muslims drove the Christian armies from the Holy Land once and for all.

For the Templars, it was the beginning of the end. . . .

1. The Fall

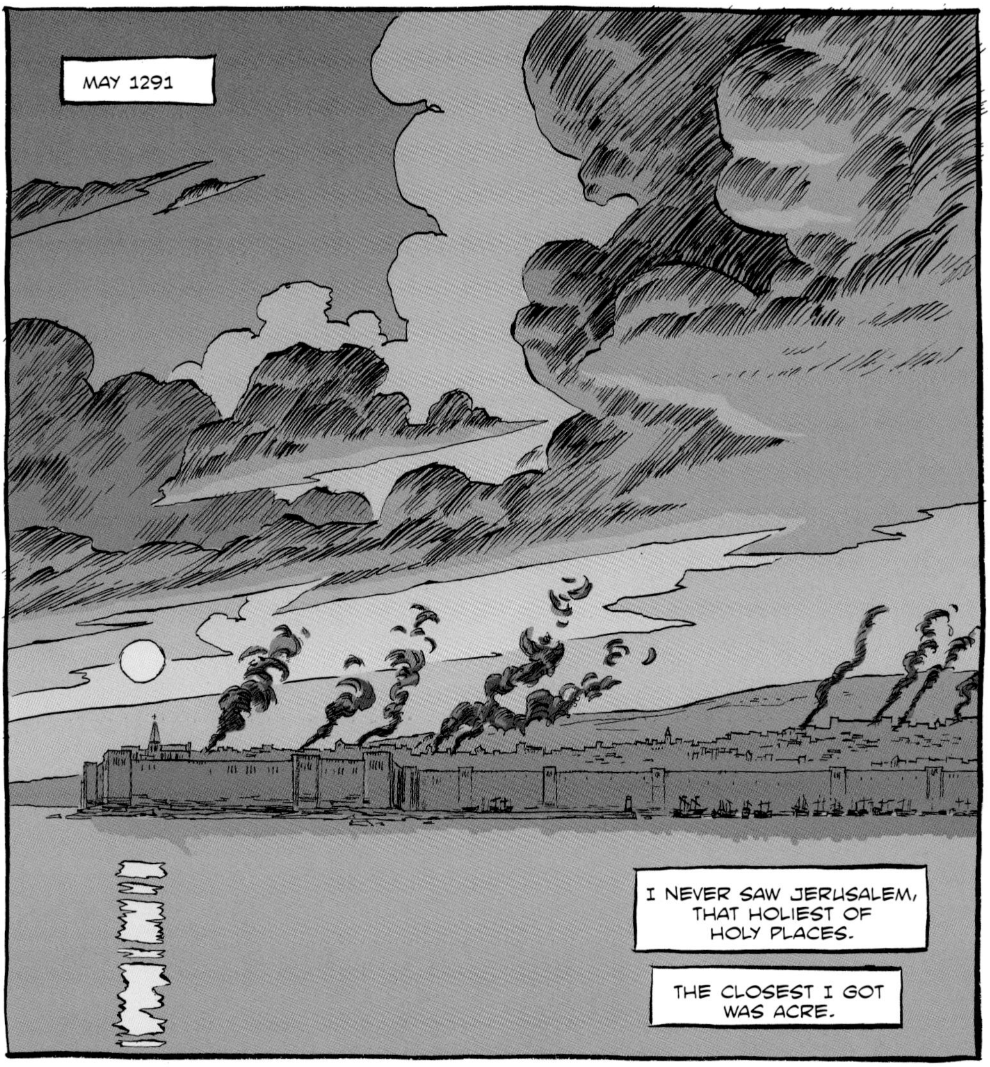
MAY 1291
I NEVER SAW JERUSALEM, THAT HOLIEST OF HOLY PLACES.
THE CLOSEST I GOT WAS ACRE.

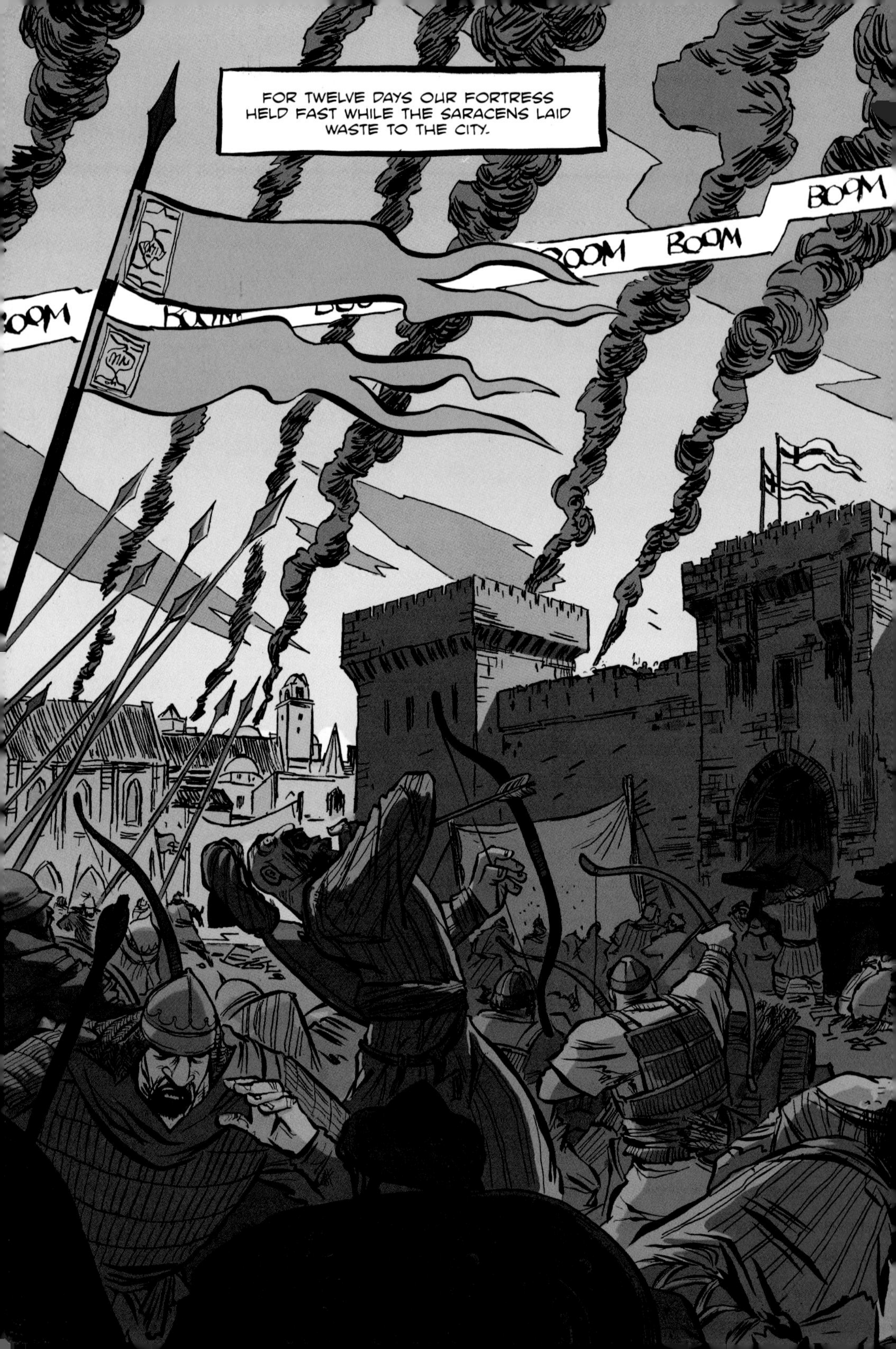
FOR TWELVE DAYS OUR FORTRESS HELD FAST WHILE THE SARACENS LAID WASTE TO THE CITY.
BOOM
BOOM
BOOM
BOOM

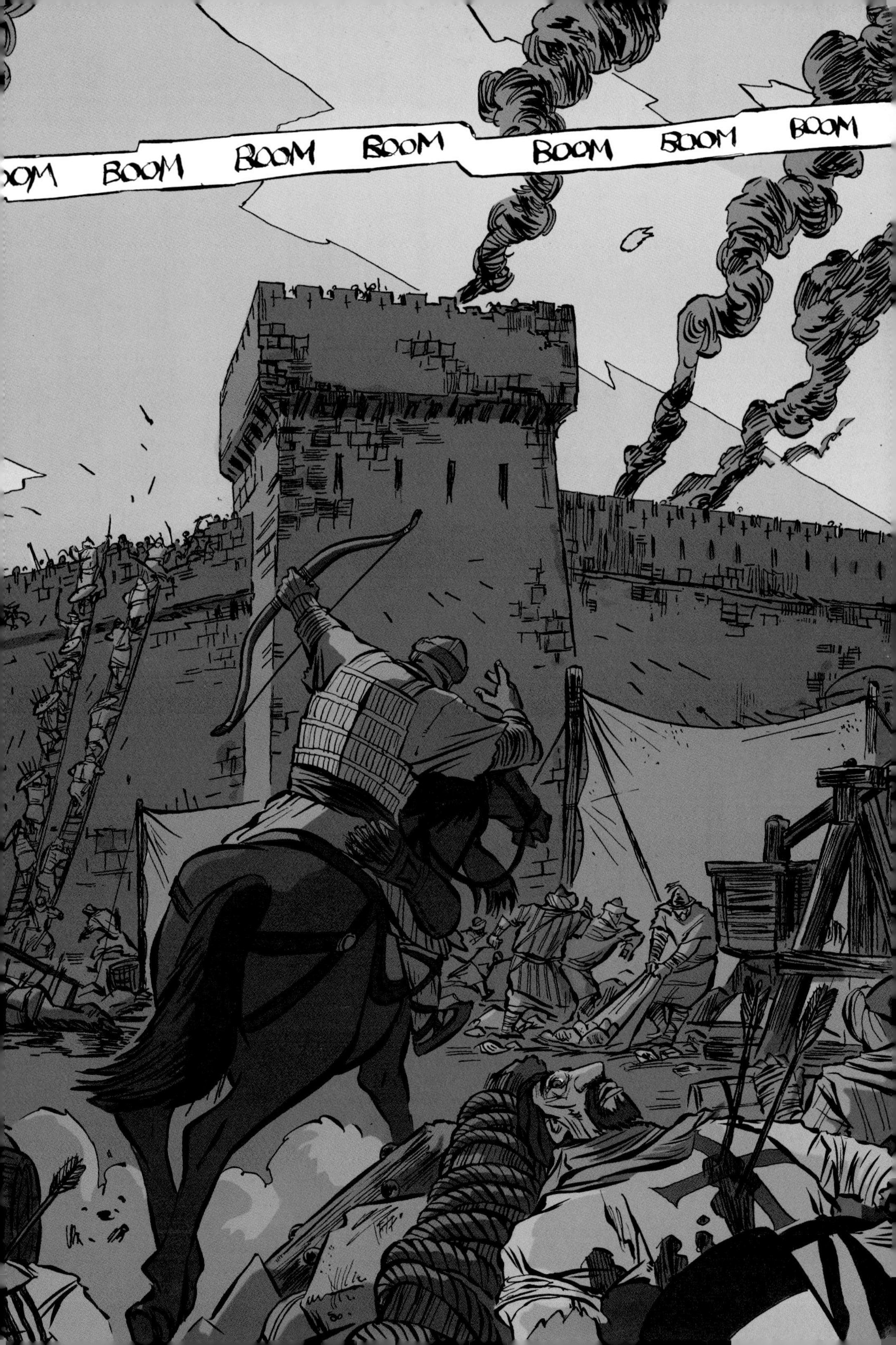
BOOM
BOOM
BOOM
BOOM
BOOM
BOOM
BOOM

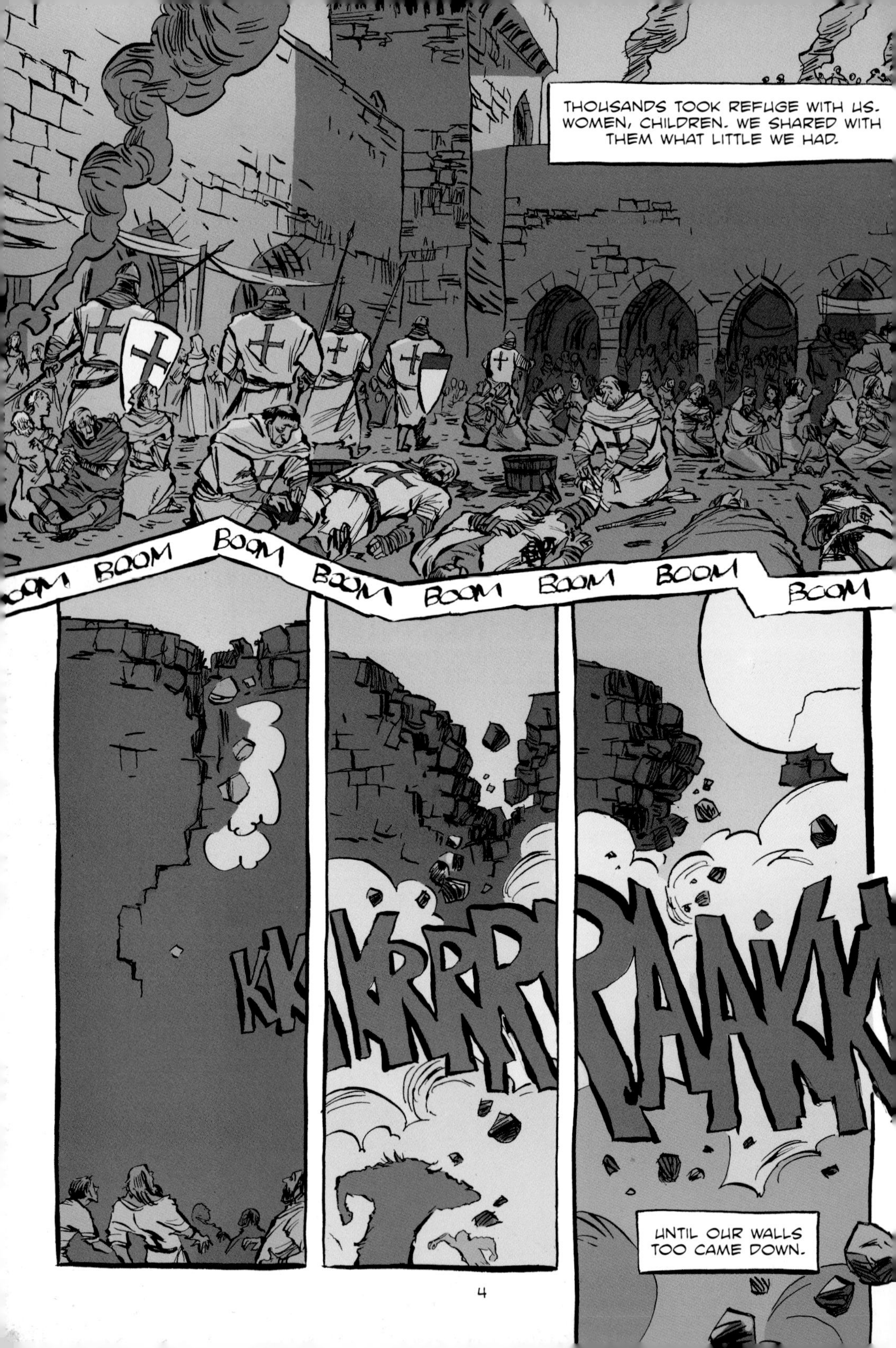

THOUSANDS TOOK REFUGE WITH US. WOMEN, CHILDREN. WE SHARED WITH THEM WHAT LITTLE WE HAD.
BOOM BOOM BOOM BOOM BOOM BOOM BOOM BOOM
KKRRRRAAKK
UNTIL OUR WALLS TOO CAME DOWN.

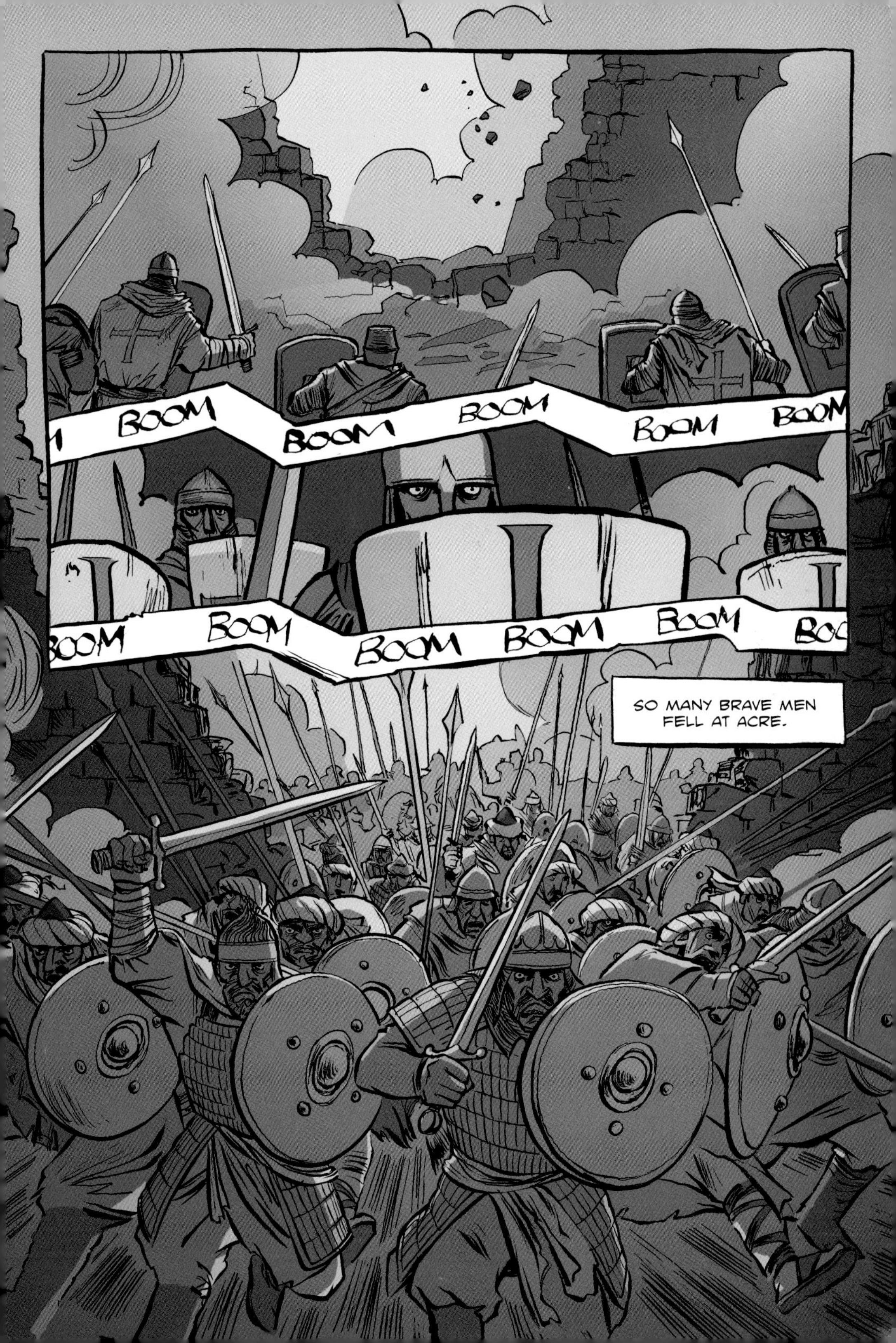
BOOM
BOOM
BOOM
BOOM
BOOM
BOOM
BOOM
BOOM
BOOM
SO MANY BRAVE MEN FELL AT ACRE.

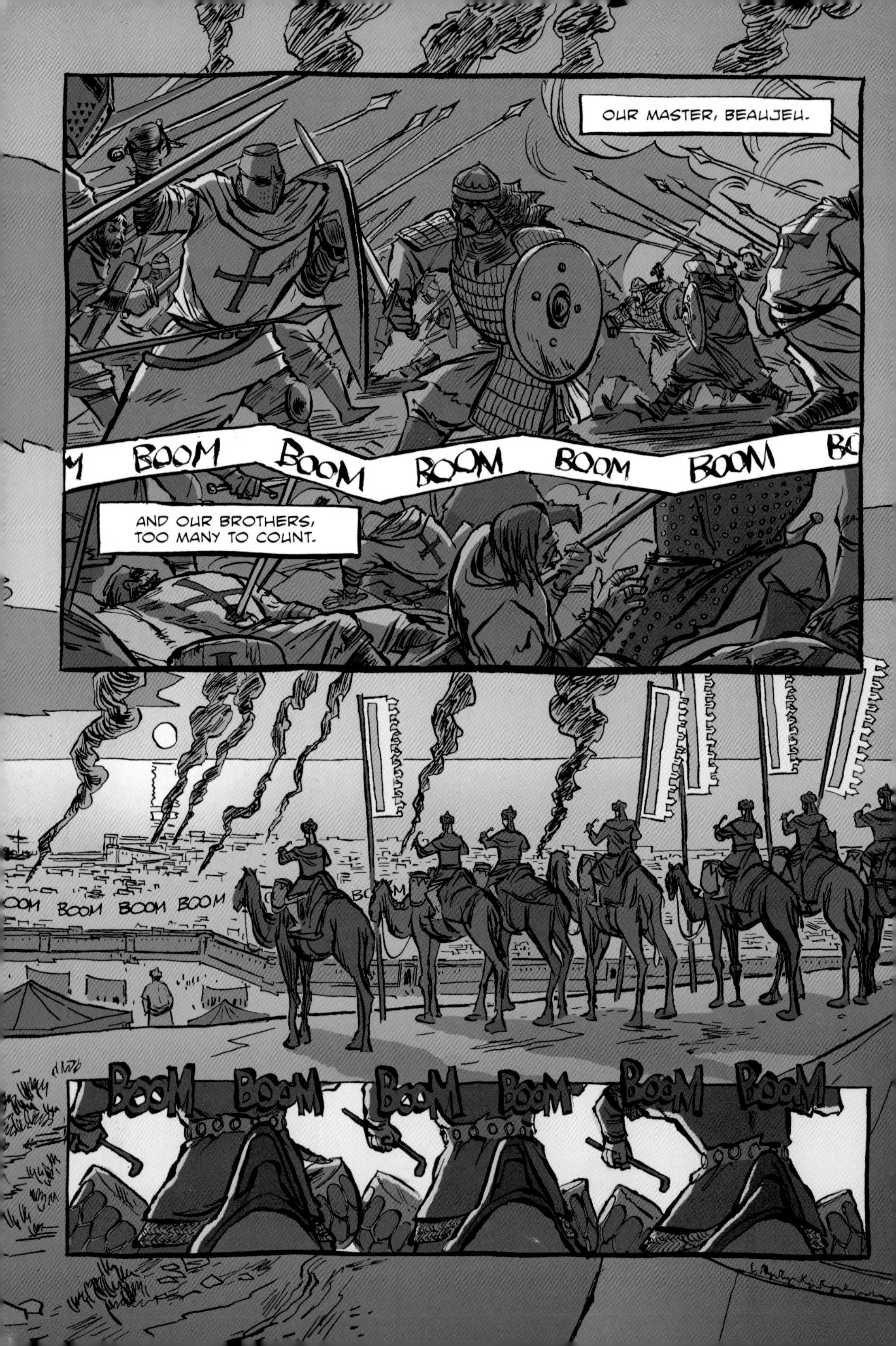
OUR MASTER, BEAUJEU.
BOOM BOOM BOOM BOOM BOOM
AND OUR BROTHERS, TOO MANY TO COUNT.
BOOM BOOM BOOM BOOM
BOOM BOOM BOOM BOOM BOOM BOOM

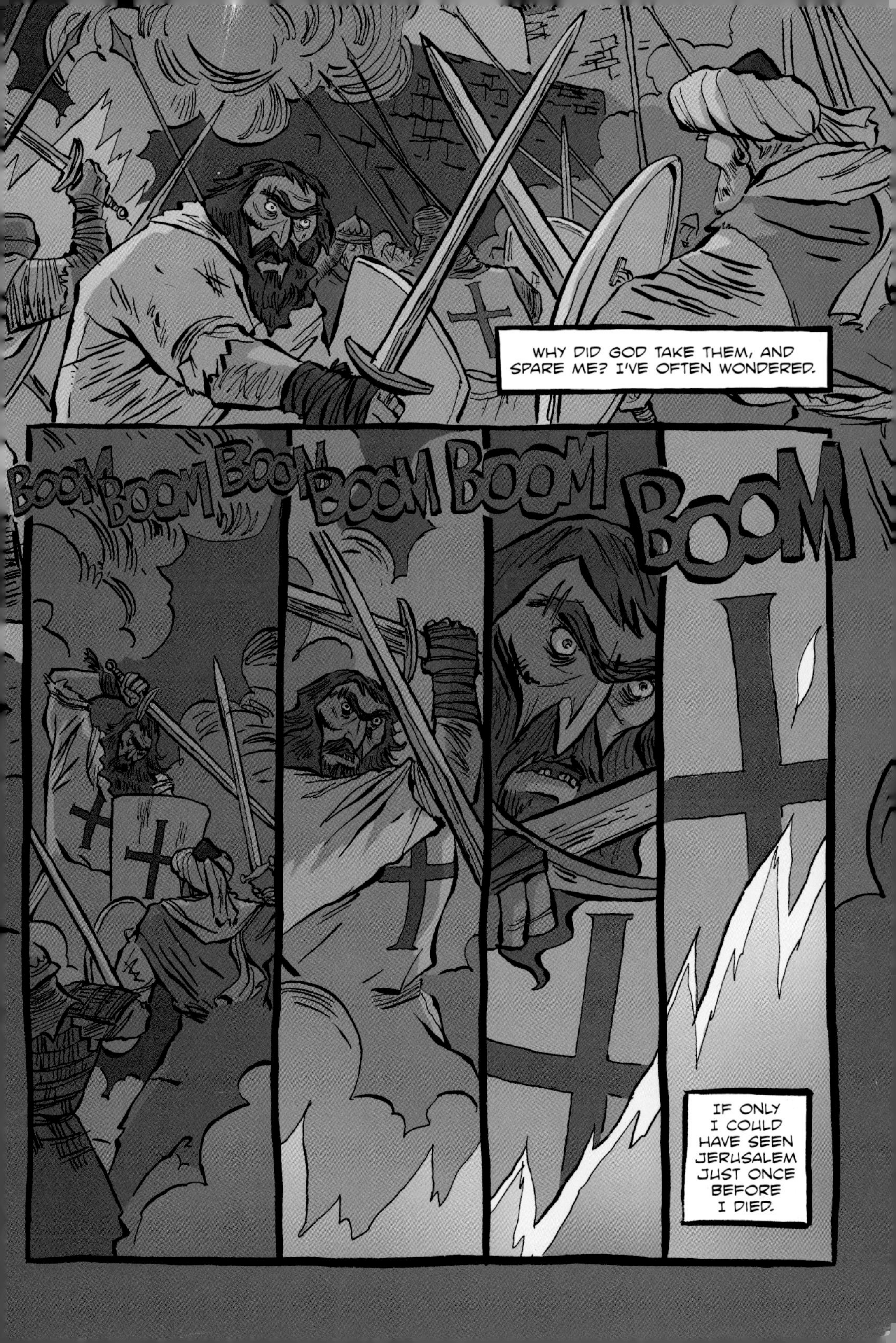
WHY DID GOD TAKE THEM, AND SPARE ME? I'VE OFTEN WONDERED.
BOOM BOOM BOOM BOOM BOOM BOOM
IF ONLY I COULD HAVE SEEN JERUSALEM JUST ONCE BEFORE I DIED.

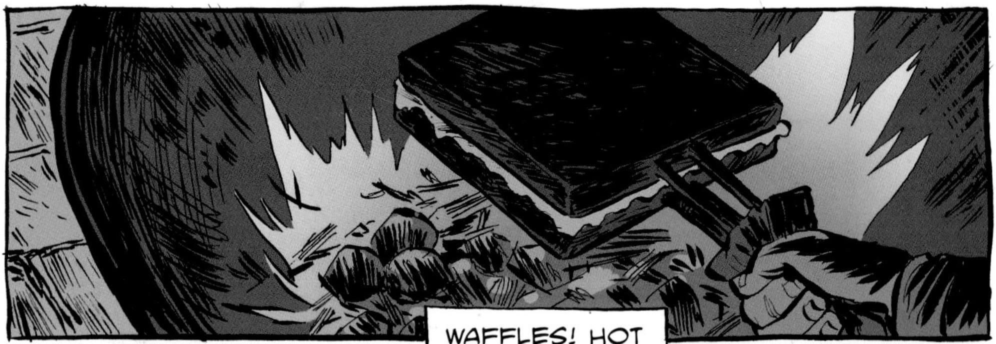

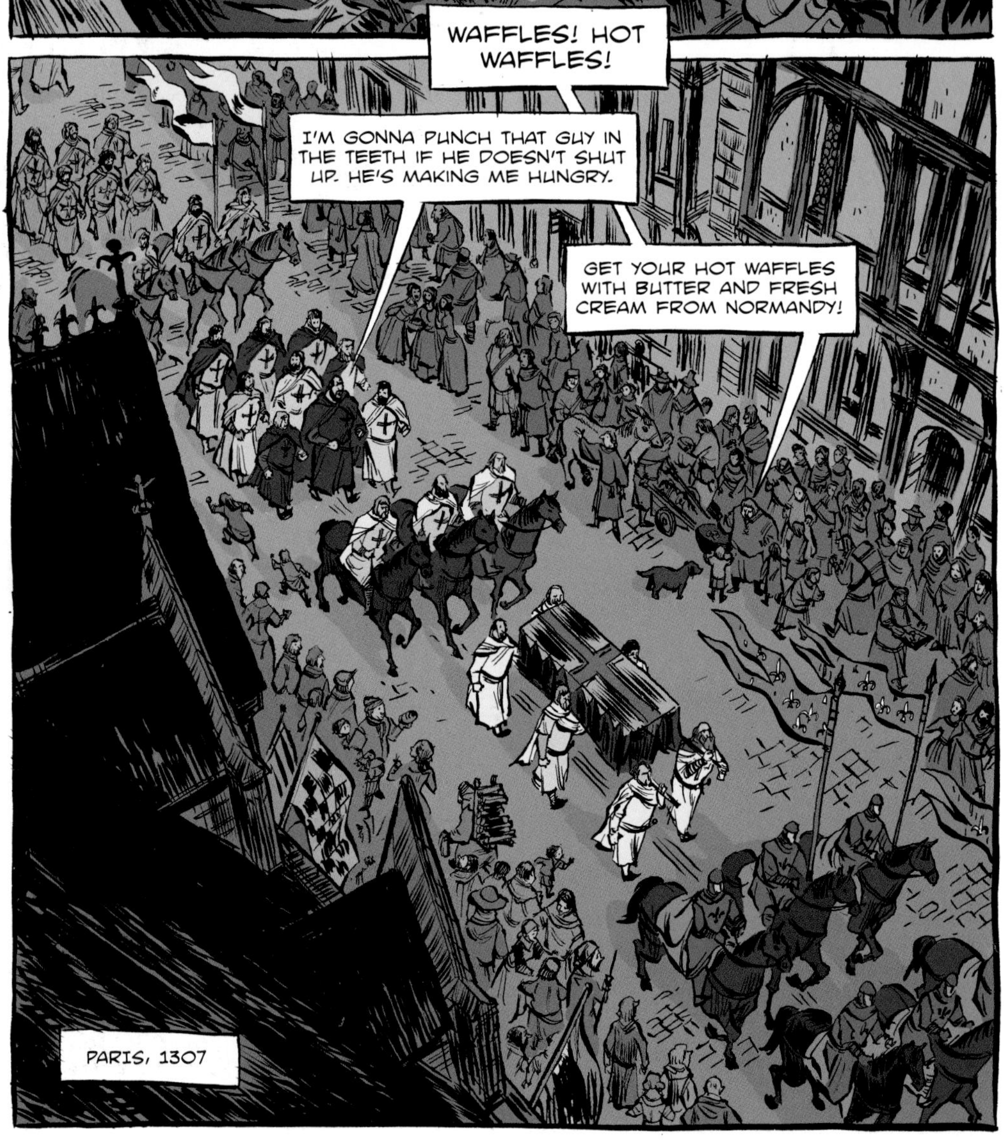
WAFFLES! HOT WAFFLES!
I'M GONNA PUNCH THAT GUY IN THE TEETH IF HE DOESN'T SHUT UP. HE'S MAKING ME HUNGRY.
GET YOUR HOT WAFFLES WITH BUTTER AND FRESH CREAM FROM NORMANDY!
PARIS, 1307

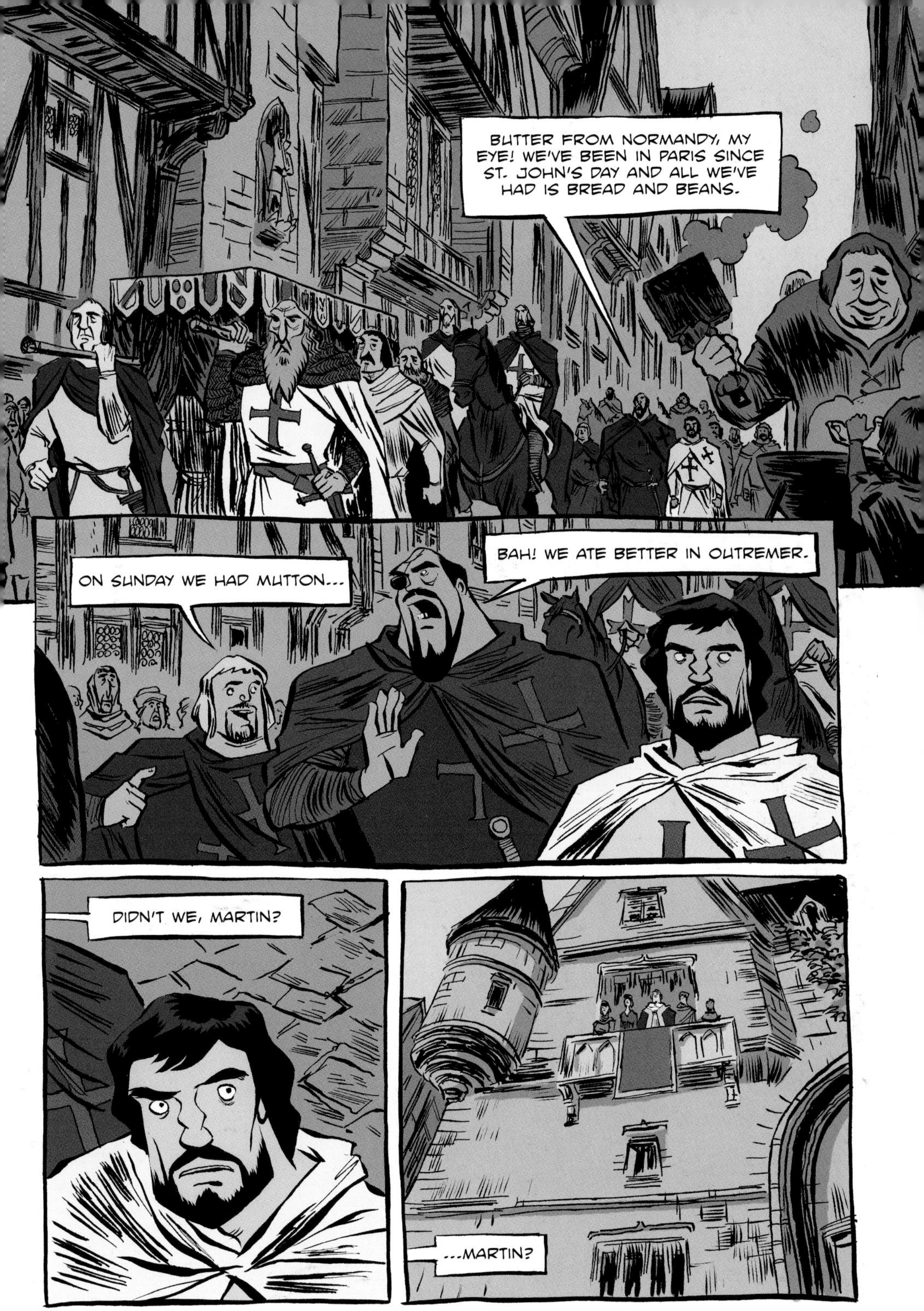

BUTTER FROM NORMANDY, MY EYE! WE'VE BEEN IN PARIS SINCE ST. JOHN'S DAY AND ALL WE'VE HAD IS BREAD AND BEANS.
ON SUNDAY WE HAD MUTTON...
BAH! WE ATE BETTER IN OUTREMER.
DIDN'T WE, MARTIN?
...MARTIN?

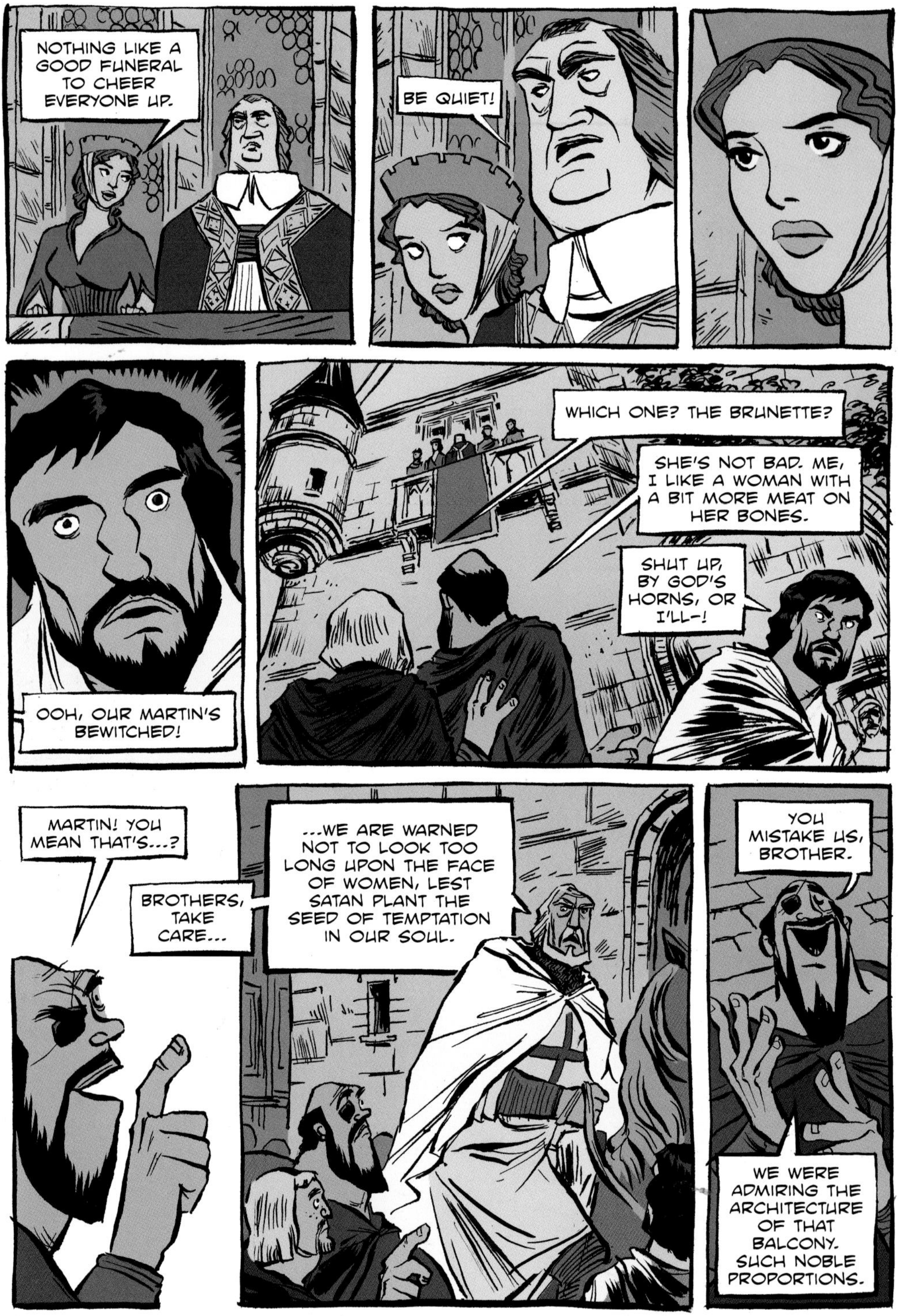
NOTHING LIKE A GOOD FUNERAL TO CHEER EVERYONE UP.
BE QUIET!
OOH, OUR MARTIN'S BEWITCHED!
WHICH ONE? THE BRUNETTE?
SHE'S NOT BAD. ME, I LIKE A WOMAN WITH A BIT MORE MEAT ON HER BONES.
SHUT UP, BY GOD'S HORNS, OR I'LL--!
MARTIN! YOU MEAN THAT'S...?
BROTHERS, TAKE CARE...
...WE ARE WARNED NOT TO LOOK TOO LONG UPON THE FACE OF WOMEN, LEST SATAN PLANT THE SEED OF TEMPTATION IN OUR SOUL.
YOU MISTAKE US, BROTHER.
WE WERE ADMIRING THE ARCHITECTURE OF THAT BALCONY. SUCH NOBLE PROPORTIONS.

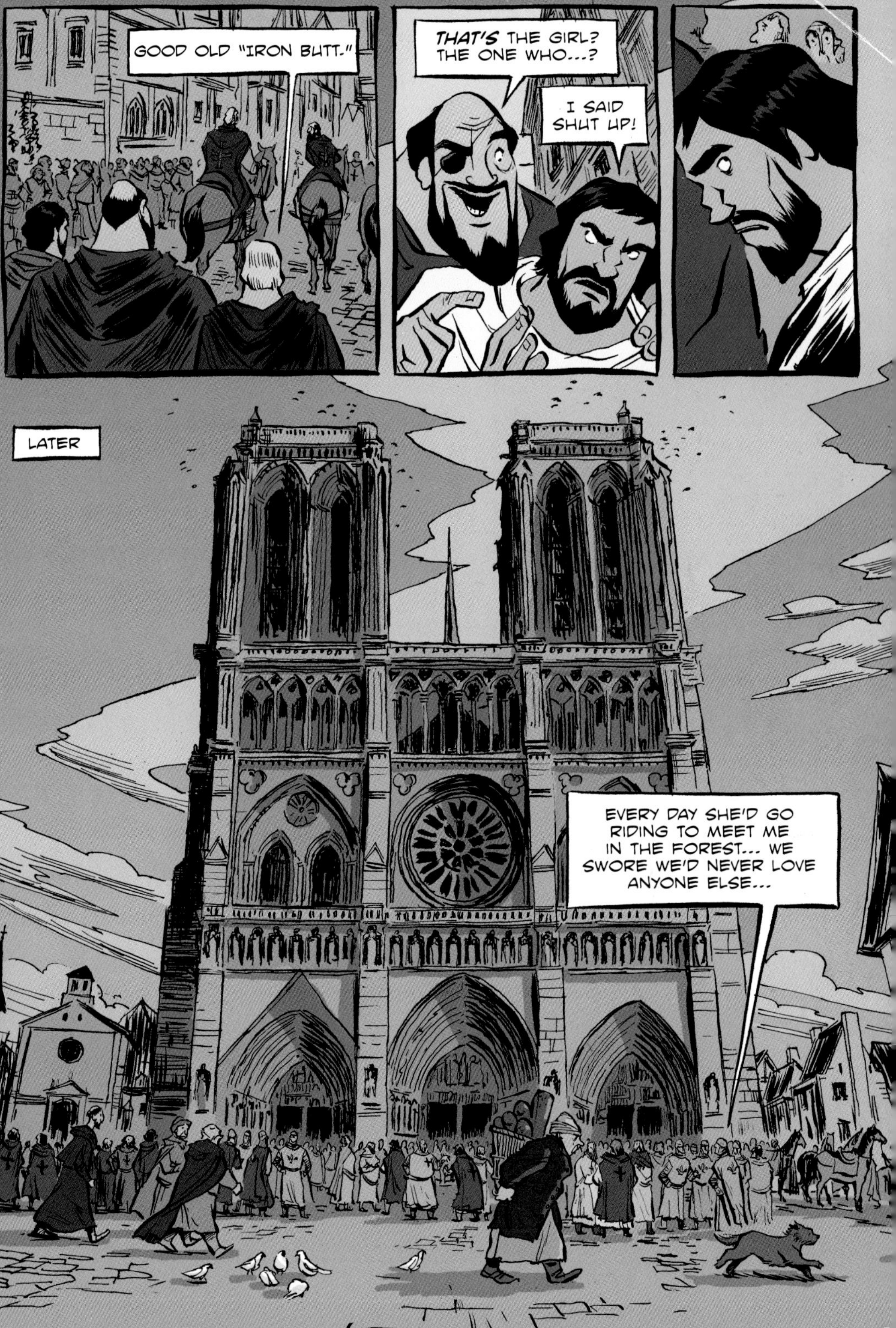
GOOD OLD "IRON BUTT."
THAT'S THE GIRL? THE ONE WHO...?
I SAID SHUT UP!
LATER
EVERY DAY SHE'D GO RIDING TO MEET ME IN THE FOREST... WE SWORE WE'D NEVER LOVE ANYONE ELSE...

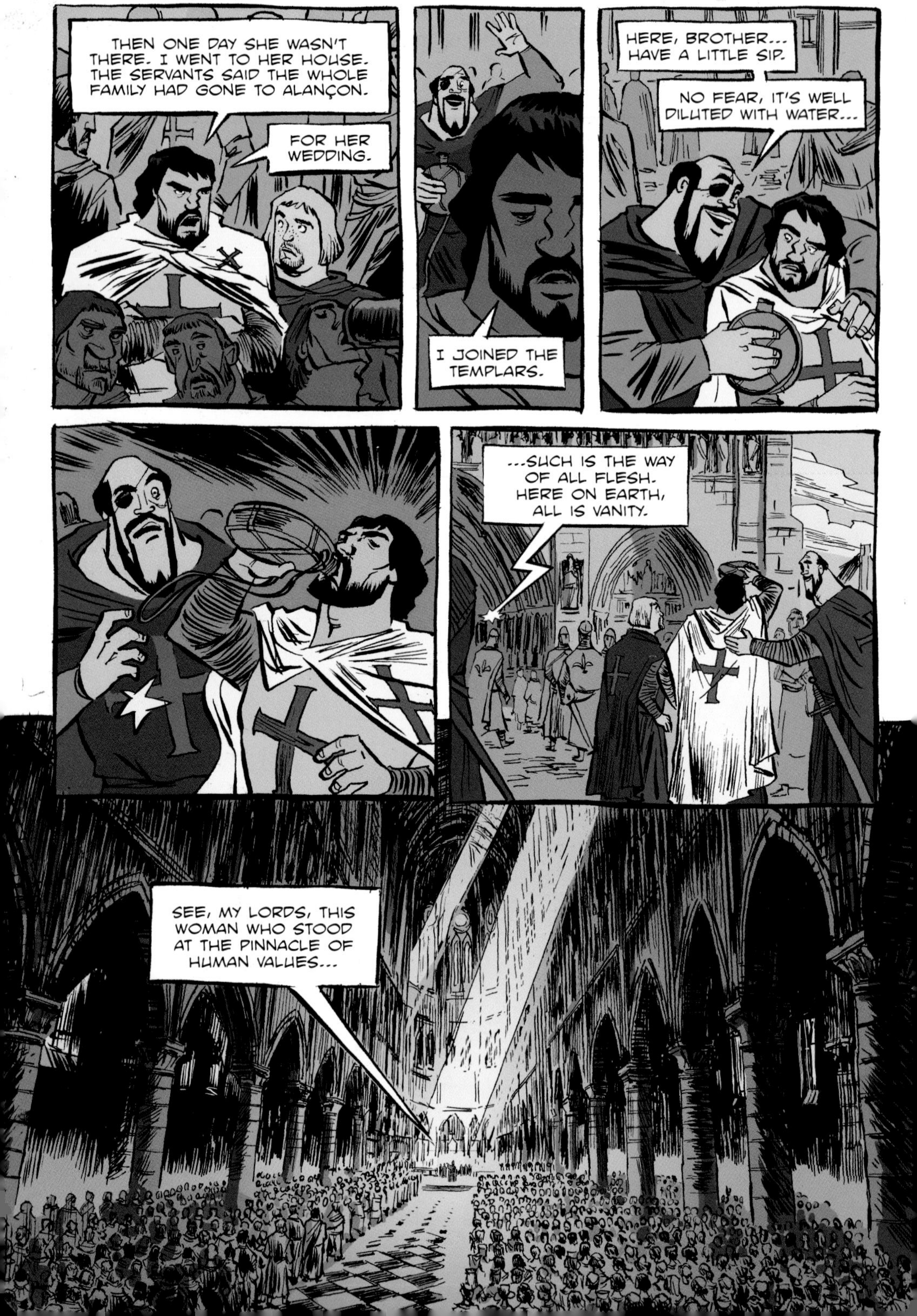
THEN ONE DAY SHE WASN'T THERE. I WENT TO HER HOUSE. THE SERVANTS SAID THE WHOLE FAMILY HAD GONE TO ALANÇON.
FOR HER WEDDING.
I JOINED THE TEMPLARS.
HERE, BROTHER... HAVE A LITTLE SIP.
NO FEAR, IT'S WELL DILUTED WITH WATER...
...SUCH IS THE WAY OF ALL FLESH. HERE ON EARTH, ALL IS VANITY.
SEE, MY LORDS, THIS WOMAN WHO STOOD AT THE PINNACLE OF HUMAN VALUES...

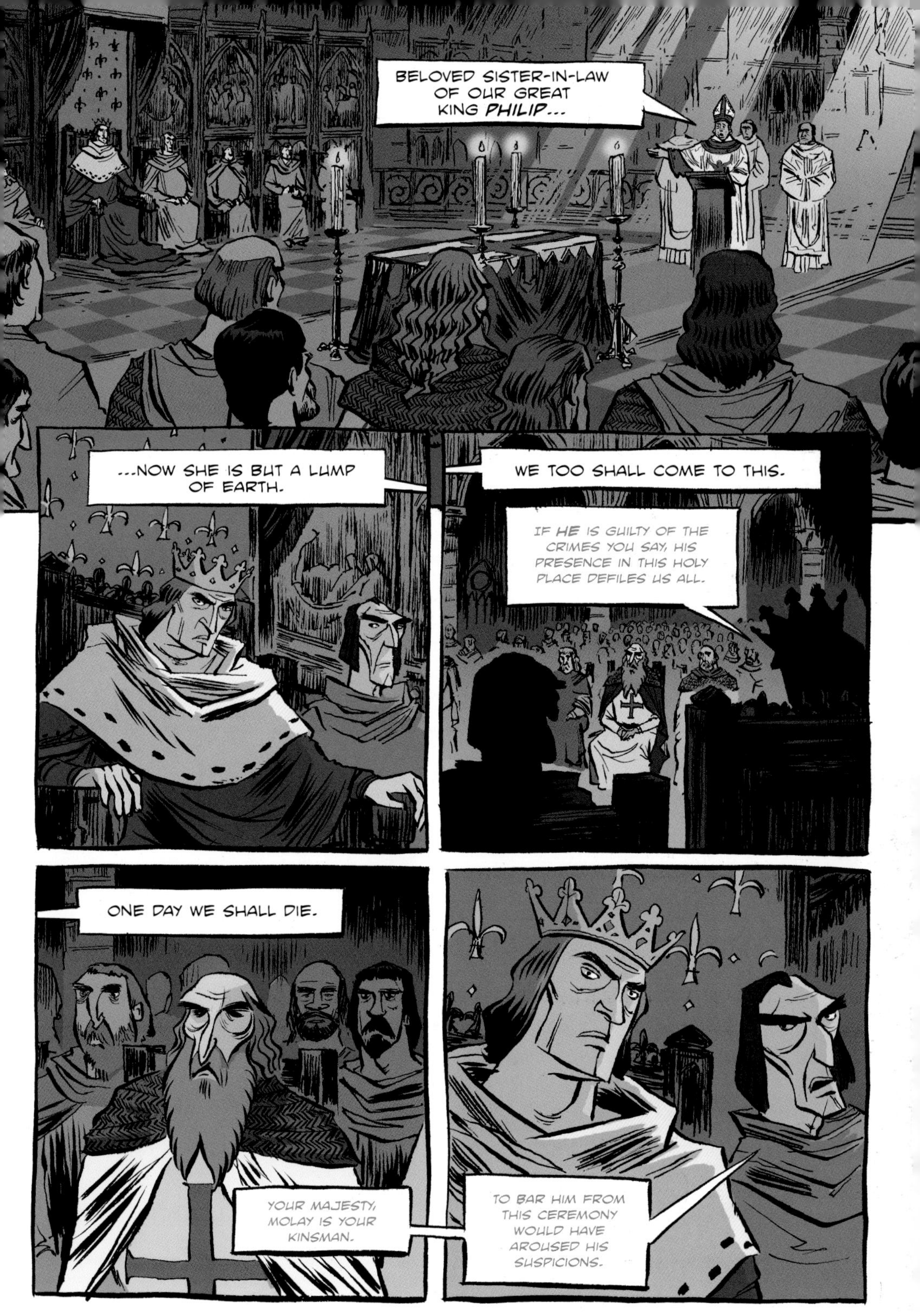
BELOVED SISTER-IN-LAW OF OUR GREAT KING *PHILIP*...
...NOW SHE IS BUT A LUMP OF EARTH.
WE TOO SHALL COME TO THIS.
IF *HE* IS GUILTY OF THE CRIMES YOU SAY, HIS PRESENCE IN THIS HOLY PLACE DEFILES US ALL.
ONE DAY WE SHALL DIE.
YOUR MAJESTY, MOLAY IS YOUR KINSMAN.
TO BAR HIM FROM THIS CEREMONY WOULD HAVE AROUSED HIS SUSPICIONS.

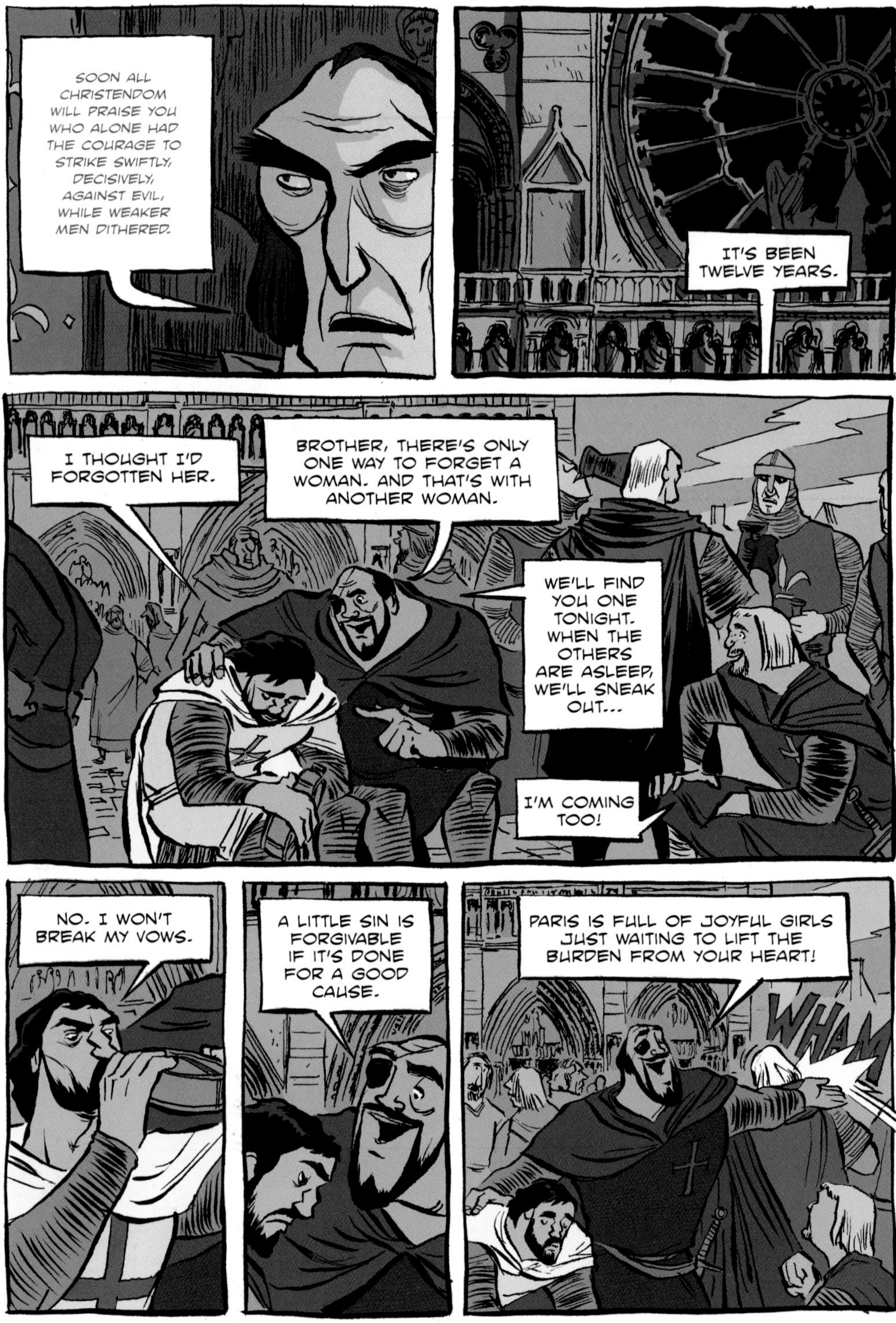
SOON ALL CHRISTENDOM WILL PRAISE YOU WHO ALONE HAD THE COURAGE TO STRIKE SWIFTLY, DECISIVELY, AGAINST EVIL, WHILE WEAKER MEN DITHERED.
IT'S BEEN TWELVE YEARS.
I THOUGHT I'D FORGOTTEN HER.
BROTHER, THERE'S ONLY ONE WAY TO FORGET A WOMAN. AND THAT'S WITH ANOTHER WOMAN.
WE'LL FIND YOU ONE TONIGHT. WHEN THE OTHERS ARE ASLEEP, WE'LL SNEAK OUT...
I'M COMING TOO!
NO. I WON'T BREAK MY VOWS.
A LITTLE SIN IS FORGIVABLE IF IT'S DONE FOR A GOOD CAUSE.
PARIS IS FULL OF JOYFUL GIRLS JUST WAITING TO LIFT THE BURDEN FROM YOUR HEART!
WHAM

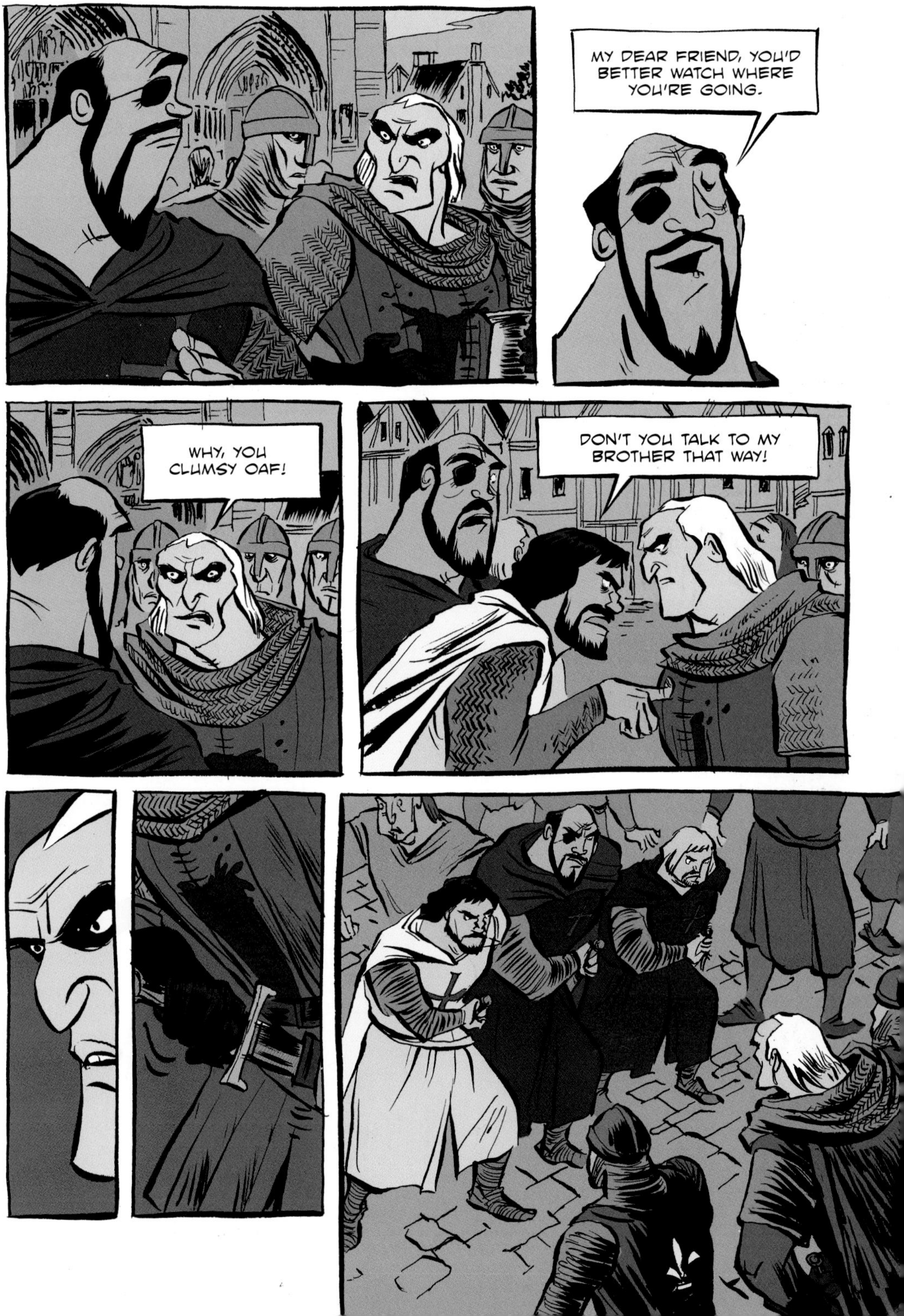
MY DEAR FRIEND, YOU'D BETTER WATCH WHERE YOU'RE GOING.
WHY, YOU CLUMSY OAF!
DON'T YOU TALK TO MY BROTHER THAT WAY!

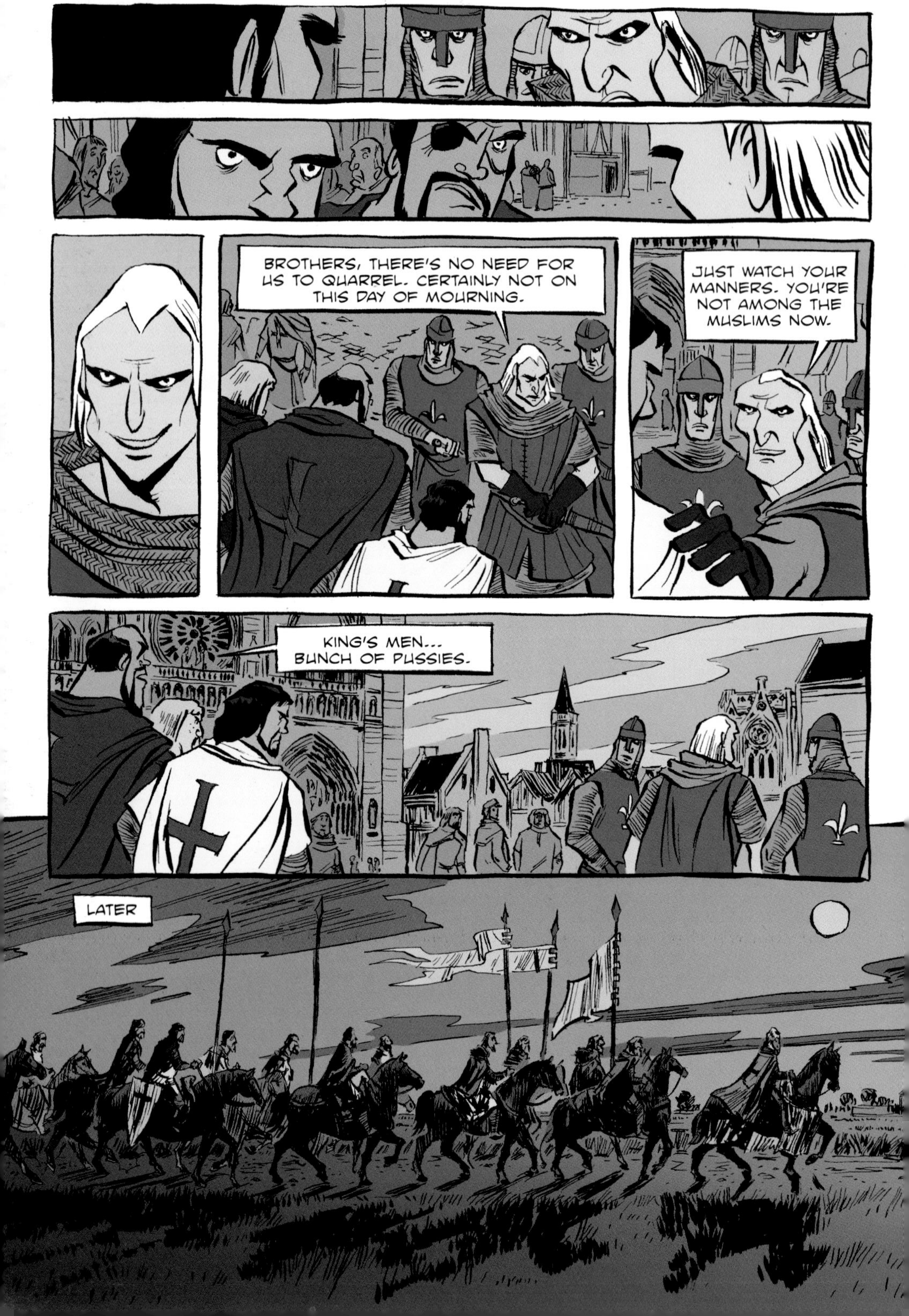
BROTHERS, THERE'S NO NEED FOR US TO QUARREL. CERTAINLY NOT ON THIS DAY OF MOURNING.
JUST WATCH YOUR MANNERS. YOU'RE NOT AMONG THE MUSLIMS NOW.
KING'S MEN... BUNCH OF PUSSIES.
LATER

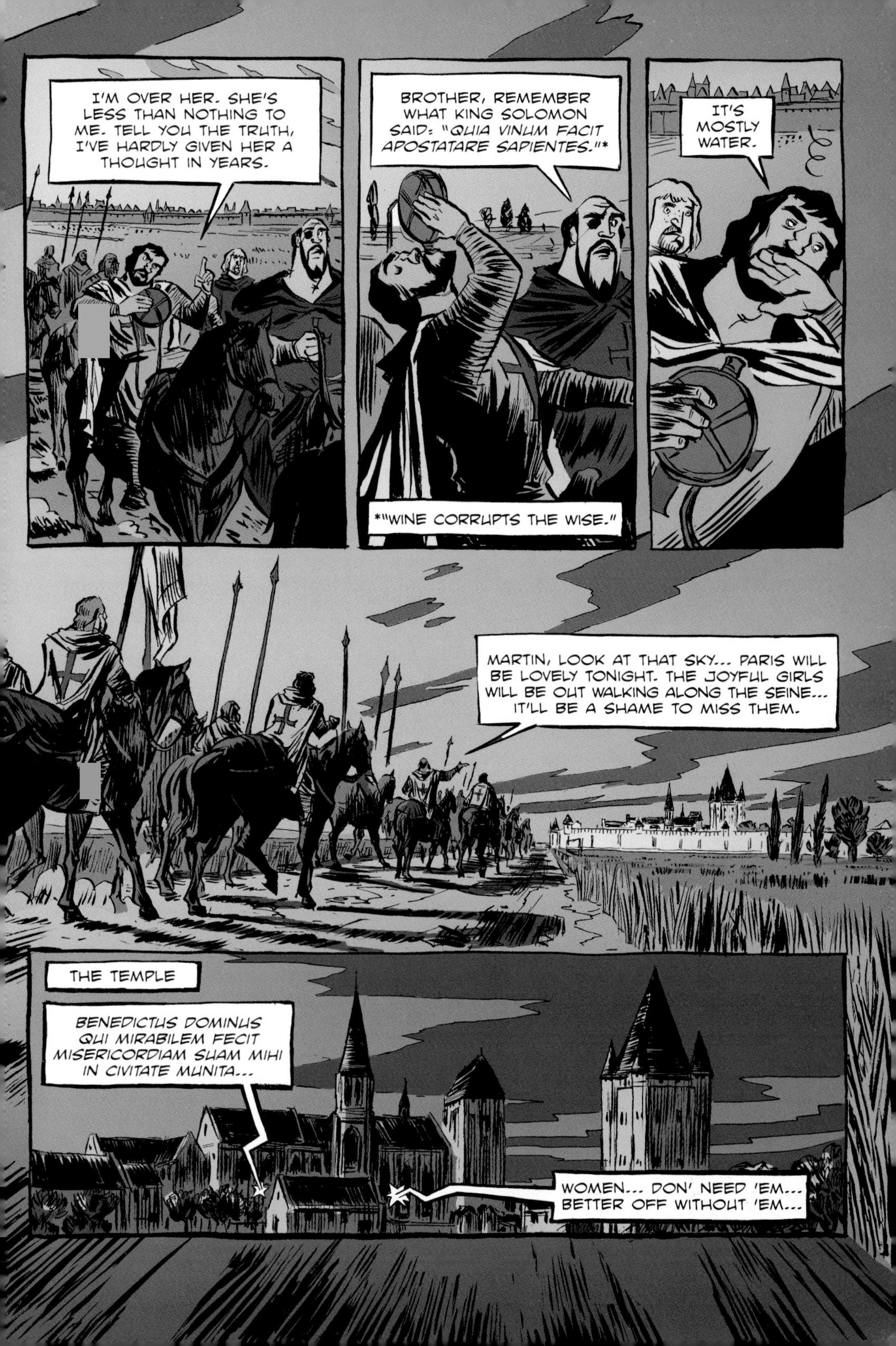
I'M OVER HER. SHE'S LESS THAN NOTHING TO ME. TELL YOU THE TRUTH, I'VE HARDLY GIVEN HER A THOUGHT IN YEARS.
BROTHER, REMEMBER WHAT KING SOLOMON SAID: "QUIA VINUM FACIT APOSTATARE SAPIENTES."*
*"WINE CORRUPTS THE WISE."
IT'S MOSTLY WATER.
MARTIN, LOOK AT THAT SKY... PARIS WILL BE LOVELY TONIGHT. THE JOYFUL GIRLS WILL BE OUT WALKING ALONG THE SEINE... IT'LL BE A SHAME TO MISS THEM.
THE TEMPLE
BENEDICTUS DOMINUS QUI MIRABILEM FECIT MISERICORDIAM SUAM MIHI IN CIVITATE MUNITA...
WOMEN... DON' NEED 'EM... BETTER OFF WITHOUT 'EM...

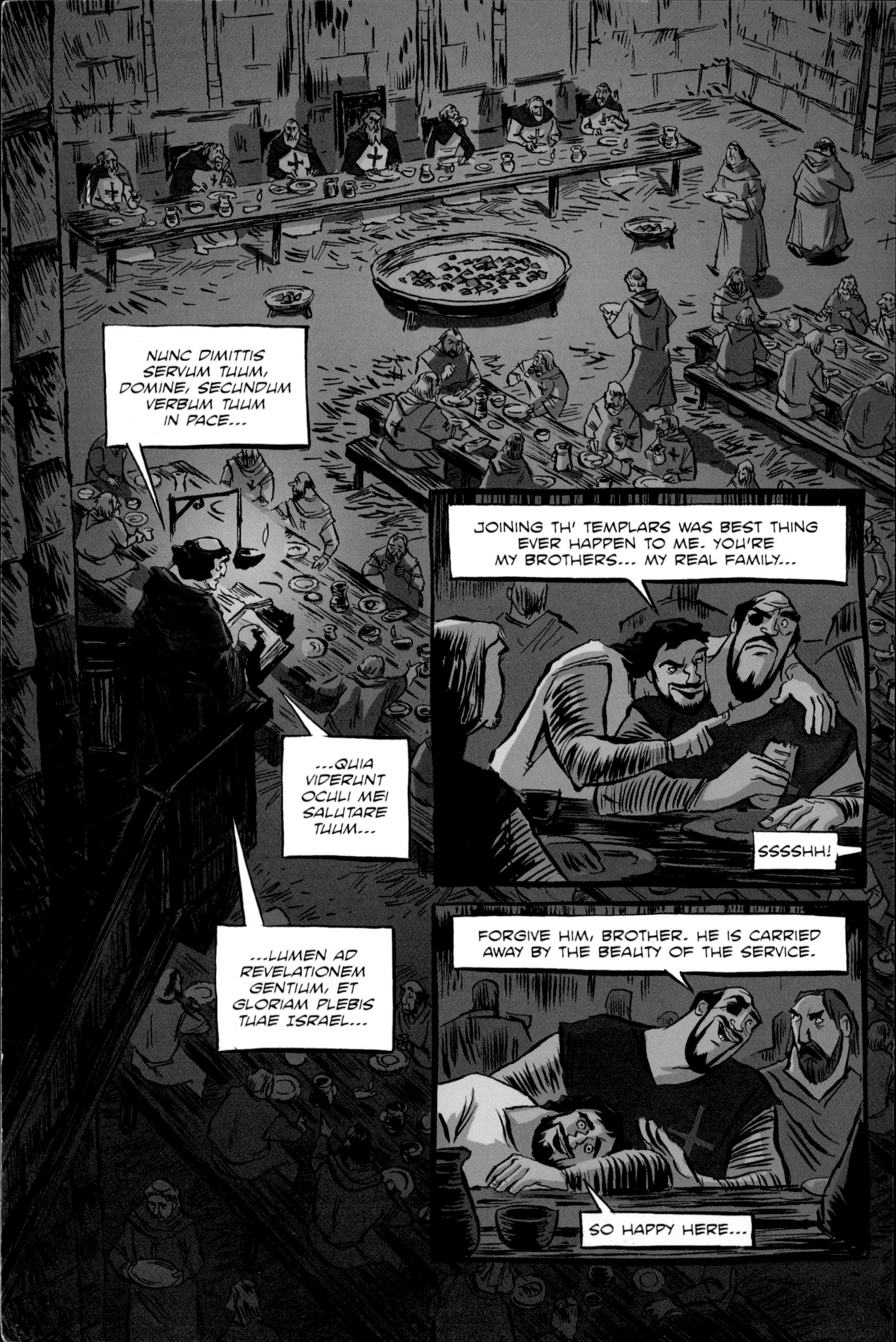
NUNC DIMITTIS SERVUM TUUM, DOMINE, SECUNDUM VERBUM TUUM IN PACE...
...QUIA VIDERUNT OCULI MEI SALUTARE TUUM...
...LUMEN AD REVELATIONEM GENTIUM, ET GLORIAM PLEBIS TUAE ISRAEL...
JOINING TH' TEMPLARS WAS BEST THING EVER HAPPEN TO ME. YOU'RE MY BROTHERS... MY REAL FAMILY...
SSSSHH!
FORGIVE HIM, BROTHER. HE IS CARRIED AWAY BY THE BEAUTY OF THE SERVICE.
SO HAPPY HERE...

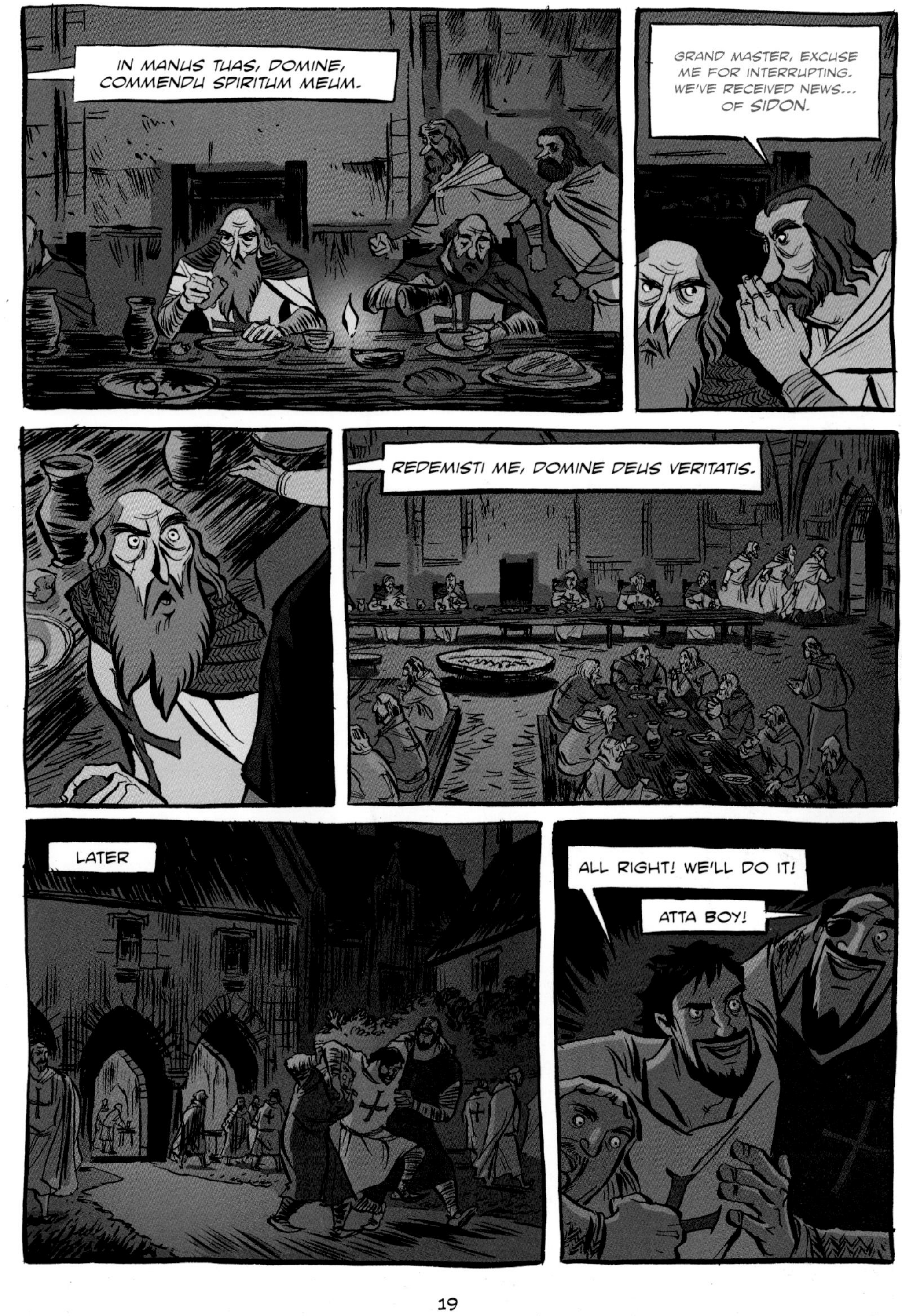
IN MANUS TUAS, DOMINE, COMMENDU SPIRITUM MEUM.
GRAND MASTER, EXCUSE ME FOR INTERRUPTING. WE'VE RECEIVED NEWS... OF SIDON.
REDEMISTI ME, DOMINE DEUS VERITATIS.
LATER
ALL RIGHT! WE'LL DO IT!
ATTA BOY!

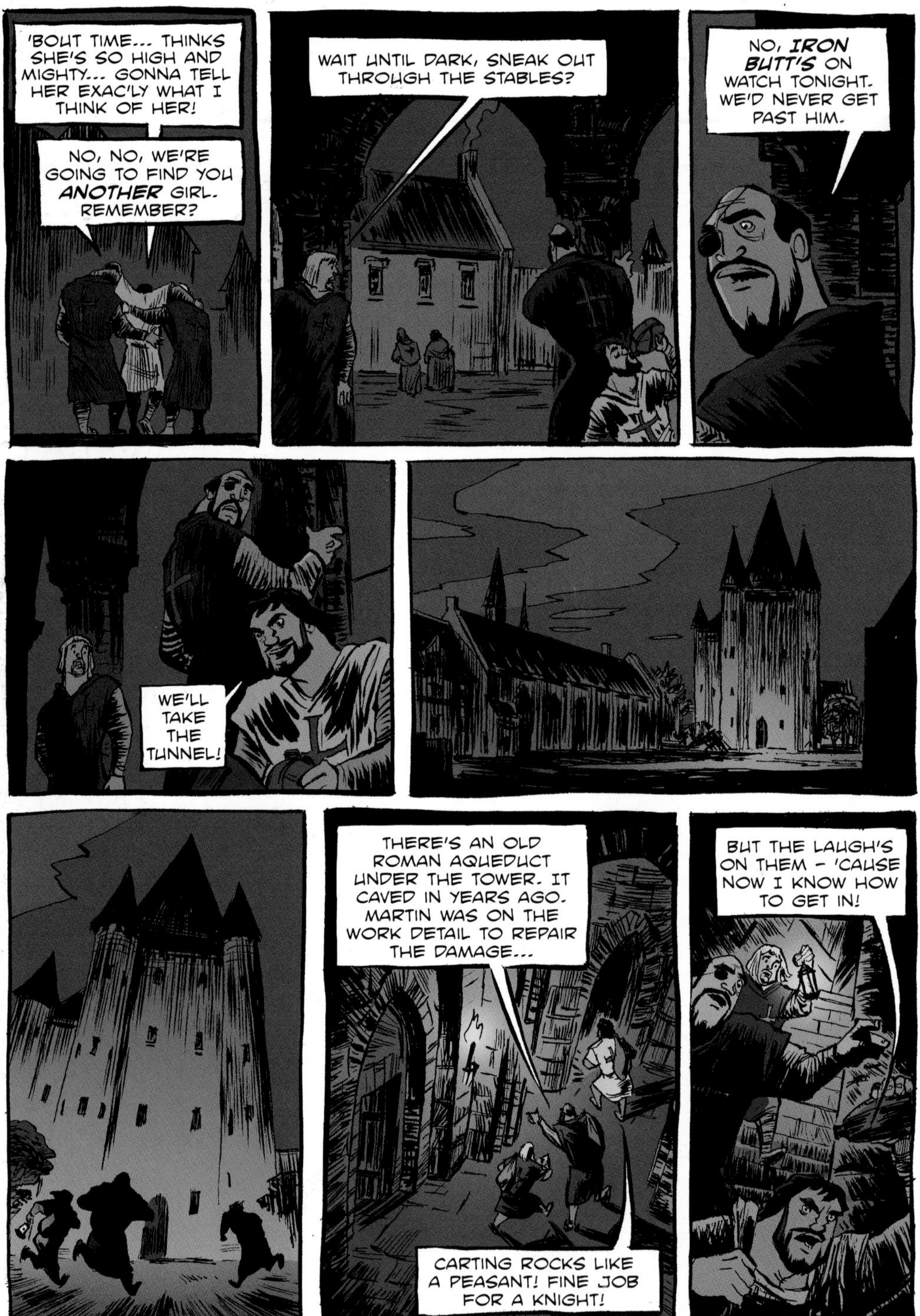
'BOUT TIME... THINKS SHE'S SO HIGH AND MIGHTY... GONNA TELL HER EXAC'LY WHAT I THINK OF HER!
NO, NO, WE'RE GOING TO FIND YOU ANOTHER GIRL. REMEMBER?
WAIT UNTIL DARK, SNEAK OUT THROUGH THE STABLES?
NO, IRON BUTT'S ON WATCH TONIGHT. WE'D NEVER GET PAST HIM.
WE'LL TAKE THE TUNNEL!
THERE'S AN OLD ROMAN AQUEDUCT UNDER THE TOWER. IT CAVED IN YEARS AGO. MARTIN WAS ON THE WORK DETAIL TO REPAIR THE DAMAGE...
CARTING ROCKS LIKE A PEASANT! FINE JOB FOR A KNIGHT!
BUT THE LAUGH'S ON THEM - 'CAUSE NOW I KNOW HOW TO GET IN!

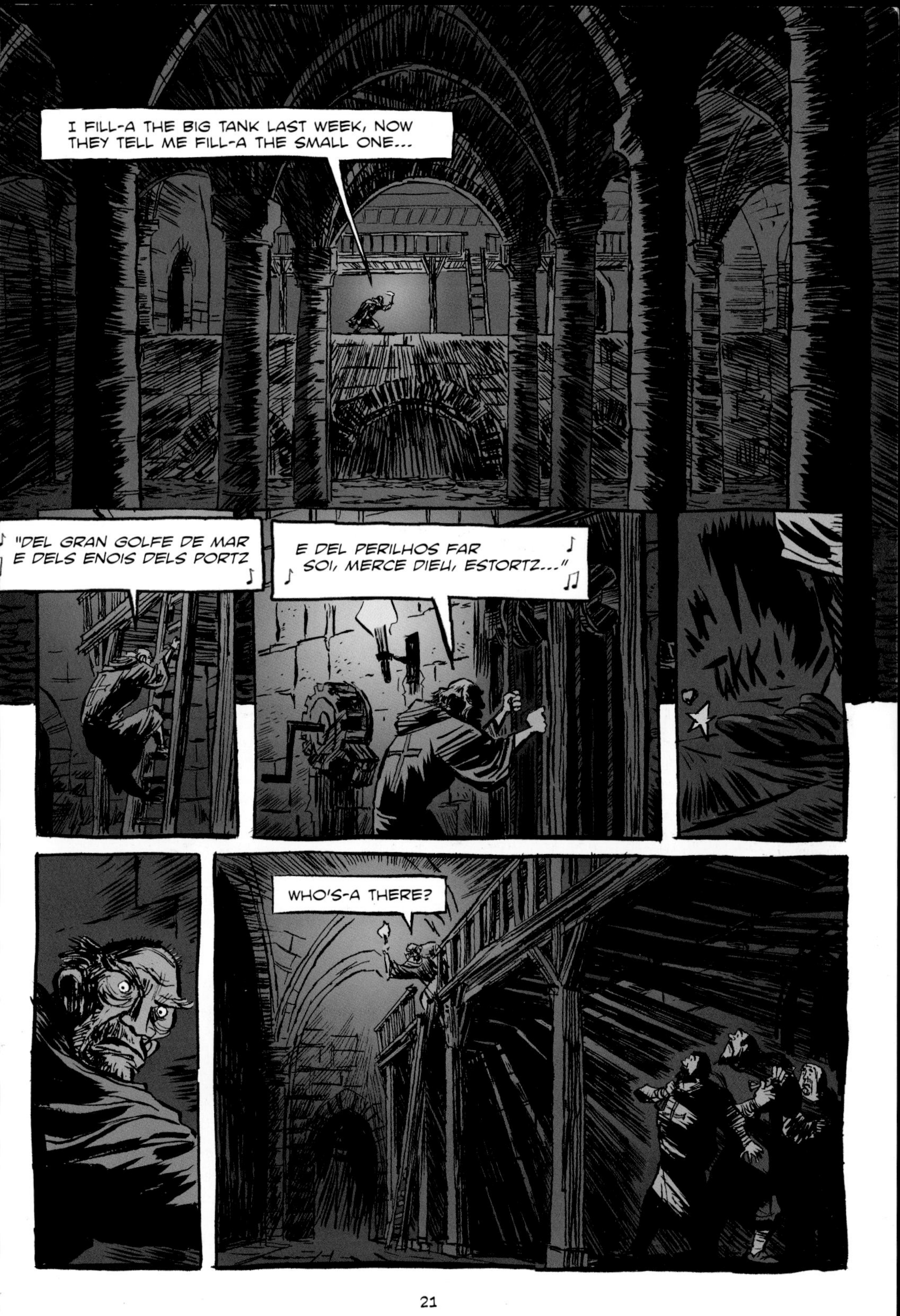
I FILL-A THE BIG TANK LAST WEEK, NOW THEY TELL ME FILL-A THE SMALL ONE...
"DEL GRAN GOLFE DE MAR E DELS ENOIS DELS PORTZ
E DEL PERILHOS FAR SOI, MERCE DIEU, ESTORTZ..."
TAKK!
WHO'S-A THERE?

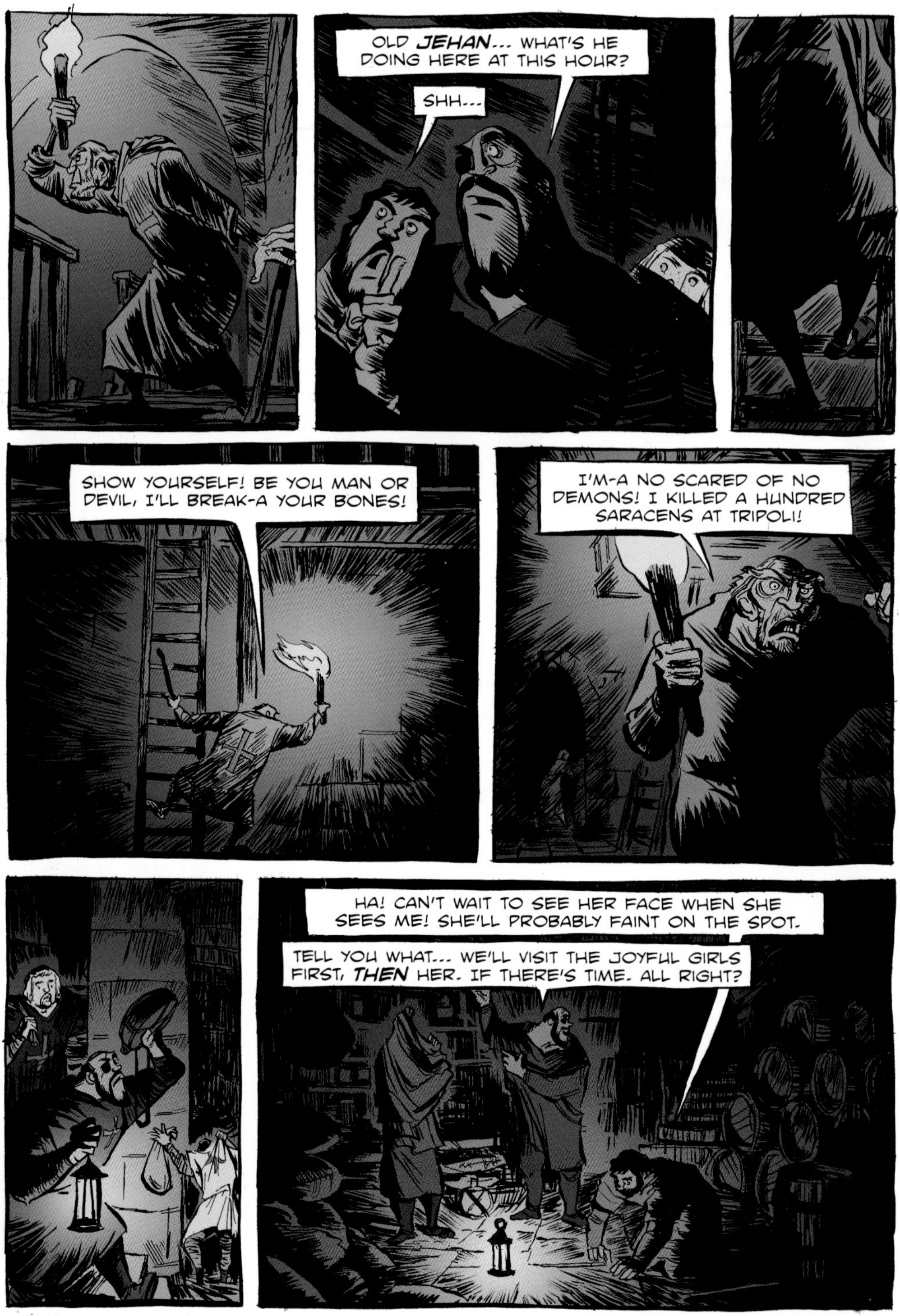
OLD JEHAN... WHAT'S HE DOING HERE AT THIS HOUR?
SHH...
SHOW YOURSELF! BE YOU MAN OR DEVIL, I'LL BREAK-A YOUR BONES!
I'M-A NO SCARED OF NO DEMONS! I KILLED A HUNDRED SARACENS AT TRIPOLI!
HA! CAN'T WAIT TO SEE HER FACE WHEN SHE SEES ME! SHE'LL PROBABLY FAINT ON THE SPOT.
TELL YOU WHAT... WE'LL VISIT THE JOYFUL GIRLS FIRST, THEN HER. IF THERE'S TIME. ALL RIGHT?

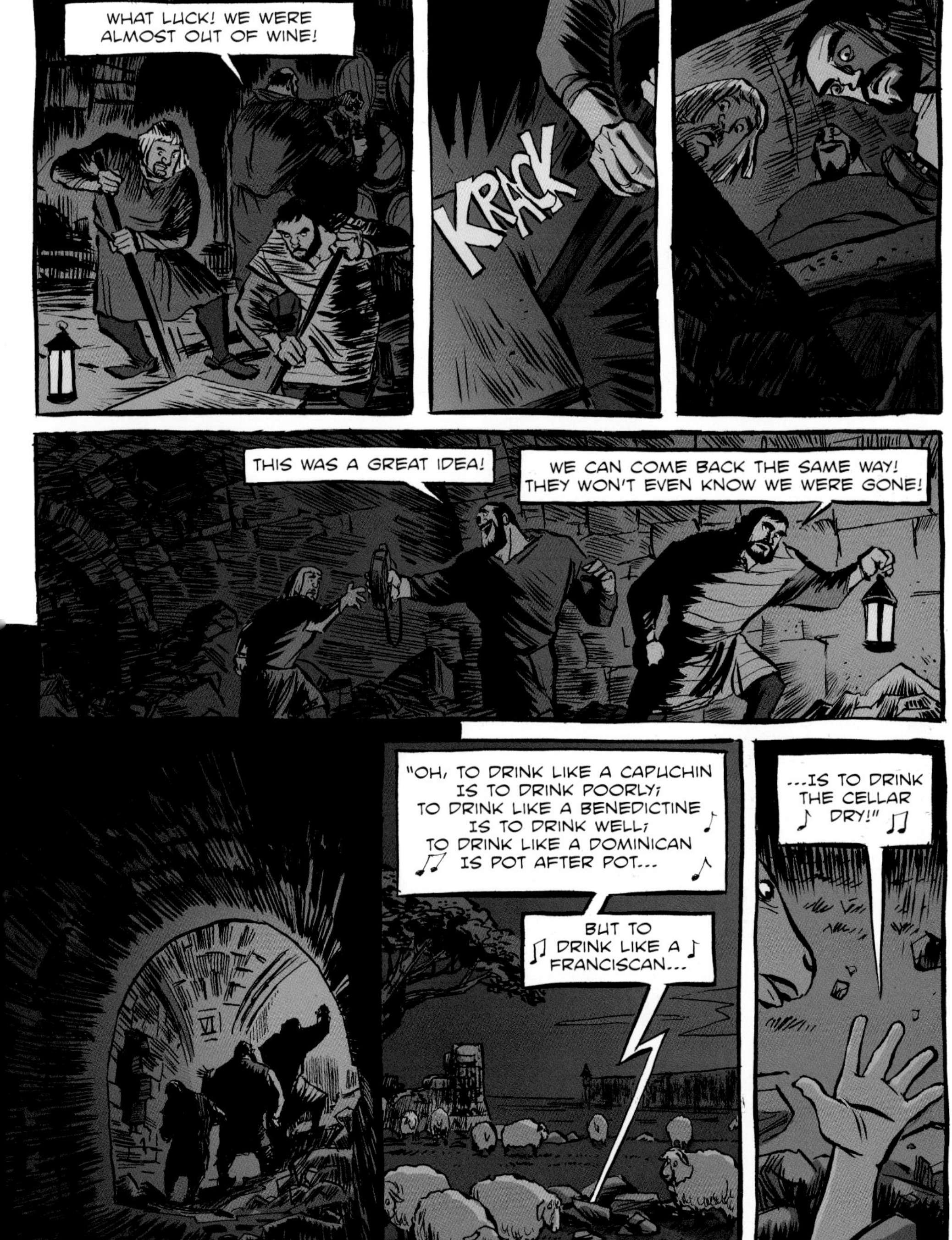
WHAT LUCK! WE WERE ALMOST OUT OF WINE!
KRACK
THIS WAS A GREAT IDEA!
WE CAN COME BACK THE SAME WAY! THEY WON'T EVEN KNOW WE WERE GONE!
VI
"OH, TO DRINK LIKE A CAPUCHIN IS TO DRINK POORLY; TO DRINK LIKE A BENEDICTINE IS TO DRINK WELL; TO DRINK LIKE A DOMINICAN IS POT AFTER POT...
BUT TO DRINK LIKE A FRANCISCAN...
...IS TO DRINK THE CELLAR DRY!"

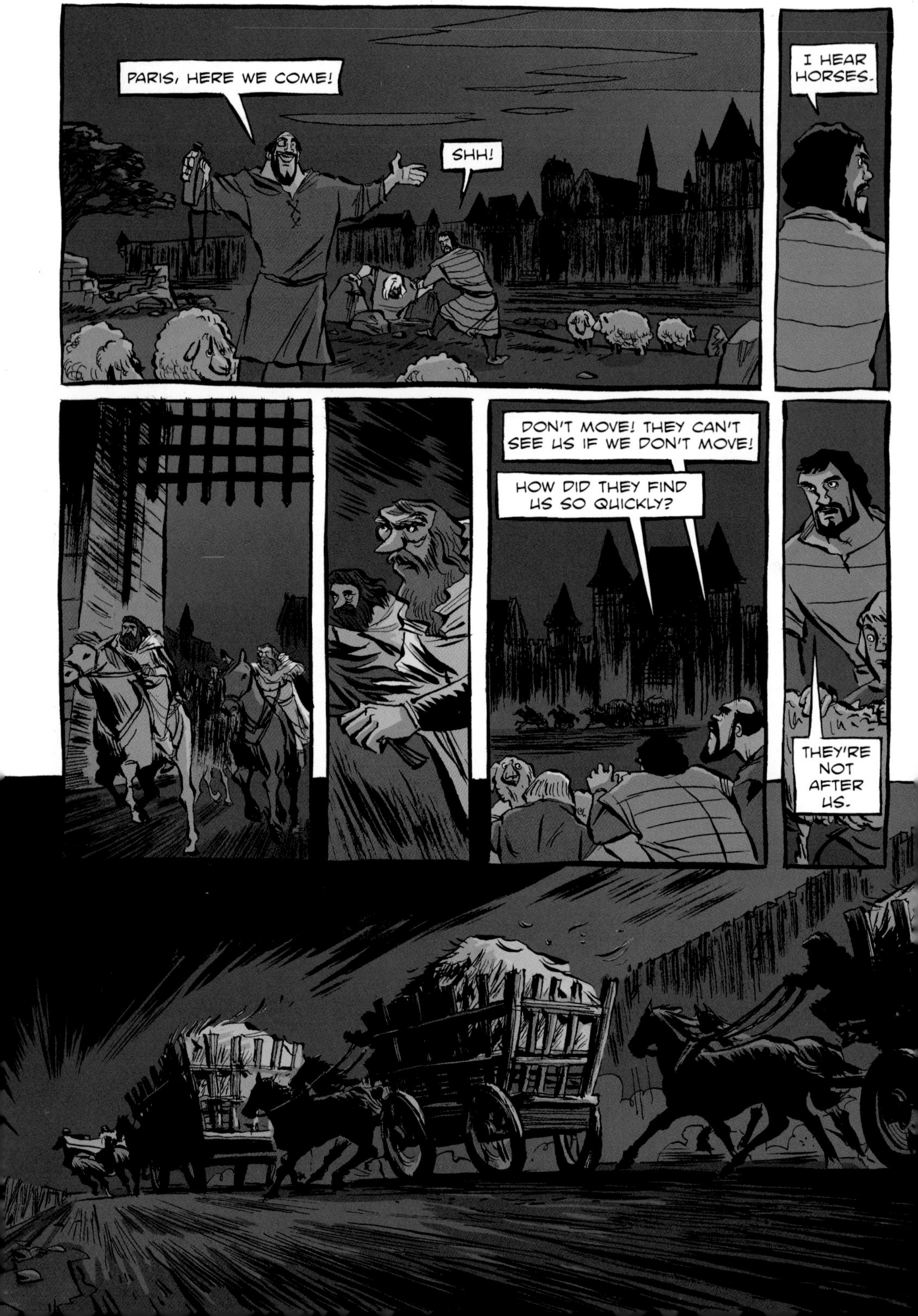
PARIS, HERE WE COME!
SHH!
I HEAR HORSES.
DON'T MOVE! THEY CAN'T SEE US IF WE DON'T MOVE!
HOW DID THEY FIND US SO QUICKLY?
THEY'RE NOT AFTER US.

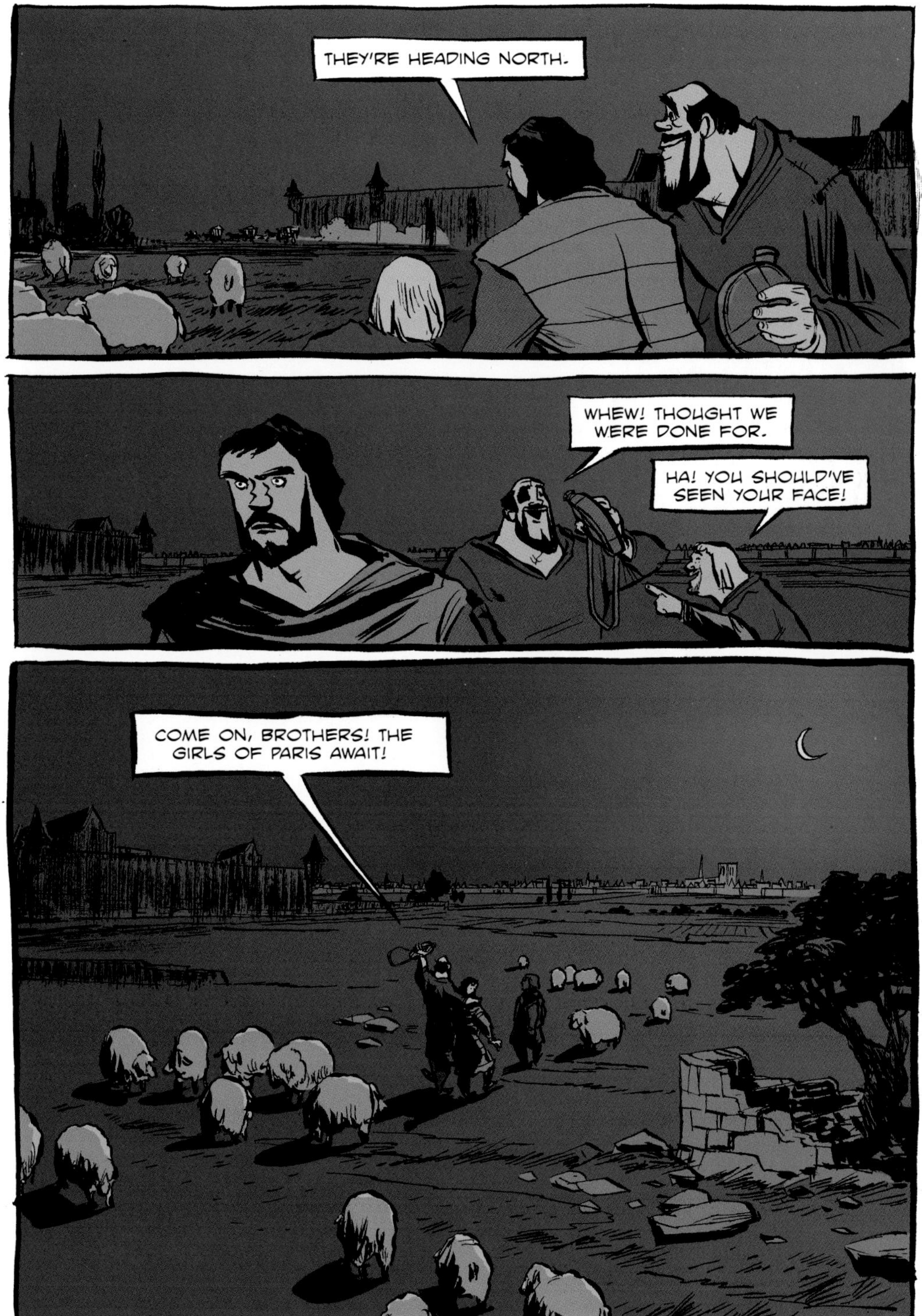
THEY'RE HEADING NORTH.
WHEW! THOUGHT WE WERE DONE FOR.
HA! YOU SHOULD'VE SEEN YOUR FACE!
COME ON, BROTHERS! THE GIRLS OF PARIS AWAIT!

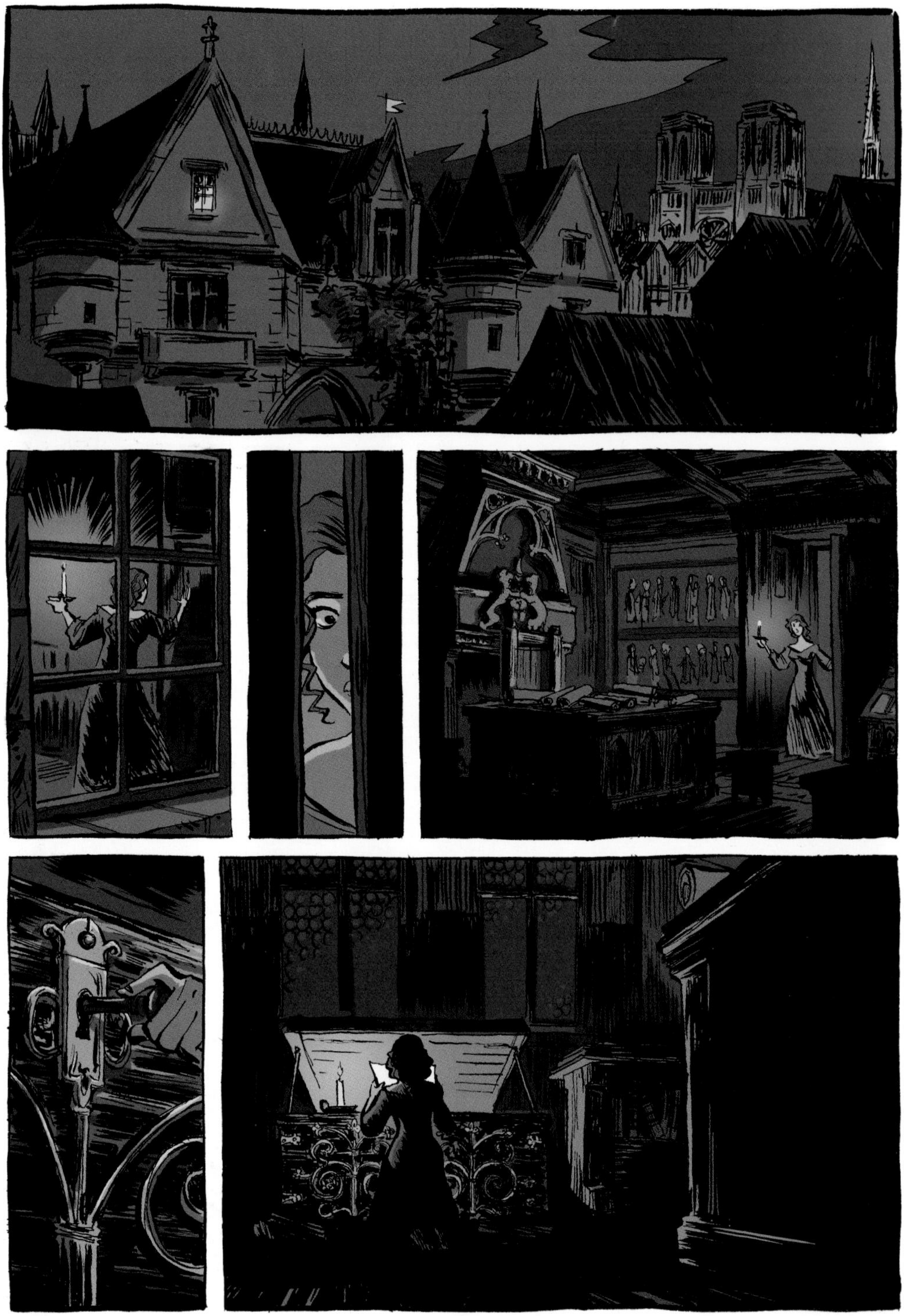

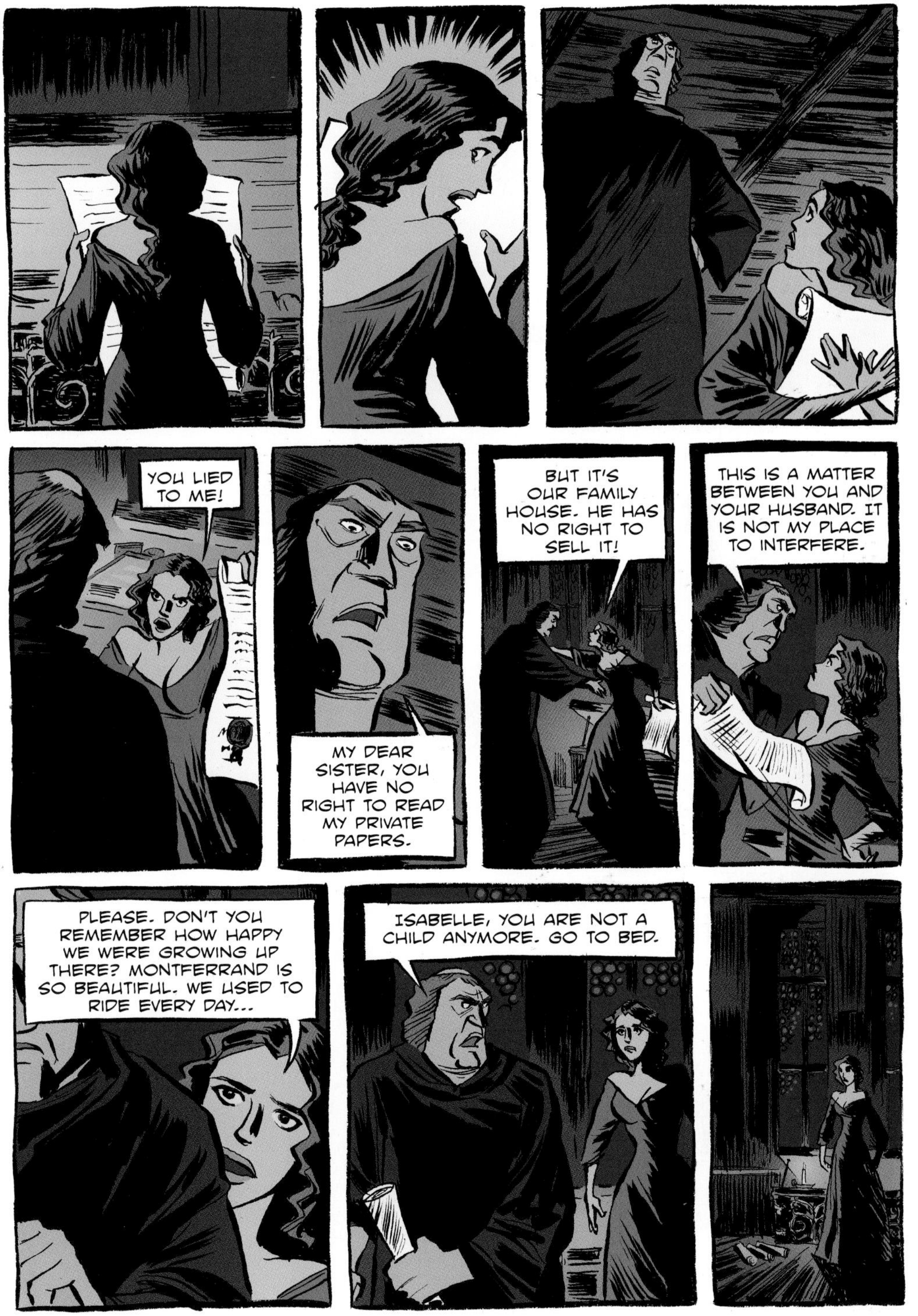
YOU LIED TO ME!
MY DEAR SISTER, YOU HAVE NO RIGHT TO READ MY PRIVATE PAPERS.
BUT IT'S OUR FAMILY HOUSE. HE HAS NO RIGHT TO SELL IT!
THIS IS A MATTER BETWEEN YOU AND YOUR HUSBAND. IT IS NOT MY PLACE TO INTERFERE.
PLEASE. DON'T YOU REMEMBER HOW HAPPY WE WERE GROWING UP THERE? MONTFERRAND IS SO BEAUTIFUL. WE USED TO RIDE EVERY DAY...
ISABELLE, YOU ARE NOT A CHILD ANYMORE. GO TO BED.

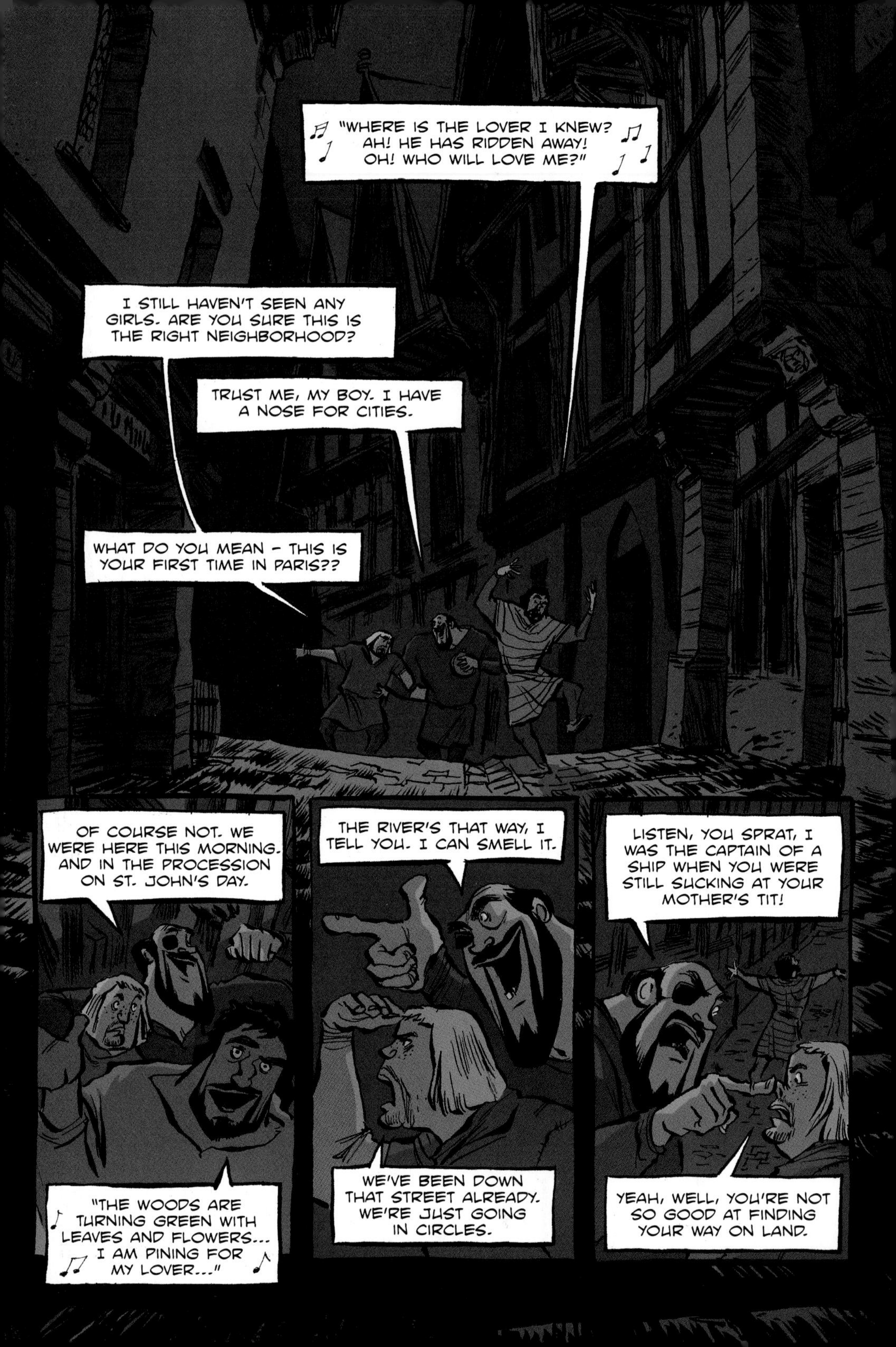
"WHERE IS THE LOVER I KNEW? AH! HE HAS RIDDEN AWAY! OH! WHO WILL LOVE ME?"
I STILL HAVEN'T SEEN ANY GIRLS. ARE YOU SURE THIS IS THE RIGHT NEIGHBORHOOD?
TRUST ME, MY BOY. I HAVE A NOSE FOR CITIES.
WHAT DO YOU MEAN - THIS IS YOUR FIRST TIME IN PARIS??
OF COURSE NOT. WE WERE HERE THIS MORNING. AND IN THE PROCESSION ON ST. JOHN'S DAY.
"THE WOODS ARE TURNING GREEN WITH LEAVES AND FLOWERS... I AM PINING FOR MY LOVER..."
THE RIVER'S THAT WAY, I TELL YOU. I CAN SMELL IT.
WE'VE BEEN DOWN THAT STREET ALREADY. WE'RE JUST GOING IN CIRCLES.
LISTEN, YOU SPRAT, I WAS THE CAPTAIN OF A SHIP WHEN YOU WERE STILL SUCKING AT YOUR MOTHER'S TIT!
YEAH, WELL, YOU'RE NOT SO GOOD AT FINDING YOUR WAY ON LAND.

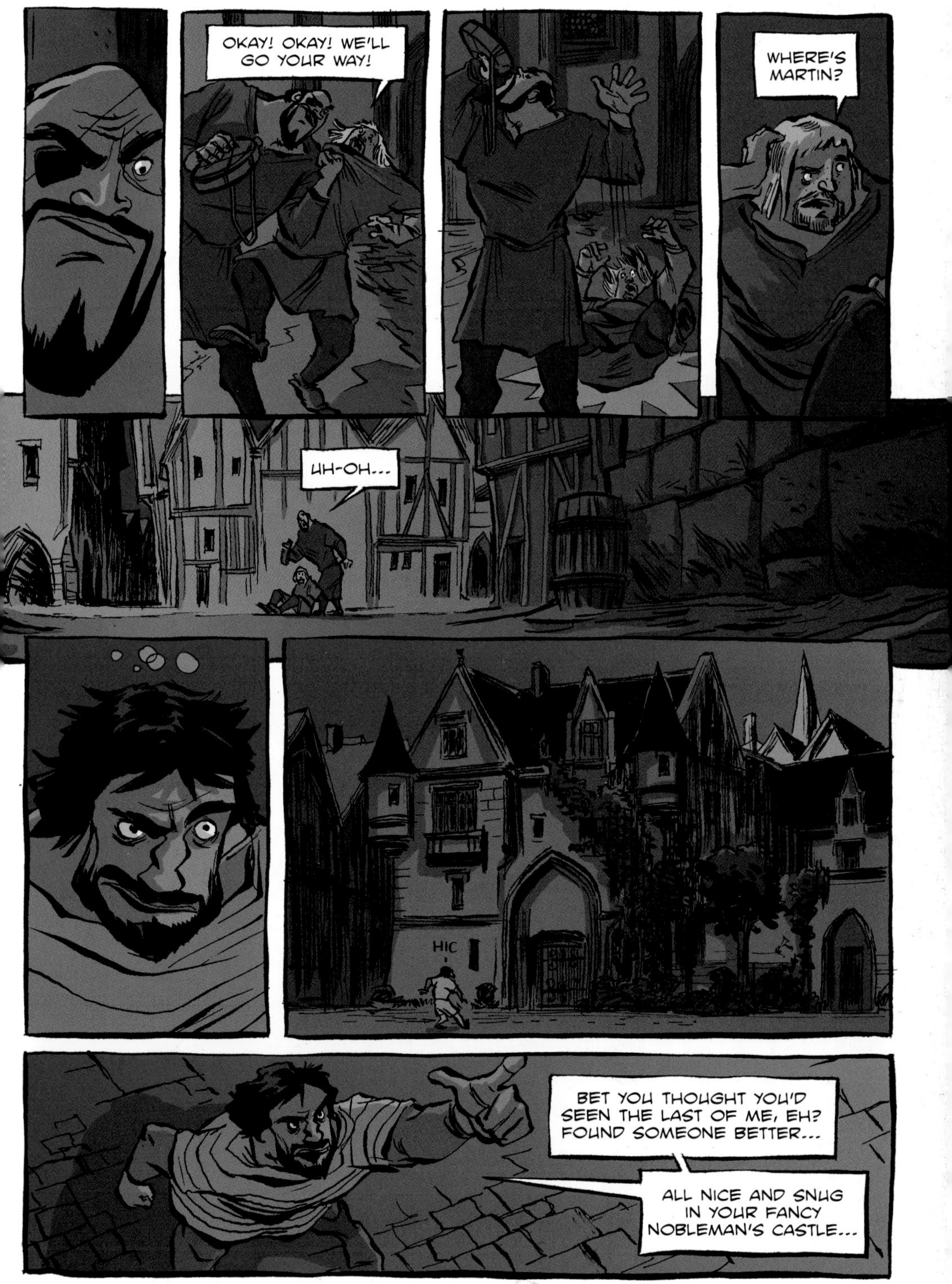
OKAY! OKAY! WE'LL GO YOUR WAY!
WHERE'S MARTIN?
UH-OH...
HIC
BET YOU THOUGHT YOU'D SEEN THE LAST OF ME, EH? FOUND SOMEONE BETTER...
ALL NICE AND SNUG IN YOUR FANCY NOBLEMAN'S CASTLE...

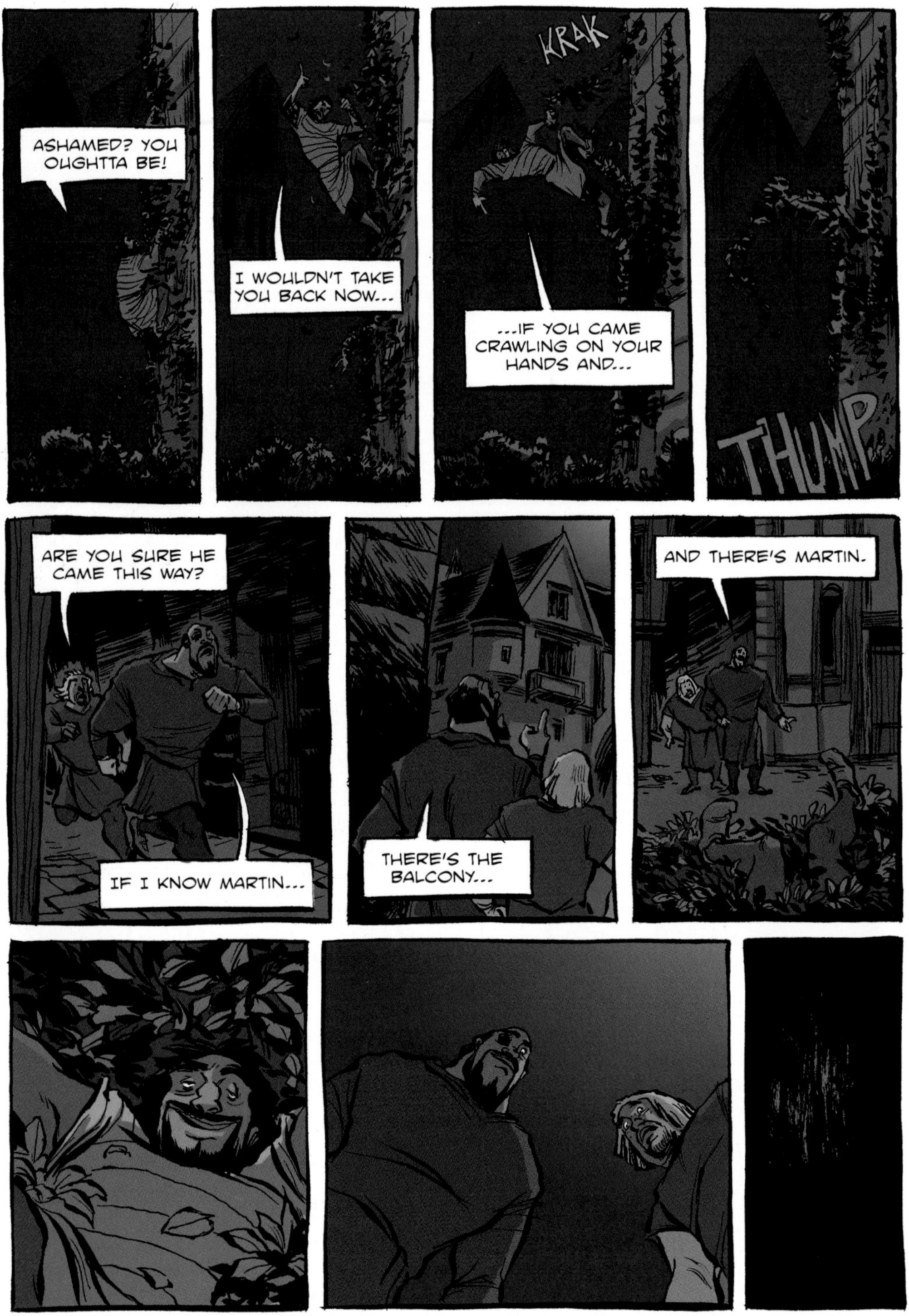

ASHAMED? YOU OUGHTTA BE!
I WOULDN'T TAKE YOU BACK NOW...
KRAK
...IF YOU CAME CRAWLING ON YOUR HANDS AND...
THUMP
ARE YOU SURE HE CAME THIS WAY?
IF I KNOW MARTIN...
THERE'S THE BALCONY...
AND THERE'S MARTIN.

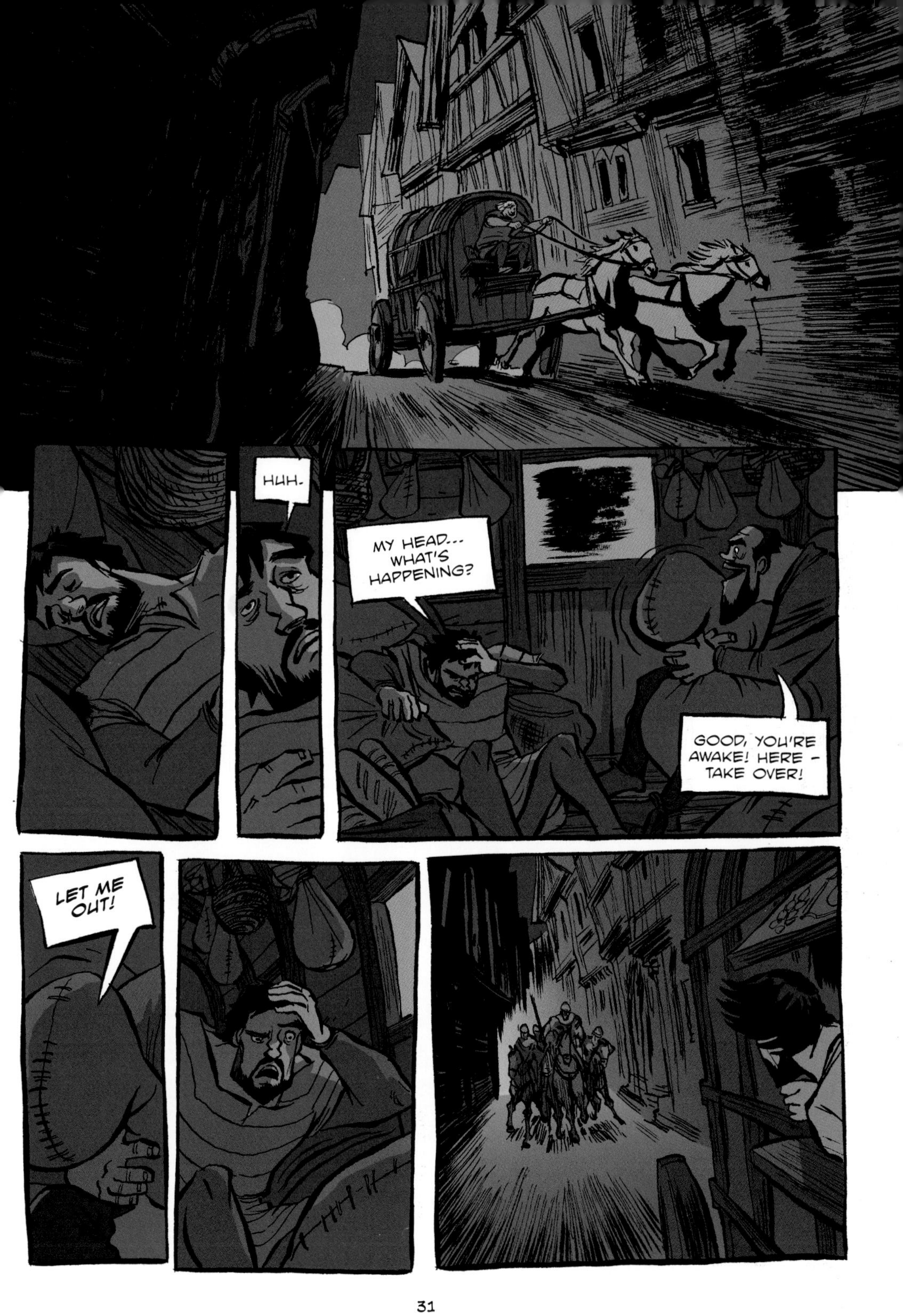
HUH.
MY HEAD... WHAT'S HAPPENING?
GOOD, YOU'RE AWAKE! HERE - TAKE OVER!
LET ME OUT!

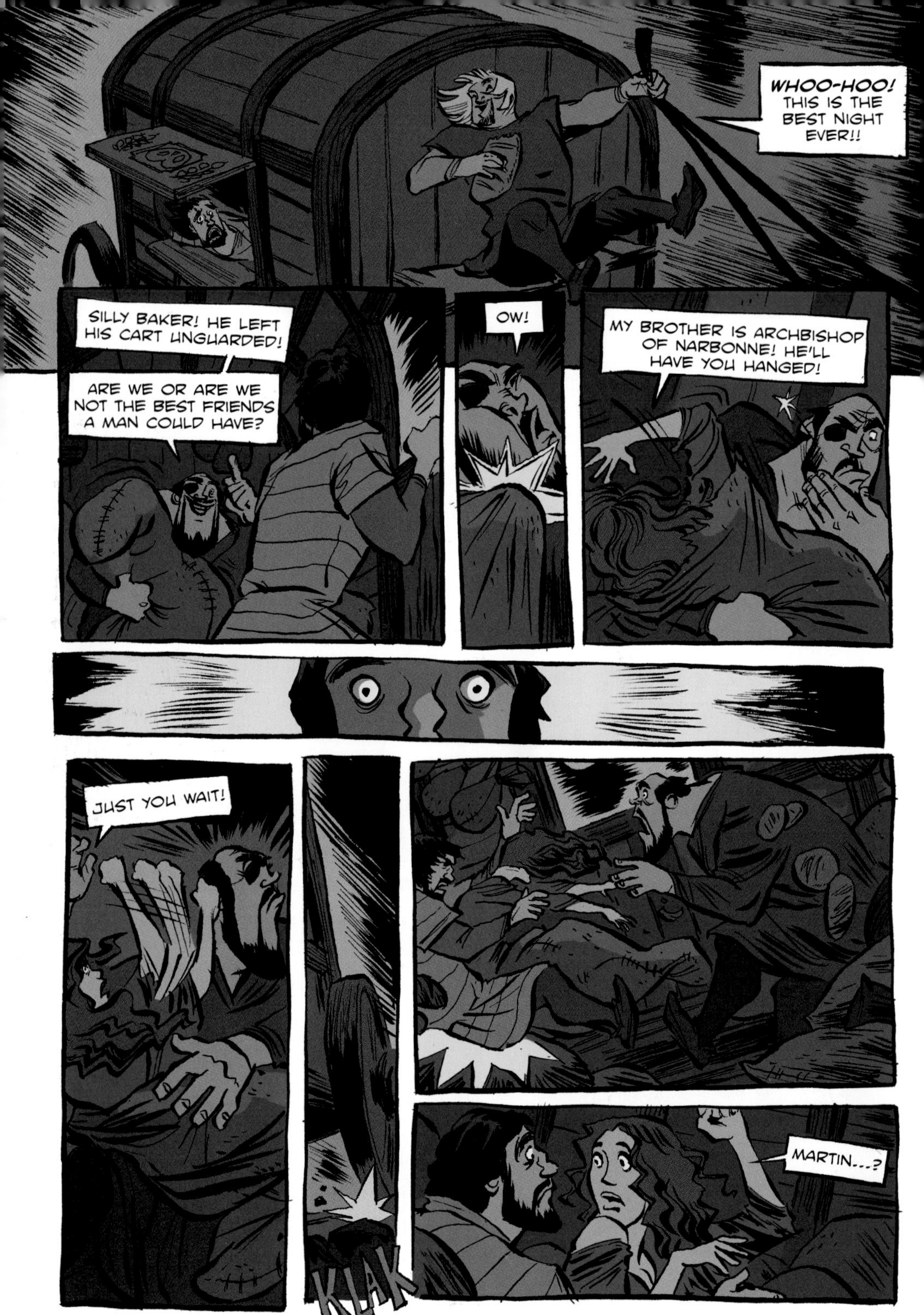
WHOO-HOO! THIS IS THE BEST NIGHT EVER!!
SILLY BAKER! HE LEFT HIS CART UNGUARDED!
ARE WE OR ARE WE NOT THE BEST FRIENDS A MAN COULD HAVE?
OW!
MY BROTHER IS ARCHBISHOP OF NARBONNE! HE'LL HAVE YOU HANGED!
JUST YOU WAIT!
KLAK
MARTIN...?

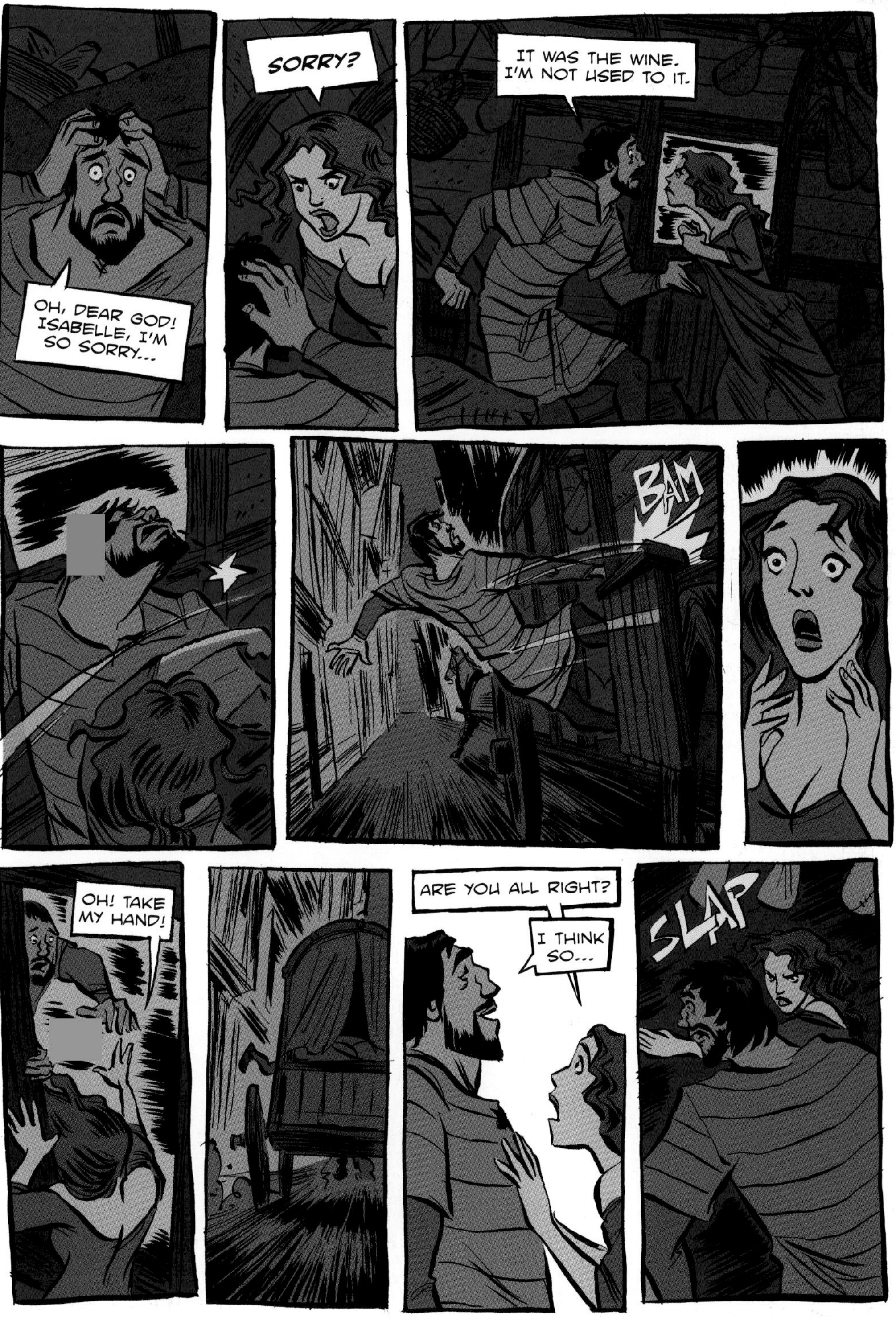
OH, DEAR GOD! ISABELLE, I'M SO SORRY...
SORRY?
IT WAS THE WINE. I'M NOT USED TO IT.
BAM
OH! TAKE MY HAND!
ARE YOU ALL RIGHT?
I THINK SO...
SLAP

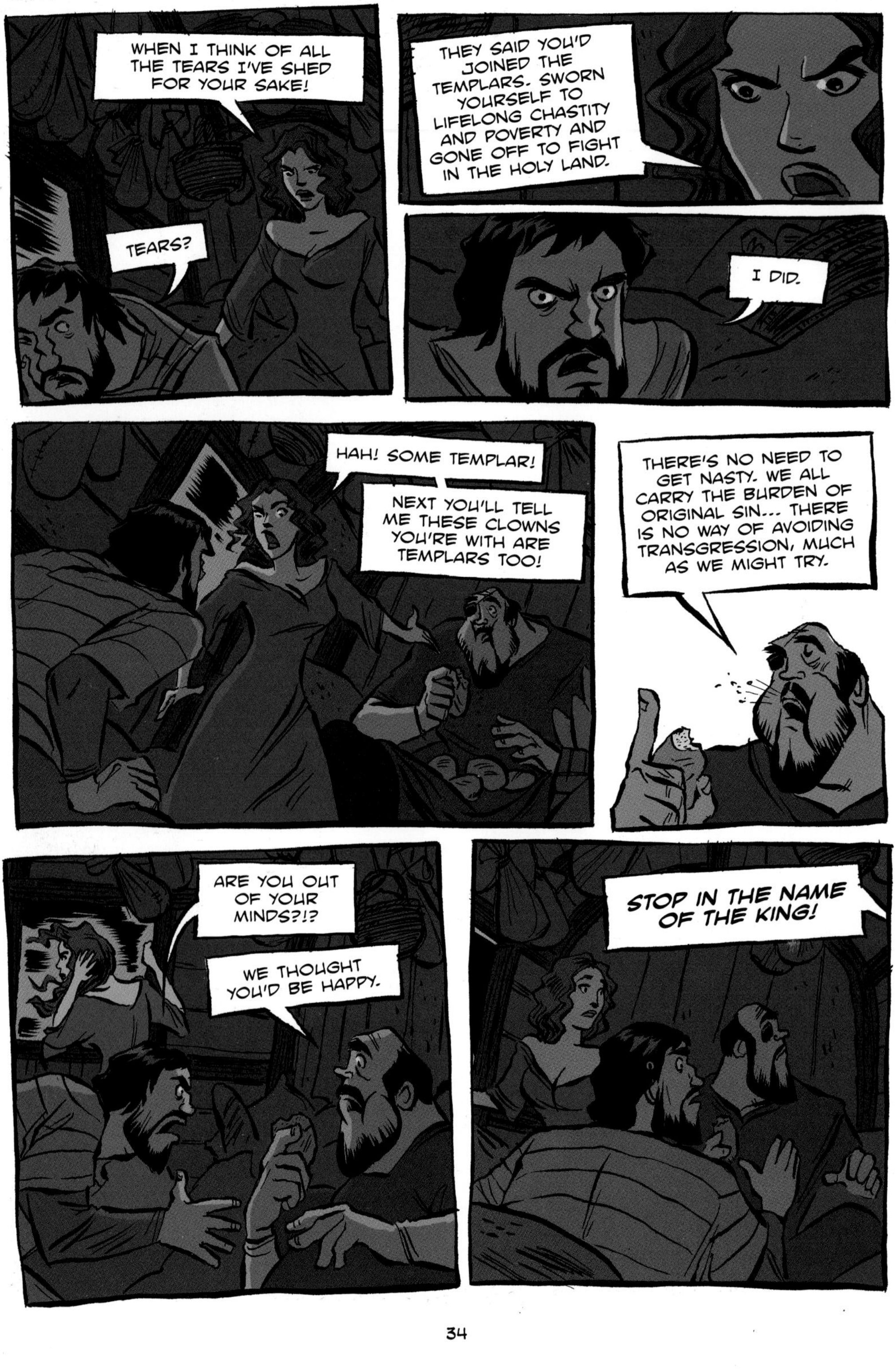

WHEN I THINK OF ALL THE TEARS I'VE SHED FOR YOUR SAKE!
TEARS?
THEY SAID YOU'D JOINED THE TEMPLARS. SWORN YOURSELF TO LIFELONG CHASTITY AND POVERTY AND GONE OFF TO FIGHT IN THE HOLY LAND.
I DID.
HAH! SOME TEMPLAR!
NEXT YOU'LL TELL ME THESE CLOWNS YOU'RE WITH ARE TEMPLARS TOO!
THERE'S NO NEED TO GET NASTY. WE ALL CARRY THE BURDEN OF ORIGINAL SIN... THERE IS NO WAY OF AVOIDING TRANSGRESSION, MUCH AS WE MIGHT TRY.
ARE YOU OUT OF YOUR MINDS?!?
WE THOUGHT YOU'D BE HAPPY.
STOP IN THE NAME OF THE KING!

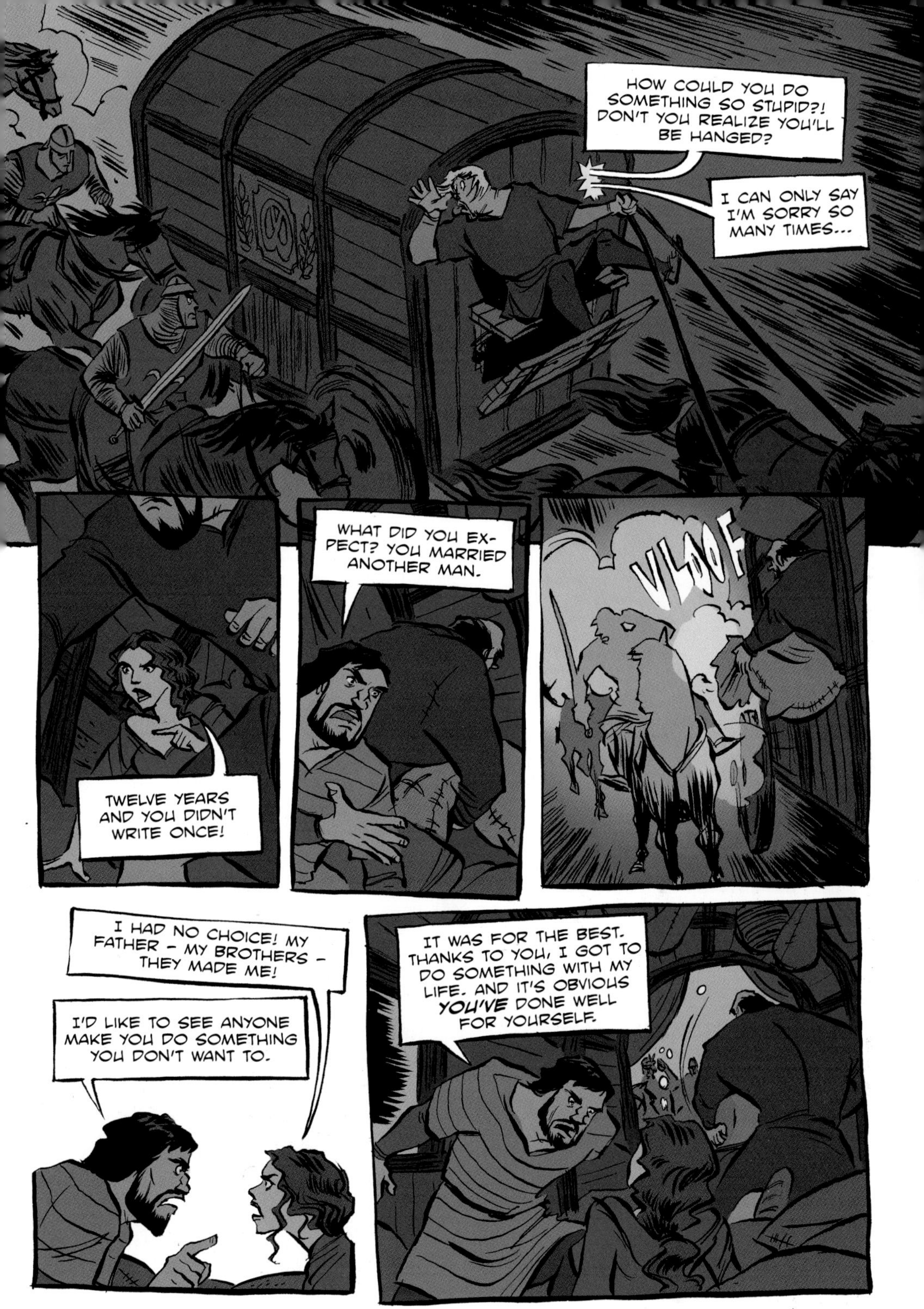
HOW COULD YOU DO SOMETHING SO STUPID?! DON'T YOU REALIZE YOU'LL BE HANGED?
I CAN ONLY SAY I'M SORRY SO MANY TIMES...
TWELVE YEARS AND YOU DIDN'T WRITE ONCE!
WHAT DID YOU EXPECT? YOU MARRIED ANOTHER MAN.
VLOOF
I HAD NO CHOICE! MY FATHER – MY BROTHERS – THEY MADE ME!
I'D LIKE TO SEE ANYONE MAKE YOU DO SOMETHING YOU DON'T WANT TO.
IT WAS FOR THE BEST. THANKS TO YOU, I GOT TO DO SOMETHING WITH MY LIFE. AND IT'S OBVIOUS *YOU'VE* DONE WELL FOR YOURSELF.

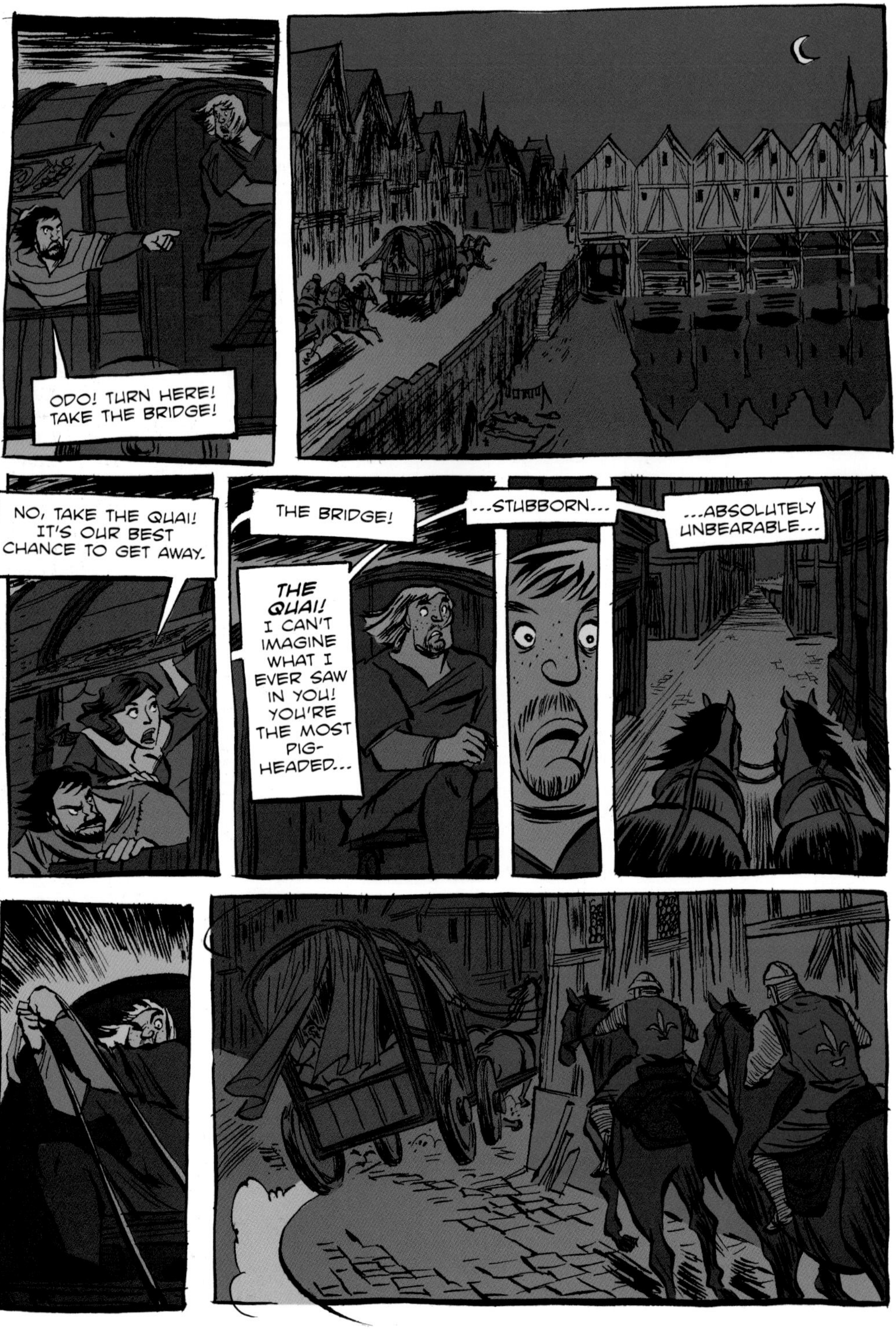

ODO! TURN HERE! TAKE THE BRIDGE!
NO, TAKE THE QUAI! IT'S OUR BEST CHANCE TO GET AWAY.
THE BRIDGE!
THE QUAI! I CAN'T IMAGINE WHAT I EVER SAW IN YOU! YOU'RE THE MOST PIG-HEADED...
...STUBBORN...
...ABSOLUTELY UNBEARABLE...

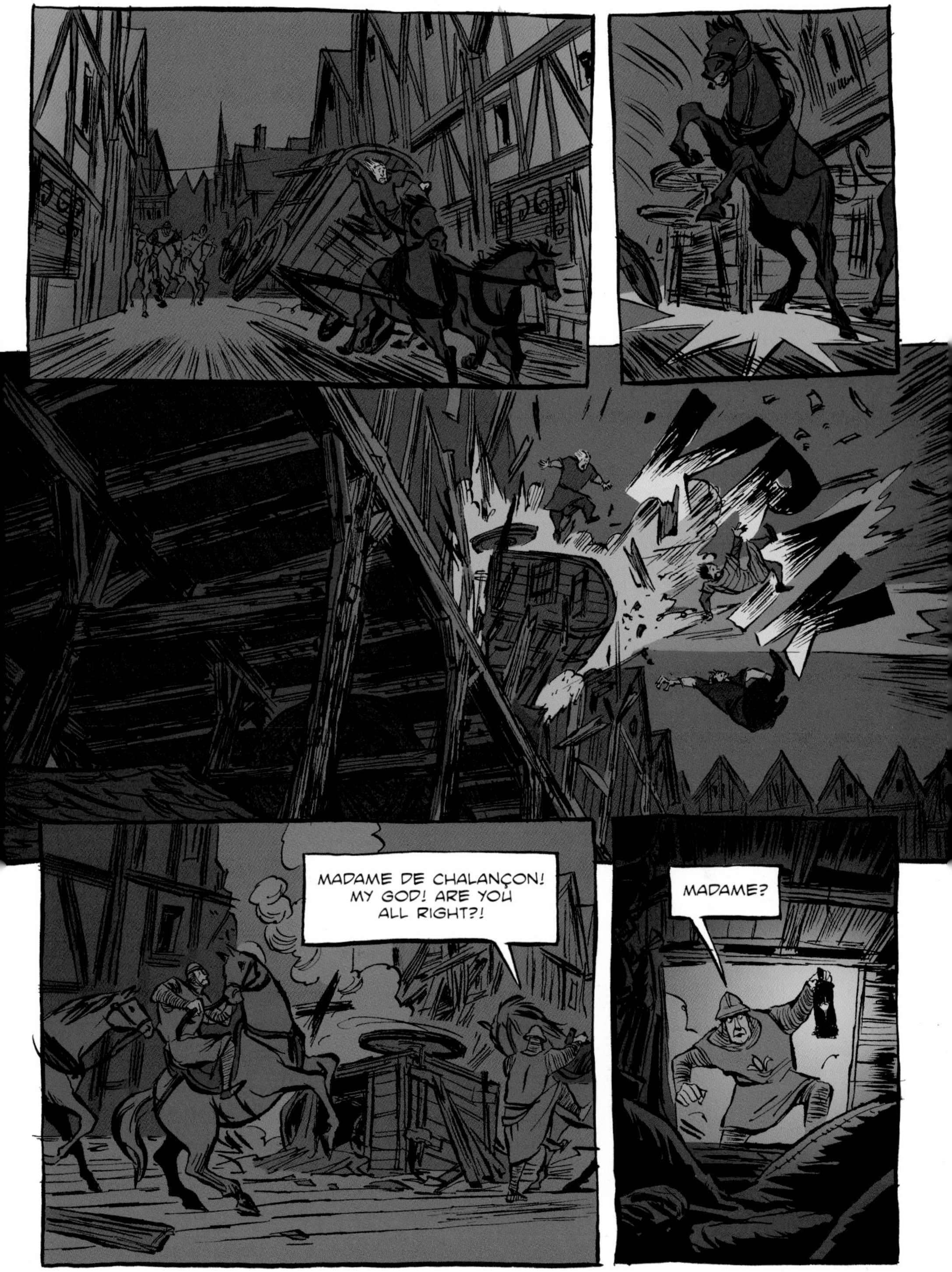
MADAME DE CHALANÇON! MY GOD! ARE YOU ALL RIGHT?!
MADAME?

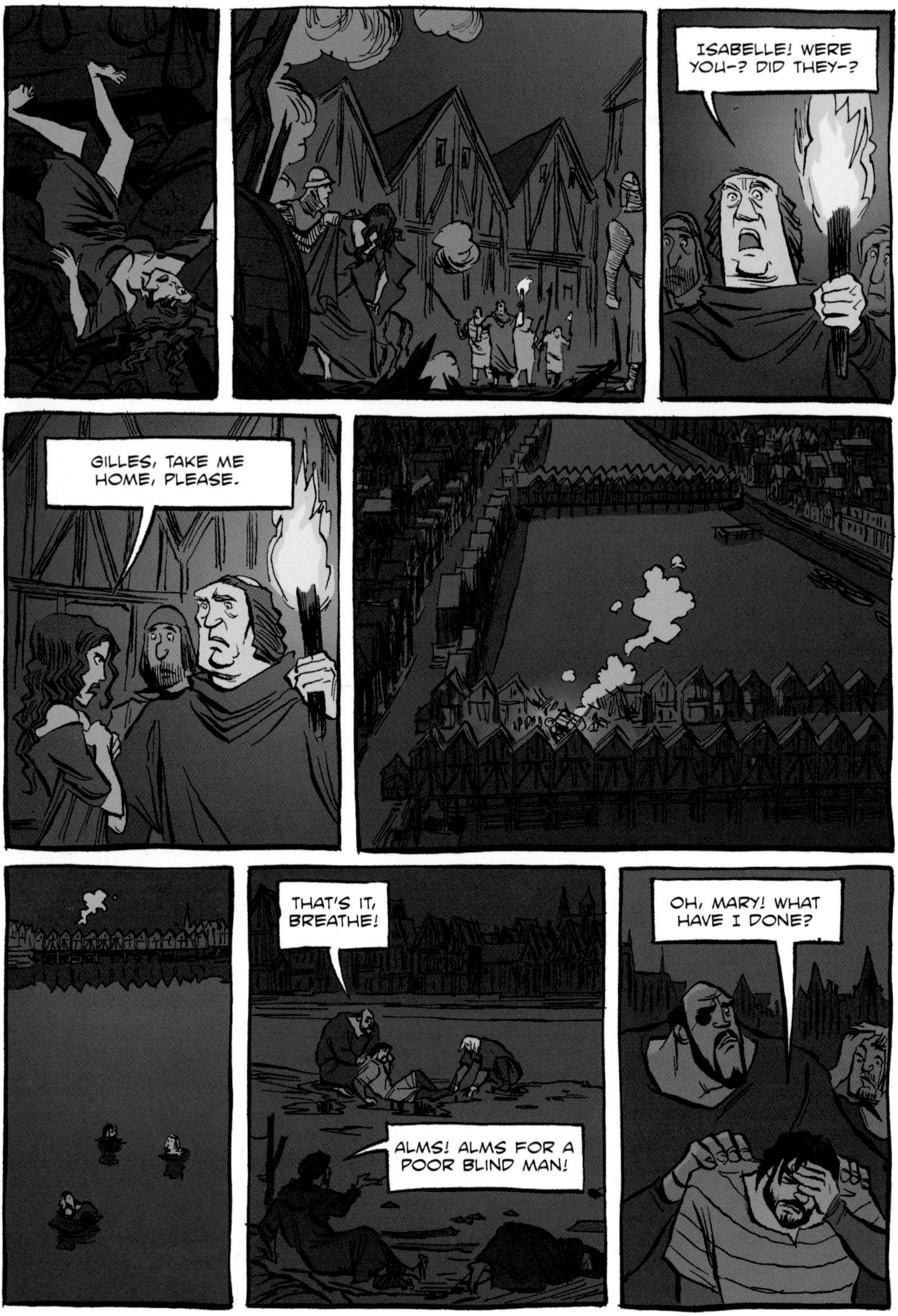
ISABELLE! WERE YOU-? DID THEY-?
GILLES, TAKE ME HOME, PLEASE.
THAT'S IT, BREATHE!
ALMS! ALMS FOR A POOR BLIND MAN!
OH, MARY! WHAT HAVE I DONE?

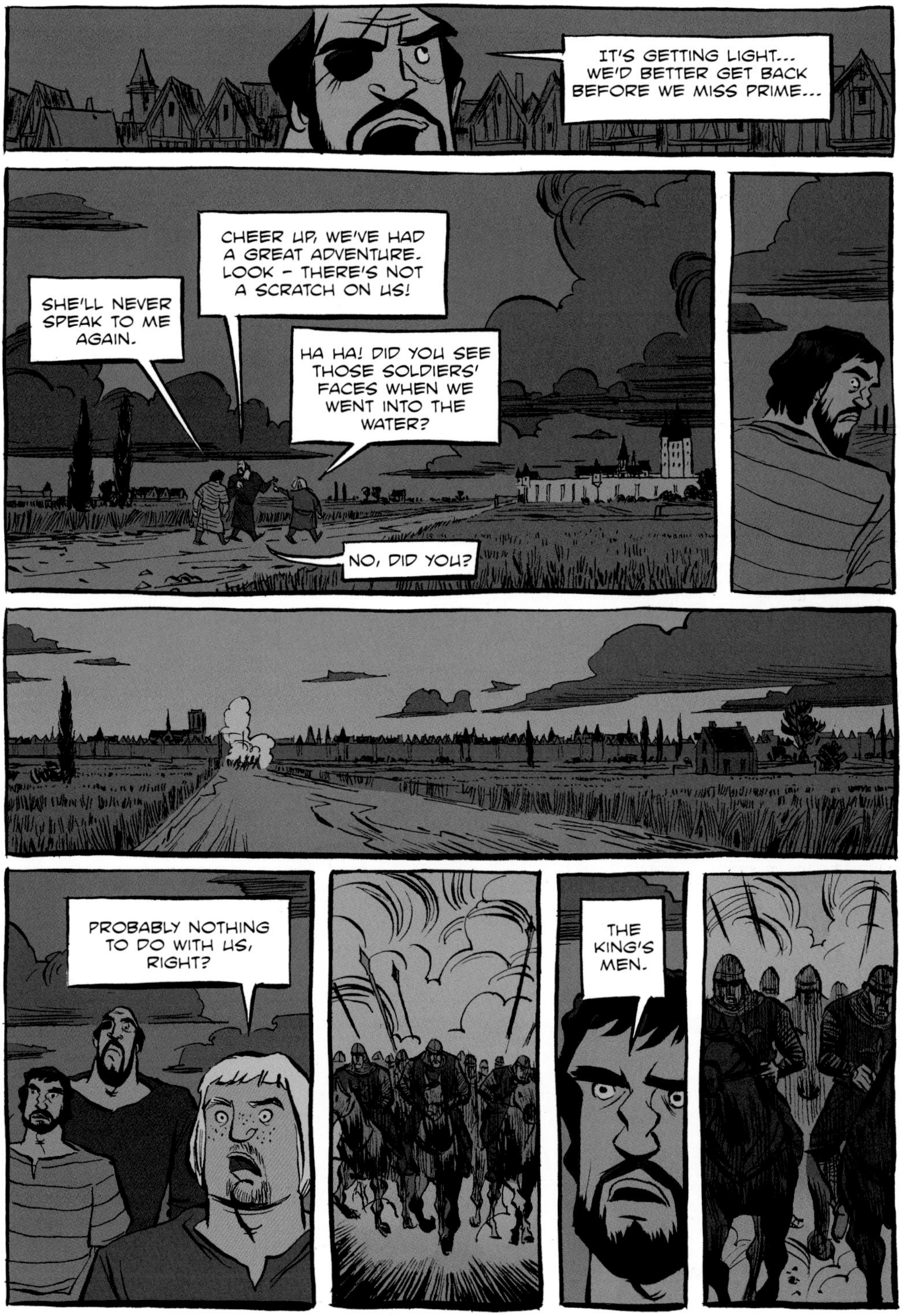
IT'S GETTING LIGHT... WE'D BETTER GET BACK BEFORE WE MISS PRIME...
SHE'LL NEVER SPEAK TO ME AGAIN.
CHEER UP, WE'VE HAD A GREAT ADVENTURE. LOOK - THERE'S NOT A SCRATCH ON US!
HA HA! DID YOU SEE THOSE SOLDIERS' FACES WHEN WE WENT INTO THE WATER?
NO, DID YOU?
PROBABLY NOTHING TO DO WITH US, RIGHT?
THE KING'S MEN.

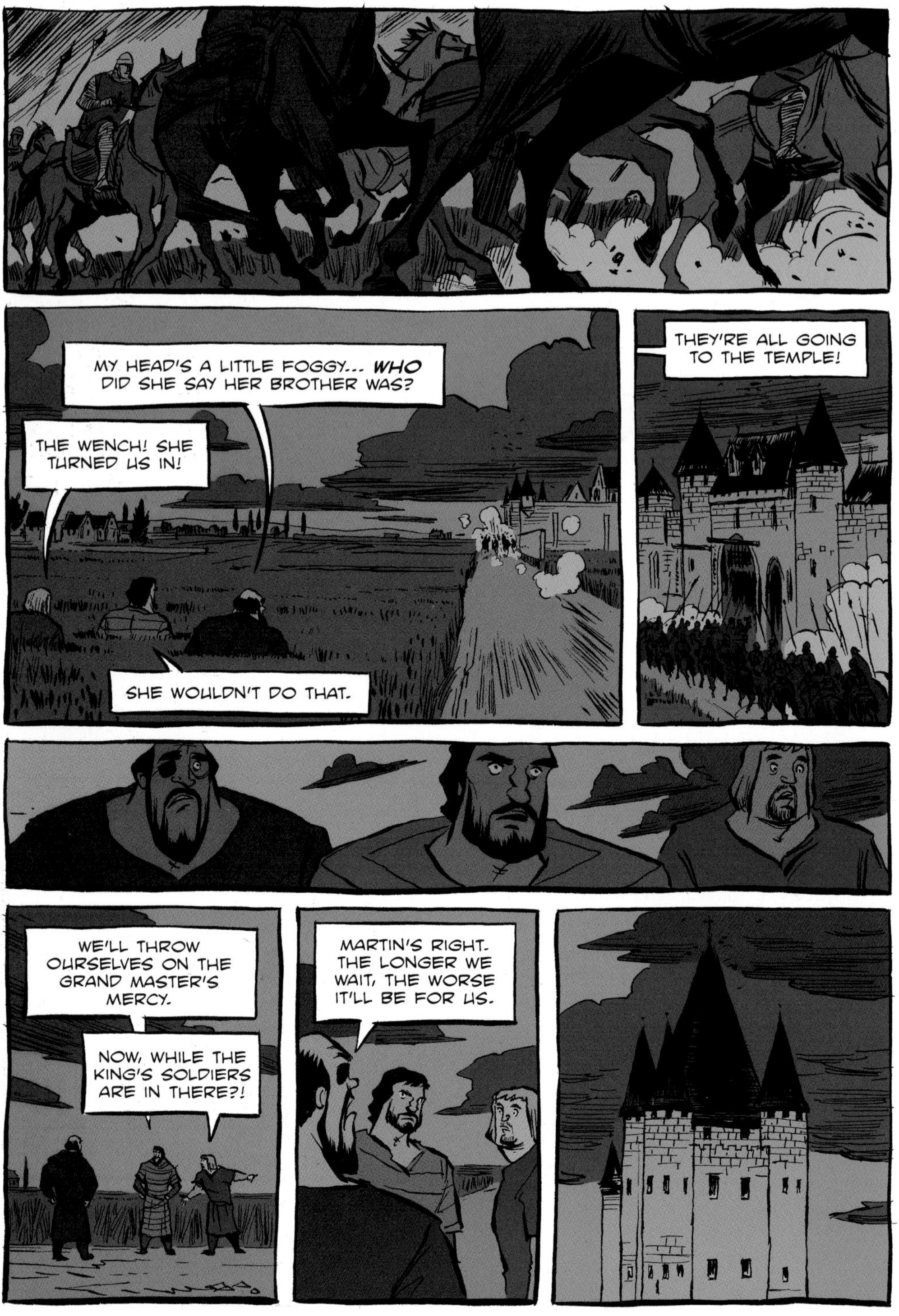
MY HEAD'S A LITTLE FOGGY... WHO DID SHE SAY HER BROTHER WAS?
THE WENCH! SHE TURNED US IN!
SHE WOULDN'T DO THAT.
THEY'RE ALL GOING TO THE TEMPLE!
WE'LL THROW OURSELVES ON THE GRAND MASTER'S MERCY.
NOW, WHILE THE KING'S SOLDIERS ARE IN THERE?!
MARTIN'S RIGHT. THE LONGER WE WAIT, THE WORSE IT'LL BE FOR US.

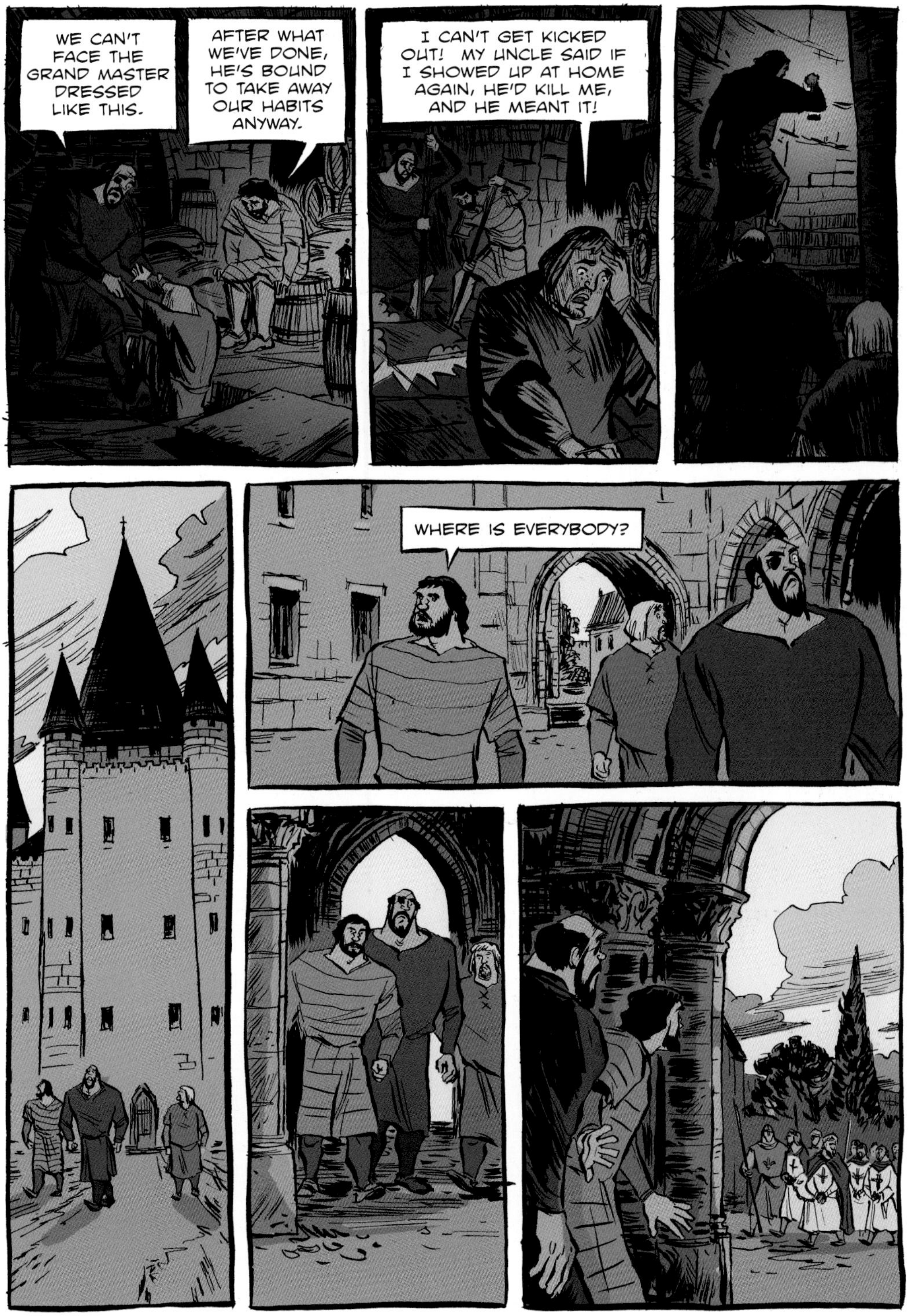
WE CAN'T FACE THE GRAND MASTER DRESSED LIKE THIS.
AFTER WHAT WE'VE DONE, HE'S BOUND TO TAKE AWAY OUR HABITS ANYWAY.
I CAN'T GET KICKED OUT! MY UNCLE SAID IF I SHOWED UP AT HOME AGAIN, HE'D KILL ME, AND HE MEANT IT!
WHERE IS EVERYBODY?

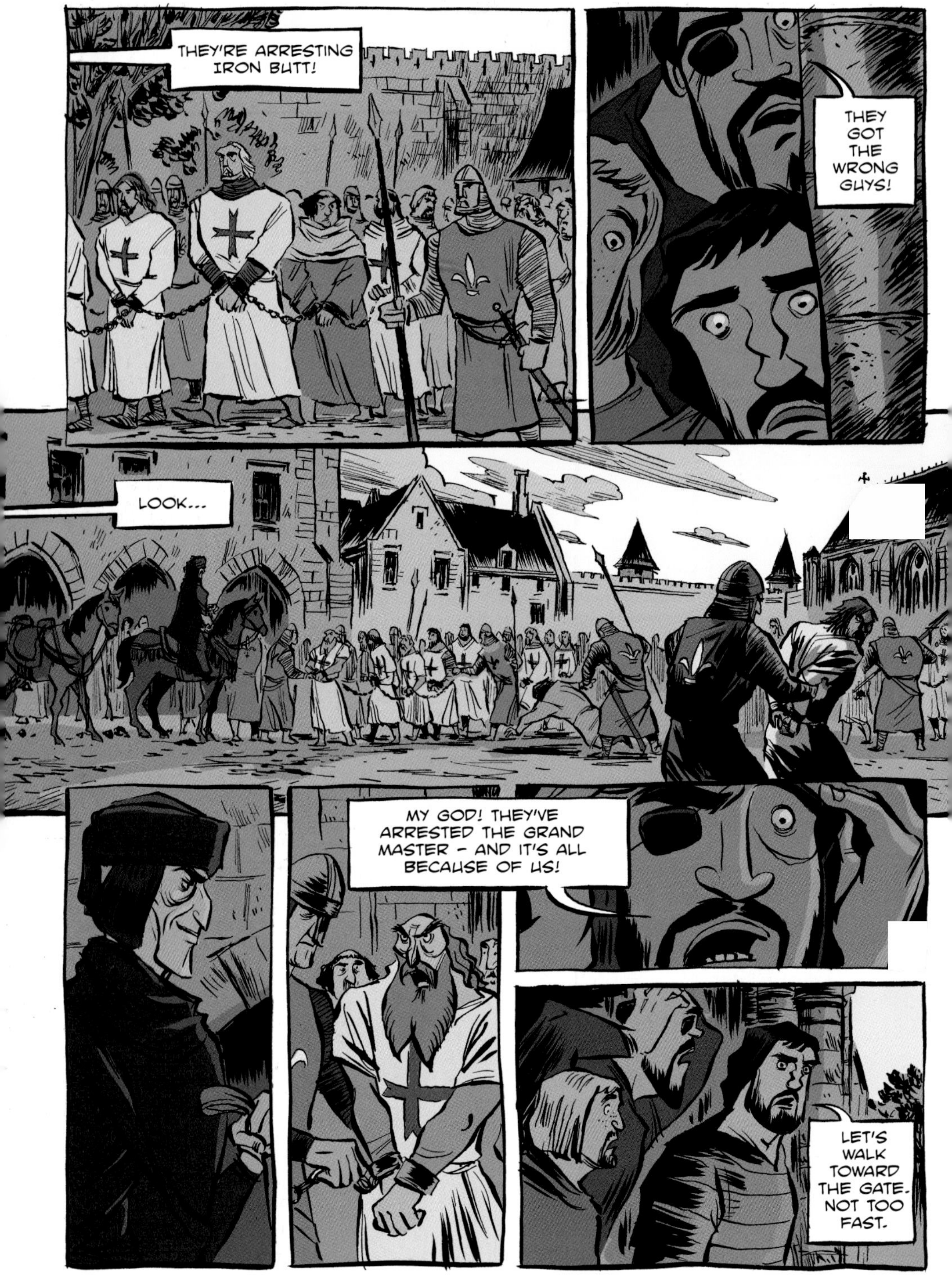
THEY'RE ARRESTING IRON BUTT!
THEY GOT THE WRONG GUYS!
LOOK...
MY GOD! THEY'VE ARRESTED THE GRAND MASTER - AND IT'S ALL BECAUSE OF US!
LET'S WALK TOWARD THE GATE. NOT TOO FAST.

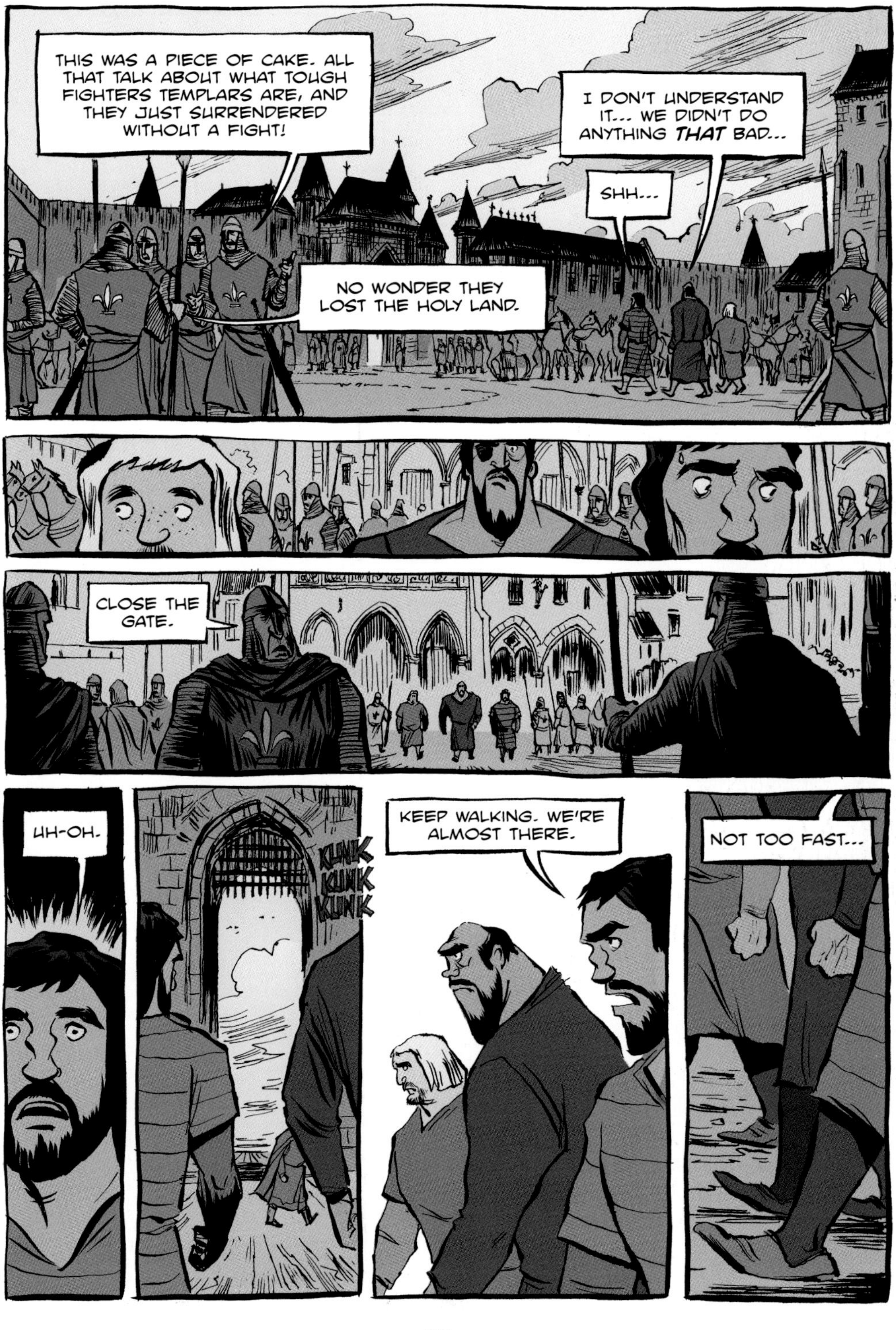
THIS WAS A PIECE OF CAKE. ALL THAT TALK ABOUT WHAT TOUGH FIGHTERS TEMPLARS ARE, AND THEY JUST SURRENDERED WITHOUT A FIGHT!
I DON'T UNDERSTAND IT... WE DIDN'T DO ANYTHING *THAT* BAD...
SHH...
NO WONDER THEY LOST THE HOLY LAND.
CLOSE THE GATE.
UH-OH.
KLUNK KLUNK KLUNK
KEEP WALKING. WE'RE ALMOST THERE.
NOT TOO FAST...

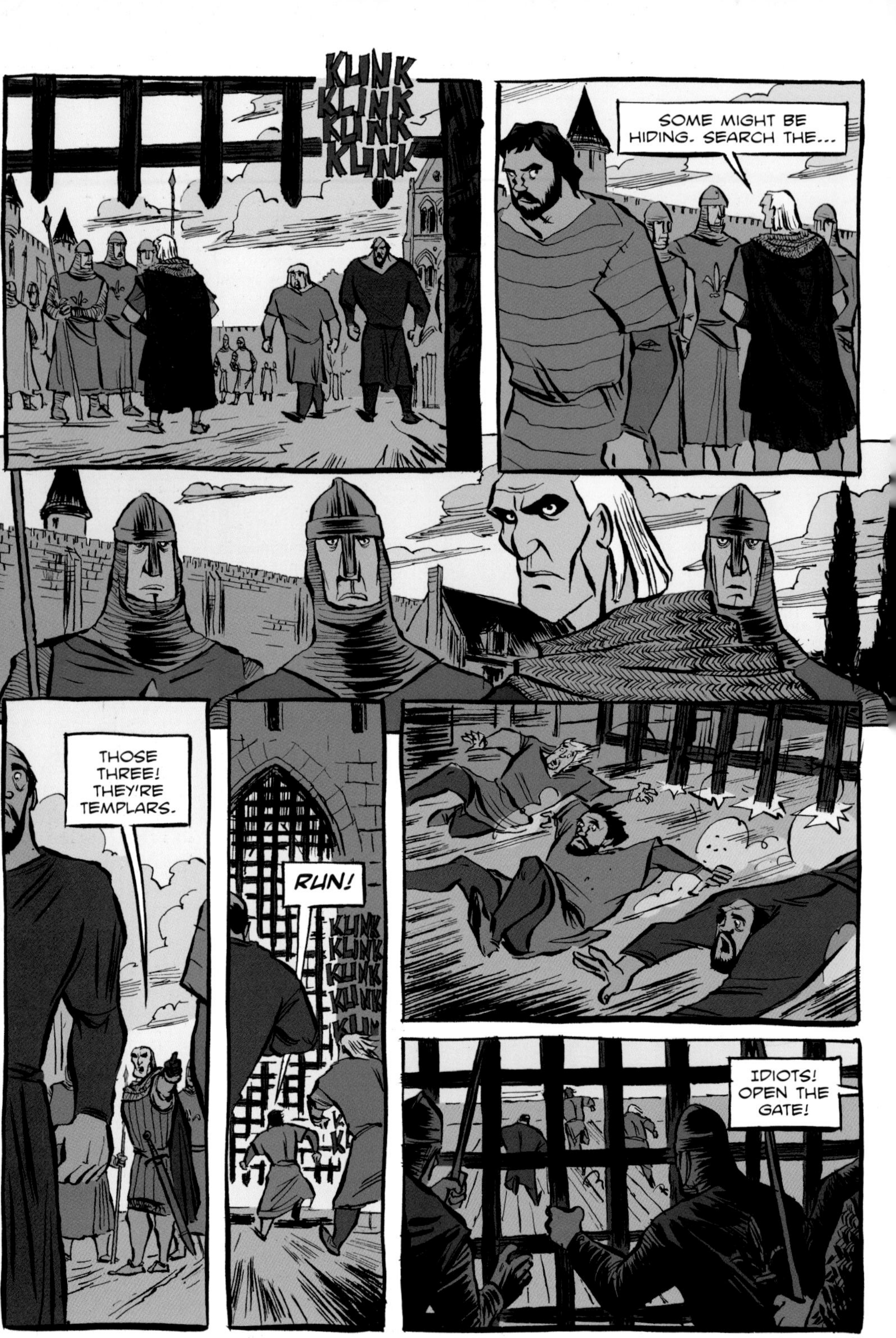
KLINK
KLINK
KLINK
KLINK
SOME MIGHT BE HIDING. SEARCH THE...
THOSE THREE! THEY'RE TEMPLARS.
RUN!
KLINK
KLINK
KLINK
KLINK
IDIOTS! OPEN THE GATE!

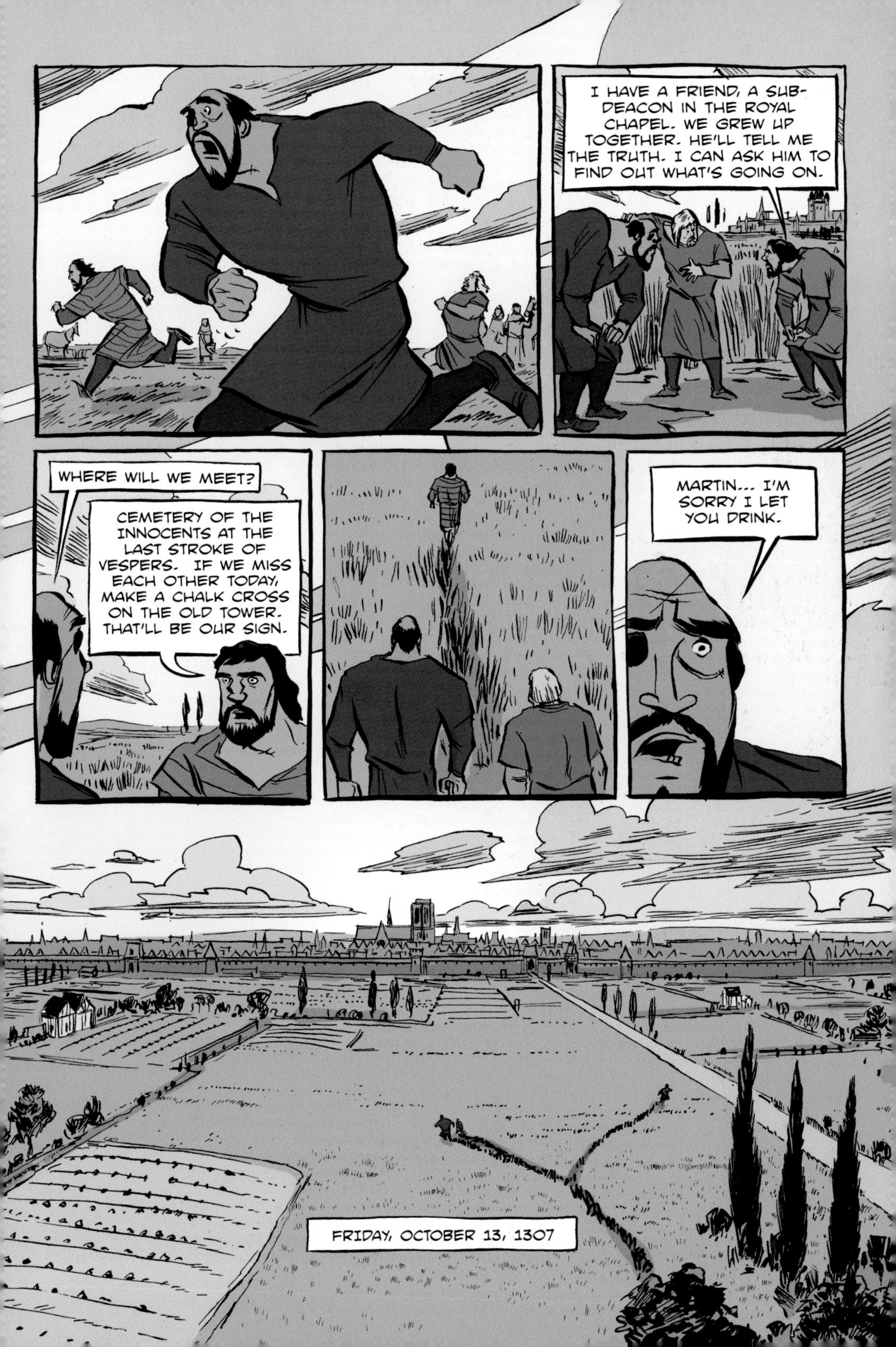
I HAVE A FRIEND, A SUB-DEACON IN THE ROYAL CHAPEL. WE GREW UP TOGETHER. HE'LL TELL ME THE TRUTH. I CAN ASK HIM TO FIND OUT WHAT'S GOING ON.
WHERE WILL WE MEET?
CEMETERY OF THE INNOCENTS AT THE LAST STROKE OF VESPERS. IF WE MISS EACH OTHER TODAY, MAKE A CHALK CROSS ON THE OLD TOWER. THAT'LL BE OUR SIGN.
MARTIN... I'M SORRY I LET YOU DRINK.
FRIDAY, OCTOBER 13, 1307

2.

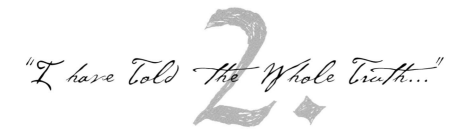

"I have Told the Whole Truth..."

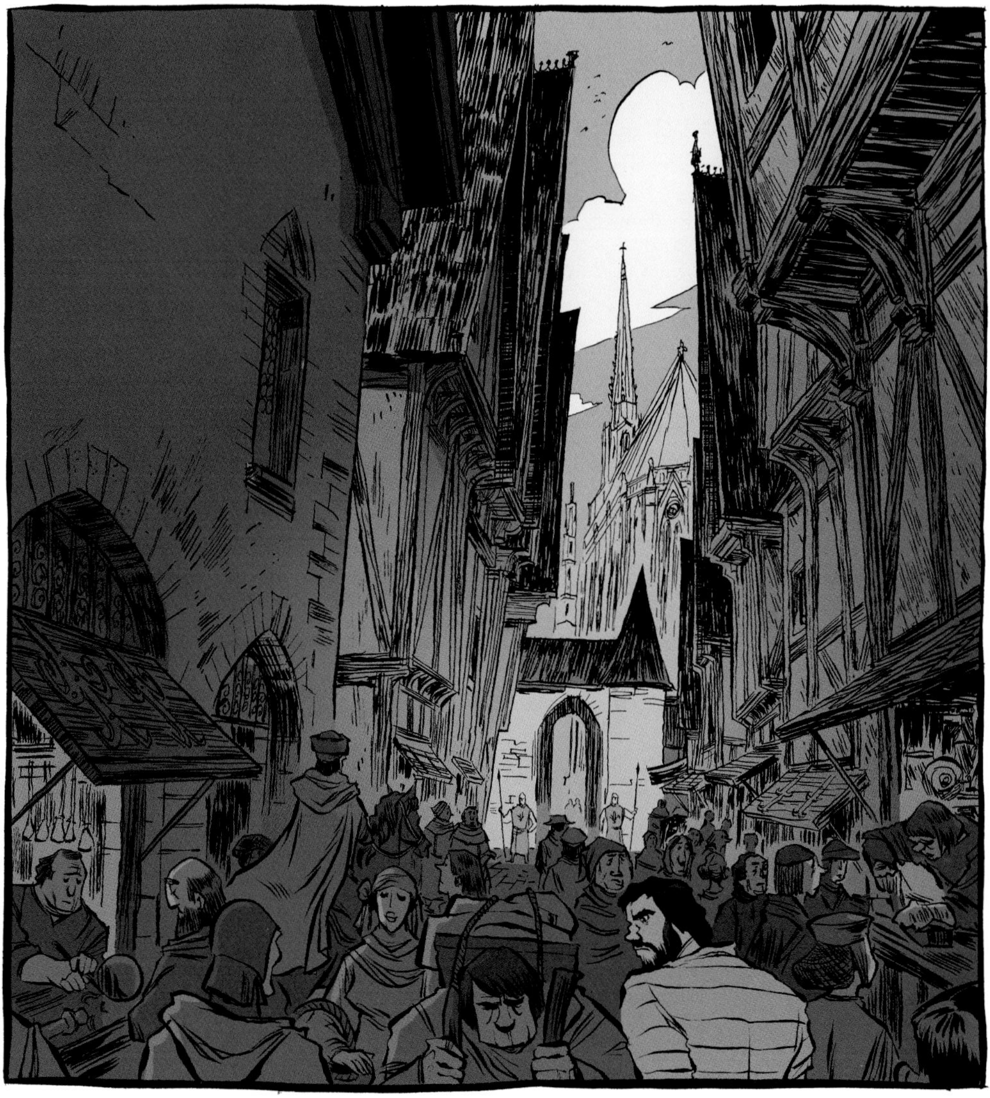

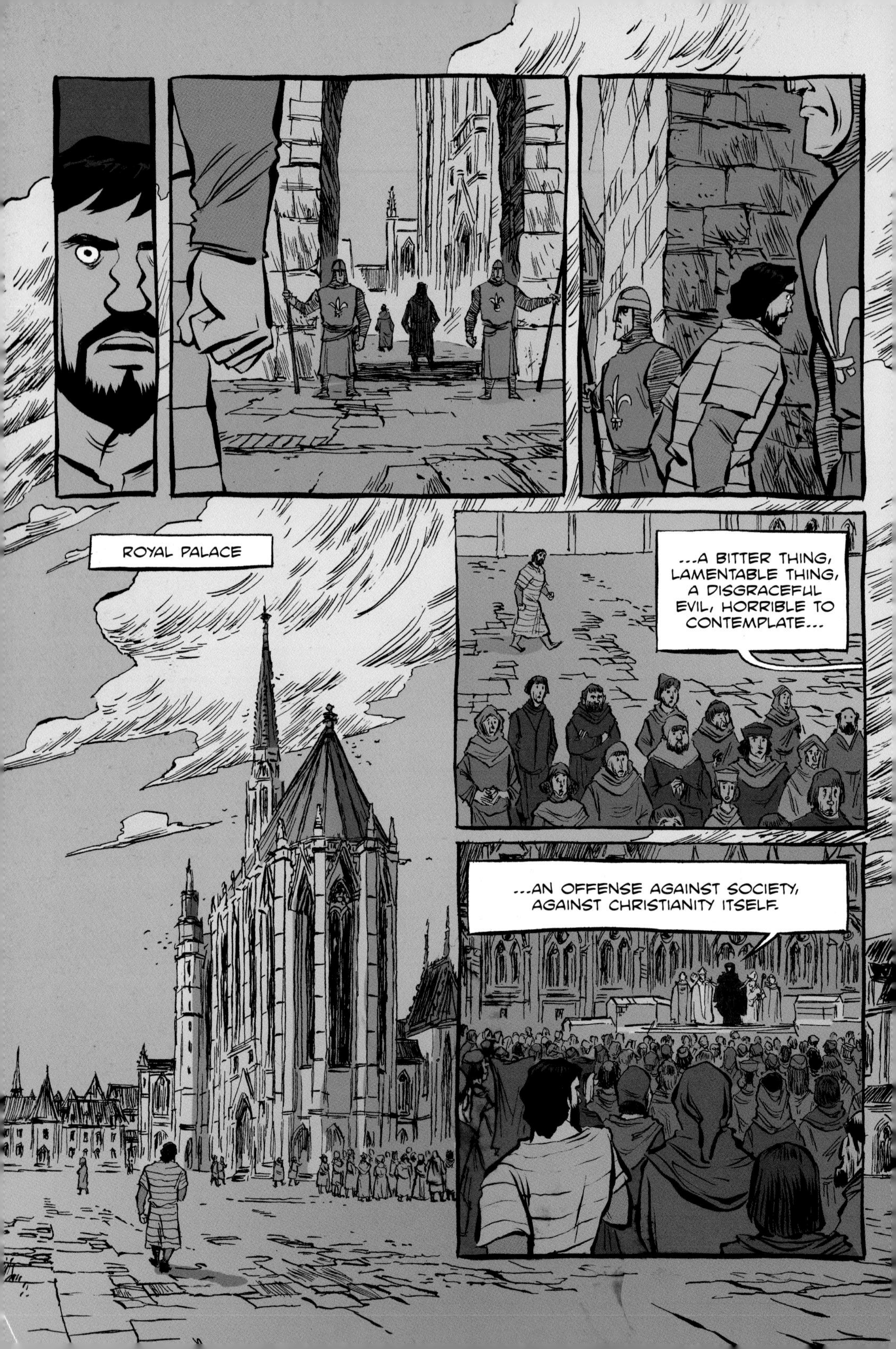
ROYAL PALACE
...A BITTER THING, LAMENTABLE THING, A DISGRACEFUL EVIL, HORRIBLE TO CONTEMPLATE...
...AN OFFENSE AGAINST SOCIETY, AGAINST CHRISTIANITY ITSELF.

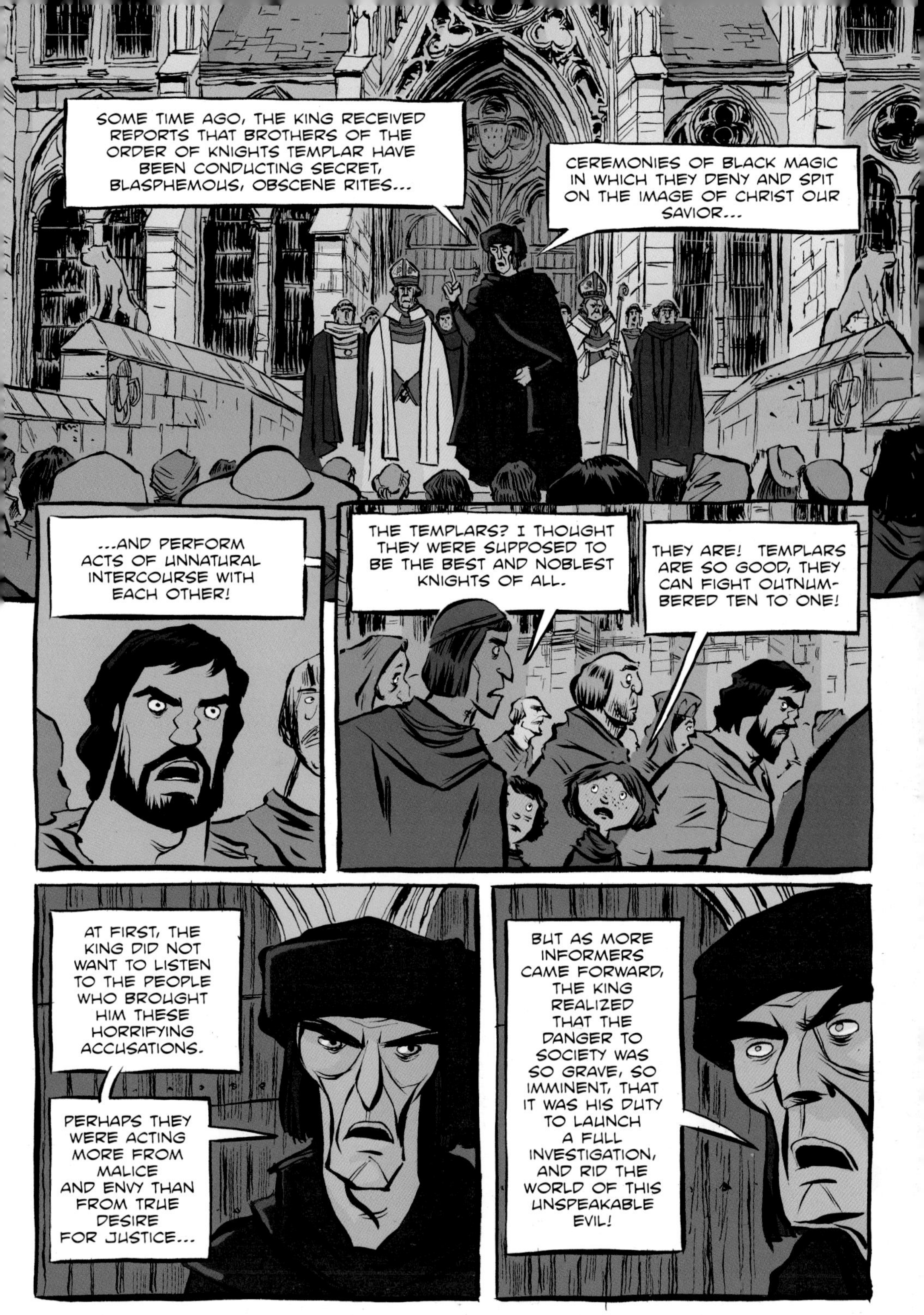
SOME TIME AGO, THE KING RECEIVED REPORTS THAT BROTHERS OF THE ORDER OF KNIGHTS TEMPLAR HAVE BEEN CONDUCTING SECRET, BLASPHEMOUS, OBSCENE RITES...
CEREMONIES OF BLACK MAGIC IN WHICH THEY DENY AND SPIT ON THE IMAGE OF CHRIST OUR SAVIOR...
...AND PERFORM ACTS OF UNNATURAL INTERCOURSE WITH EACH OTHER!
THE TEMPLARS? I THOUGHT THEY WERE SUPPOSED TO BE THE BEST AND NOBLEST KNIGHTS OF ALL.
THEY ARE! TEMPLARS ARE SO GOOD, THEY CAN FIGHT OUTNUMBERED TEN TO ONE!
AT FIRST, THE KING DID NOT WANT TO LISTEN TO THE PEOPLE WHO BROUGHT HIM THESE HORRIFYING ACCUSATIONS.
PERHAPS THEY WERE ACTING MORE FROM MALICE AND ENVY THAN FROM TRUE DESIRE FOR JUSTICE...
BUT AS MORE INFORMERS CAME FORWARD, THE KING REALIZED THAT THE DANGER TO SOCIETY WAS SO GRAVE, SO IMMINENT, THAT IT WAS HIS DUTY TO LAUNCH A FULL INVESTIGATION, AND RID THE WORLD OF THIS UNSPEAKABLE EVIL!

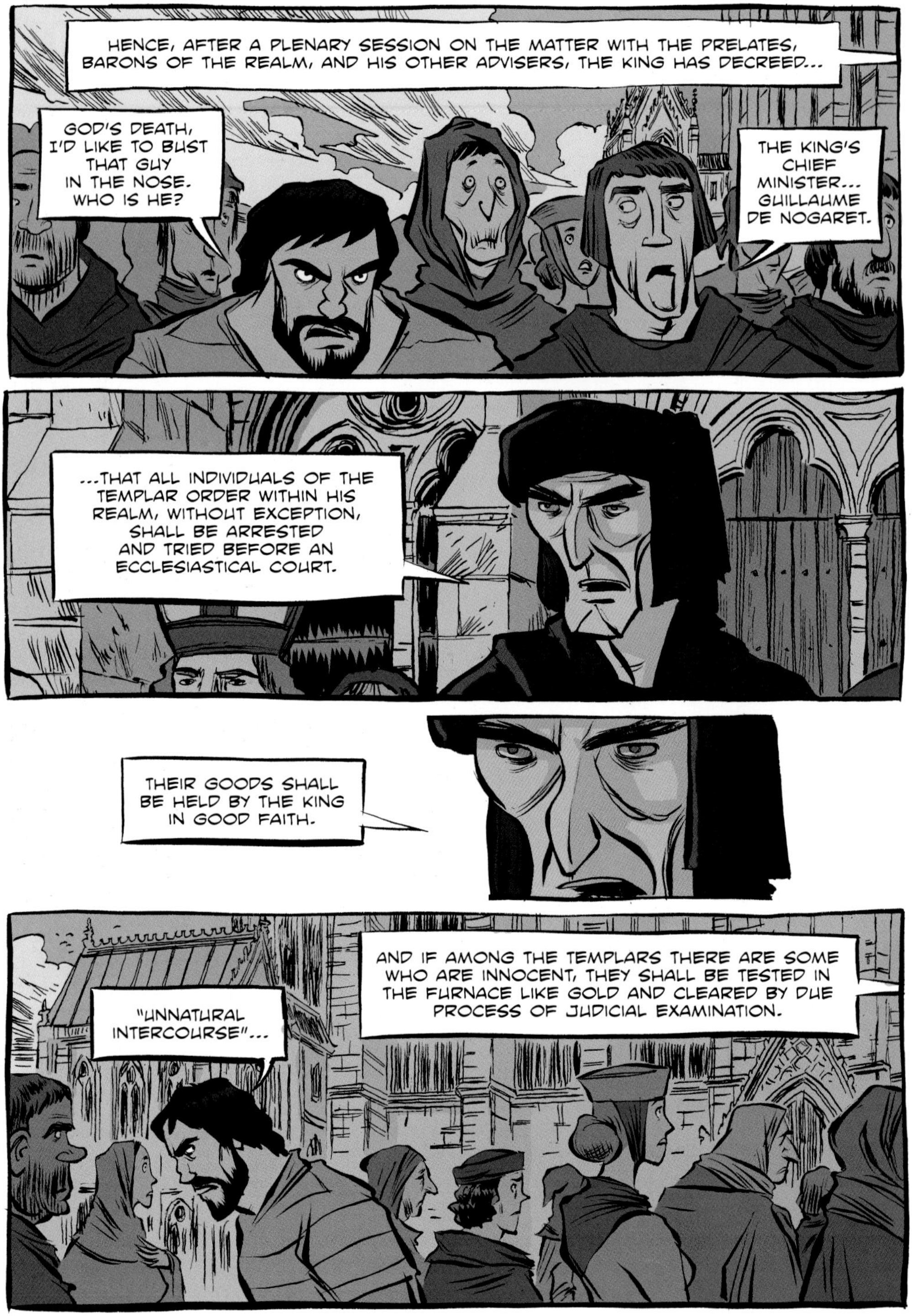
HENCE, AFTER A PLENARY SESSION ON THE MATTER WITH THE PRELATES, BARONS OF THE REALM, AND HIS OTHER ADVISERS, THE KING HAS DECREED...
GOD'S DEATH, I'D LIKE TO BUST THAT GUY IN THE NOSE. WHO IS HE?
THE KING'S CHIEF MINISTER... GUILLAUME DE NOGARET.
...THAT ALL INDIVIDUALS OF THE TEMPLAR ORDER WITHIN HIS REALM, WITHOUT EXCEPTION, SHALL BE ARRESTED AND TRIED BEFORE AN ECCLESIASTICAL COURT.
THEIR GOODS SHALL BE HELD BY THE KING IN GOOD FAITH.
AND IF AMONG THE TEMPLARS THERE ARE SOME WHO ARE INNOCENT, THEY SHALL BE TESTED IN THE FURNACE LIKE GOLD AND CLEARED BY DUE PROCESS OF JUDICIAL EXAMINATION.
"UNNATURAL INTERCOURSE"...

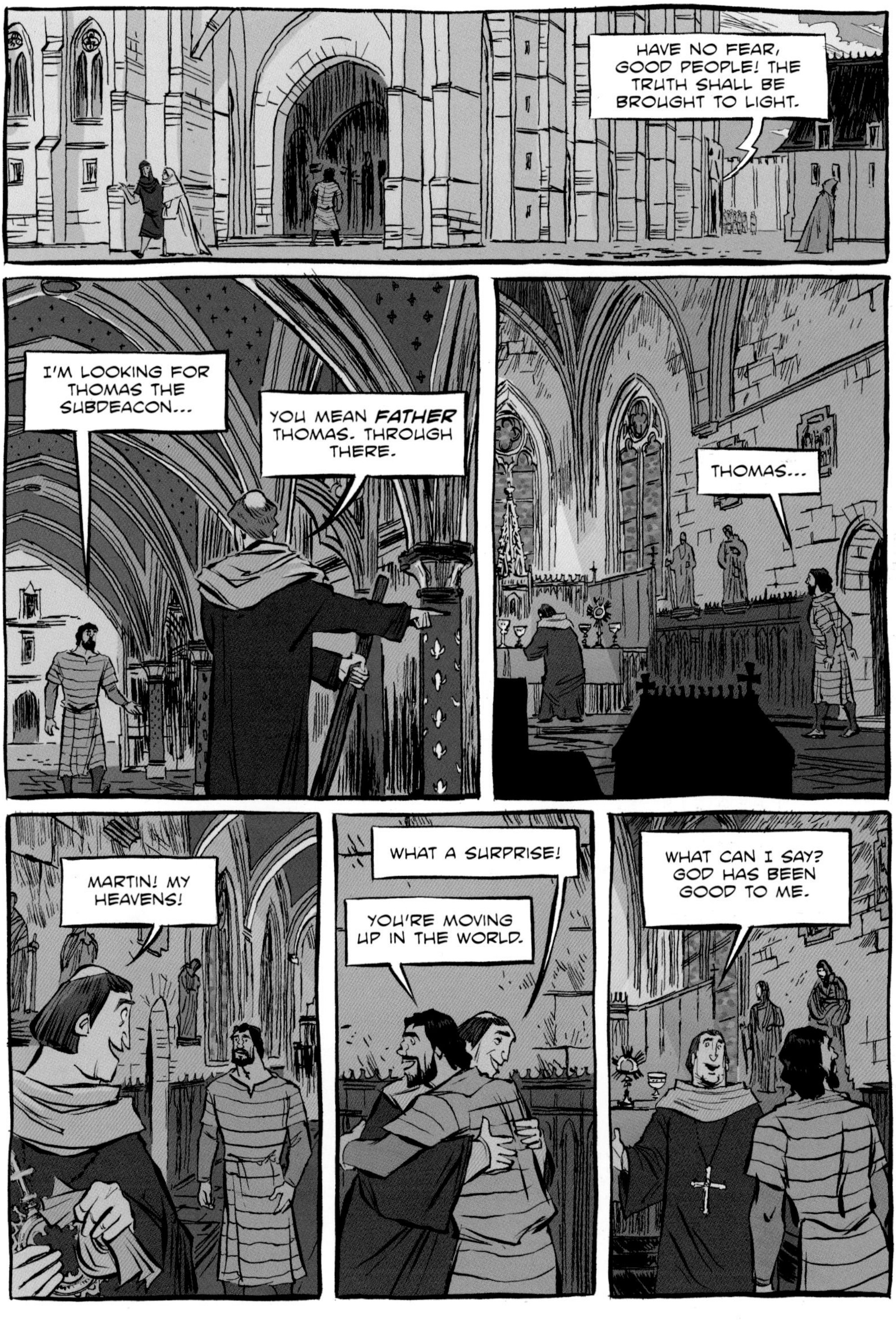
HAVE NO FEAR, GOOD PEOPLE! THE TRUTH SHALL BE BROUGHT TO LIGHT.
I'M LOOKING FOR THOMAS THE SUBDEACON...
YOU MEAN FATHER THOMAS. THROUGH THERE.
THOMAS...
MARTIN! MY HEAVENS!
WHAT A SURPRISE!
YOU'RE MOVING UP IN THE WORLD.
WHAT CAN I SAY? GOD HAS BEEN GOOD TO ME.

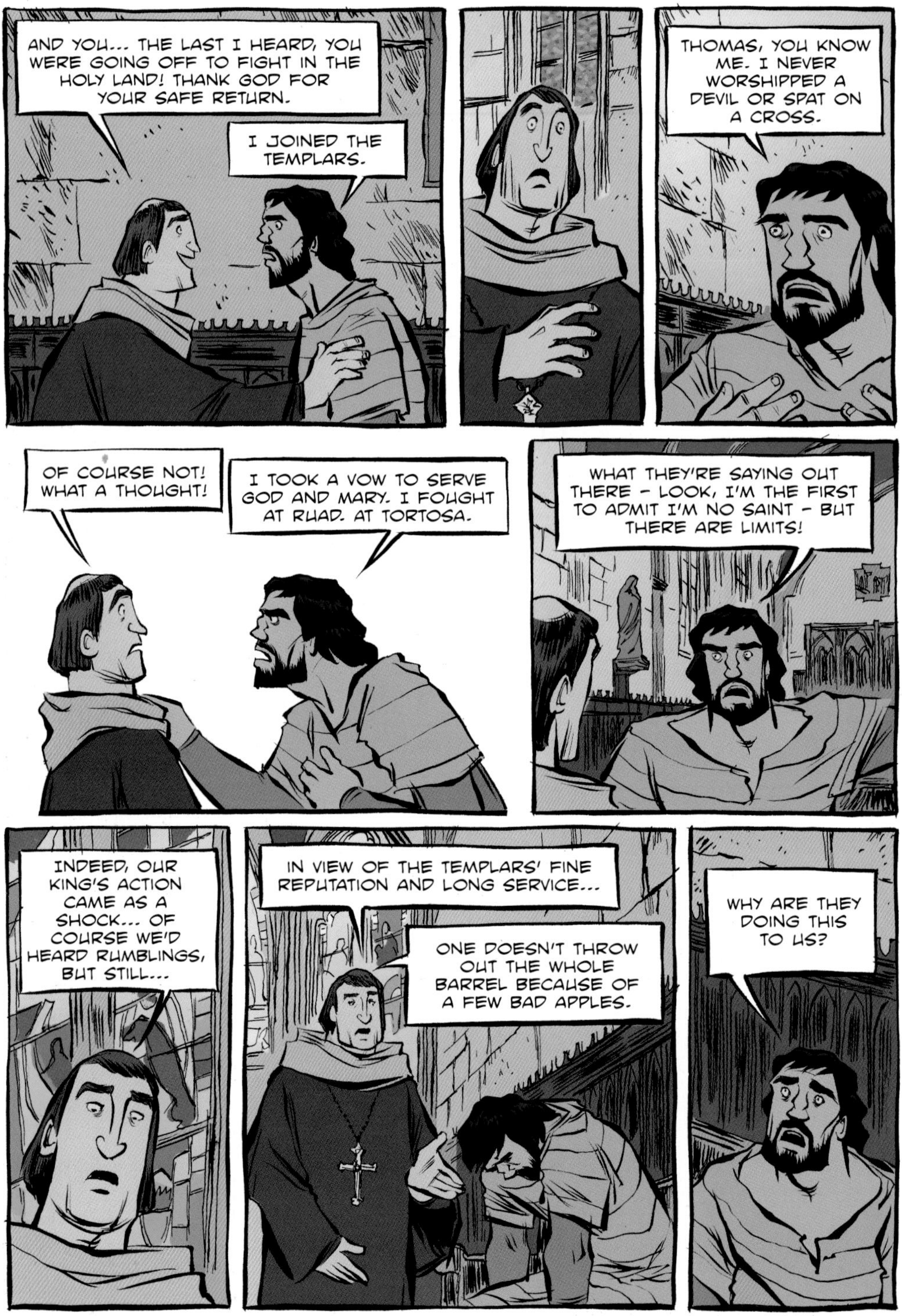
AND YOU... THE LAST I HEARD, YOU WERE GOING OFF TO FIGHT IN THE HOLY LAND! THANK GOD FOR YOUR SAFE RETURN.
I JOINED THE TEMPLARS.
THOMAS, YOU KNOW ME. I NEVER WORSHIPPED A DEVIL OR SPAT ON A CROSS.
OF COURSE NOT! WHAT A THOUGHT!
I TOOK A VOW TO SERVE GOD AND MARY. I FOUGHT AT RUAD. AT TORTOSA.
WHAT THEY'RE SAYING OUT THERE – LOOK, I'M THE FIRST TO ADMIT I'M NO SAINT – BUT THERE ARE LIMITS!
INDEED, OUR KING'S ACTION CAME AS A SHOCK... OF COURSE WE'D HEARD RUMBLINGS, BUT STILL...
IN VIEW OF THE TEMPLARS' FINE REPUTATION AND LONG SERVICE...
ONE DOESN'T THROW OUT THE WHOLE BARREL BECAUSE OF A FEW BAD APPLES.
WHY ARE THEY DOING THIS TO US?

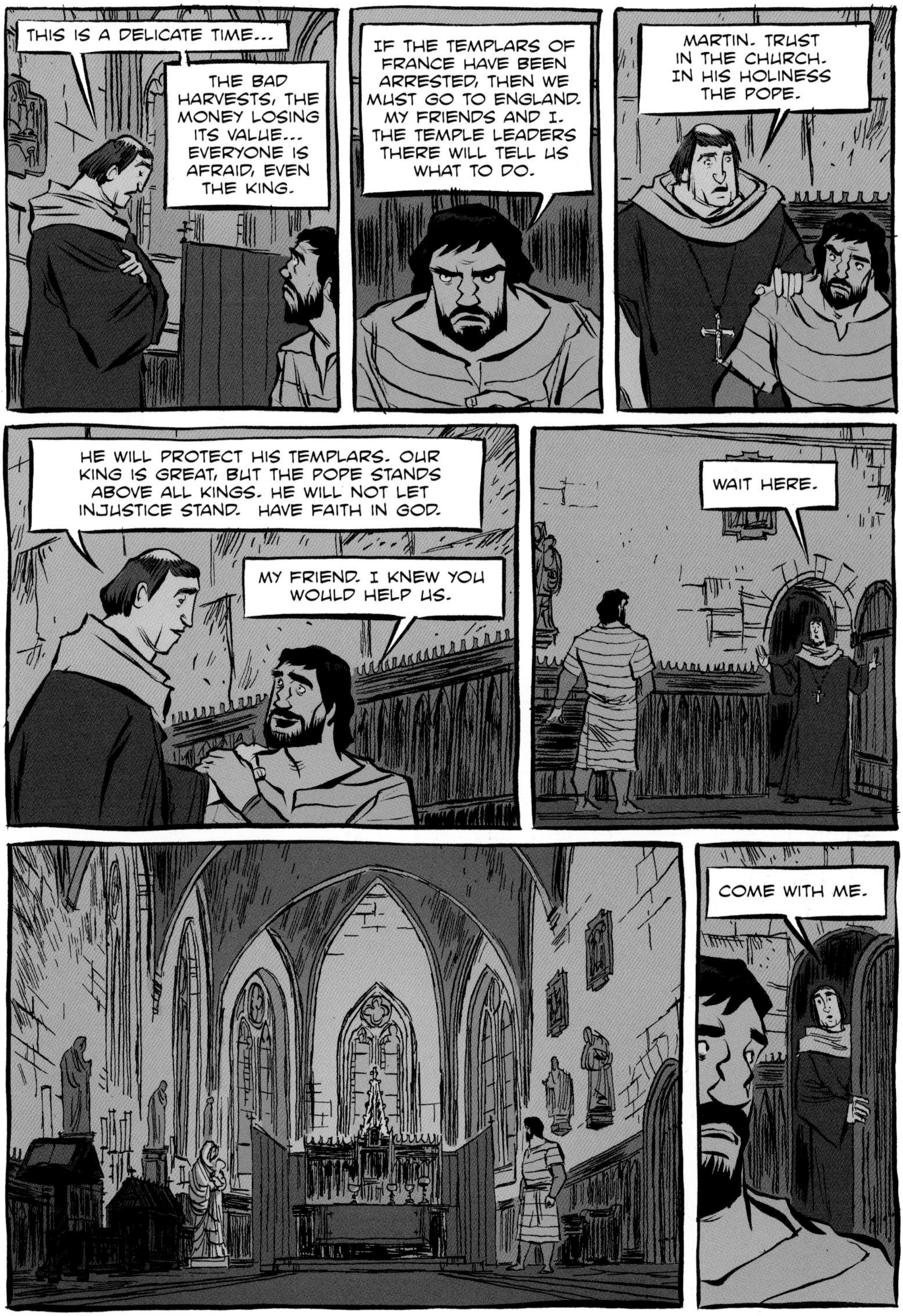
THIS IS A DELICATE TIME...
THE BAD HARVESTS, THE MONEY LOSING ITS VALUE... EVERYONE IS AFRAID, EVEN THE KING.
IF THE TEMPLARS OF FRANCE HAVE BEEN ARRESTED, THEN WE MUST GO TO ENGLAND. MY FRIENDS AND I. THE TEMPLE LEADERS THERE WILL TELL US WHAT TO DO.
MARTIN. TRUST IN THE CHURCH. IN HIS HOLINESS THE POPE.
HE WILL PROTECT HIS TEMPLARS. OUR KING IS GREAT, BUT THE POPE STANDS ABOVE ALL KINGS. HE WILL NOT LET INJUSTICE STAND. HAVE FAITH IN GOD.
MY FRIEND. I KNEW YOU WOULD HELP US.
WAIT HERE.
COME WITH ME.

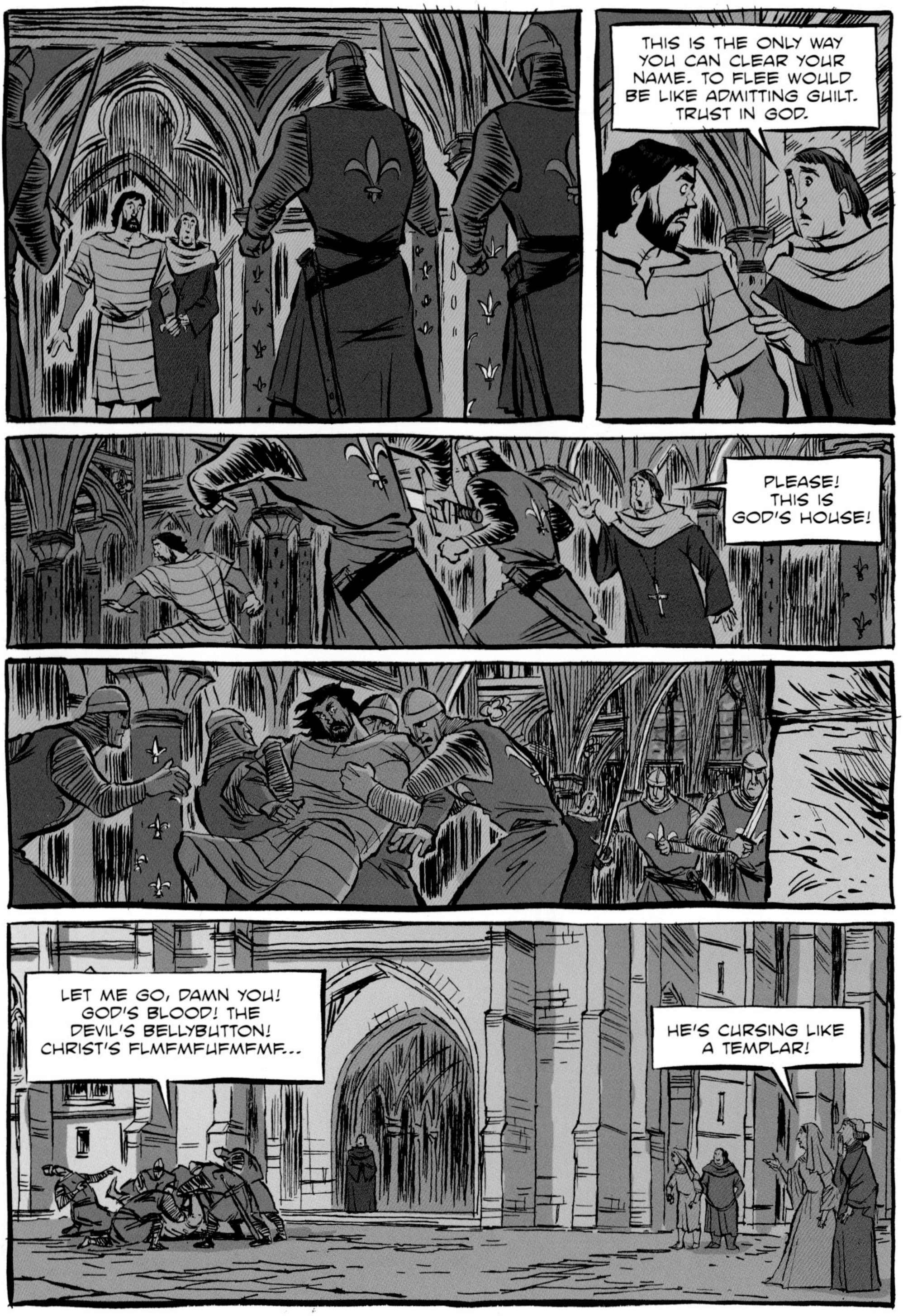
THIS IS THE ONLY WAY YOU CAN CLEAR YOUR NAME. TO FLEE WOULD BE LIKE ADMITTING GUILT. TRUST IN GOD.
PLEASE! THIS IS GOD'S HOUSE!
LET ME GO, DAMN YOU! GOD'S BLOOD! THE DEVIL'S BELLYBUTTON! CHRIST'S FLMFMFUFMFMF...
HE'S CURSING LIKE A TEMPLAR!

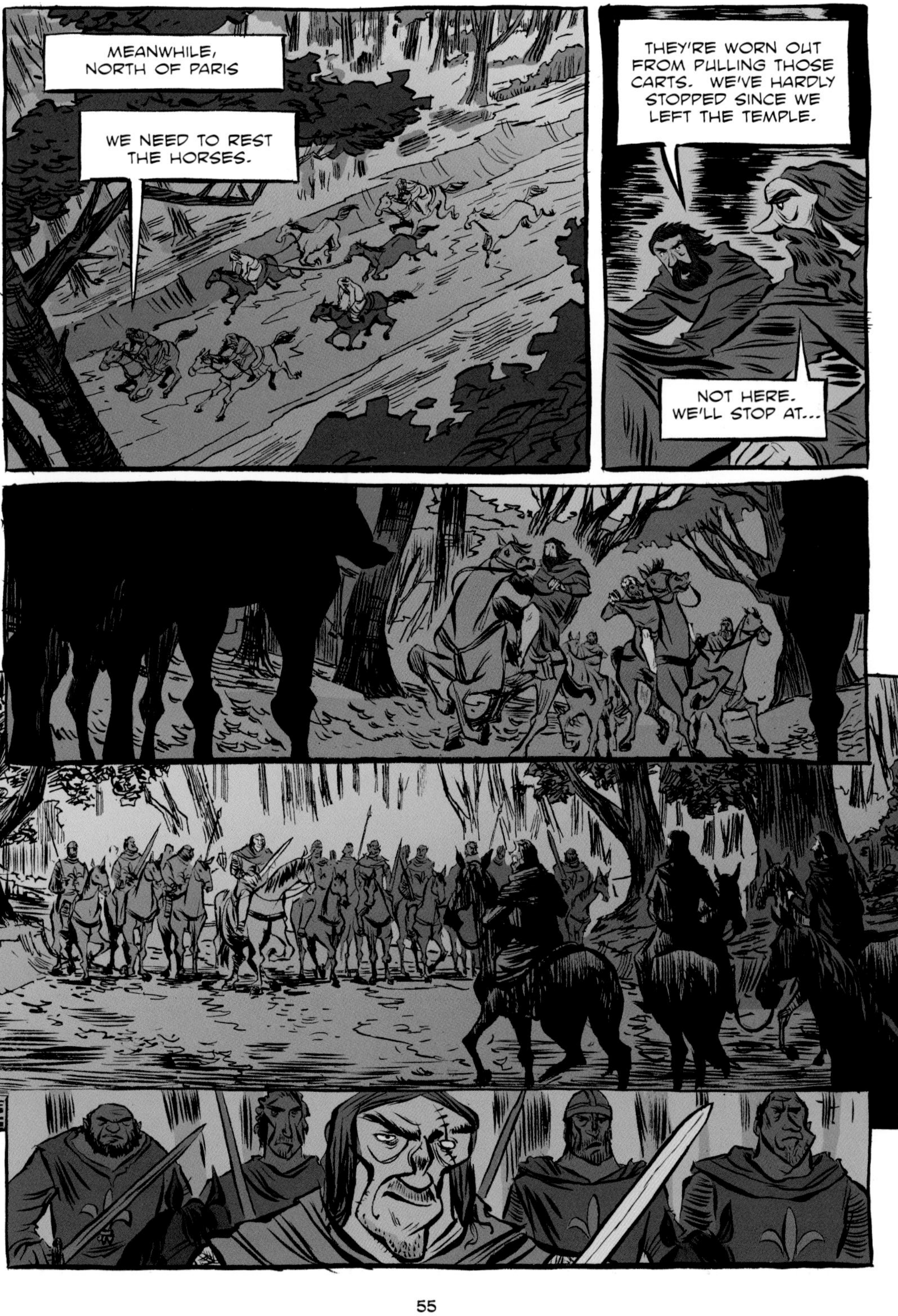
MEANWHILE, NORTH OF PARIS
WE NEED TO REST THE HORSES.
THEY'RE WORN OUT FROM PULLING THOSE CARTS. WE'VE HARDLY STOPPED SINCE WE LEFT THE TEMPLE.
NOT HERE. WE'LL STOP AT...

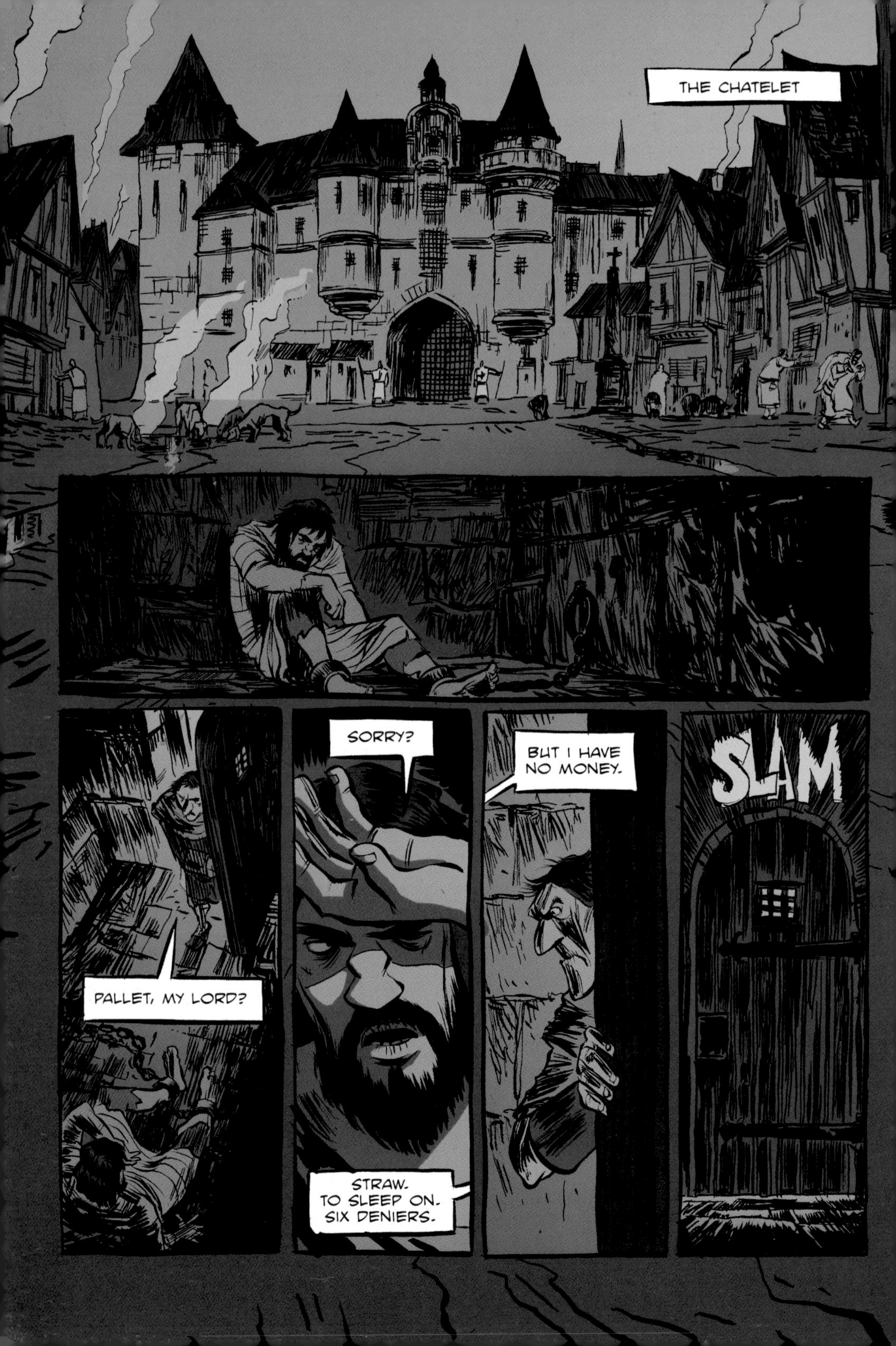
THE CHATELET
PALLET, MY LORD?
SORRY?
STRAW. TO SLEEP ON. SIX DENIERS.
BUT I HAVE NO MONEY.
SLAM

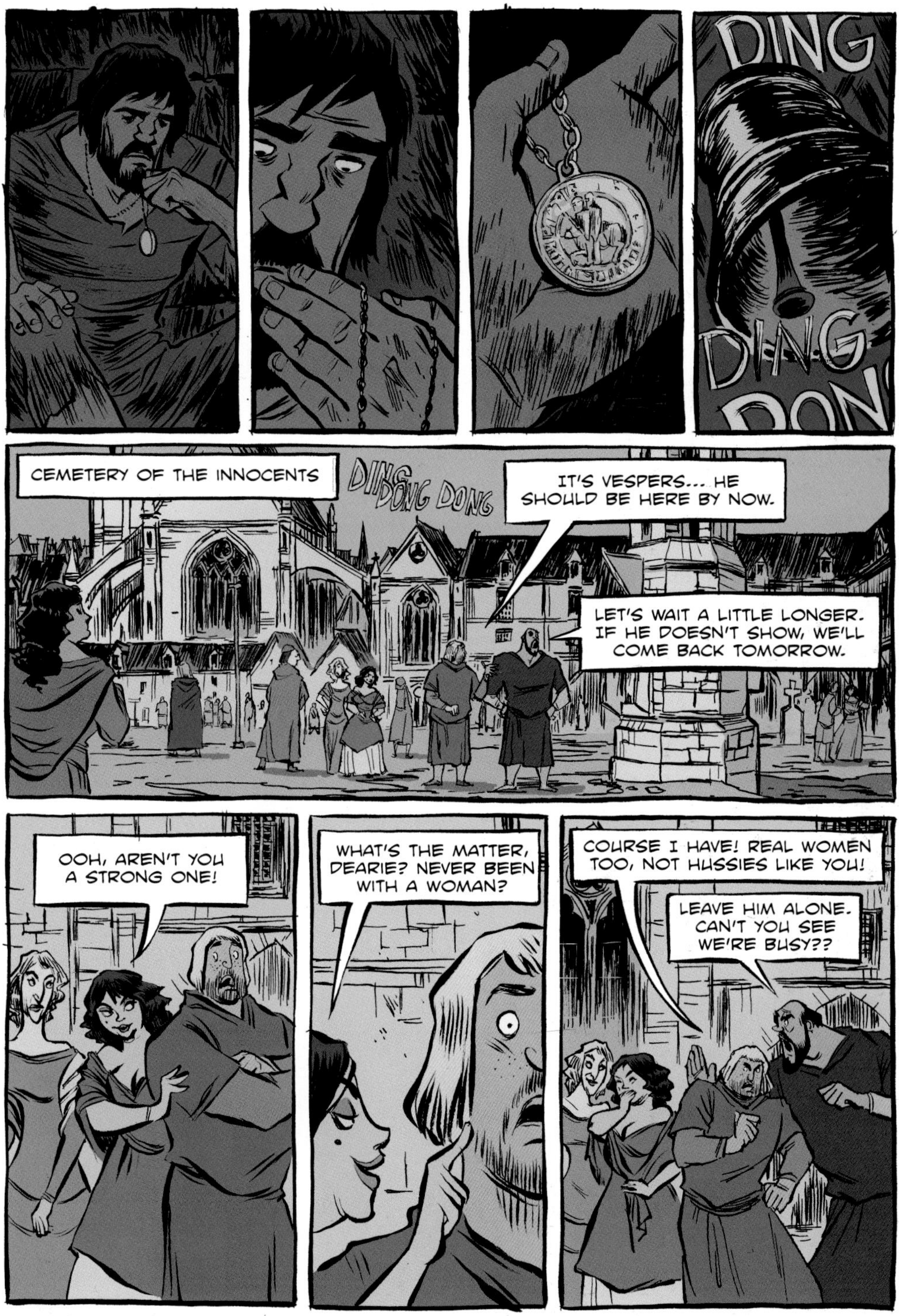
DING
DING
DONG
CEMETERY OF THE INNOCENTS
DING DONG DONG
IT'S VESPERS... HE SHOULD BE HERE BY NOW.
LET'S WAIT A LITTLE LONGER. IF HE DOESN'T SHOW, WE'LL COME BACK TOMORROW.
OOH, AREN'T YOU A STRONG ONE!
WHAT'S THE MATTER, DEARIE? NEVER BEEN WITH A WOMAN?
COURSE I HAVE! REAL WOMEN TOO, NOT HUSSIES LIKE YOU!
LEAVE HIM ALONE. CAN'T YOU SEE WE'RE BUSY??

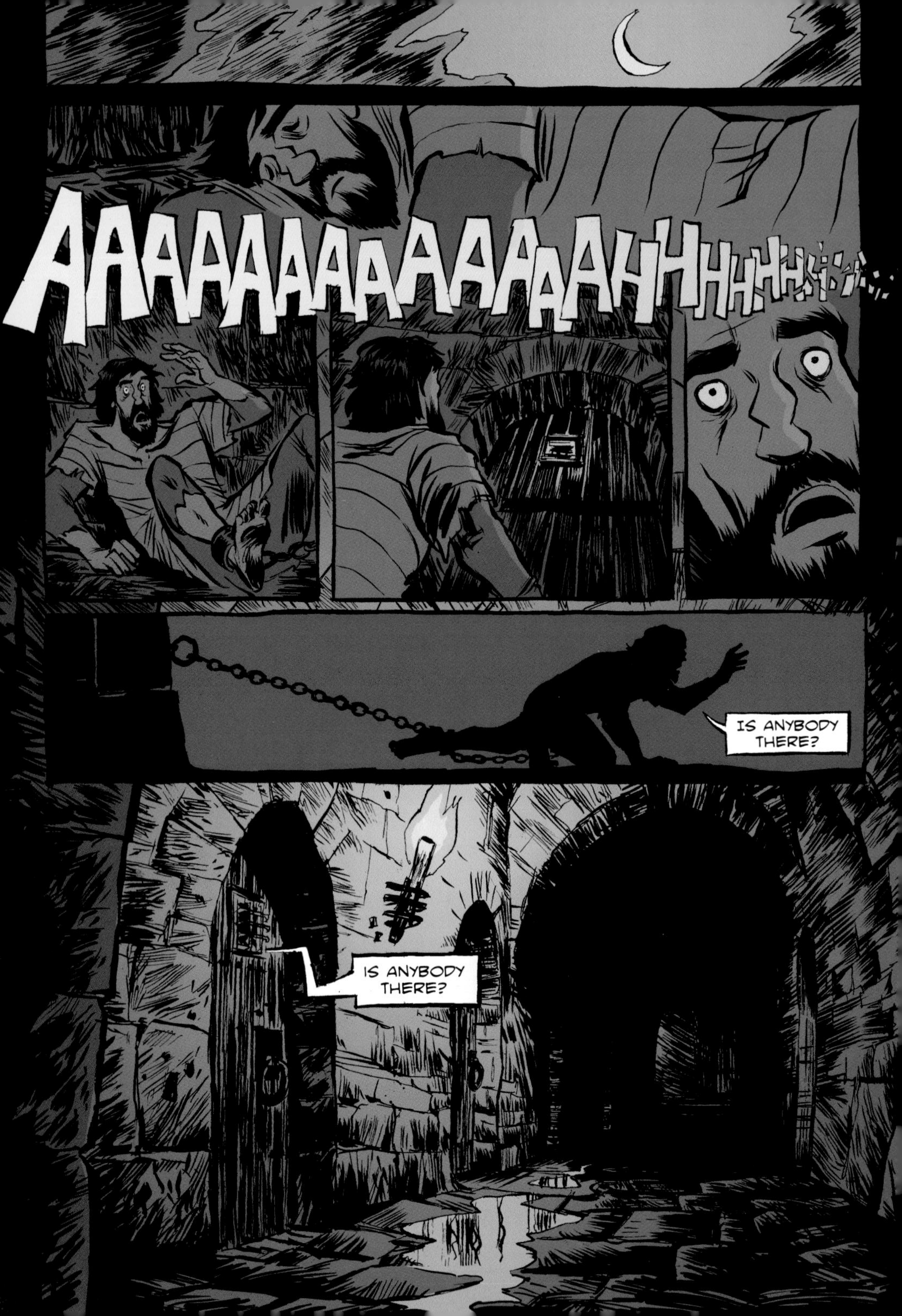
AAAAAAAAAAAAAAHHHH
IS ANYBODY THERE?
IS ANYBODY THERE?

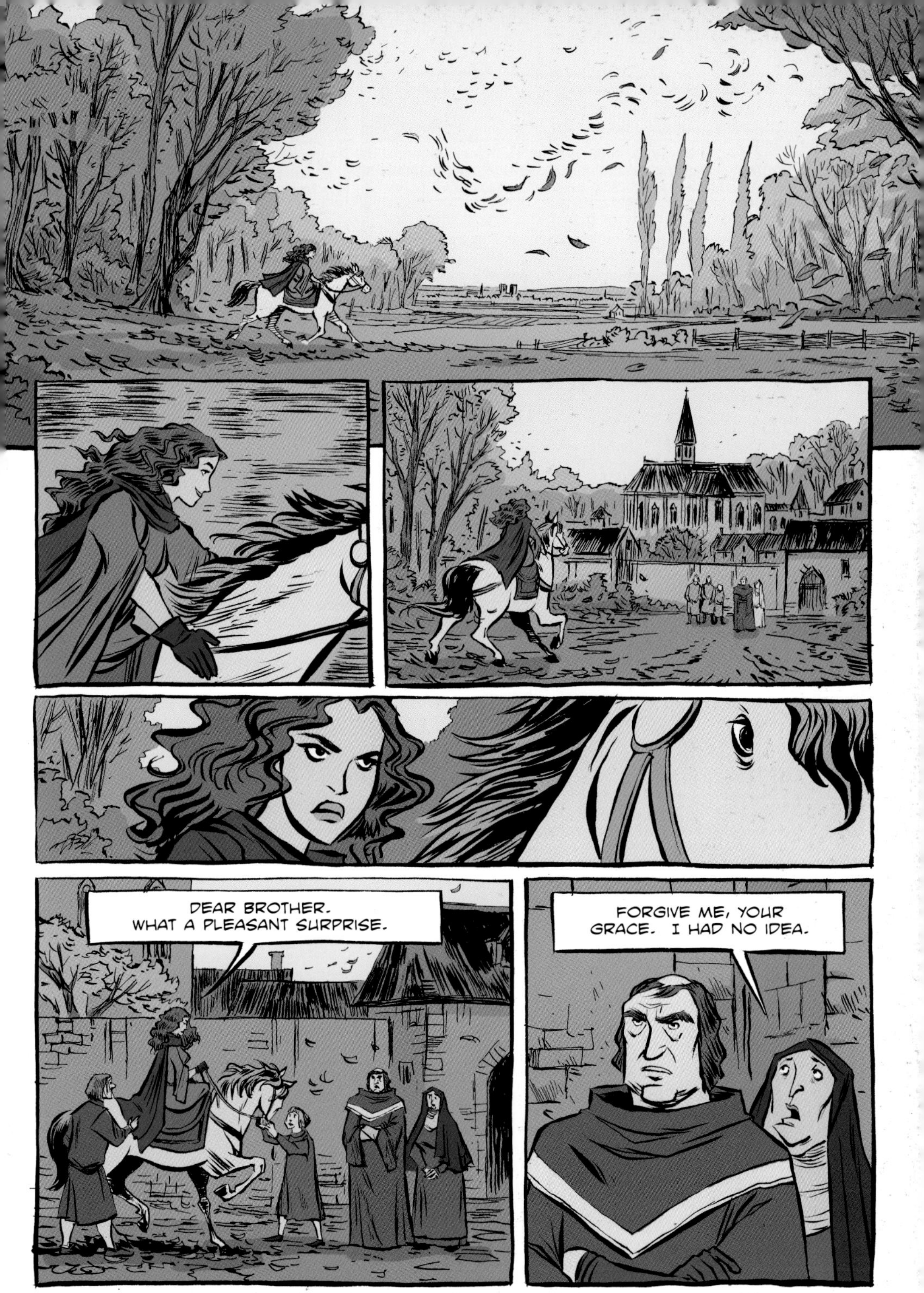
DEAR BROTHER. WHAT A PLEASANT SURPRISE.
FORGIVE ME, YOUR GRACE. I HAD NO IDEA.

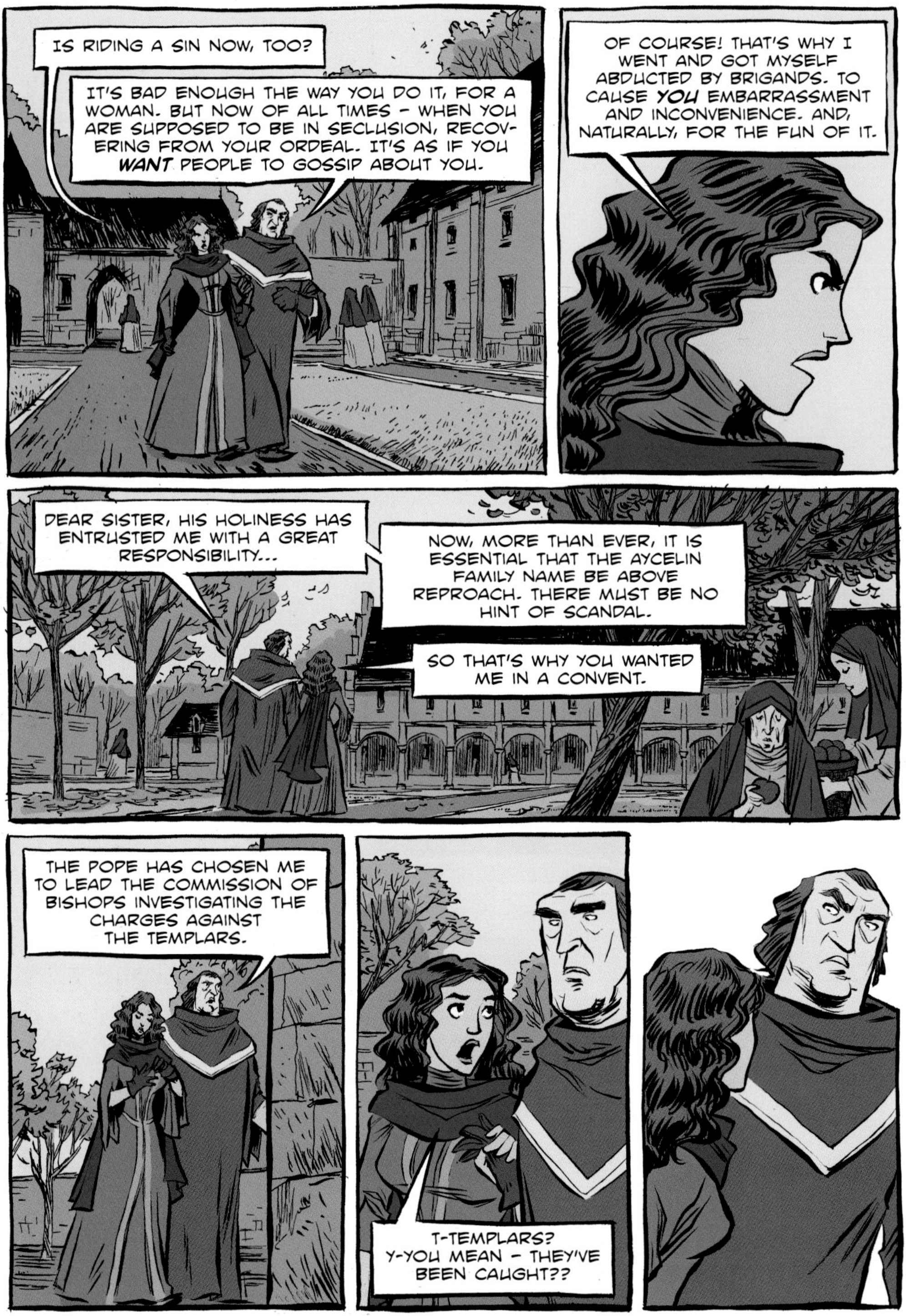
IS RIDING A SIN NOW, TOO?
IT'S BAD ENOUGH THE WAY YOU DO IT, FOR A WOMAN. BUT NOW OF ALL TIMES - WHEN YOU ARE SUPPOSED TO BE IN SECLUSION, RECOVERING FROM YOUR ORDEAL. IT'S AS IF YOU WANT PEOPLE TO GOSSIP ABOUT YOU.
OF COURSE! THAT'S WHY I WENT AND GOT MYSELF ABDUCTED BY BRIGANDS. TO CAUSE YOU EMBARRASSMENT AND INCONVENIENCE. AND, NATURALLY, FOR THE FUN OF IT.
DEAR SISTER, HIS HOLINESS HAS ENTRUSTED ME WITH A GREAT RESPONSIBILITY...
NOW, MORE THAN EVER, IT IS ESSENTIAL THAT THE AYCELIN FAMILY NAME BE ABOVE REPROACH. THERE MUST BE NO HINT OF SCANDAL.
SO THAT'S WHY YOU WANTED ME IN A CONVENT.
THE POPE HAS CHOSEN ME TO LEAD THE COMMISSION OF BISHOPS INVESTIGATING THE CHARGES AGAINST THE TEMPLARS.
T-TEMPLARS? Y-YOU MEAN - THEY'VE BEEN CAUGHT??

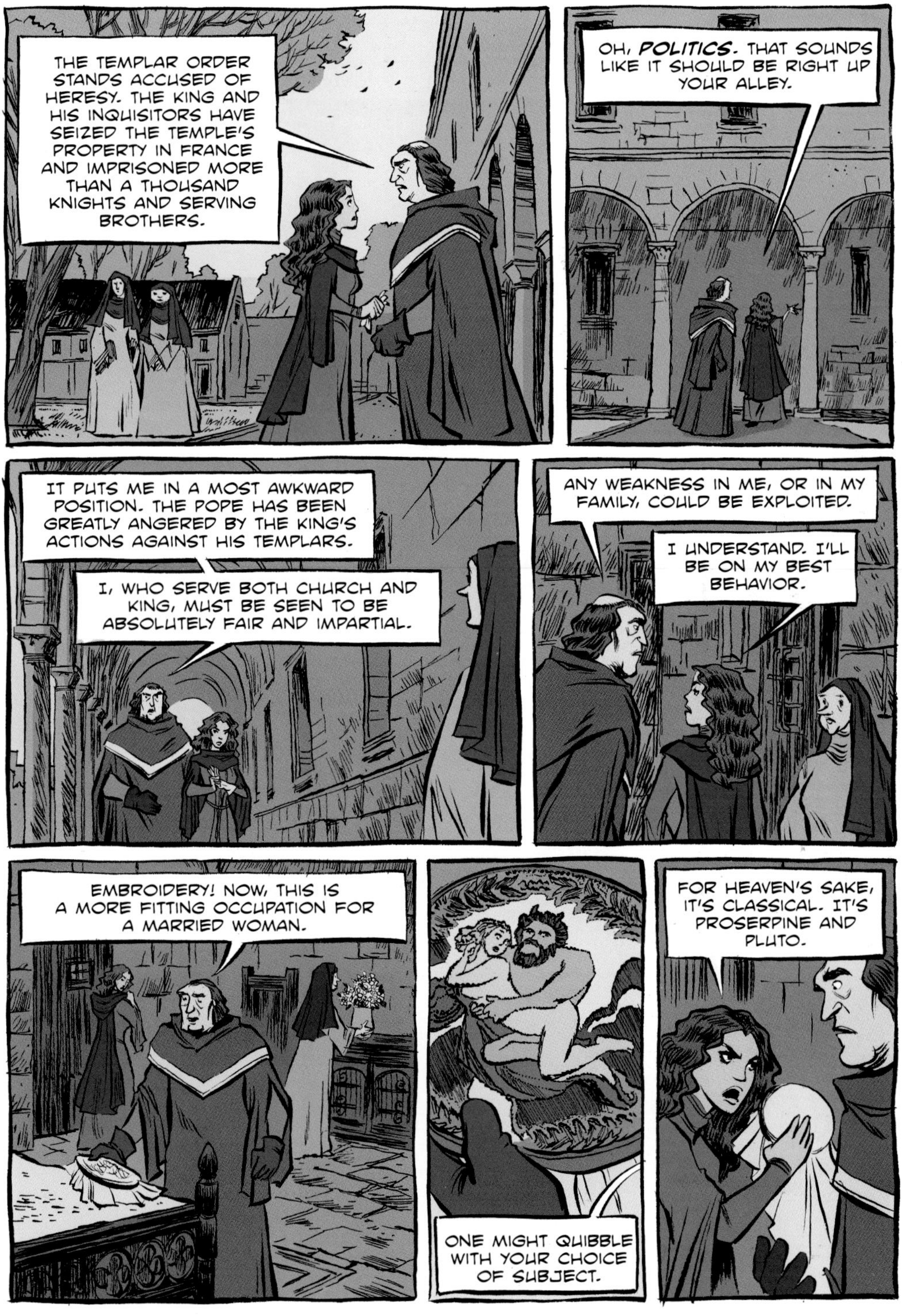
THE TEMPLAR ORDER STANDS ACCUSED OF HERESY. THE KING AND HIS INQUISITORS HAVE SEIZED THE TEMPLE'S PROPERTY IN FRANCE AND IMPRISONED MORE THAN A THOUSAND KNIGHTS AND SERVING BROTHERS.
OH, POLITICS. THAT SOUNDS LIKE IT SHOULD BE RIGHT UP YOUR ALLEY.
IT PUTS ME IN A MOST AWKWARD POSITION. THE POPE HAS BEEN GREATLY ANGERED BY THE KING'S ACTIONS AGAINST HIS TEMPLARS.
I, WHO SERVE BOTH CHURCH AND KING, MUST BE SEEN TO BE ABSOLUTELY FAIR AND IMPARTIAL.
ANY WEAKNESS IN ME, OR IN MY FAMILY, COULD BE EXPLOITED.
I UNDERSTAND. I'LL BE ON MY BEST BEHAVIOR.
EMBROIDERY! NOW, THIS IS A MORE FITTING OCCUPATION FOR A MARRIED WOMAN.
ONE MIGHT QUIBBLE WITH YOUR CHOICE OF SUBJECT.
FOR HEAVEN'S SAKE, IT'S CLASSICAL. IT'S PROSERPINE AND PLUTO.

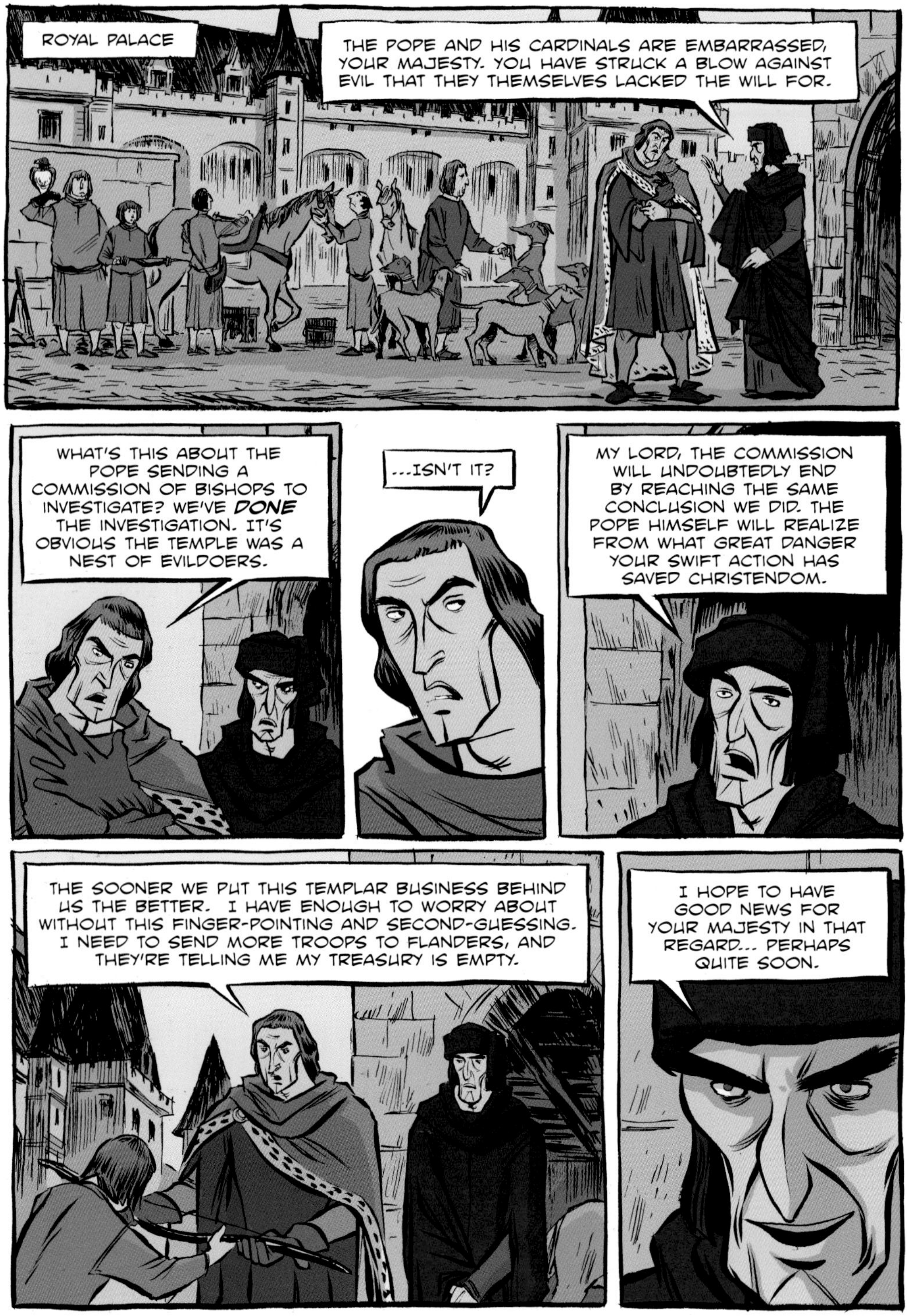
ROYAL PALACE
THE POPE AND HIS CARDINALS ARE EMBARRASSED, YOUR MAJESTY. YOU HAVE STRUCK A BLOW AGAINST EVIL THAT THEY THEMSELVES LACKED THE WILL FOR.
WHAT'S THIS ABOUT THE POPE SENDING A COMMISSION OF BISHOPS TO INVESTIGATE? WE'VE *DONE* THE INVESTIGATION. IT'S OBVIOUS THE TEMPLE WAS A NEST OF EVILDOERS.
...ISN'T IT?
MY LORD, THE COMMISSION WILL UNDOUBTEDLY END BY REACHING THE SAME CONCLUSION WE DID. THE POPE HIMSELF WILL REALIZE FROM WHAT GREAT DANGER YOUR SWIFT ACTION HAS SAVED CHRISTENDOM.
THE SOONER WE PUT THIS TEMPLAR BUSINESS BEHIND US THE BETTER. I HAVE ENOUGH TO WORRY ABOUT WITHOUT THIS FINGER-POINTING AND SECOND-GUESSING. I NEED TO SEND MORE TROOPS TO FLANDERS, AND THEY'RE TELLING ME MY TREASURY IS EMPTY.
I HOPE TO HAVE GOOD NEWS FOR YOUR MAJESTY IN THAT REGARD... PERHAPS QUITE SOON.

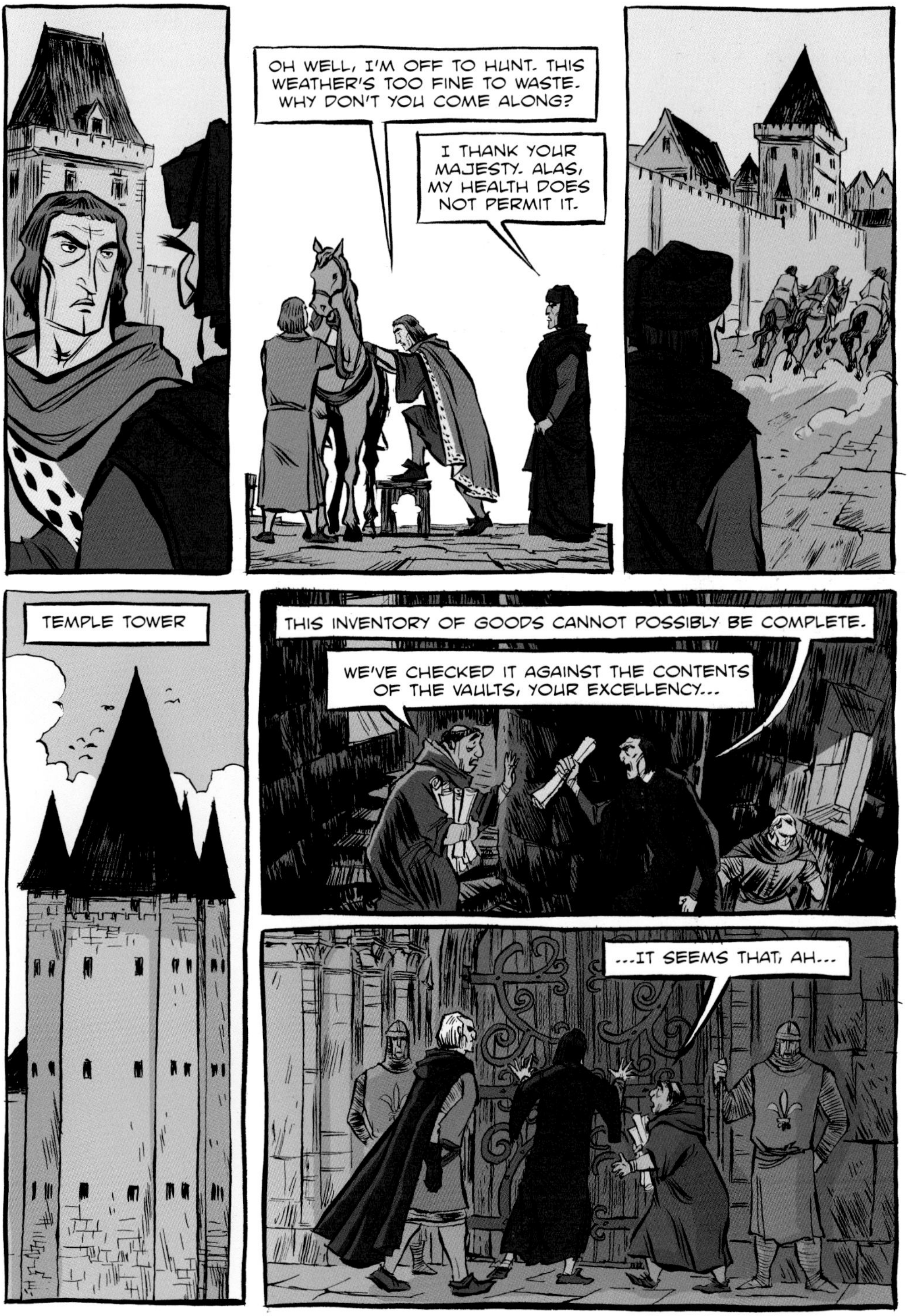
OH WELL, I'M OFF TO HUNT. THIS WEATHER'S TOO FINE TO WASTE. WHY DON'T YOU COME ALONG?
I THANK YOUR MAJESTY. ALAS, MY HEALTH DOES NOT PERMIT IT.
TEMPLE TOWER
THIS INVENTORY OF GOODS CANNOT POSSIBLY BE COMPLETE.
WE'VE CHECKED IT AGAINST THE CONTENTS OF THE VAULTS, YOUR EXCELLENCY...
...IT SEEMS THAT, AH...

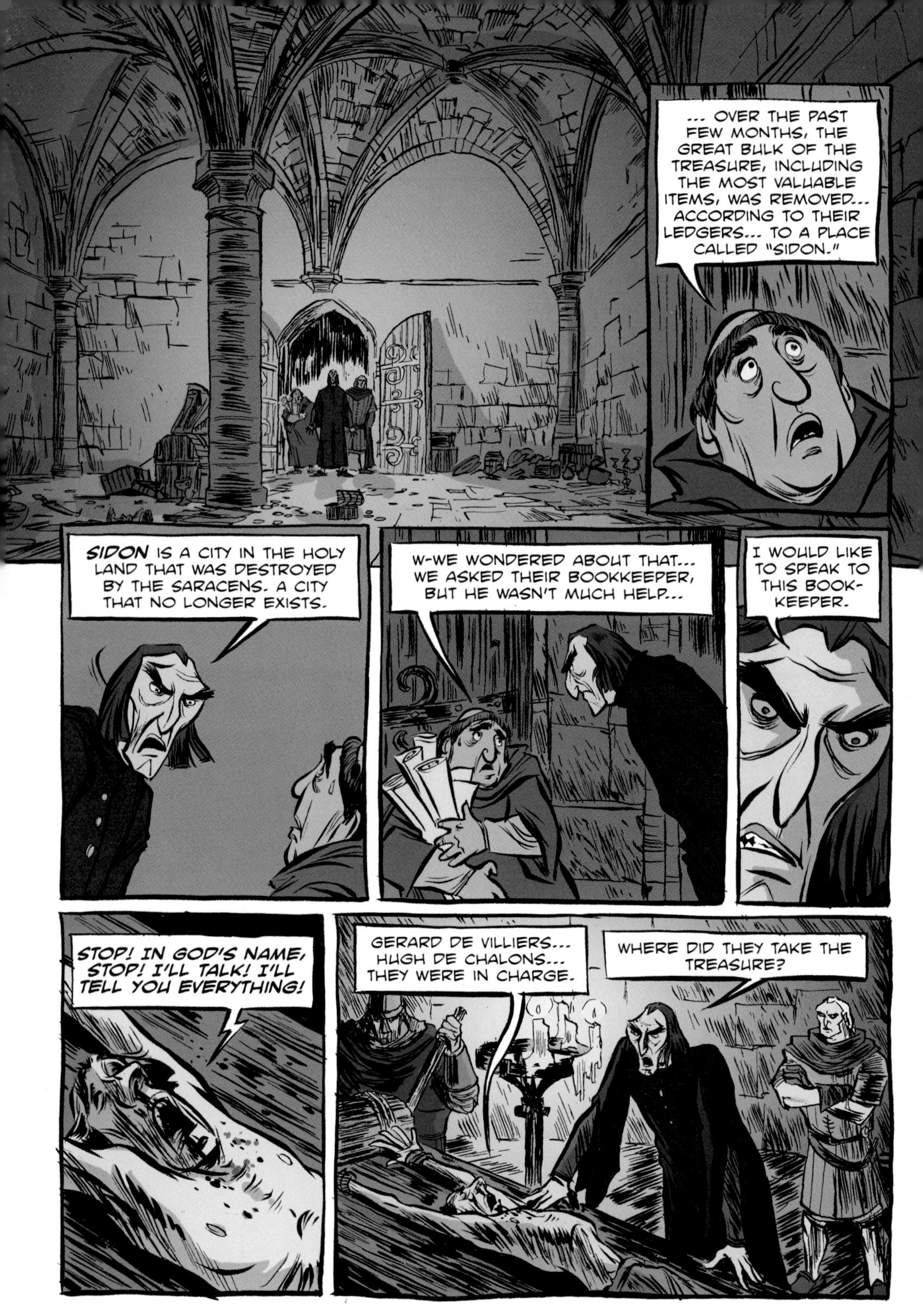
... OVER THE PAST FEW MONTHS, THE GREAT BULK OF THE TREASURE, INCLUDING THE MOST VALUABLE ITEMS, WAS REMOVED... ACCORDING TO THEIR LEDGERS... TO A PLACE CALLED "SIDON."
SIDON IS A CITY IN THE HOLY LAND THAT WAS DESTROYED BY THE SARACENS. A CITY THAT NO LONGER EXISTS.
W-WE WONDERED ABOUT THAT... WE ASKED THEIR BOOKKEEPER, BUT HE WASN'T MUCH HELP...
I WOULD LIKE TO SPEAK TO THIS BOOK-KEEPER.
STOP! IN GOD'S NAME, STOP! I'LL TALK! I'LL TELL YOU EVERYTHING!
GERARD DE VILLIERS... HUGH DE CHALONS... THEY WERE IN CHARGE.
WHERE DID THEY TAKE THE TREASURE?

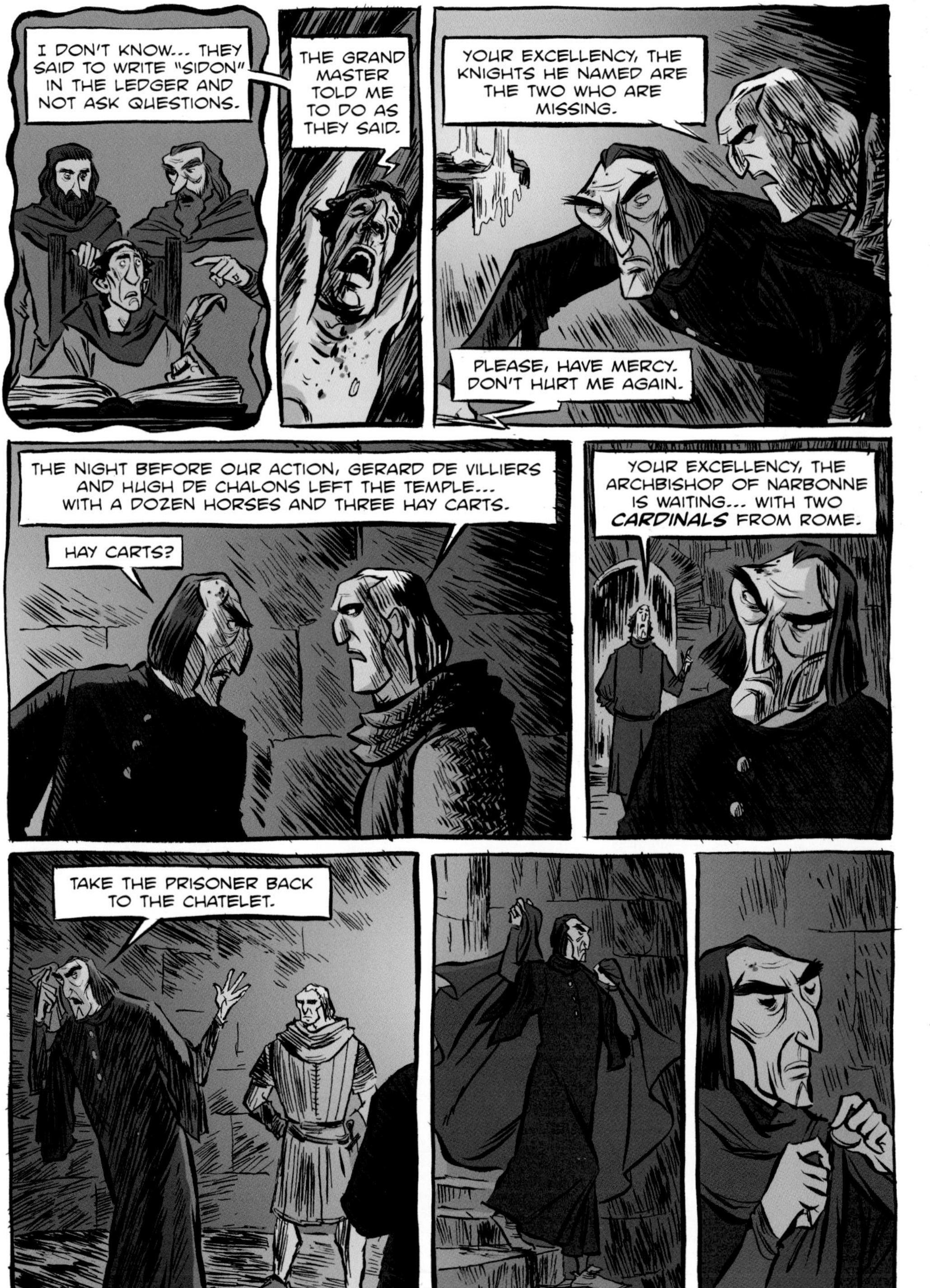
I DON'T KNOW... THEY SAID TO WRITE "SIDON" IN THE LEDGER AND NOT ASK QUESTIONS.
THE GRAND MASTER TOLD ME TO DO AS THEY SAID.
YOUR EXCELLENCY, THE KNIGHTS HE NAMED ARE THE TWO WHO ARE MISSING.
PLEASE, HAVE MERCY. DON'T HURT ME AGAIN.
THE NIGHT BEFORE OUR ACTION, GERARD DE VILLIERS AND HUGH DE CHALONS LEFT THE TEMPLE... WITH A DOZEN HORSES AND THREE HAY CARTS.
HAY CARTS?
YOUR EXCELLENCY, THE ARCHBISHOP OF NARBONNE IS WAITING... WITH TWO CARDINALS FROM ROME.
TAKE THE PRISONER BACK TO THE CHATELET.

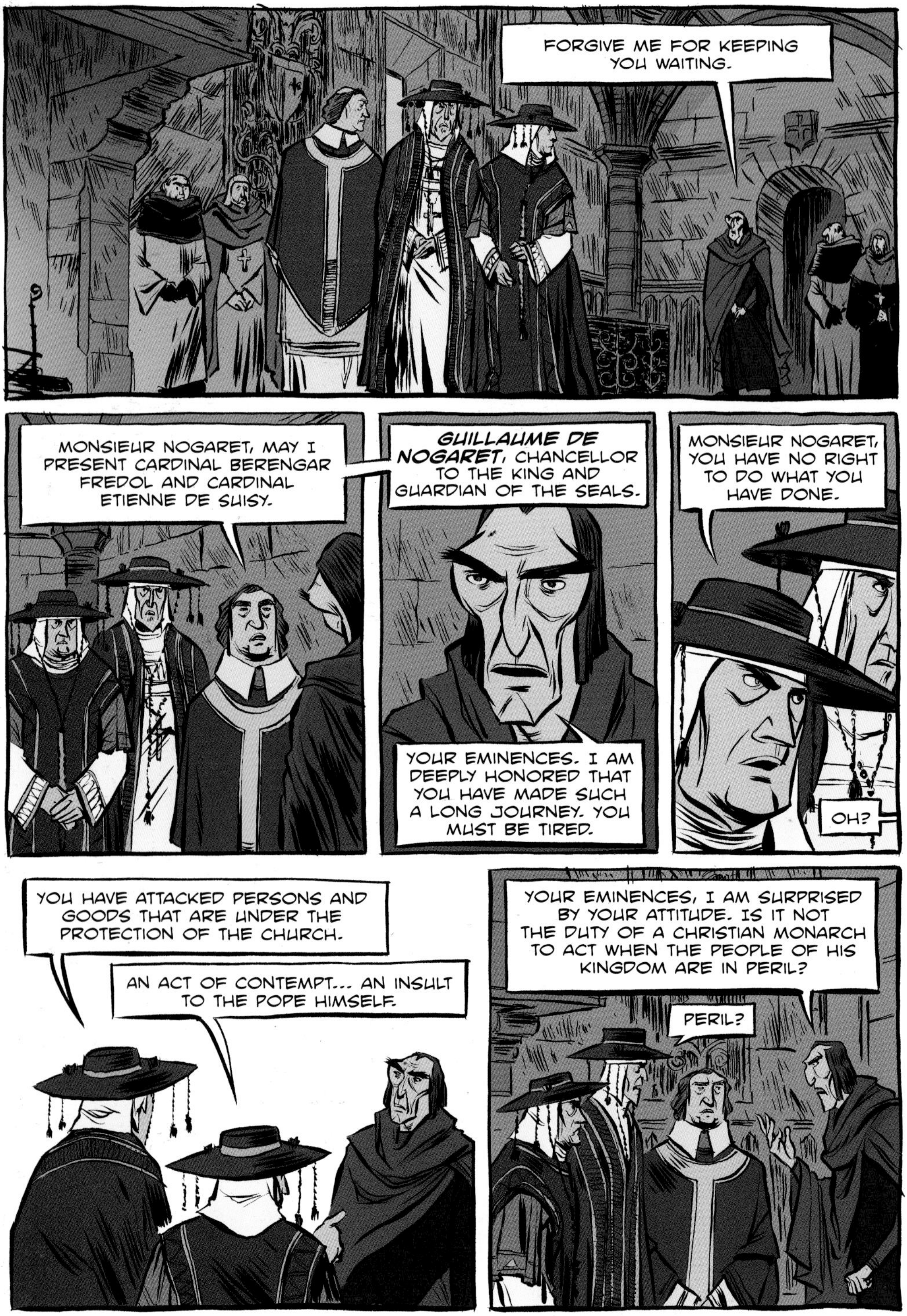

FORGIVE ME FOR KEEPING YOU WAITING.
MONSIEUR NOGARET, MAY I PRESENT CARDINAL BERENGAR FREDOL AND CARDINAL ETIENNE DE SUISY.
GUILLAUME DE NOGARET, CHANCELLOR TO THE KING AND GUARDIAN OF THE SEALS.
YOUR EMINENCES. I AM DEEPLY HONORED THAT YOU HAVE MADE SUCH A LONG JOURNEY. YOU MUST BE TIRED.
MONSIEUR NOGARET, YOU HAVE NO RIGHT TO DO WHAT YOU HAVE DONE.
OH?
YOU HAVE ATTACKED PERSONS AND GOODS THAT ARE UNDER THE PROTECTION OF THE CHURCH.
AN ACT OF CONTEMPT... AN INSULT TO THE POPE HIMSELF.
YOUR EMINENCES, I AM SURPRISED BY YOUR ATTITUDE. IS IT NOT THE DUTY OF A CHRISTIAN MONARCH TO ACT WHEN THE PEOPLE OF HIS KINGDOM ARE IN PERIL?
PERIL?

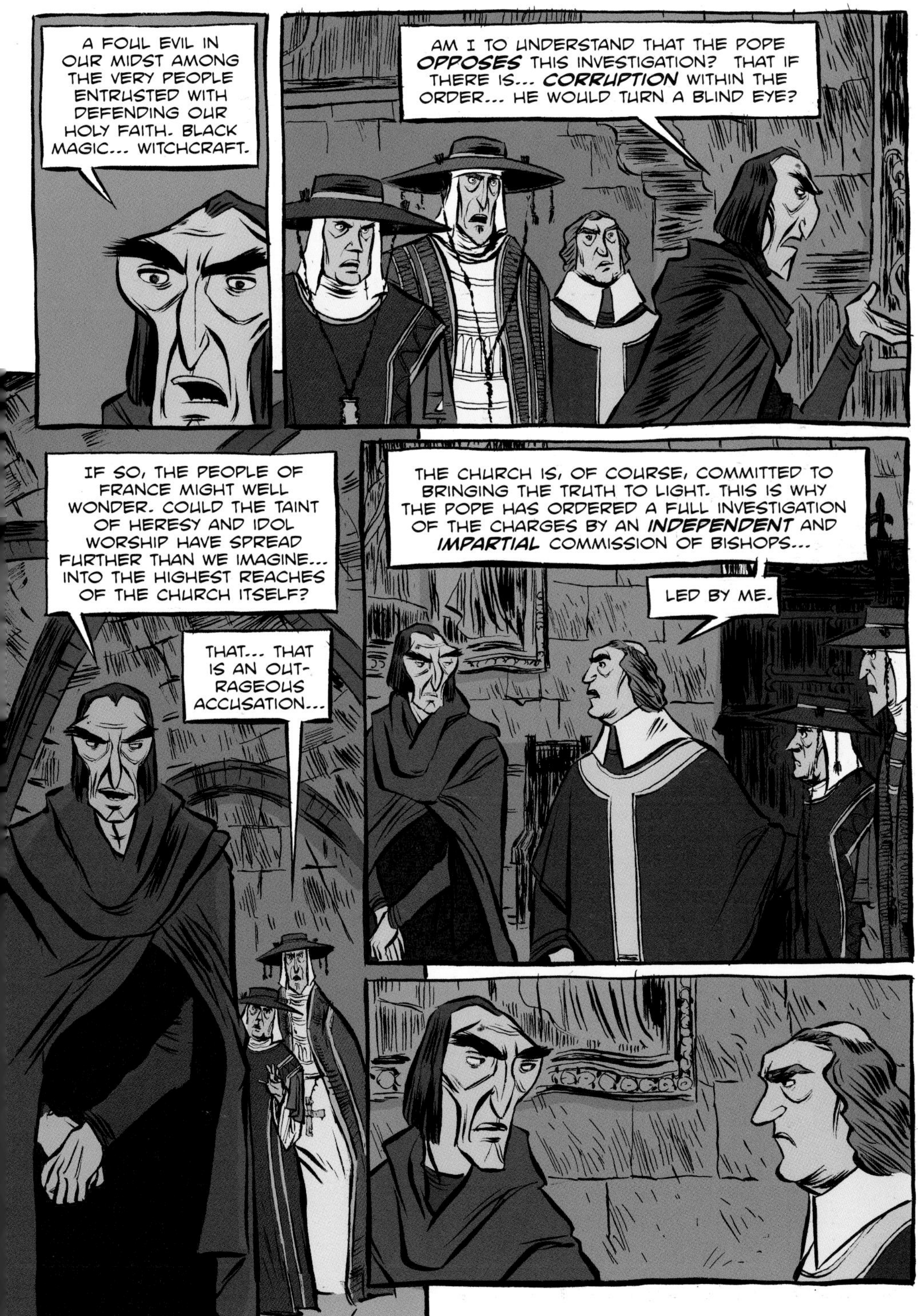
A FOUL EVIL IN OUR MIDST AMONG THE VERY PEOPLE ENTRUSTED WITH DEFENDING OUR HOLY FAITH. BLACK MAGIC... WITCHCRAFT.
AM I TO UNDERSTAND THAT THE POPE *OPPOSES* THIS INVESTIGATION? THAT IF THERE IS... *CORRUPTION* WITHIN THE ORDER... HE WOULD TURN A BLIND EYE?
IF SO, THE PEOPLE OF FRANCE MIGHT WELL WONDER. COULD THE TAINT OF HERESY AND IDOL WORSHIP HAVE SPREAD FURTHER THAN WE IMAGINE... INTO THE HIGHEST REACHES OF THE CHURCH ITSELF?
THAT... THAT IS AN OUT-RAGEOUS ACCUSATION...
THE CHURCH IS, OF COURSE, COMMITTED TO BRINGING THE TRUTH TO LIGHT. THIS IS WHY THE POPE HAS ORDERED A FULL INVESTIGATION OF THE CHARGES BY AN *INDEPENDENT* AND *IMPARTIAL* COMMISSION OF BISHOPS...
LED BY ME.

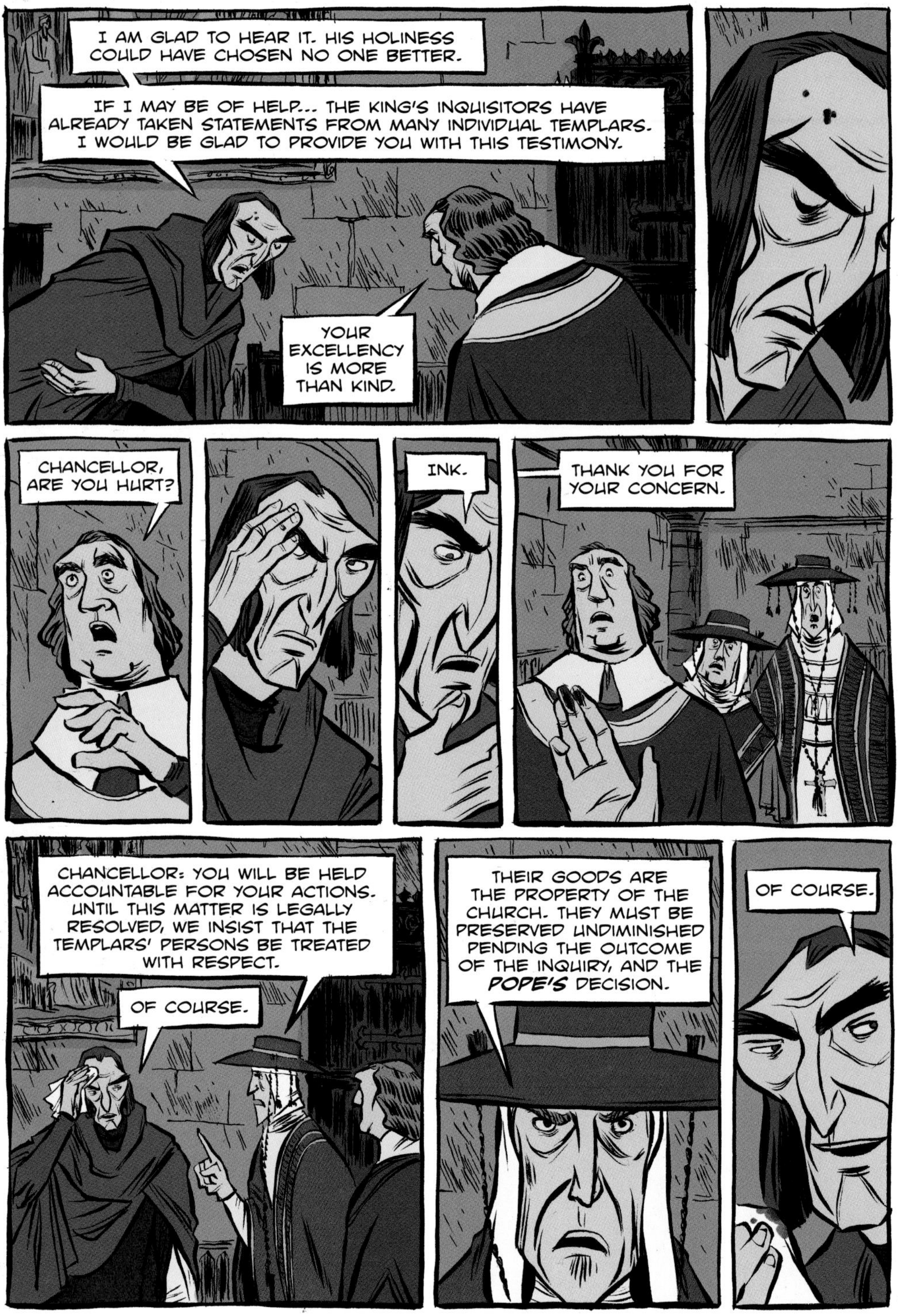
I AM GLAD TO HEAR IT. HIS HOLINESS COULD HAVE CHOSEN NO ONE BETTER.
IF I MAY BE OF HELP... THE KING'S INQUISITORS HAVE ALREADY TAKEN STATEMENTS FROM MANY INDIVIDUAL TEMPLARS. I WOULD BE GLAD TO PROVIDE YOU WITH THIS TESTIMONY.
YOUR EXCELLENCY IS MORE THAN KIND.
CHANCELLOR, ARE YOU HURT?
INK.
THANK YOU FOR YOUR CONCERN.
CHANCELLOR: YOU WILL BE HELD ACCOUNTABLE FOR YOUR ACTIONS. UNTIL THIS MATTER IS LEGALLY RESOLVED, WE INSIST THAT THE TEMPLARS' PERSONS BE TREATED WITH RESPECT.
OF COURSE.
THEIR GOODS ARE THE PROPERTY OF THE CHURCH. THEY MUST BE PRESERVED UNDIMINISHED PENDING THE OUTCOME OF THE INQUIRY, AND THE *POPE'S* DECISION.
OF COURSE.

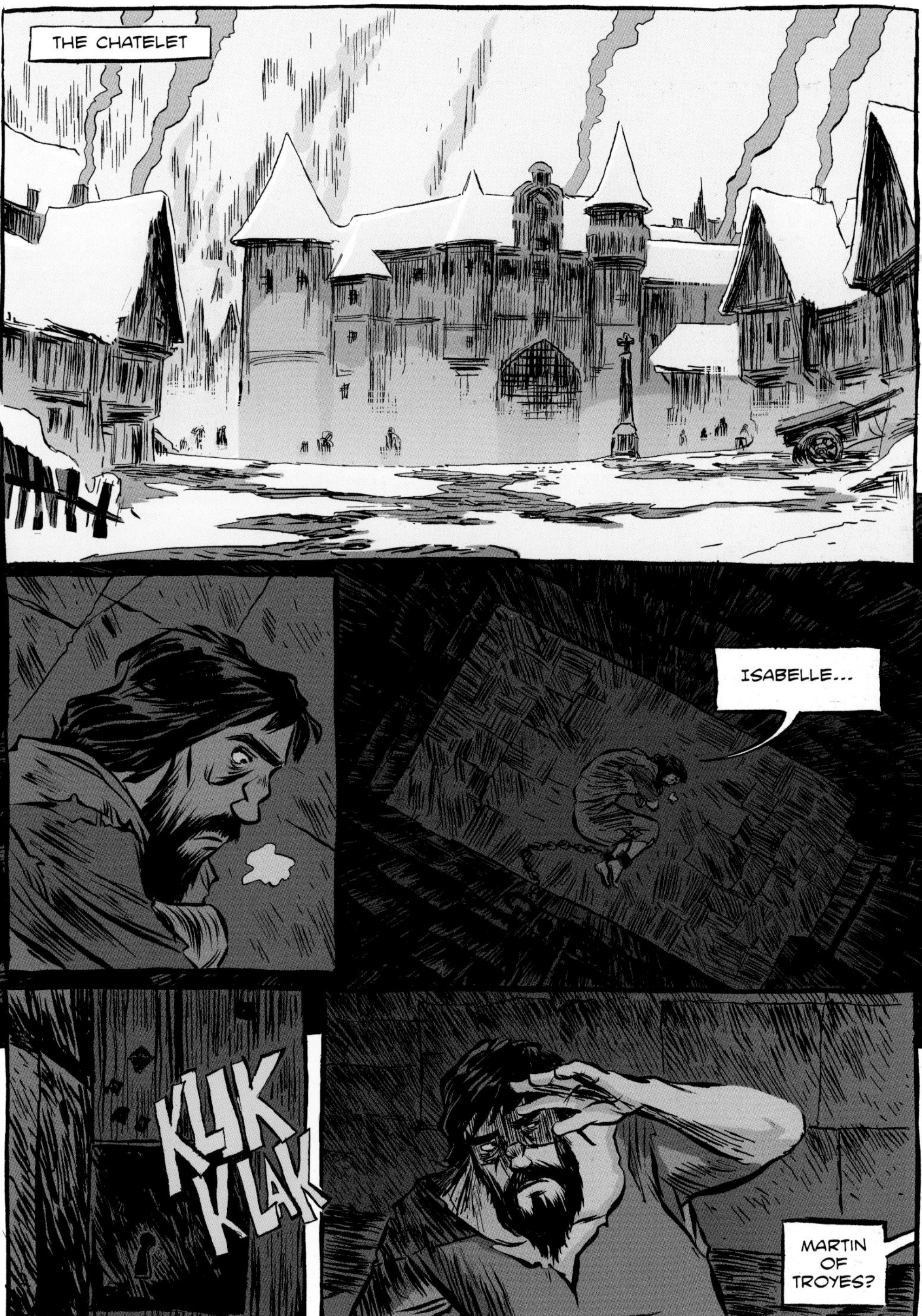
THE CHATELET
ISABELLE...
KLIK
KLAK
MARTIN OF TROYES?

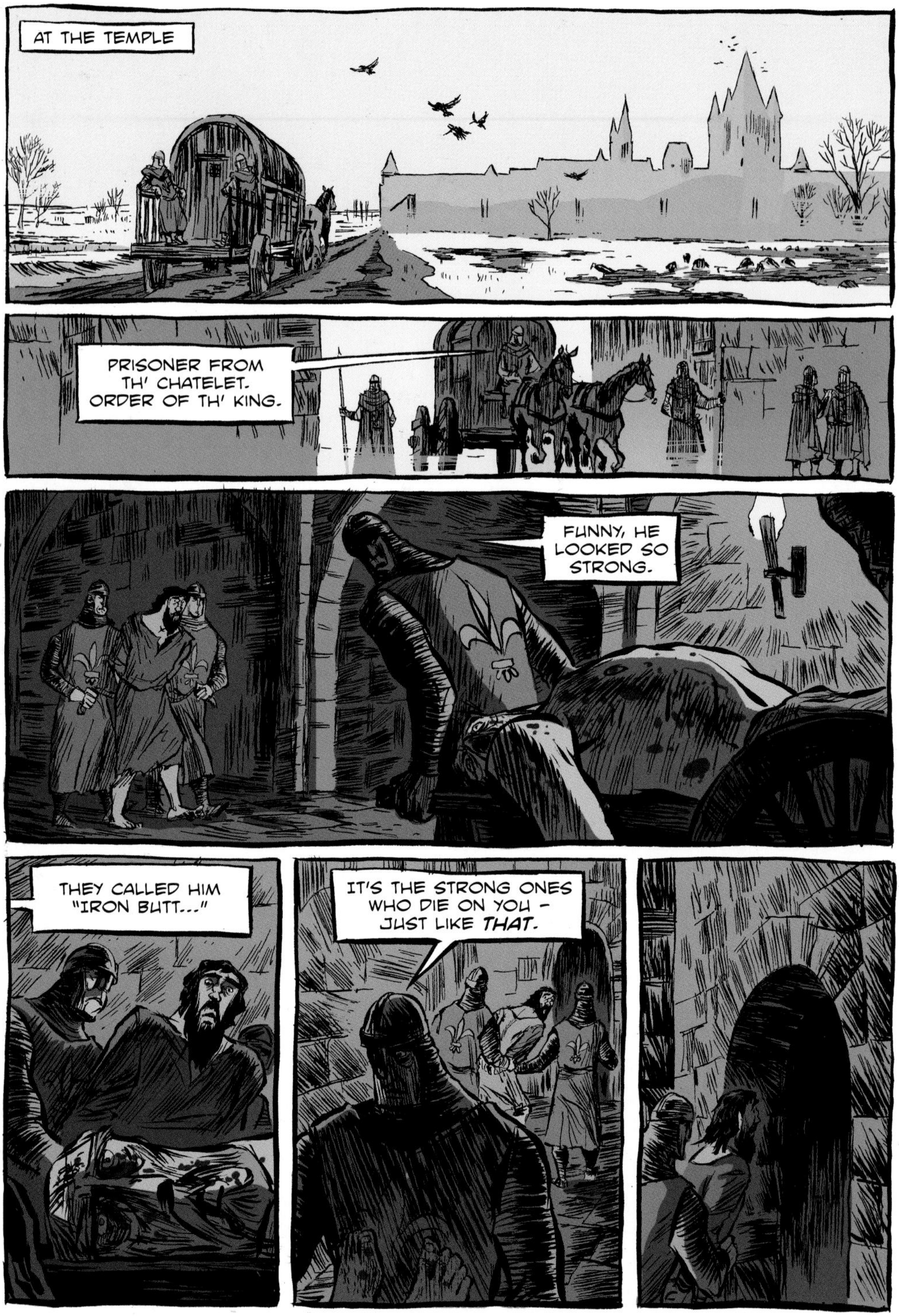
AT THE TEMPLE
PRISONER FROM TH' CHATELET. ORDER OF TH' KING.
FUNNY, HE LOOKED SO STRONG.
THEY CALLED HIM "IRON BUTT..."
IT'S THE STRONG ONES WHO DIE ON YOU - JUST LIKE *THAT*.

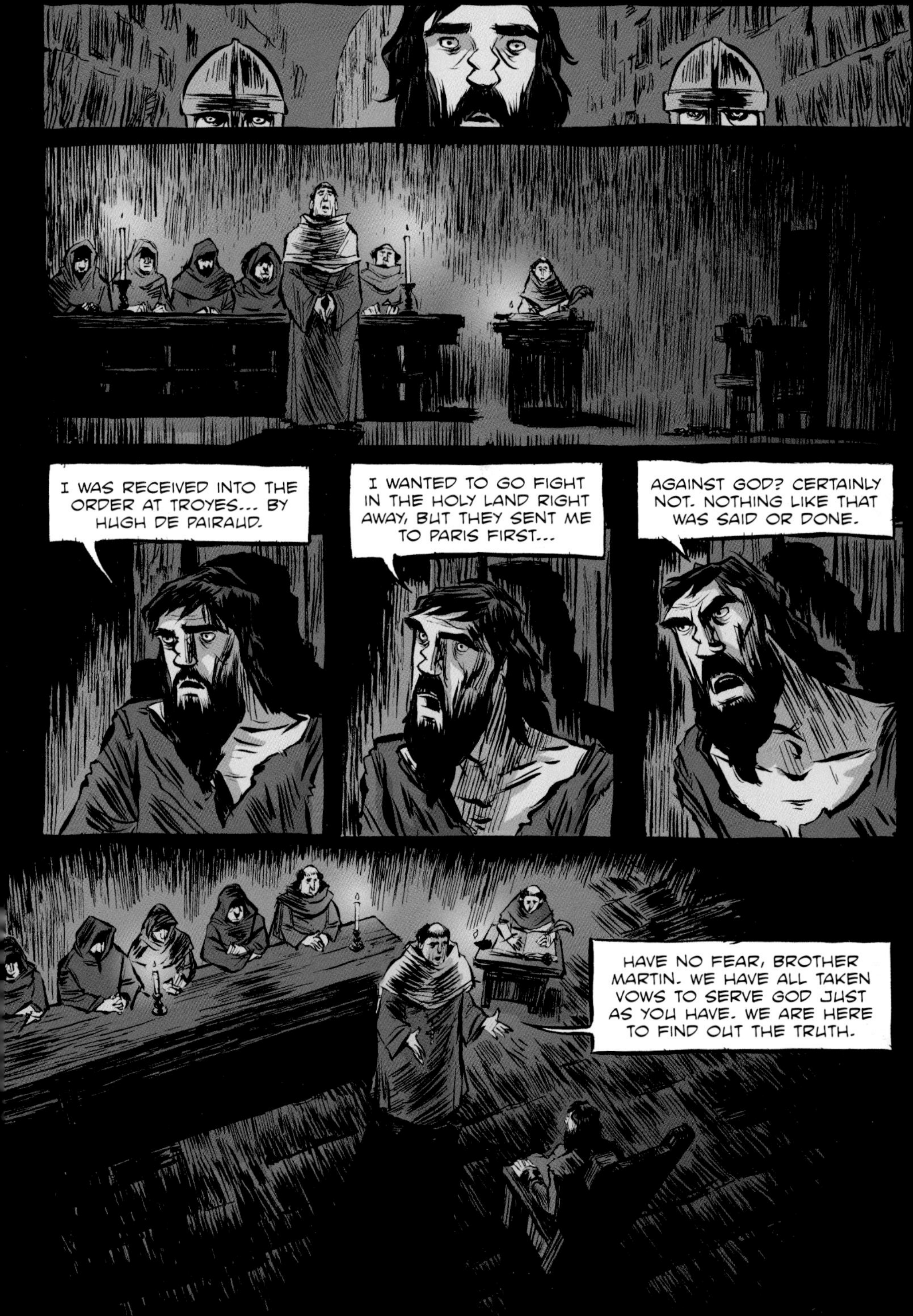
I WAS RECEIVED INTO THE ORDER AT TROYES... BY HUGH DE PAIRAUD.
I WANTED TO GO FIGHT IN THE HOLY LAND RIGHT AWAY, BUT THEY SENT ME TO PARIS FIRST...
AGAINST GOD? CERTAINLY NOT. NOTHING LIKE THAT WAS SAID OR DONE.
HAVE NO FEAR, BROTHER MARTIN. WE HAVE ALL TAKEN VOWS TO SERVE GOD JUST AS YOU HAVE. WE ARE HERE TO FIND OUT THE TRUTH.

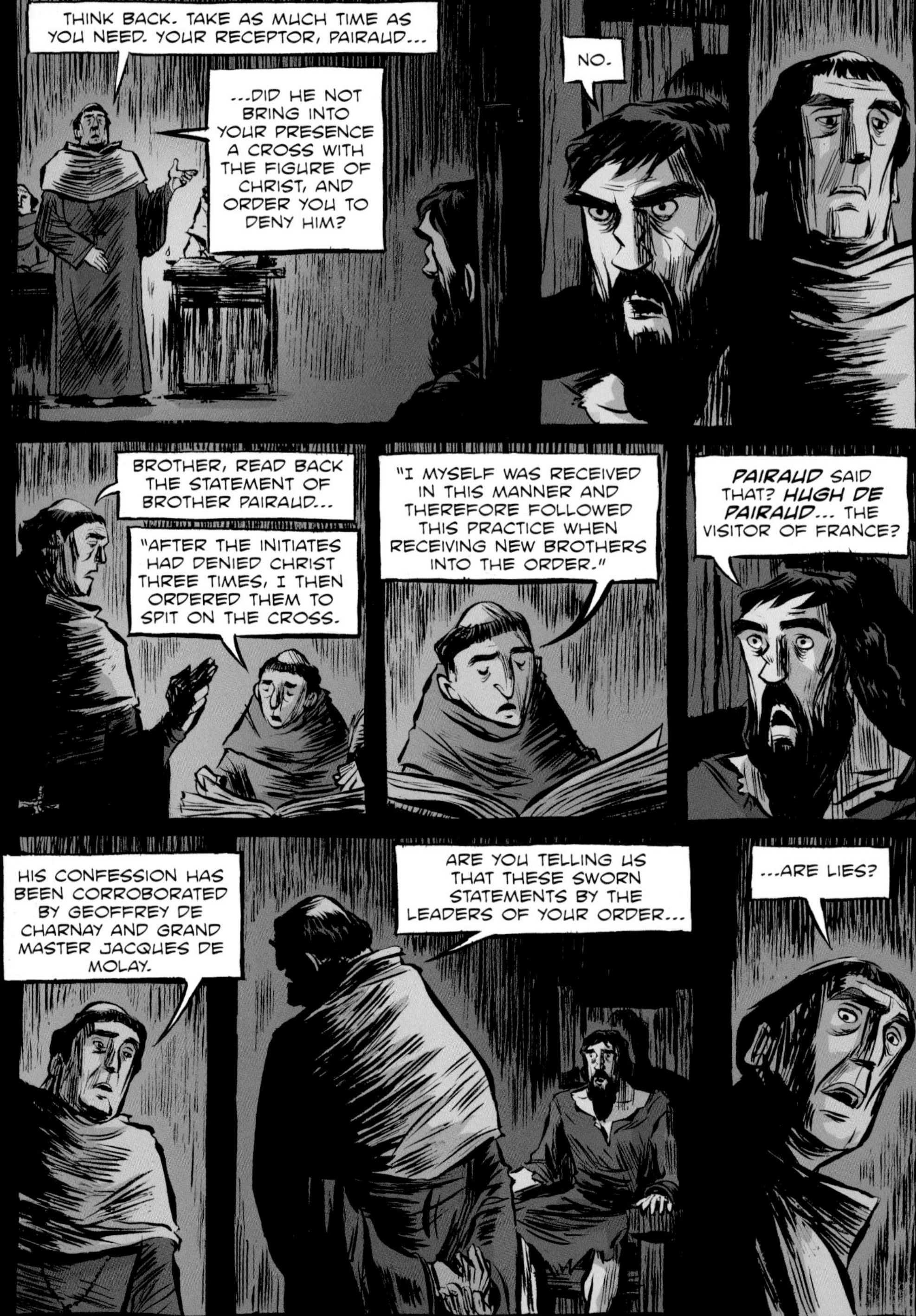
THINK BACK. TAKE AS MUCH TIME AS YOU NEED. YOUR RECEPTOR, PAIRAUD...
...DID HE NOT BRING INTO YOUR PRESENCE A CROSS WITH THE FIGURE OF CHRIST, AND ORDER YOU TO DENY HIM?
NO.
BROTHER, READ BACK THE STATEMENT OF BROTHER PAIRAUD...
"AFTER THE INITIATES HAD DENIED CHRIST THREE TIMES, I THEN ORDERED THEM TO SPIT ON THE CROSS.
"I MYSELF WAS RECEIVED IN THIS MANNER AND THEREFORE FOLLOWED THIS PRACTICE WHEN RECEIVING NEW BROTHERS INTO THE ORDER."
PAIRAUD SAID THAT? *HUGH DE PAIRAUD*... THE VISITOR OF FRANCE?
HIS CONFESSION HAS BEEN CORROBORATED BY GEOFFREY DE CHARNAY AND GRAND MASTER JACQUES DE MOLAY.
ARE YOU TELLING US THAT THESE SWORN STATEMENTS BY THE LEADERS OF YOUR ORDER...
...ARE LIES?

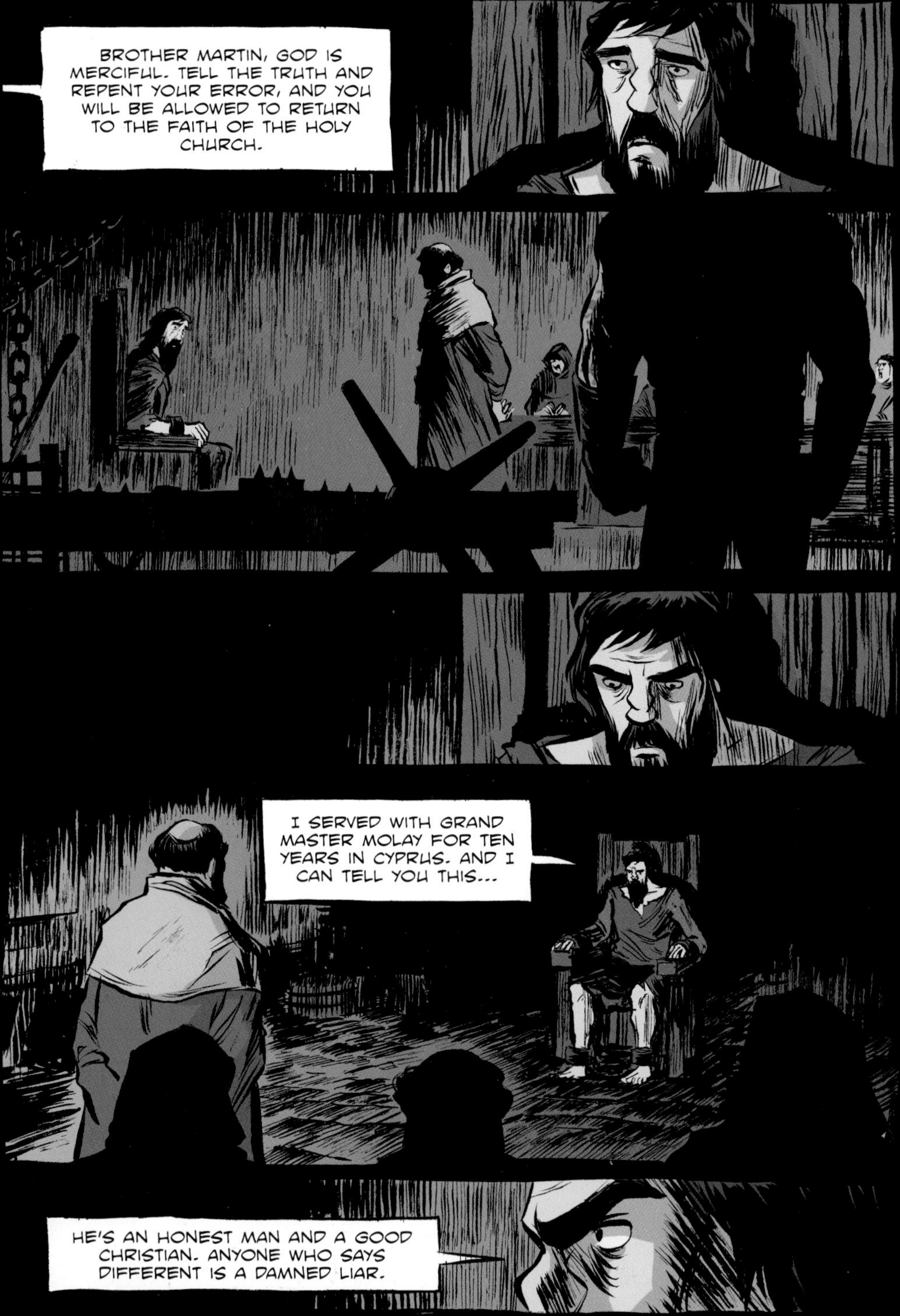
BROTHER MARTIN, GOD IS MERCIFUL. TELL THE TRUTH AND REPENT YOUR ERROR, AND YOU WILL BE ALLOWED TO RETURN TO THE FAITH OF THE HOLY CHURCH.
I SERVED WITH GRAND MASTER MOLAY FOR TEN YEARS IN CYPRUS. AND I CAN TELL YOU THIS...
HE'S AN HONEST MAN AND A GOOD CHRISTIAN. ANYONE WHO SAYS DIFFERENT IS A DAMNED LIAR.

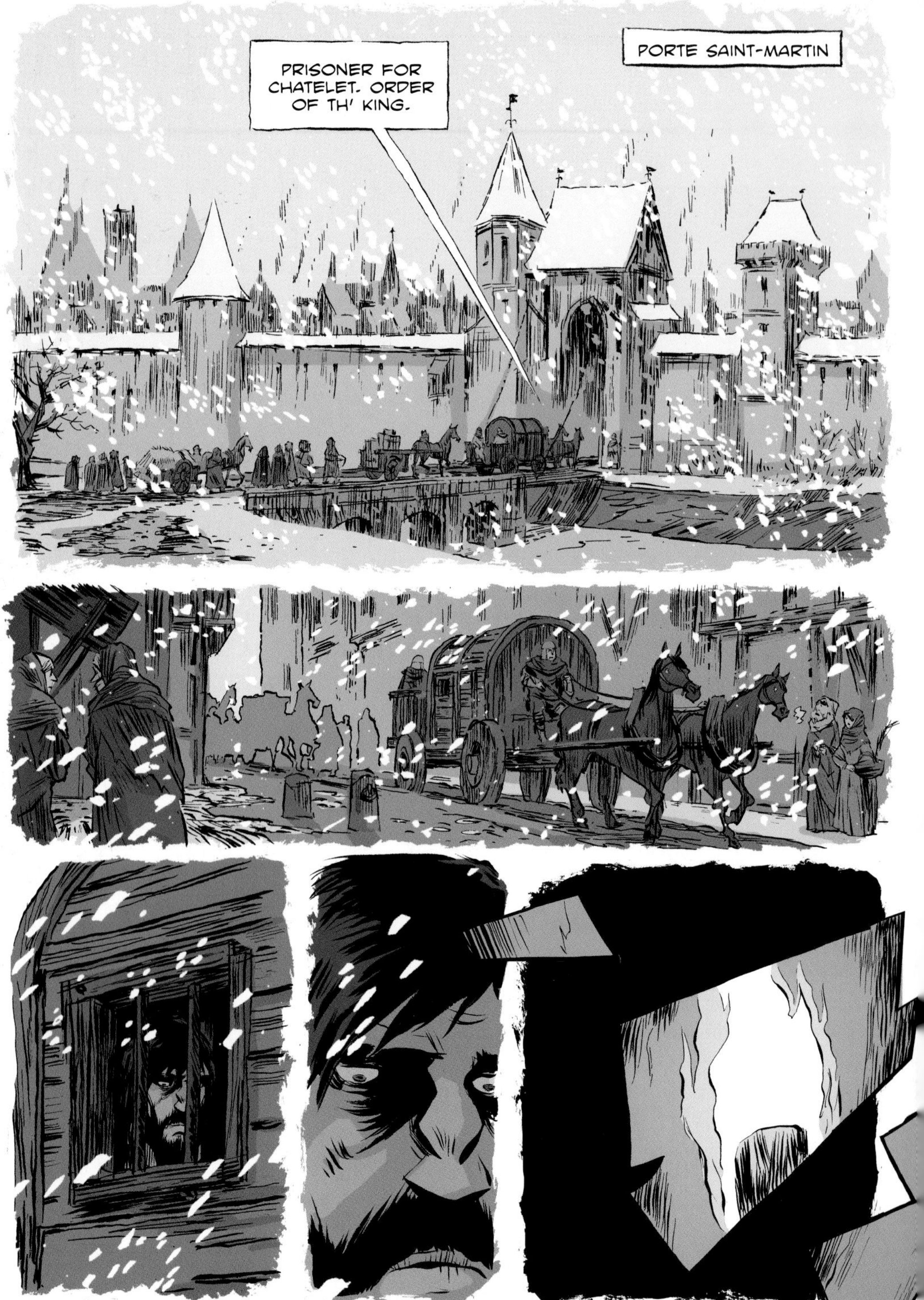
PORTE SAINT-MARTIN
PRISONER FOR CHATELET. ORDER OF TH' KING.

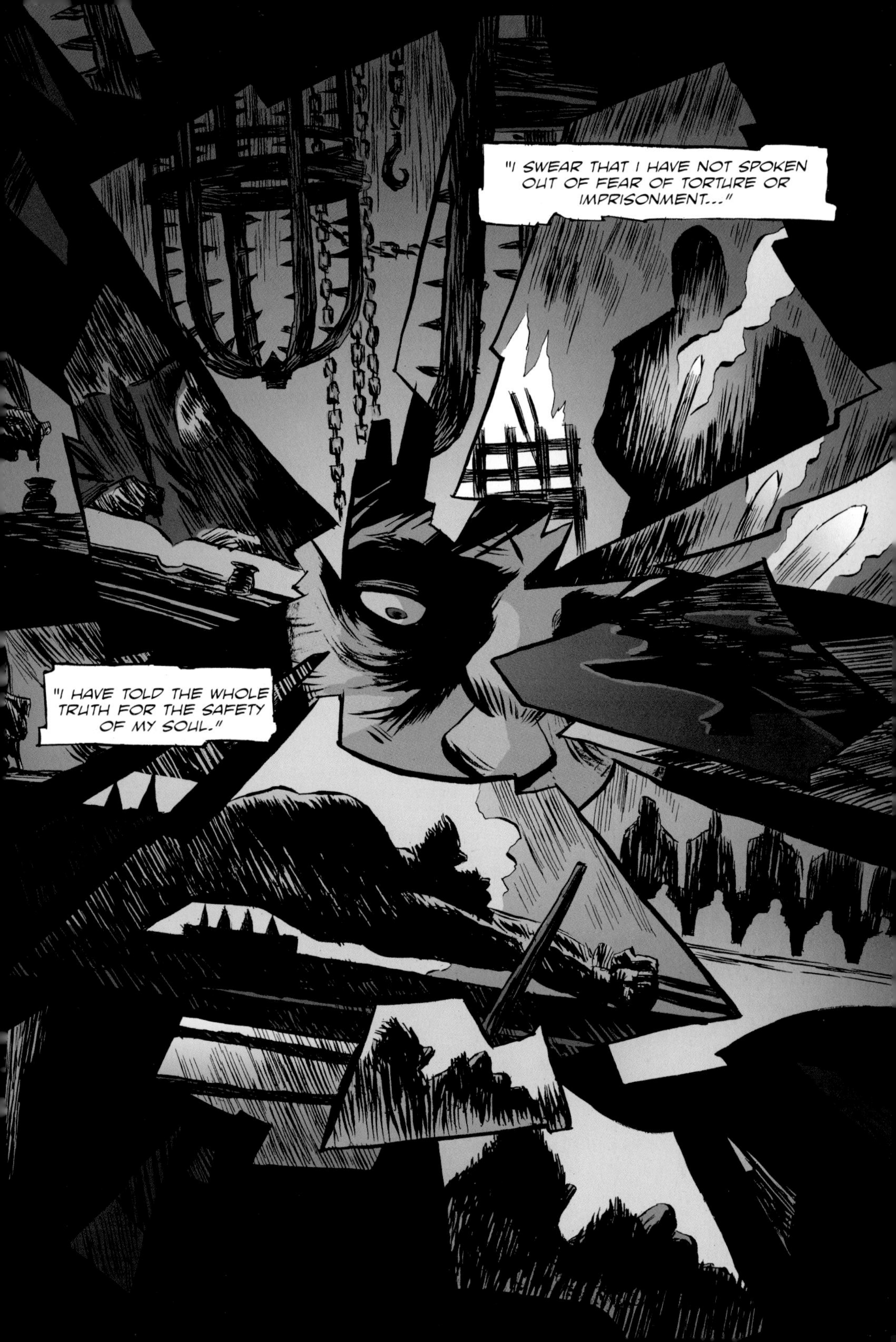
"I SWEAR THAT I HAVE NOT SPOKEN OUT OF FEAR OF TORTURE OR IMPRISONMENT..."
"I HAVE TOLD THE WHOLE TRUTH FOR THE SAFETY OF MY SOUL."

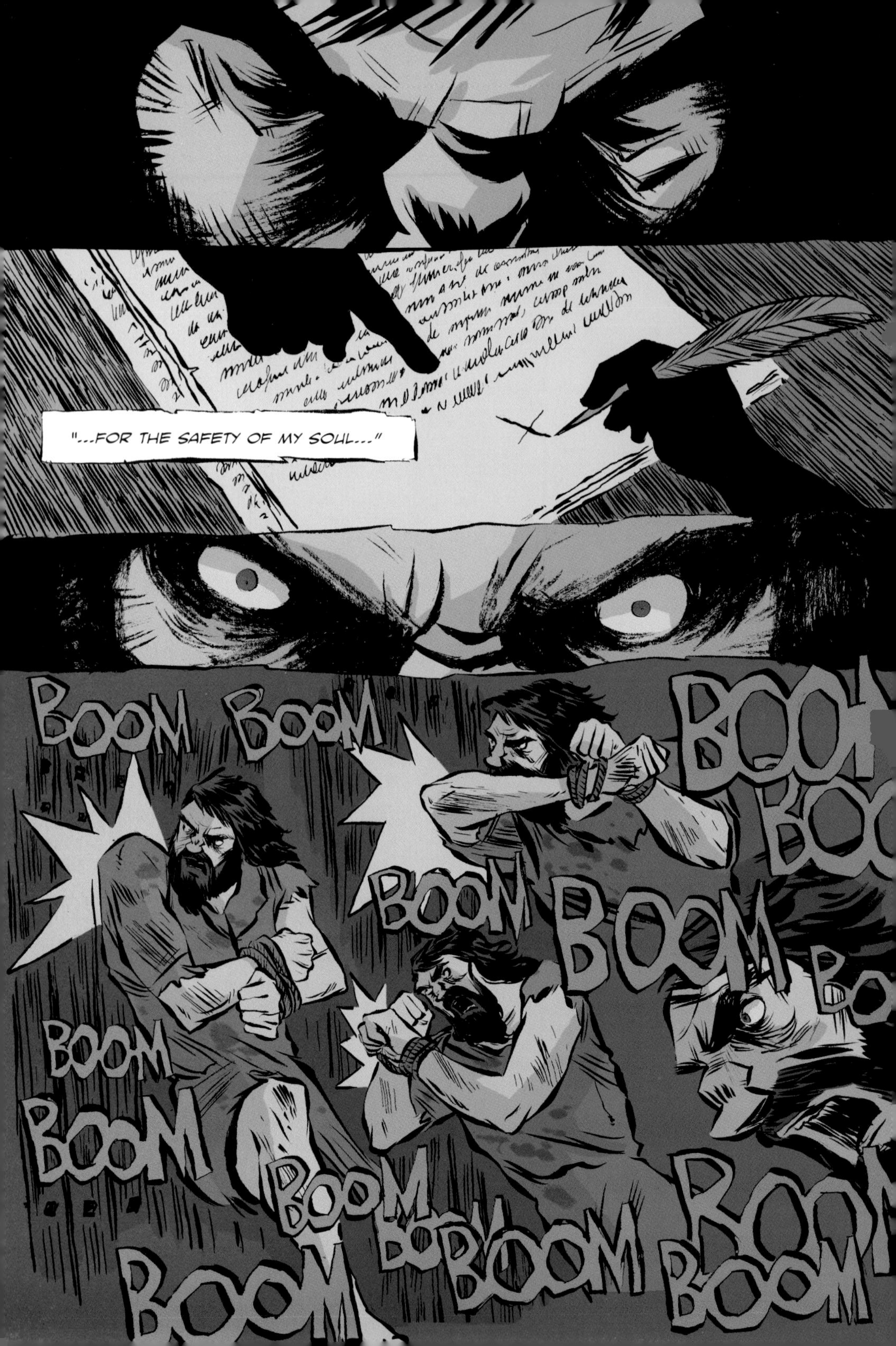
"...FOR THE SAFETY OF MY SOUL..."
BOOM BOOM
BOOM BOOM
BOOM BOOM
BOOM
BOOM
BOOM
BOOM BOOM
BOOM BOOM BOOM
BOOM BOOM

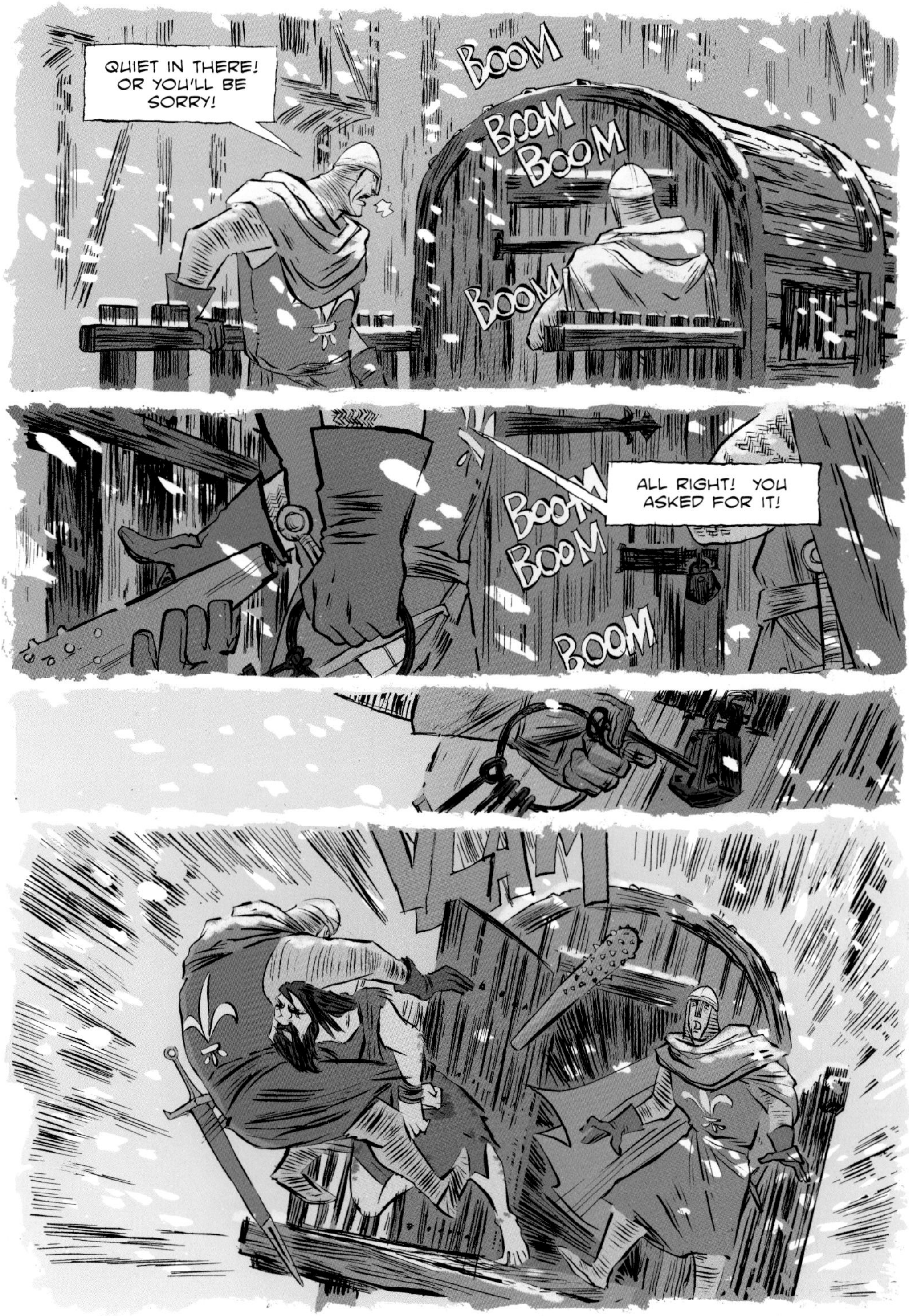
QUIET IN THERE! OR YOU'LL BE SORRY!
BOOM
BOOM
BOOM
BOOM
BOOM
BOOM
ALL RIGHT! YOU ASKED FOR IT!
BOOM

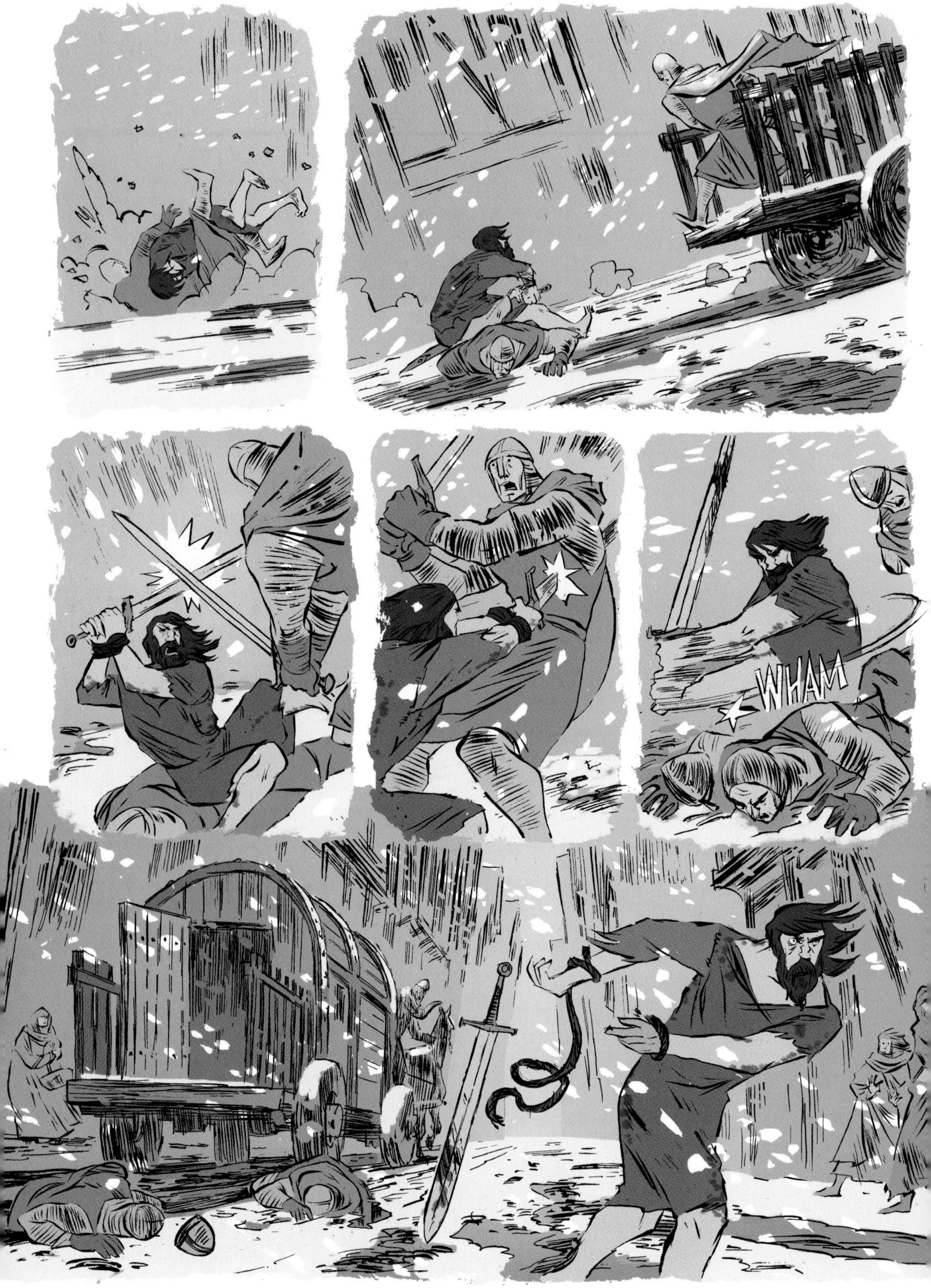
WHAM

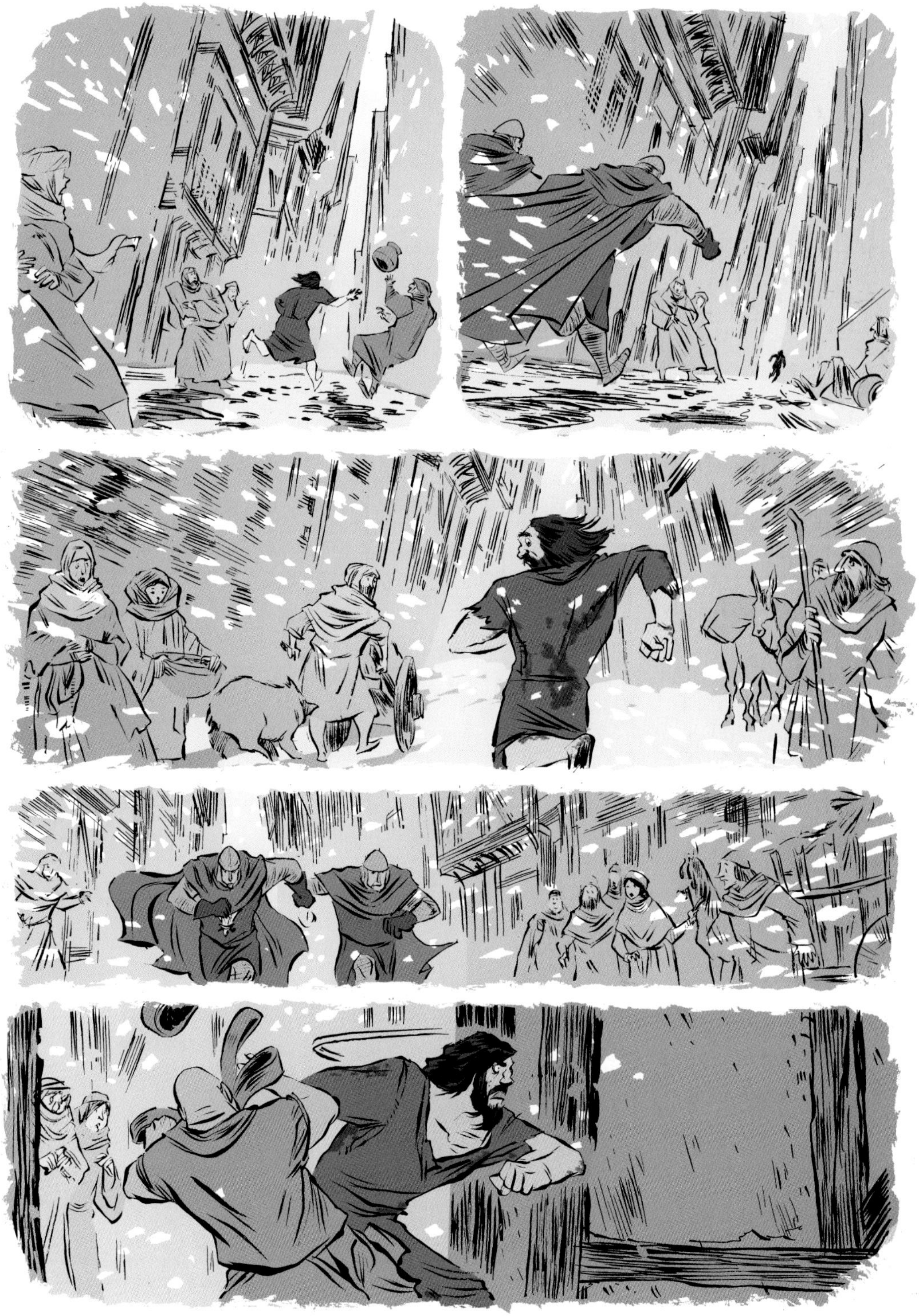

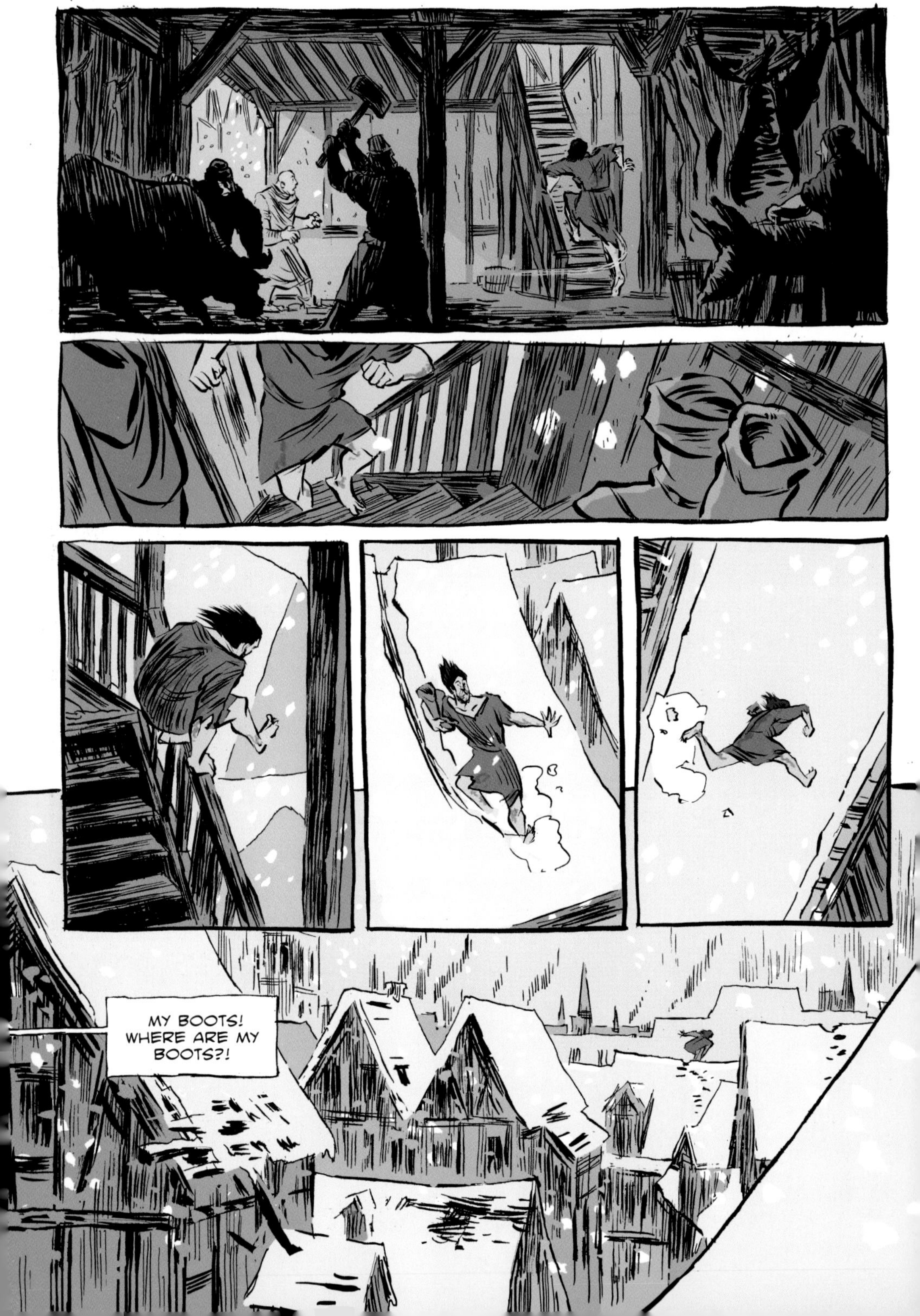
MY BOOTS!
WHERE ARE MY
BOOTS?!

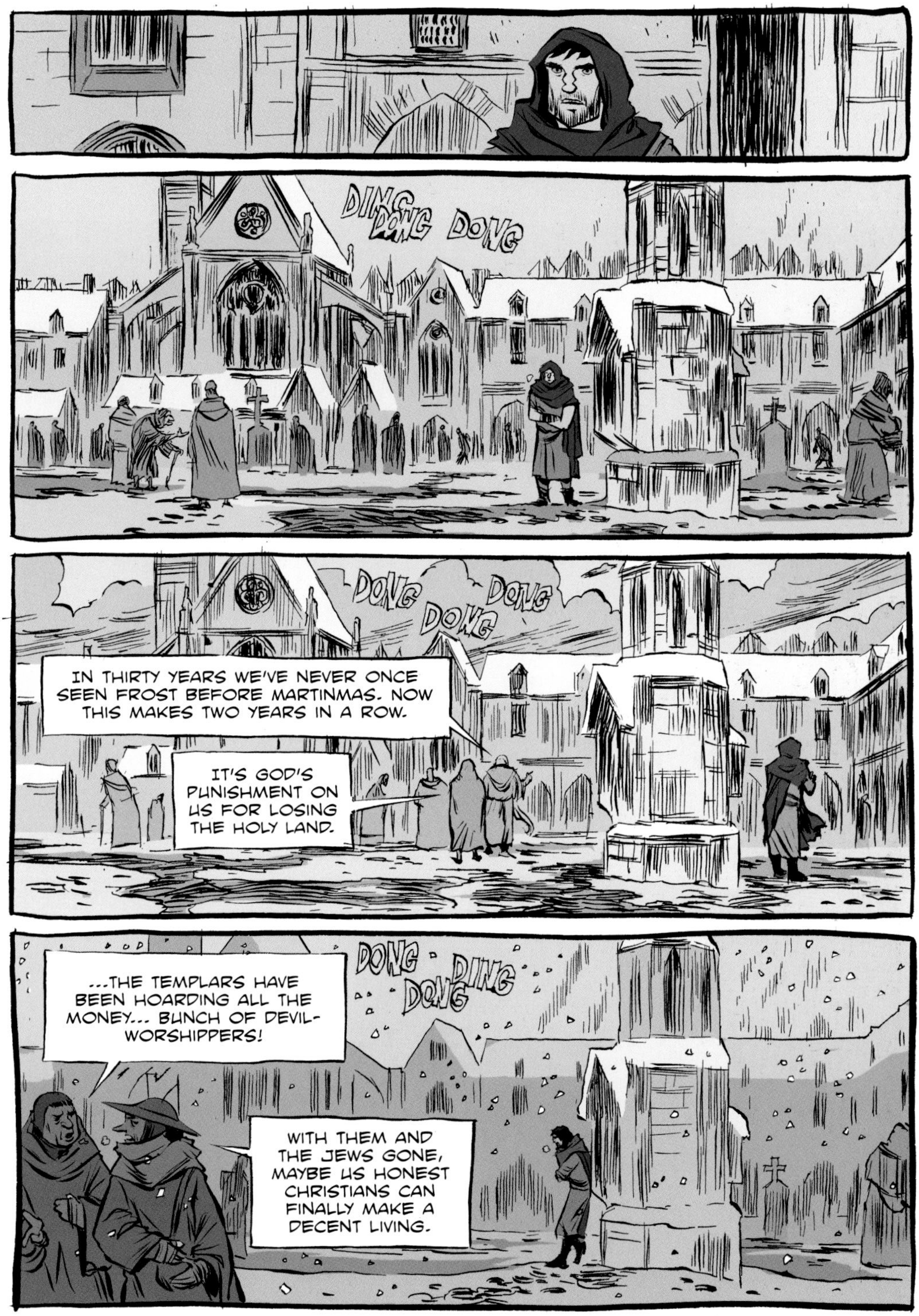
DING DONG DONG
DONG DONG DONG
IN THIRTY YEARS WE'VE NEVER ONCE SEEN FROST BEFORE MARTINMAS. NOW THIS MAKES TWO YEARS IN A ROW.
IT'S GOD'S PUNISHMENT ON US FOR LOSING THE HOLY LAND.
DONG DONG DING
...THE TEMPLARS HAVE BEEN HOARDING ALL THE MONEY... BUNCH OF DEVIL-WORSHIPPERS!
WITH THEM AND THE JEWS GONE, MAYBE US HONEST CHRISTIANS CAN FINALLY MAKE A DECENT LIVING.

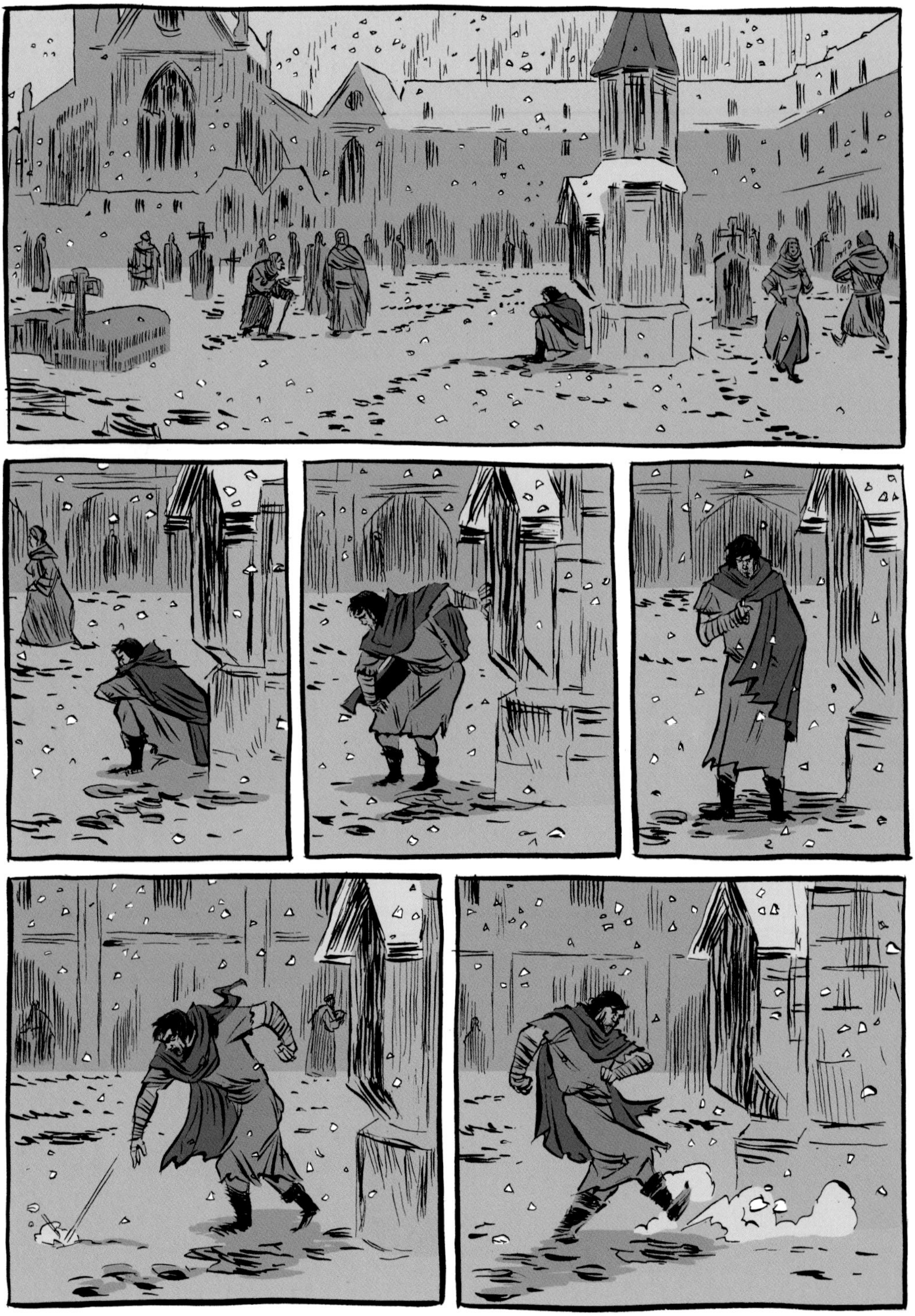

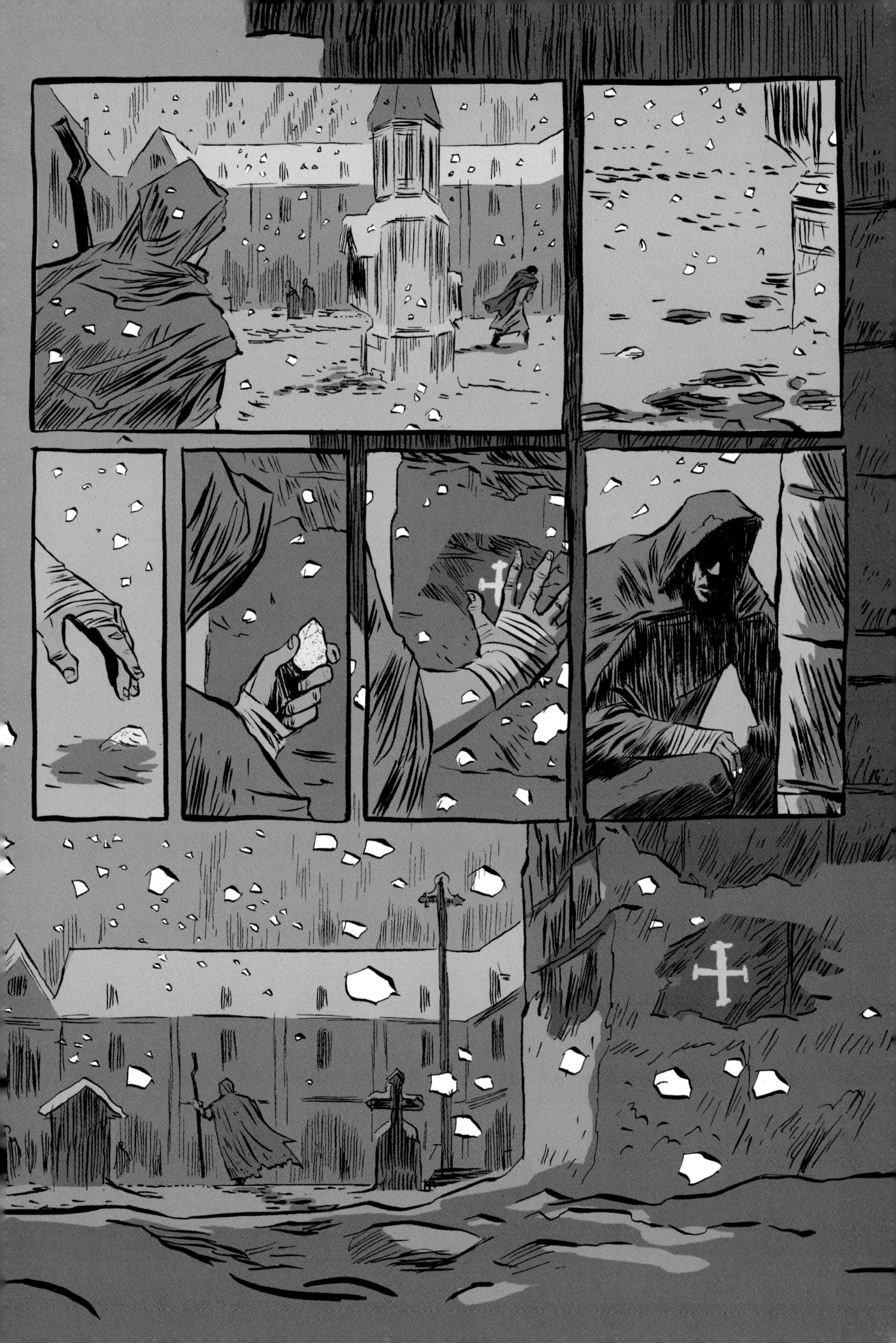

3. The Secret

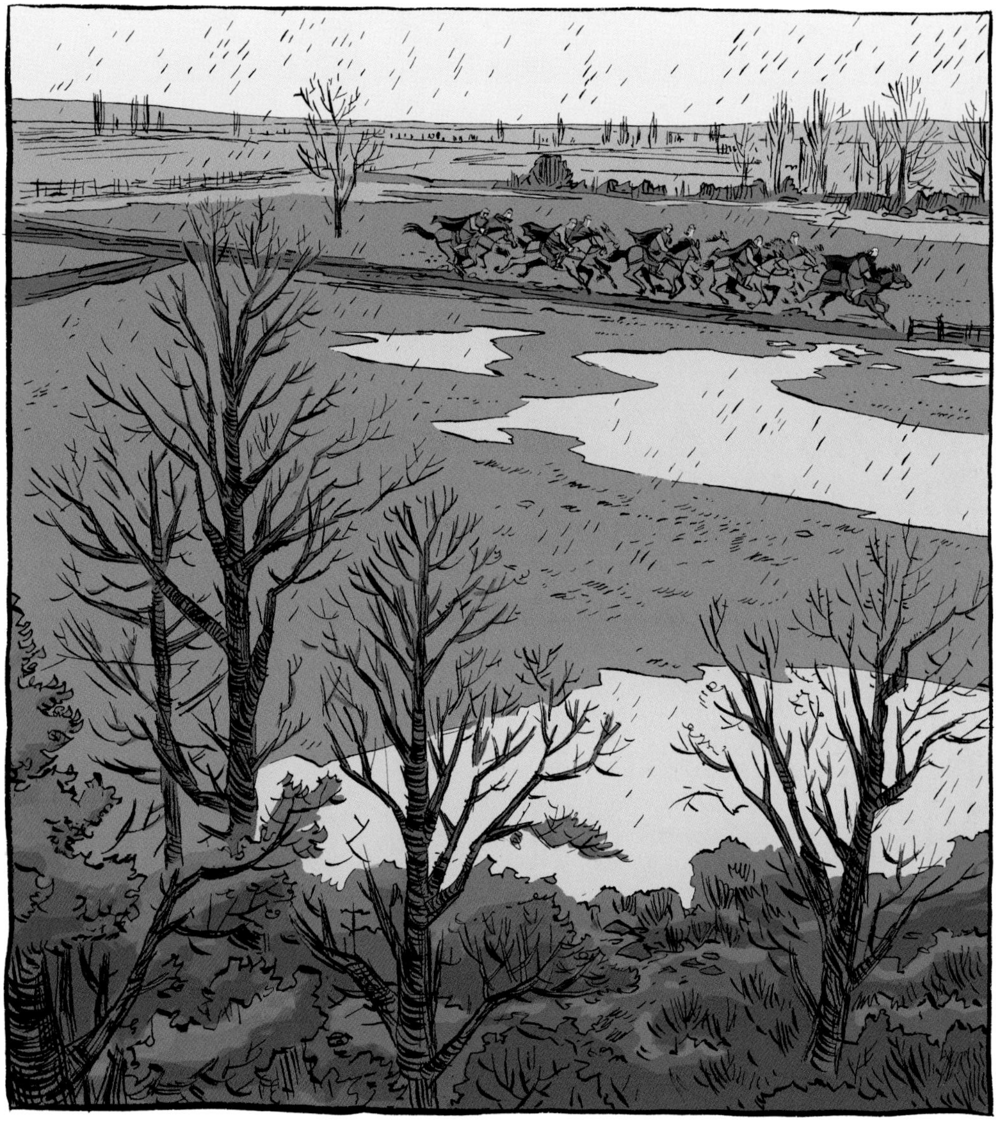

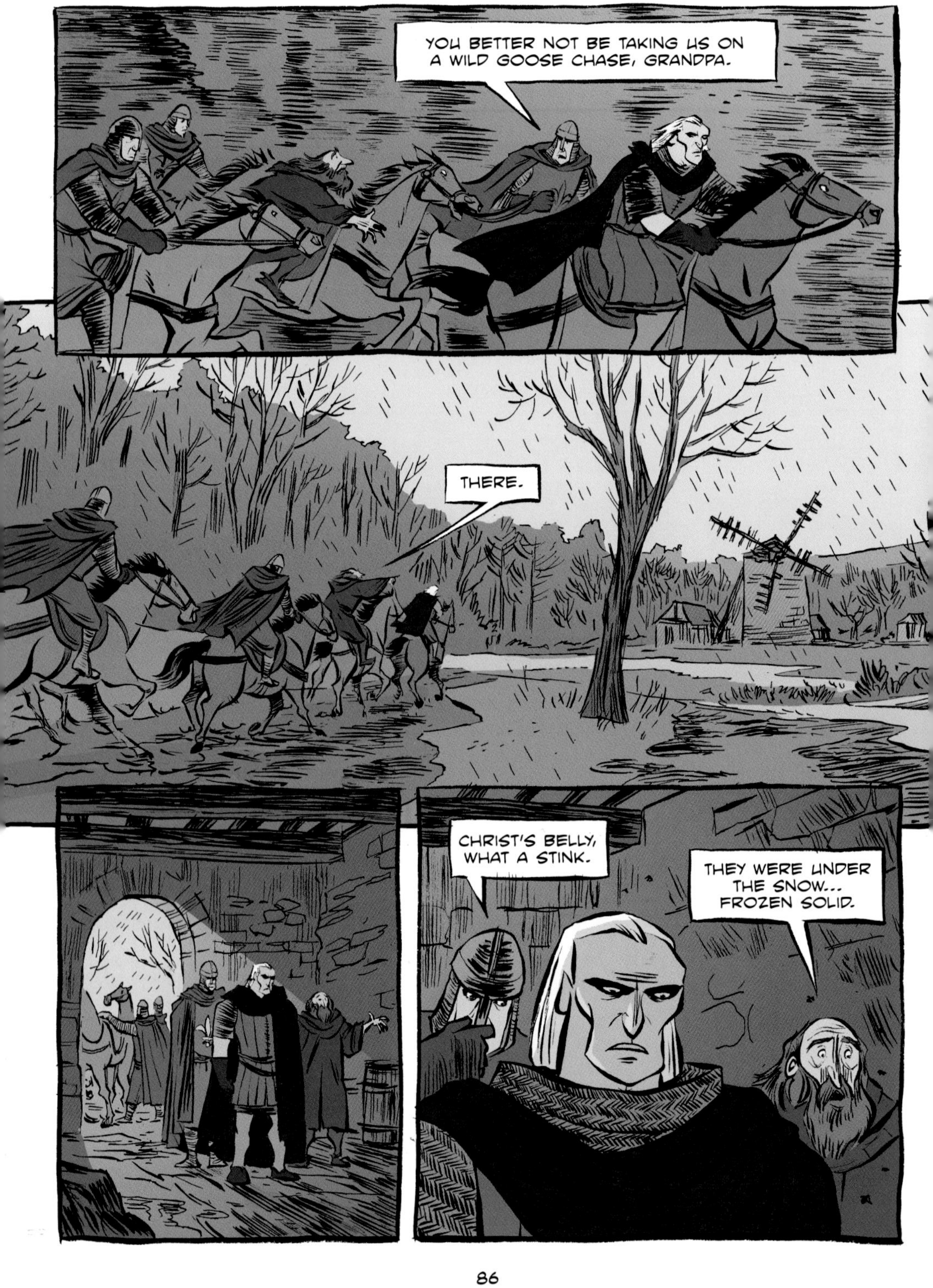
YOU BETTER NOT BE TAKING US ON A WILD GOOSE CHASE, GRANDPA.
THERE.
CHRIST'S BELLY, WHAT A STINK.
THEY WERE UNDER THE SNOW... FROZEN SOLID.

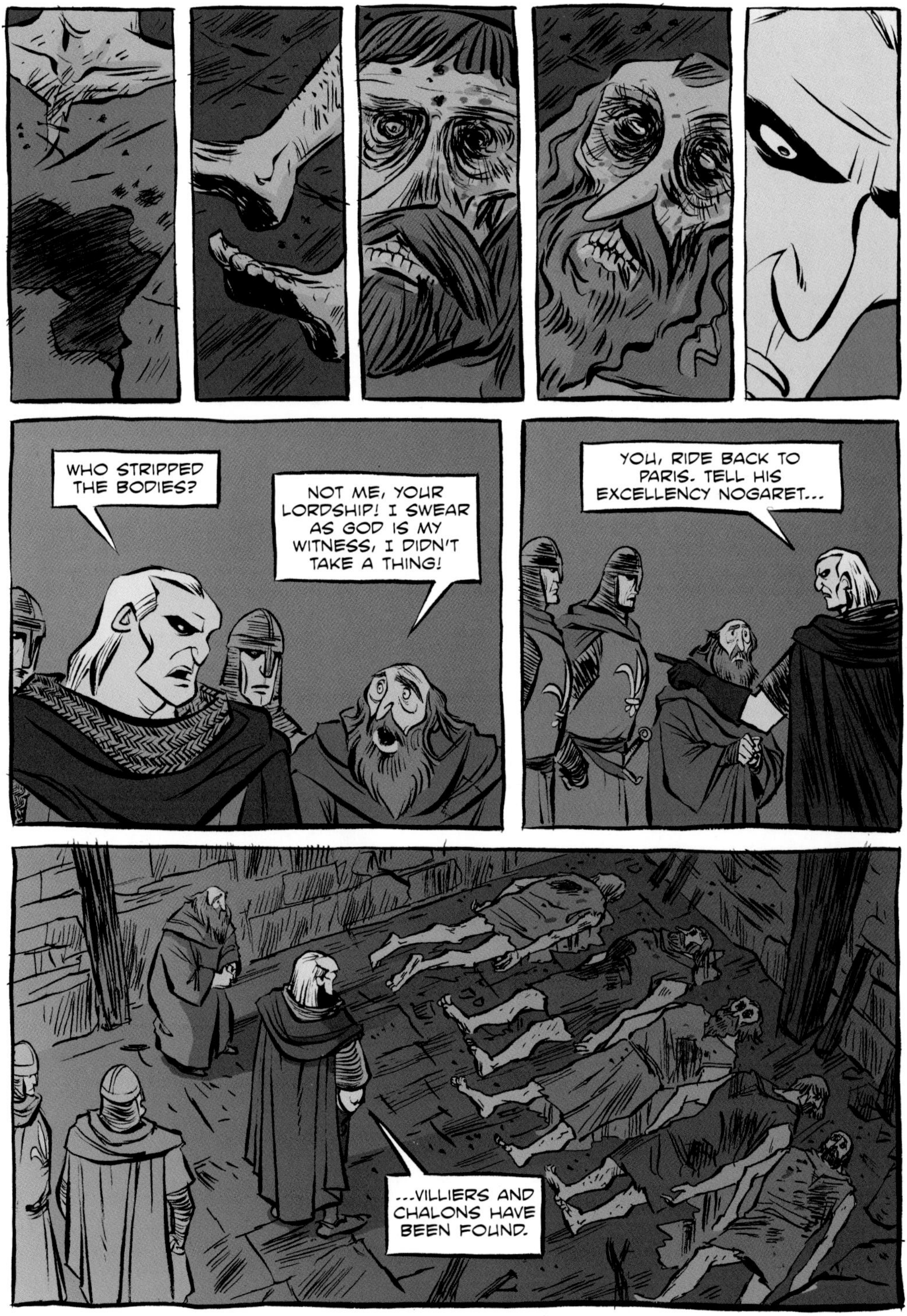

WHO STRIPPED THE BODIES?
NOT ME, YOUR LORDSHIP! I SWEAR AS GOD IS MY WITNESS, I DIDN'T TAKE A THING!
YOU, RIDE BACK TO PARIS. TELL HIS EXCELLENCY NOGARET...
...VILLIERS AND CHALONS HAVE BEEN FOUND.

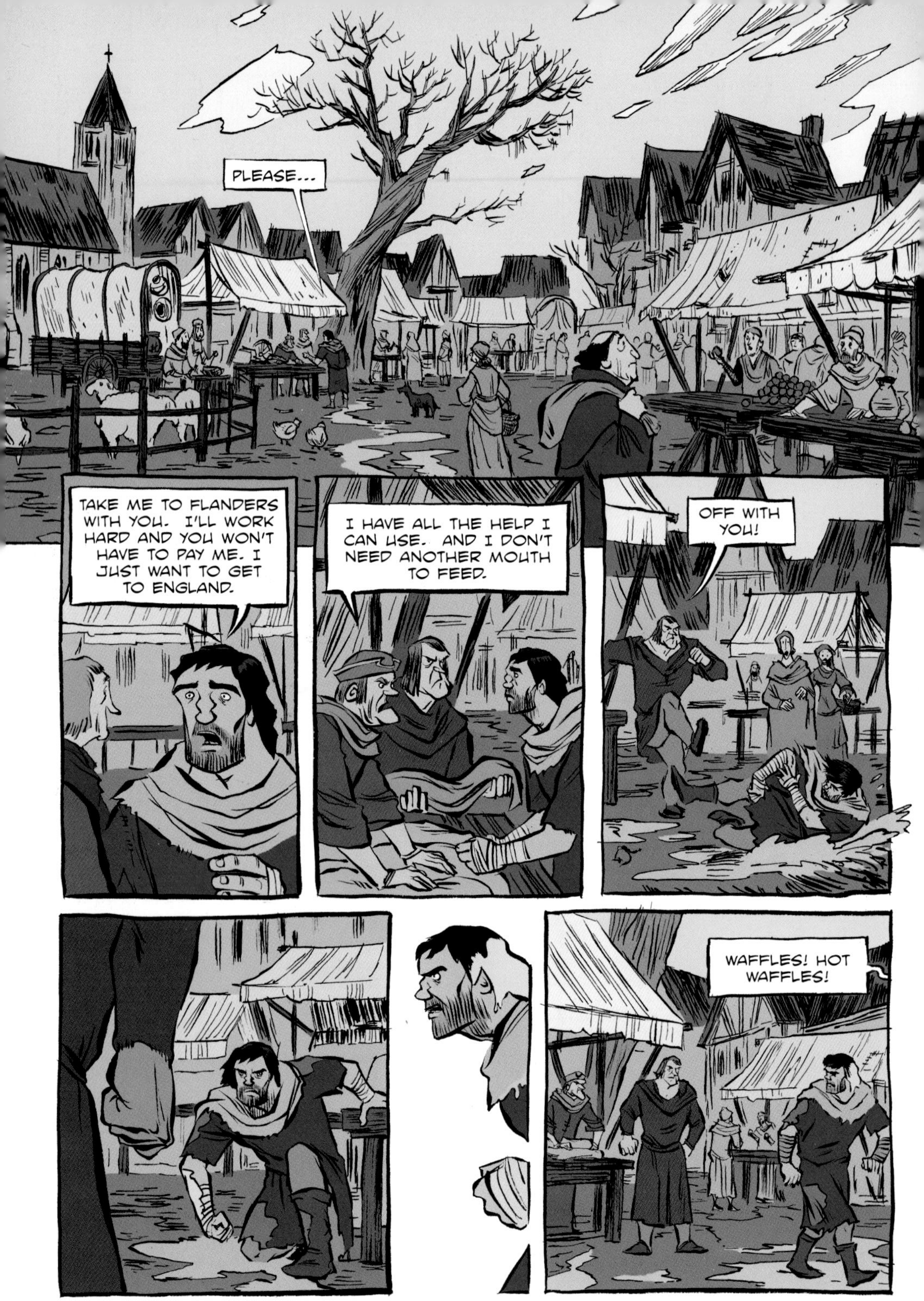
PLEASE...
TAKE ME TO FLANDERS WITH YOU. I'LL WORK HARD AND YOU WON'T HAVE TO PAY ME. I JUST WANT TO GET TO ENGLAND.
I HAVE ALL THE HELP I CAN USE. AND I DON'T NEED ANOTHER MOUTH TO FEED.
OFF WITH YOU!
WAFFLES! HOT WAFFLES!

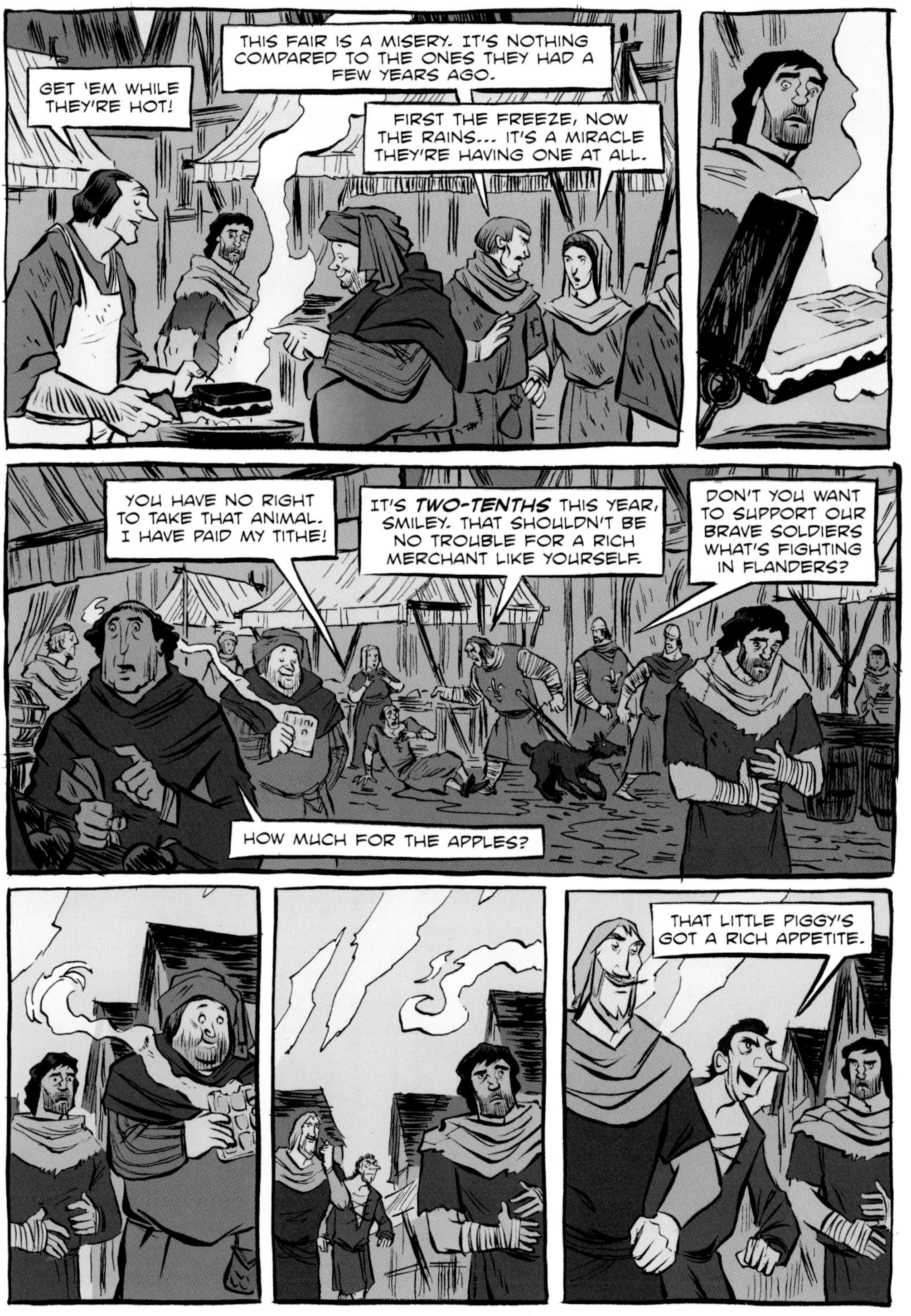
GET 'EM WHILE THEY'RE HOT!
THIS FAIR IS A MISERY. IT'S NOTHING COMPARED TO THE ONES THEY HAD A FEW YEARS AGO.
FIRST THE FREEZE, NOW THE RAINS... IT'S A MIRACLE THEY'RE HAVING ONE AT ALL.
YOU HAVE NO RIGHT TO TAKE THAT ANIMAL. I HAVE PAID MY TITHE!
IT'S TWO-TENTHS THIS YEAR, SMILEY. THAT SHOULDN'T BE NO TROUBLE FOR A RICH MERCHANT LIKE YOURSELF.
DON'T YOU WANT TO SUPPORT OUR BRAVE SOLDIERS WHAT'S FIGHTING IN FLANDERS?
HOW MUCH FOR THE APPLES?
THAT LITTLE PIGGY'S GOT A RICH APPETITE.

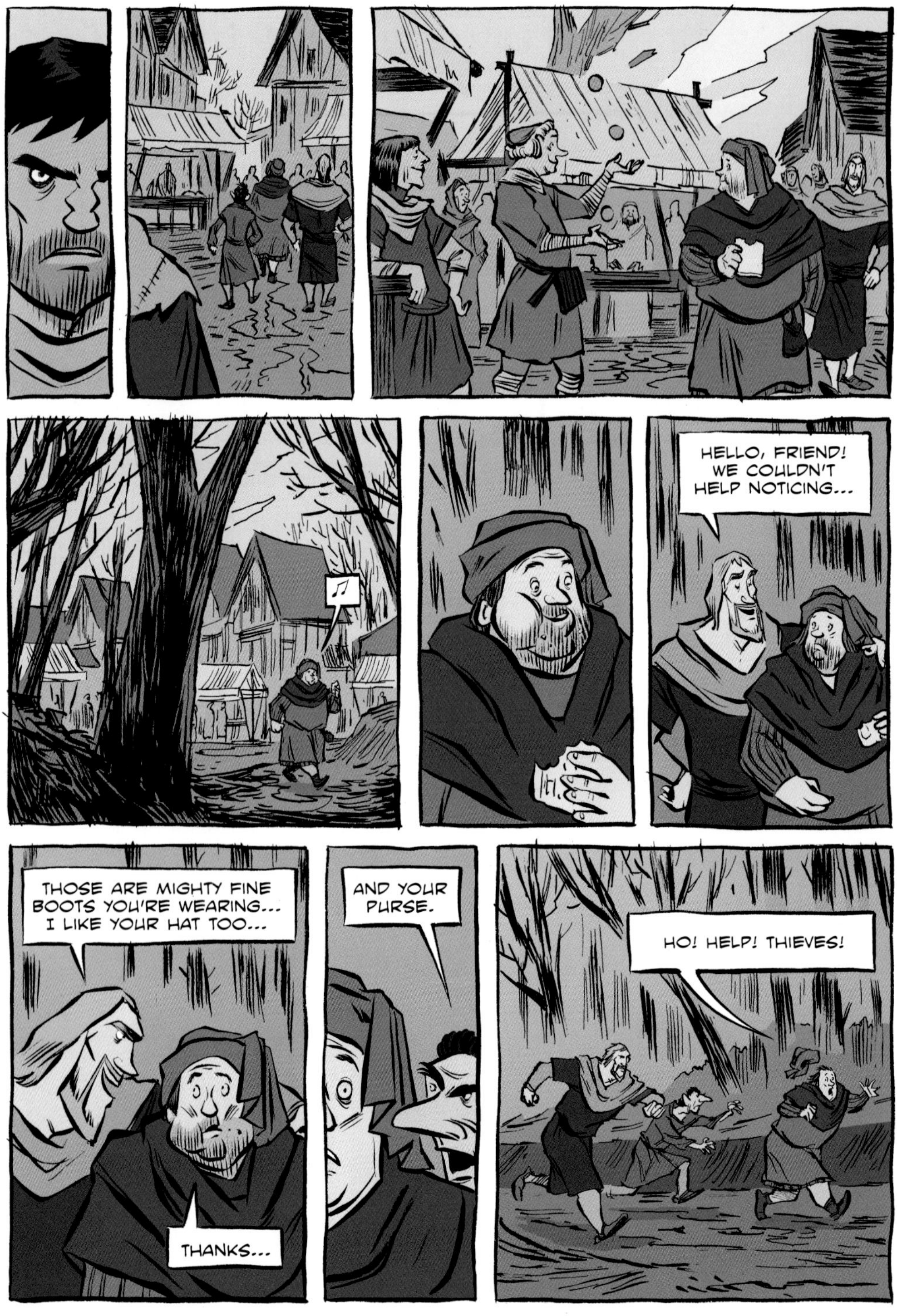

♪
HELLO, FRIEND! WE COULDN'T HELP NOTICING...
THOSE ARE MIGHTY FINE BOOTS YOU'RE WEARING... I LIKE YOUR HAT TOO...
THANKS...
AND YOUR PURSE.
HO! HELP! THIEVES!

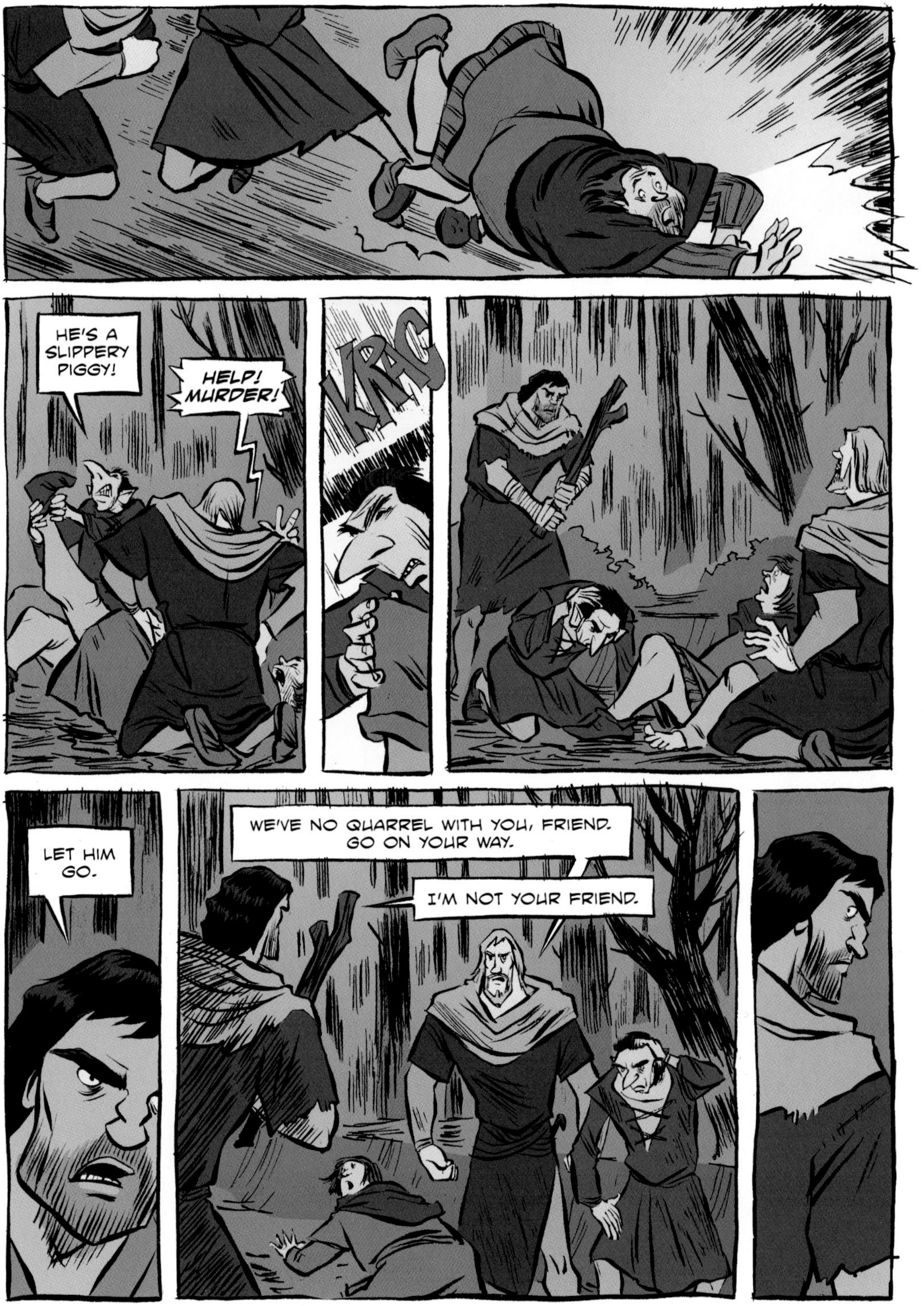
HE'S A SLIPPERY PIGGY!
HELP! MURDER!
KRAG
LET HIM GO.
WE'VE NO QUARREL WITH YOU, FRIEND. GO ON YOUR WAY.
I'M NOT YOUR FRIEND.

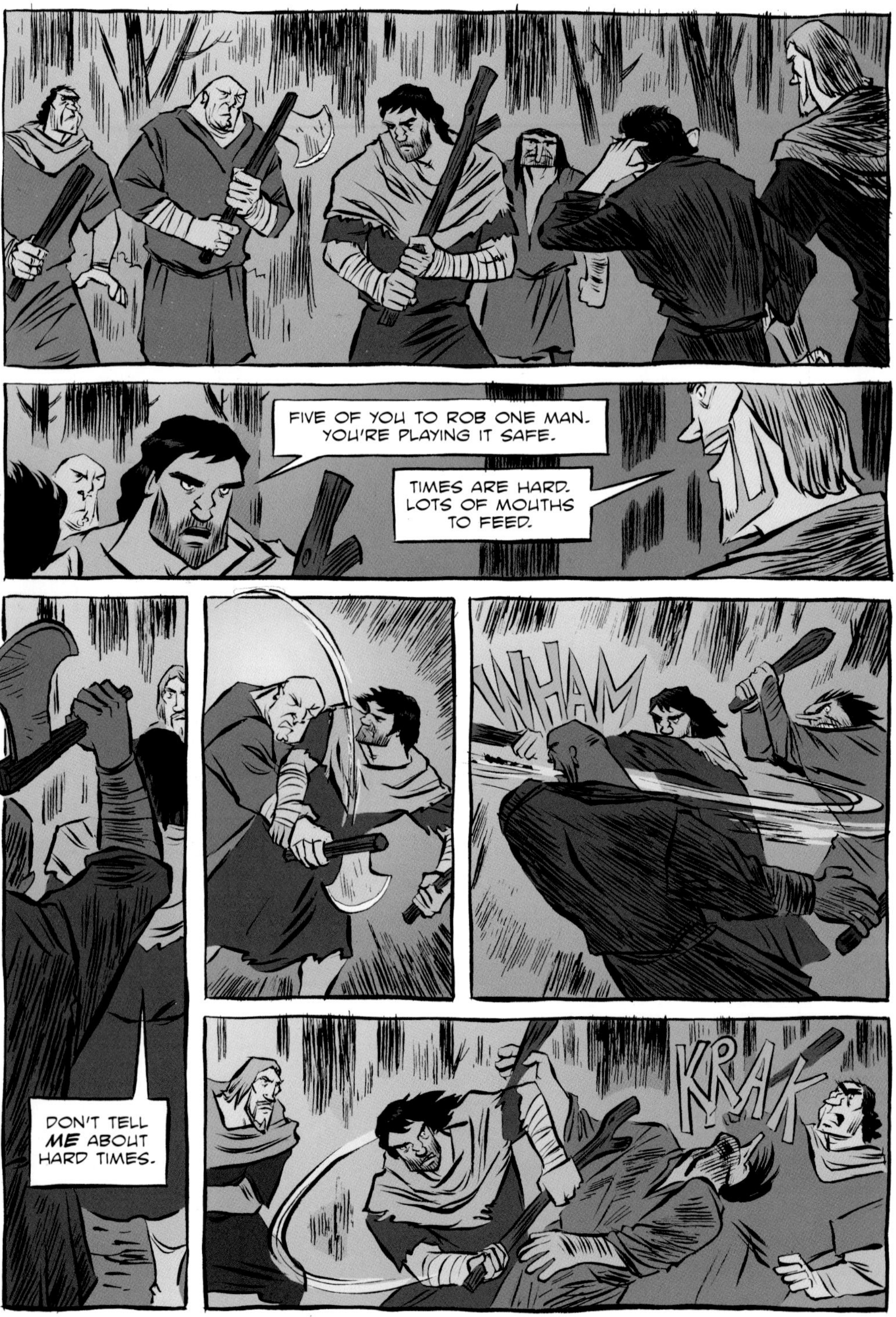
FIVE OF YOU TO ROB ONE MAN. YOU'RE PLAYING IT SAFE.
TIMES ARE HARD. LOTS OF MOUTHS TO FEED.
DON'T TELL *ME* ABOUT HARD TIMES.
WHAM
KRAK

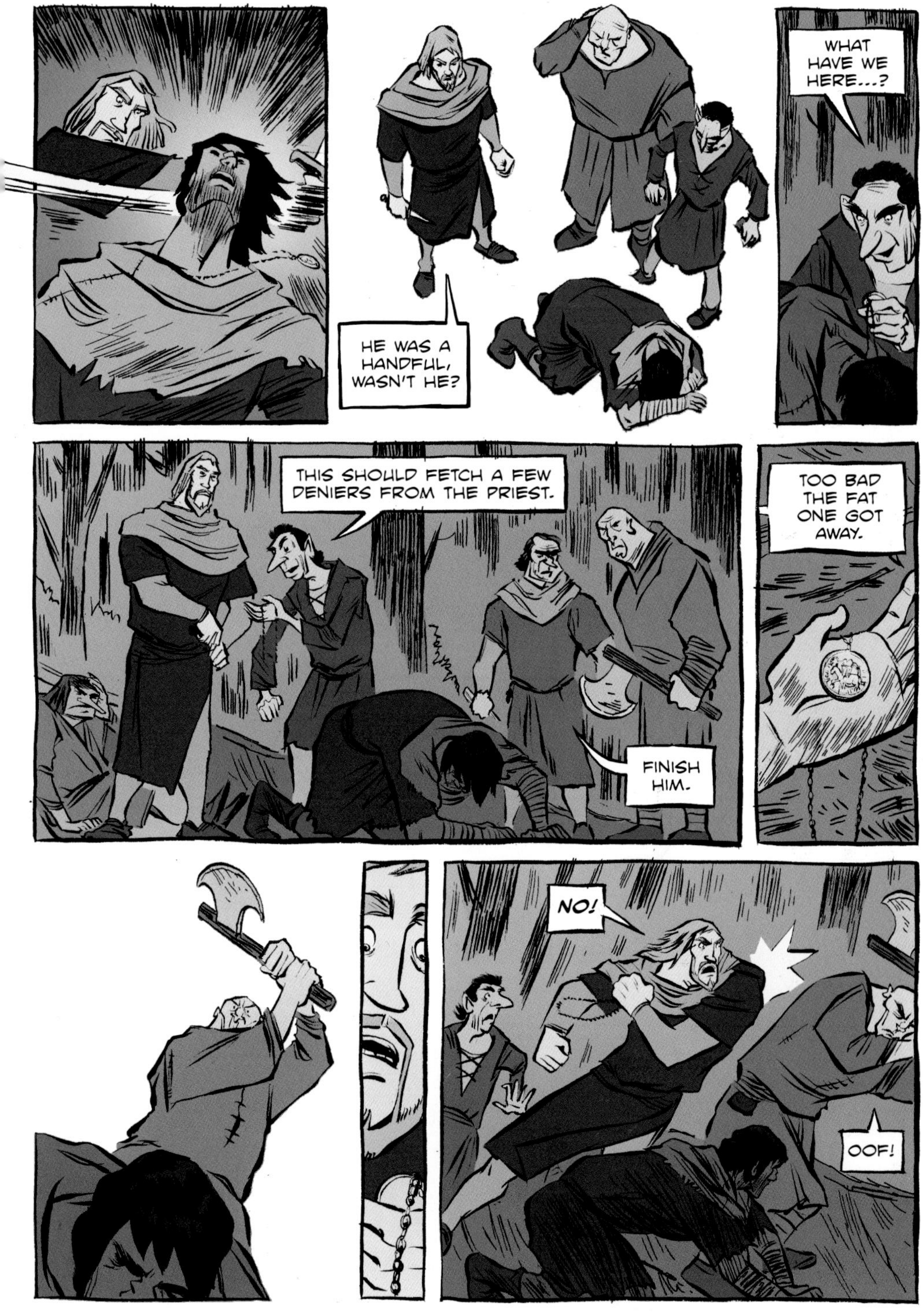

HE WAS A HANDFUL, WASN'T HE?
WHAT HAVE WE HERE...?
THIS SHOULD FETCH A FEW DENIERS FROM THE PRIEST.
FINISH HIM.
TOO BAD THE FAT ONE GOT AWAY.
NO!
OOF!

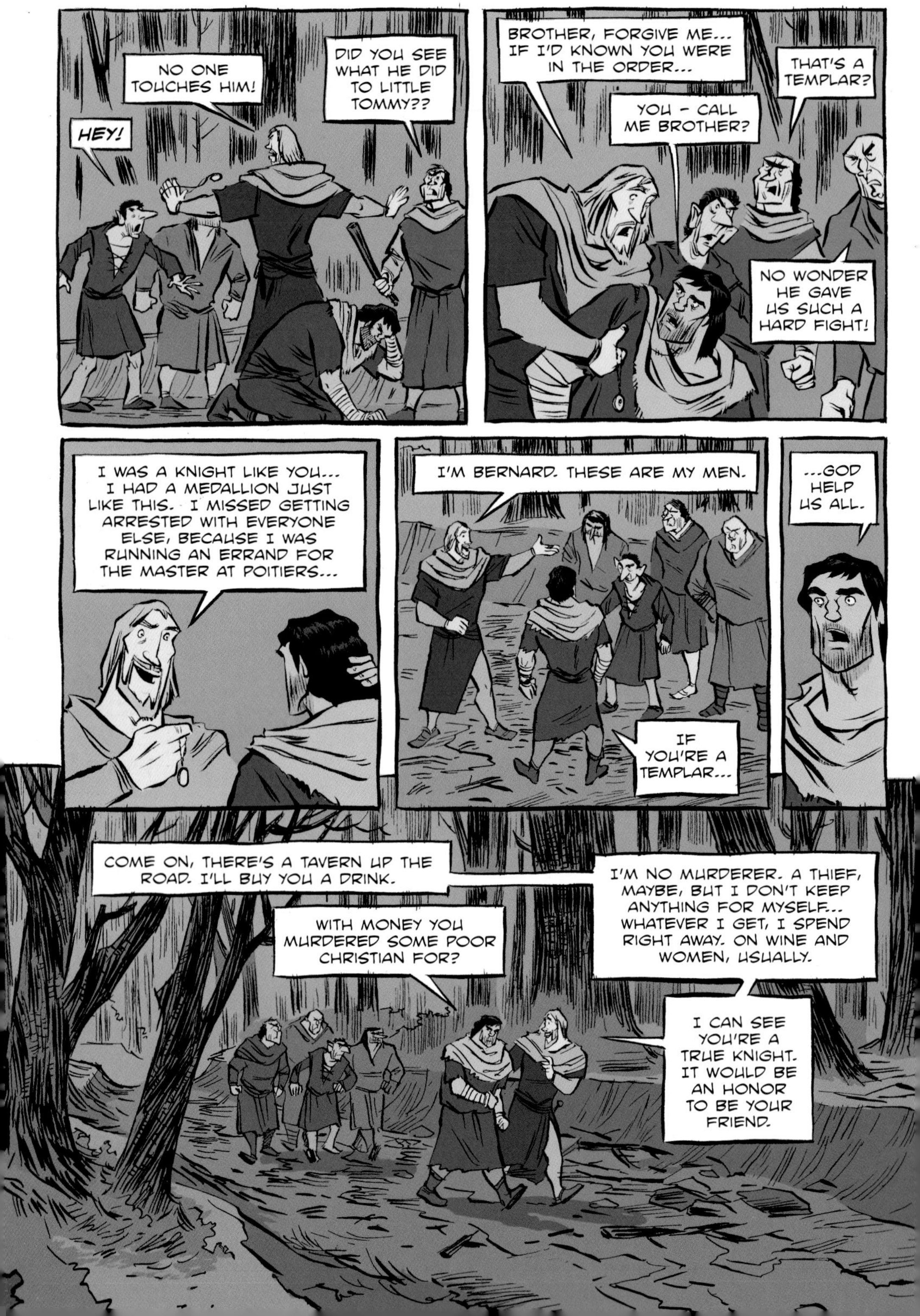
HEY!
NO ONE TOUCHES HIM!
DID YOU SEE WHAT HE DID TO LITTLE TOMMY??
BROTHER, FORGIVE ME... IF I'D KNOWN YOU WERE IN THE ORDER...
YOU - CALL ME BROTHER?
THAT'S A TEMPLAR?
NO WONDER HE GAVE US SUCH A HARD FIGHT!
I WAS A KNIGHT LIKE YOU... I HAD A MEDALLION JUST LIKE THIS. I MISSED GETTING ARRESTED WITH EVERYONE ELSE, BECAUSE I WAS RUNNING AN ERRAND FOR THE MASTER AT POITIERS...
I'M BERNARD. THESE ARE MY MEN.
IF YOU'RE A TEMPLAR...
...GOD HELP US ALL.
COME ON, THERE'S A TAVERN UP THE ROAD. I'LL BUY YOU A DRINK.
WITH MONEY YOU MURDERED SOME POOR CHRISTIAN FOR?
I'M NO MURDERER. A THIEF, MAYBE, BUT I DON'T KEEP ANYTHING FOR MYSELF... WHATEVER I GET, I SPEND RIGHT AWAY. ON WINE AND WOMEN, USUALLY.
I CAN SEE YOU'RE A TRUE KNIGHT. IT WOULD BE AN HONOR TO BE YOUR FRIEND.

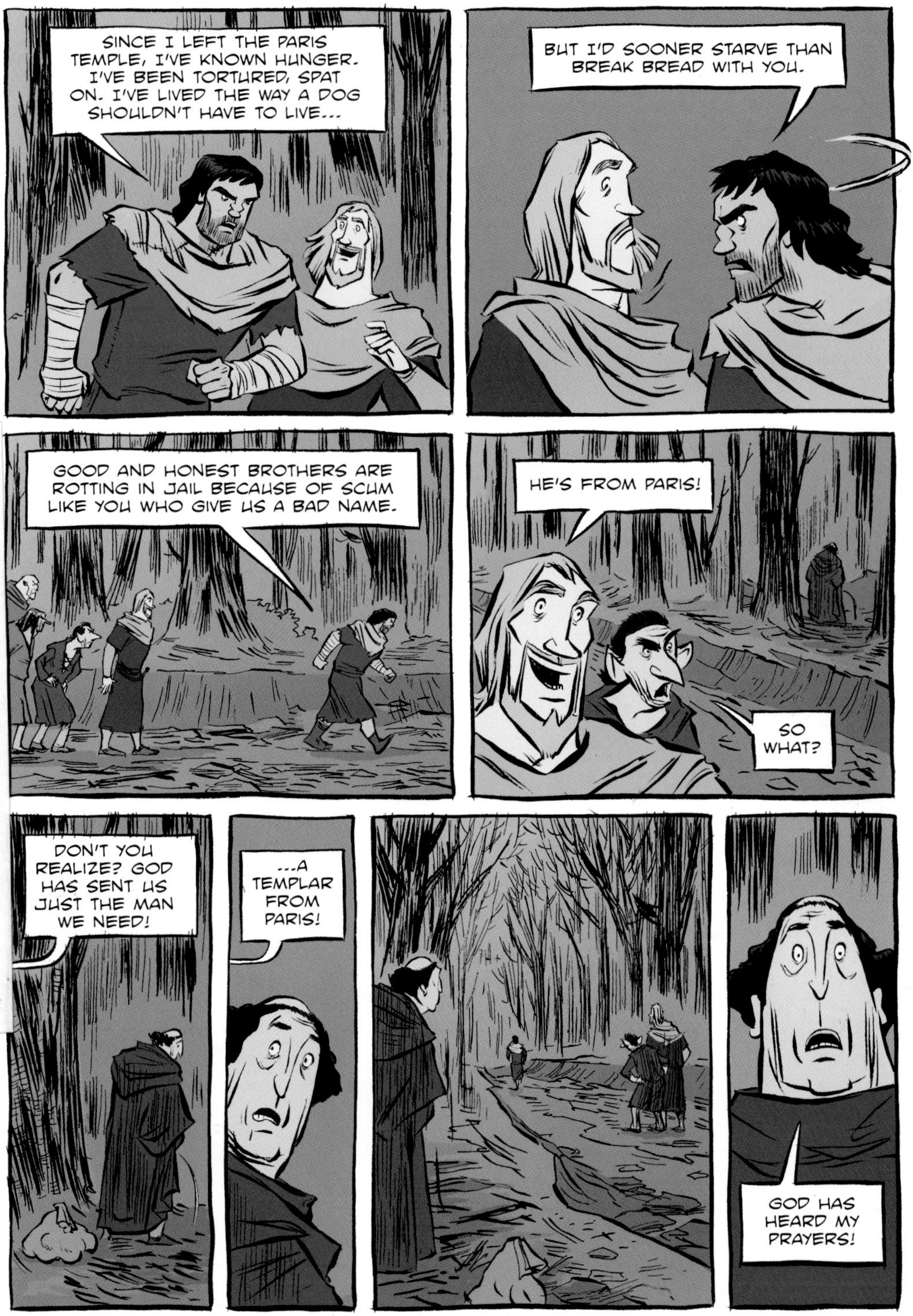
SINCE I LEFT THE PARIS TEMPLE, I'VE KNOWN HUNGER. I'VE BEEN TORTURED, SPAT ON. I'VE LIVED THE WAY A DOG SHOULDN'T HAVE TO LIVE...
BUT I'D SOONER STARVE THAN BREAK BREAD WITH YOU.
GOOD AND HONEST BROTHERS ARE ROTTING IN JAIL BECAUSE OF SCUM LIKE YOU WHO GIVE US A BAD NAME.
HE'S FROM PARIS!
SO WHAT?
DON'T YOU REALIZE? GOD HAS SENT US JUST THE MAN WE NEED!
...A TEMPLAR FROM PARIS!
GOD HAS HEARD MY PRAYERS!

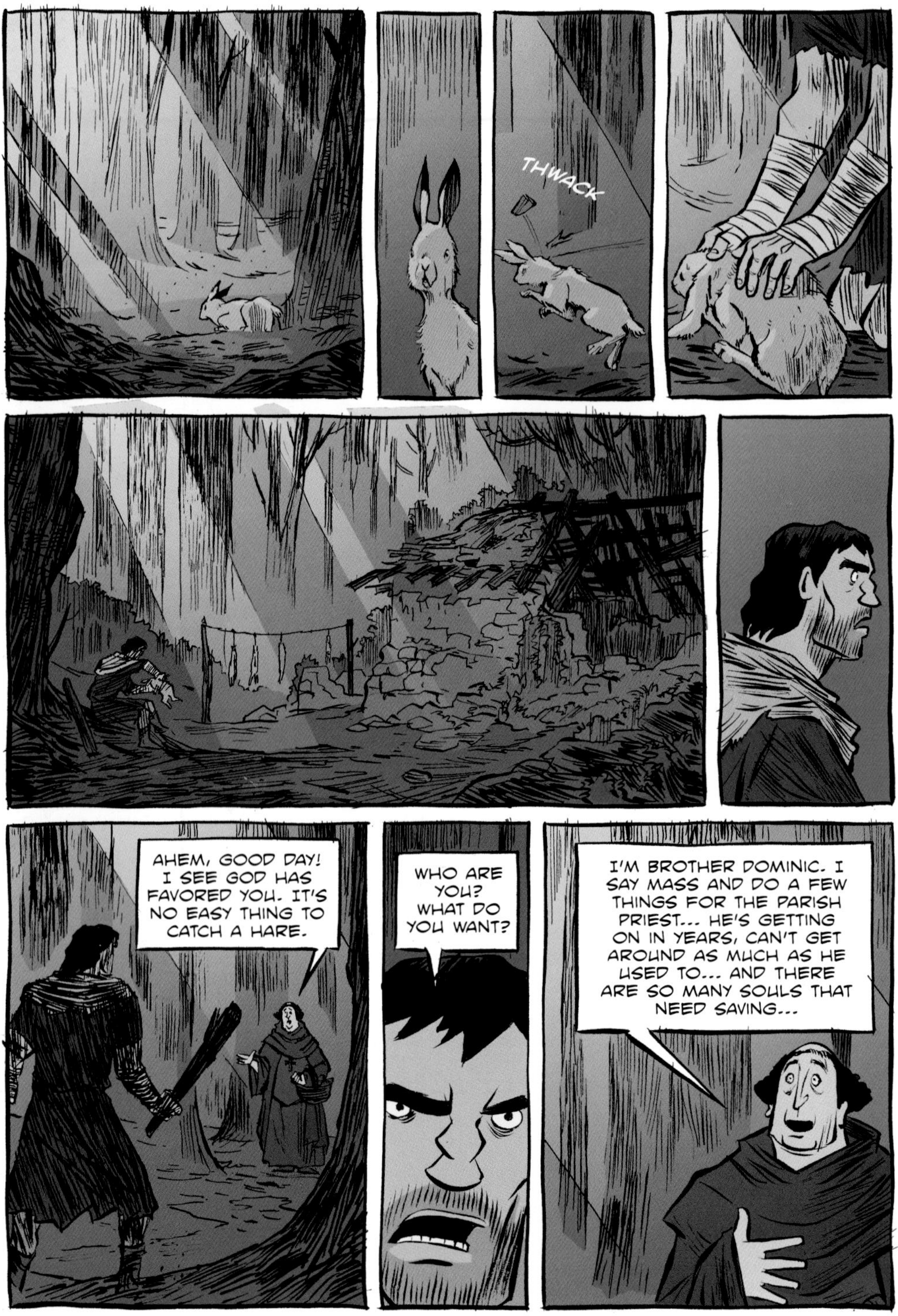
THWACK
AHEM, GOOD DAY! I SEE GOD HAS FAVORED YOU. IT'S NO EASY THING TO CATCH A HARE.
WHO ARE YOU? WHAT DO YOU WANT?
I'M BROTHER DOMINIC. I SAY MASS AND DO A FEW THINGS FOR THE PARISH PRIEST... HE'S GETTING ON IN YEARS, CAN'T GET AROUND AS MUCH AS HE USED TO... AND THERE ARE SO MANY SOULS THAT NEED SAVING...

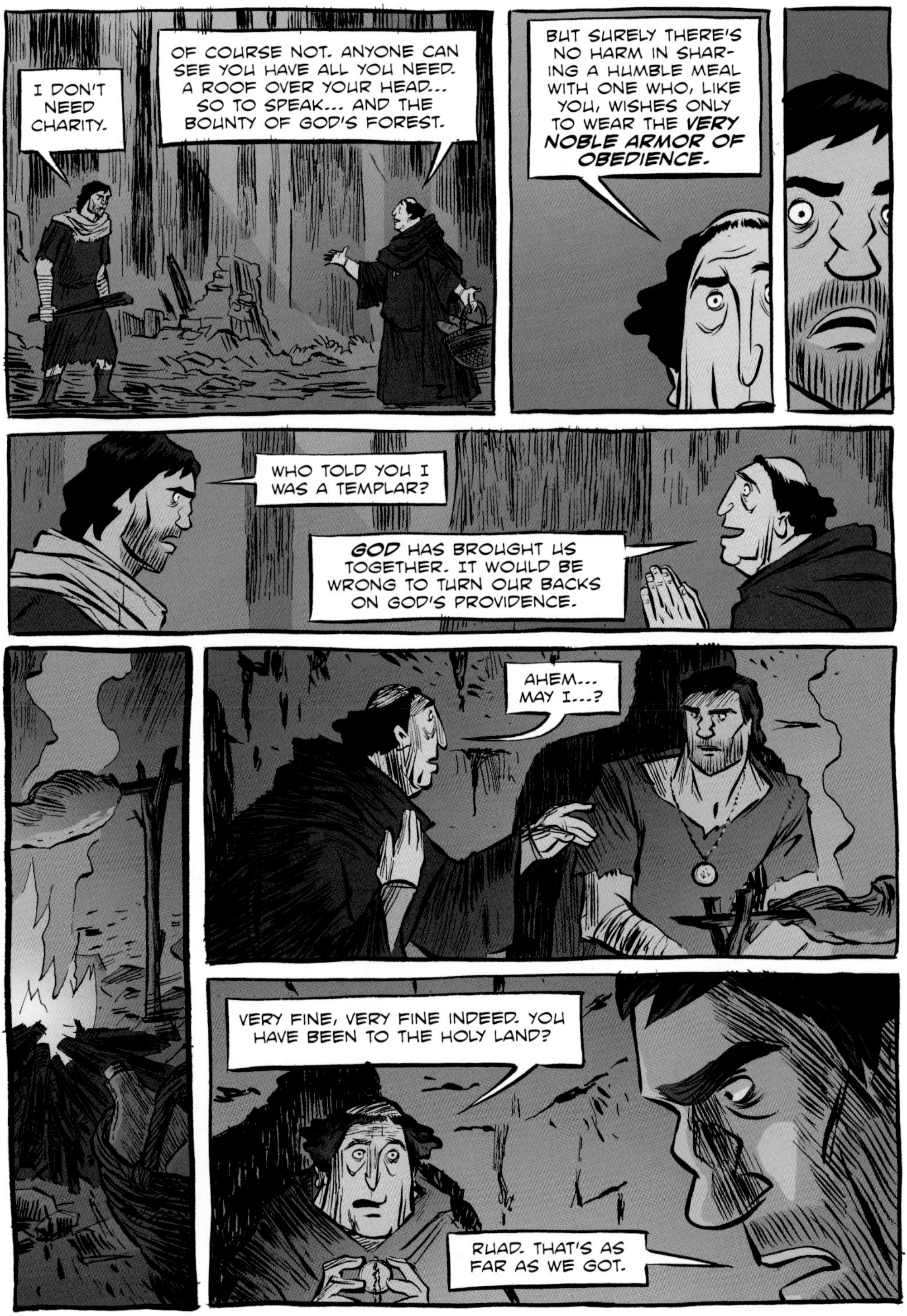
I DON'T NEED CHARITY.
OF COURSE NOT. ANYONE CAN SEE YOU HAVE ALL YOU NEED. A ROOF OVER YOUR HEAD... SO TO SPEAK... AND THE BOUNTY OF GOD'S FOREST.
BUT SURELY THERE'S NO HARM IN SHARING A HUMBLE MEAL WITH ONE WHO, LIKE YOU, WISHES ONLY TO WEAR THE VERY NOBLE ARMOR OF OBEDIENCE.
WHO TOLD YOU I WAS A TEMPLAR?
GOD HAS BROUGHT US TOGETHER. IT WOULD BE WRONG TO TURN OUR BACKS ON GOD'S PROVIDENCE.
AHEM... MAY I...?
VERY FINE, VERY FINE INDEED. YOU HAVE BEEN TO THE HOLY LAND?
RUAD. THAT'S AS FAR AS WE GOT.

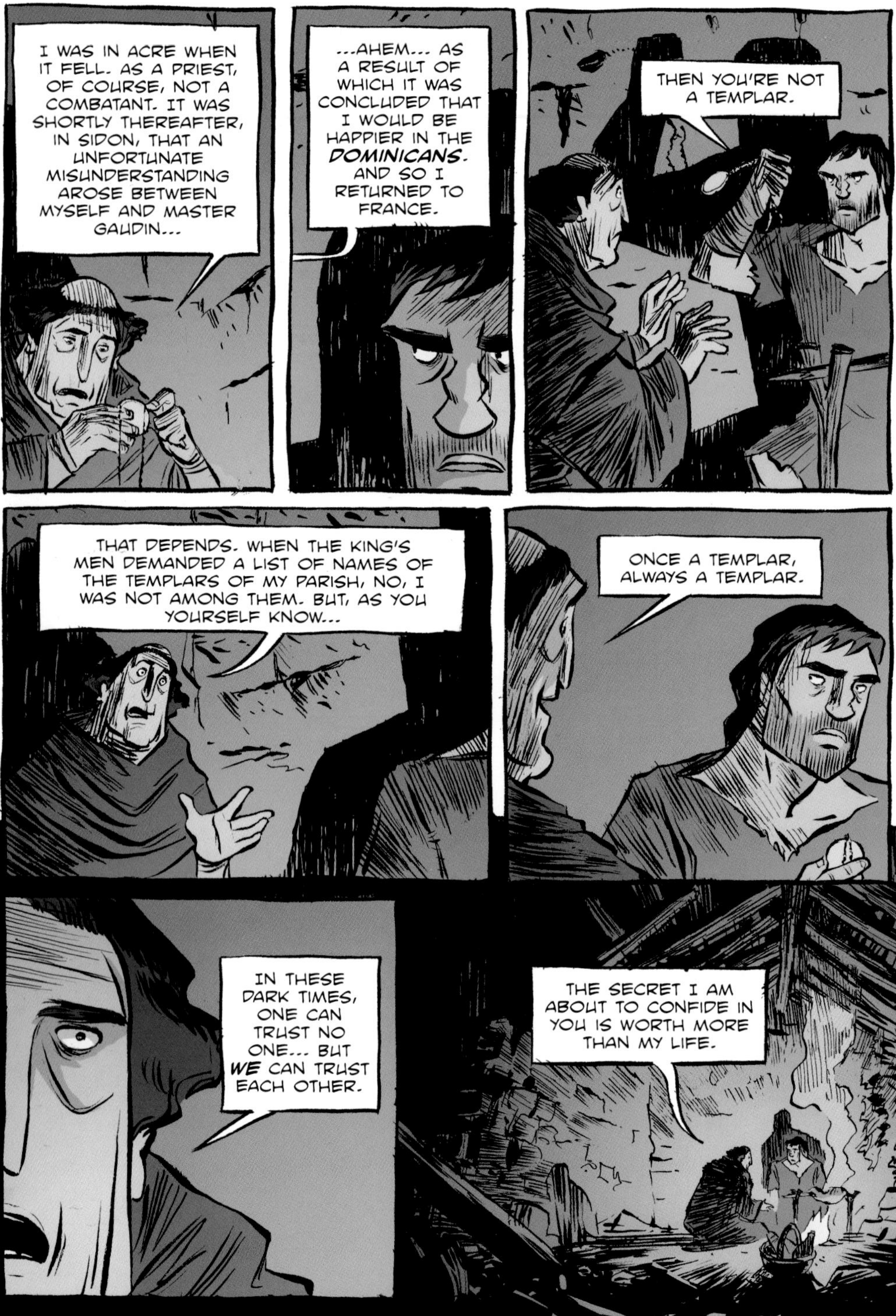
I WAS IN ACRE WHEN IT FELL. AS A PRIEST, OF COURSE, NOT A COMBATANT. IT WAS SHORTLY THEREAFTER, IN SIDON, THAT AN UNFORTUNATE MISUNDERSTANDING AROSE BETWEEN MYSELF AND MASTER GAUDIN...
...AHEM... AS A RESULT OF WHICH IT WAS CONCLUDED THAT I WOULD BE HAPPIER IN THE DOMINICANS. AND SO I RETURNED TO FRANCE.
THEN YOU'RE NOT A TEMPLAR.
THAT DEPENDS. WHEN THE KING'S MEN DEMANDED A LIST OF NAMES OF THE TEMPLARS OF MY PARISH, NO, I WAS NOT AMONG THEM. BUT, AS YOU YOURSELF KNOW...
ONCE A TEMPLAR, ALWAYS A TEMPLAR.
IN THESE DARK TIMES, ONE CAN TRUST NO ONE... BUT WE CAN TRUST EACH OTHER.
THE SECRET I AM ABOUT TO CONFIDE IN YOU IS WORTH MORE THAN MY LIFE.

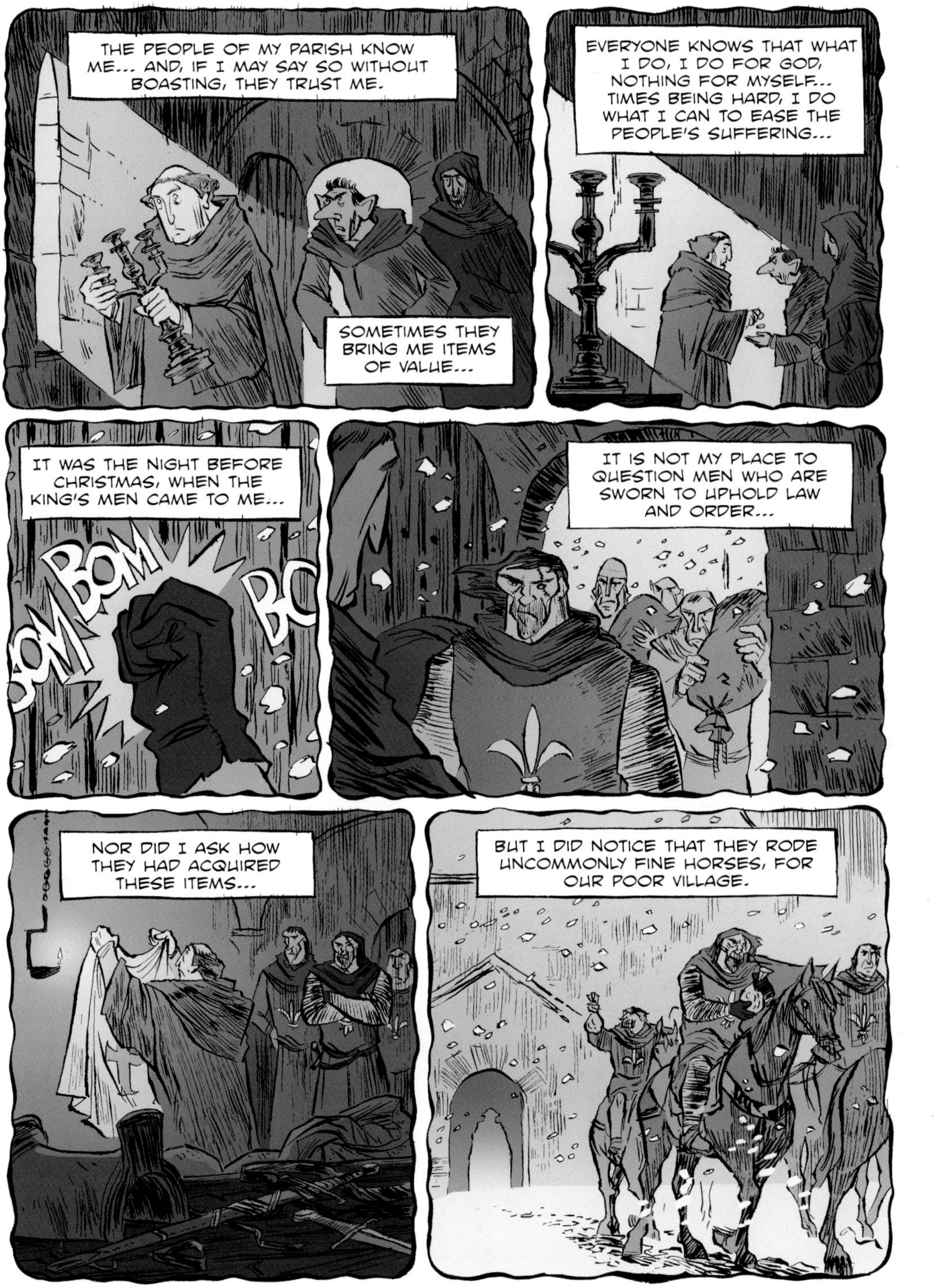
THE PEOPLE OF MY PARISH KNOW ME... AND, IF I MAY SAY SO WITHOUT BOASTING, THEY TRUST ME.
SOMETIMES THEY BRING ME ITEMS OF VALUE...
EVERYONE KNOWS THAT WHAT I DO, I DO FOR GOD, NOTHING FOR MYSELF... TIMES BEING HARD, I DO WHAT I CAN TO EASE THE PEOPLE'S SUFFERING...
IT WAS THE NIGHT BEFORE CHRISTMAS, WHEN THE KING'S MEN CAME TO ME...
BOM BOM BOM BO
IT IS NOT MY PLACE TO QUESTION MEN WHO ARE SWORN TO UPHOLD LAW AND ORDER...
NOR DID I ASK HOW THEY HAD ACQUIRED THESE ITEMS...
BUT I DID NOTICE THAT THEY RODE UNCOMMONLY FINE HORSES, FOR OUR POOR VILLAGE.

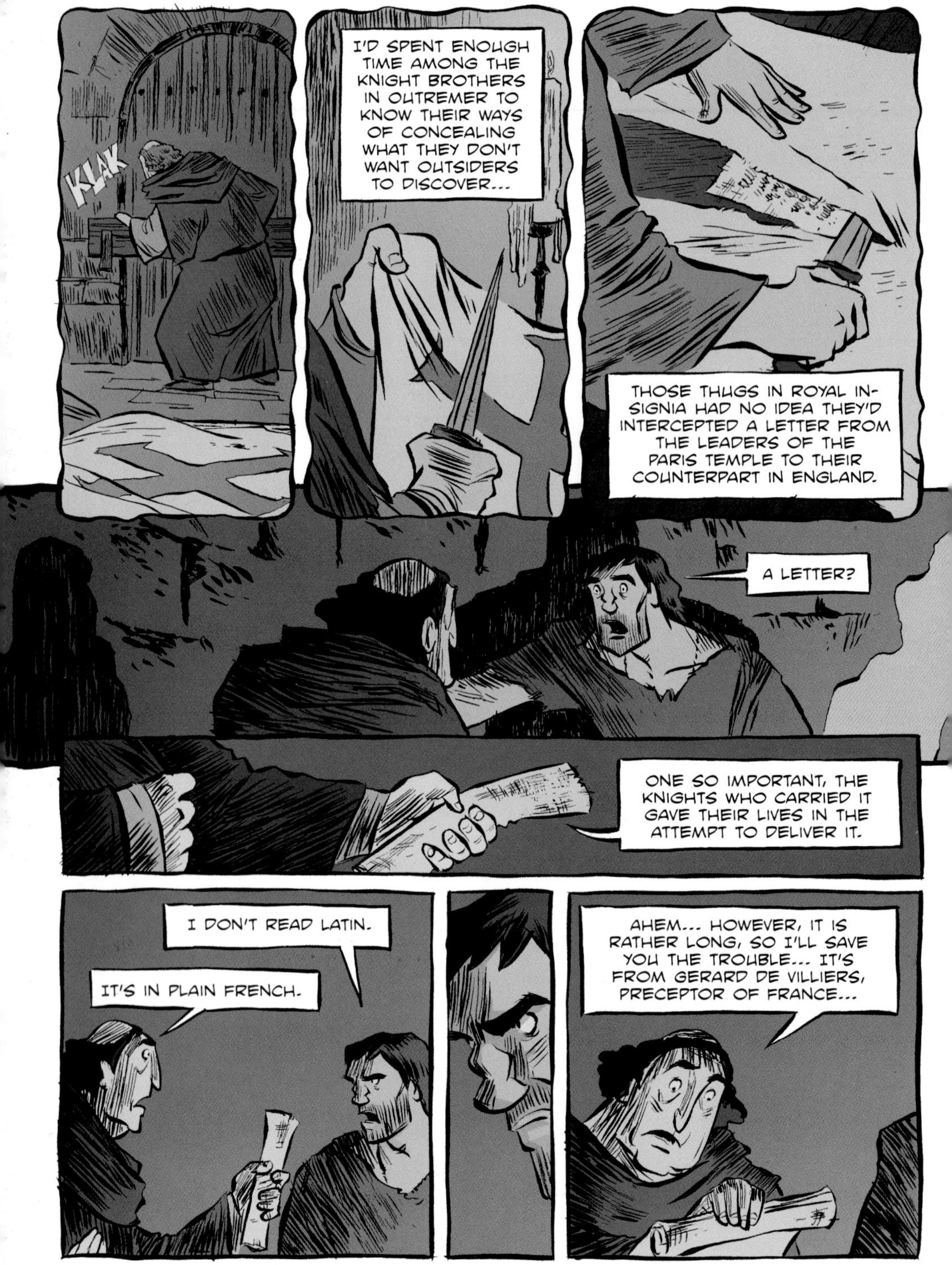
KLAK
I'D SPENT ENOUGH TIME AMONG THE KNIGHT BROTHERS IN OUTREMER TO KNOW THEIR WAYS OF CONCEALING WHAT THEY DON'T WANT OUTSIDERS TO DISCOVER...
THOSE THUGS IN ROYAL IN-SIGNIA HAD NO IDEA THEY'D INTERCEPTED A LETTER FROM THE LEADERS OF THE PARIS TEMPLE TO THEIR COUNTERPART IN ENGLAND.
A LETTER?
ONE SO IMPORTANT, THE KNIGHTS WHO CARRIED IT GAVE THEIR LIVES IN THE ATTEMPT TO DELIVER IT.
I DON'T READ LATIN.
IT'S IN PLAIN FRENCH.
AHEM... HOWEVER, IT IS RATHER LONG, SO I'LL SAVE YOU THE TROUBLE... IT'S FROM GERARD DE VILLIERS, PRECEPTOR OF FRANCE...

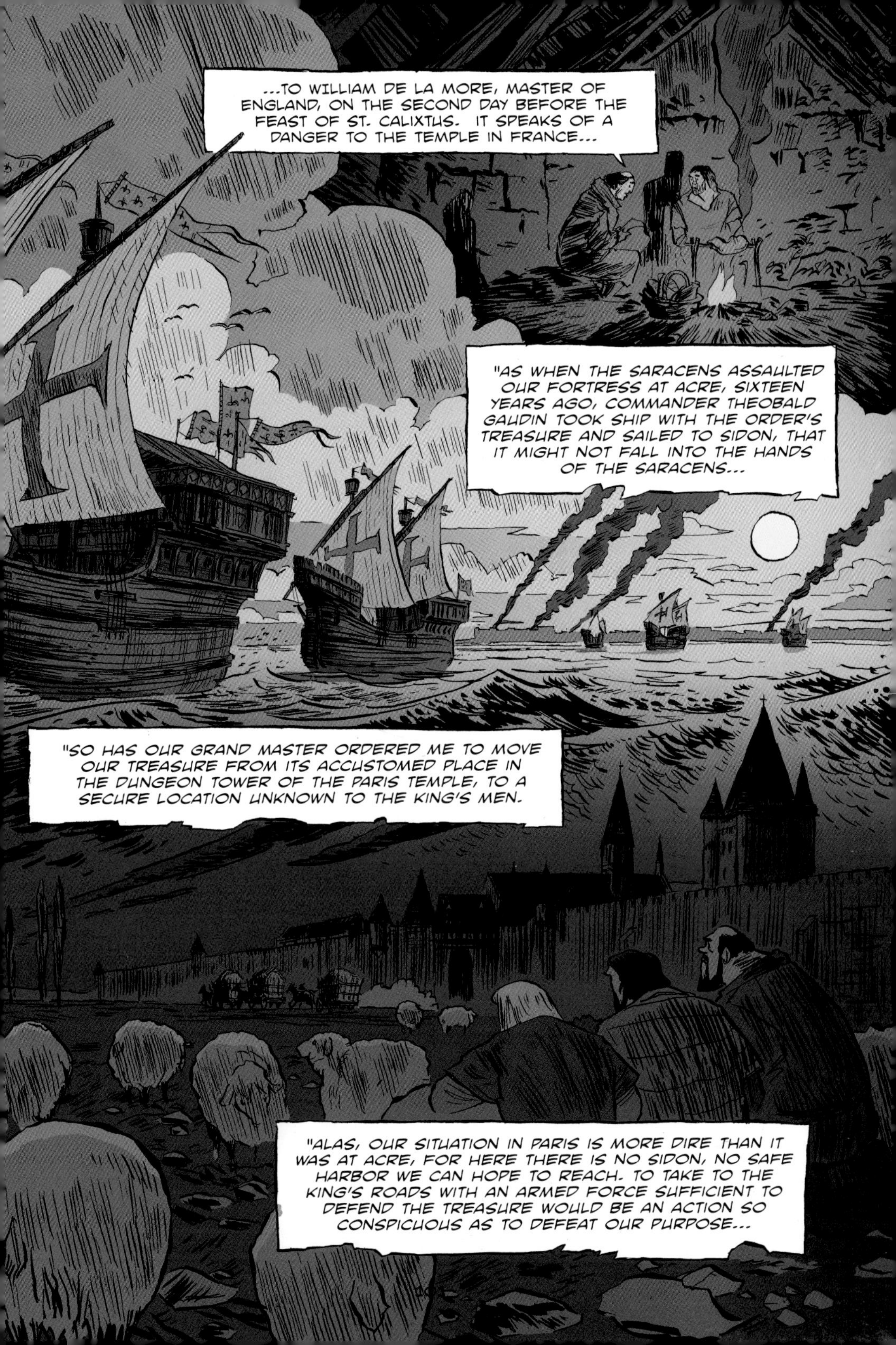
...TO WILLIAM DE LA MORE, MASTER OF ENGLAND, ON THE SECOND DAY BEFORE THE FEAST OF ST. CALIXTUS. IT SPEAKS OF A DANGER TO THE TEMPLE IN FRANCE...
"AS WHEN THE SARACENS ASSAULTED OUR FORTRESS AT ACRE, SIXTEEN YEARS AGO, COMMANDER THEOBALD GAUDIN TOOK SHIP WITH THE ORDER'S TREASURE AND SAILED TO SIDON, THAT IT MIGHT NOT FALL INTO THE HANDS OF THE SARACENS...
"SO HAS OUR GRAND MASTER ORDERED ME TO MOVE OUR TREASURE FROM ITS ACCUSTOMED PLACE IN THE DUNGEON TOWER OF THE PARIS TEMPLE, TO A SECURE LOCATION UNKNOWN TO THE KING'S MEN.
"ALAS, OUR SITUATION IN PARIS IS MORE DIRE THAN IT WAS AT ACRE, FOR HERE THERE IS NO SIDON, NO SAFE HARBOR WE CAN HOPE TO REACH. TO TAKE TO THE KING'S ROADS WITH AN ARMED FORCE SUFFICIENT TO DEFEND THE TREASURE WOULD BE AN ACTION SO CONSPICUOUS AS TO DEFEAT OUR PURPOSE...

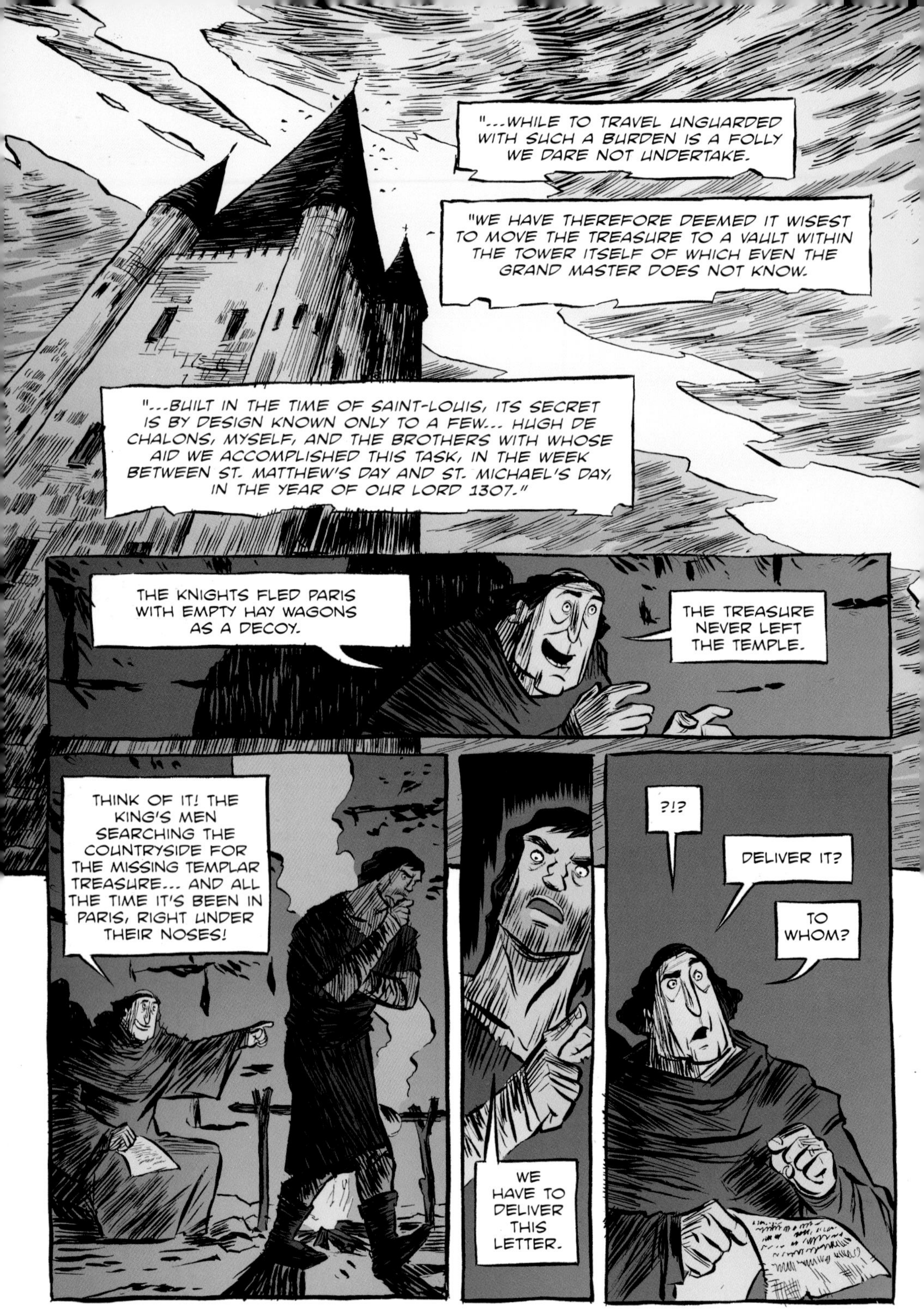
"...WHILE TO TRAVEL UNGUARDED WITH SUCH A BURDEN IS A FOLLY WE DARE NOT UNDERTAKE.
"WE HAVE THEREFORE DEEMED IT WISEST TO MOVE THE TREASURE TO A VAULT WITHIN THE TOWER ITSELF OF WHICH EVEN THE GRAND MASTER DOES NOT KNOW.
"...BUILT IN THE TIME OF SAINT-LOUIS, ITS SECRET IS BY DESIGN KNOWN ONLY TO A FEW... HUGH DE CHALONS, MYSELF, AND THE BROTHERS WITH WHOSE AID WE ACCOMPLISHED THIS TASK, IN THE WEEK BETWEEN ST. MATTHEW'S DAY AND ST. MICHAEL'S DAY, IN THE YEAR OF OUR LORD 1307."
THE KNIGHTS FLED PARIS WITH EMPTY HAY WAGONS AS A DECOY.
THE TREASURE NEVER LEFT THE TEMPLE.
THINK OF IT! THE KING'S MEN SEARCHING THE COUNTRYSIDE FOR THE MISSING TEMPLAR TREASURE... AND ALL THE TIME IT'S BEEN IN PARIS, RIGHT UNDER THEIR NOSES!
WE HAVE TO DELIVER THIS LETTER.
?!?
DELIVER IT?
TO WHOM?

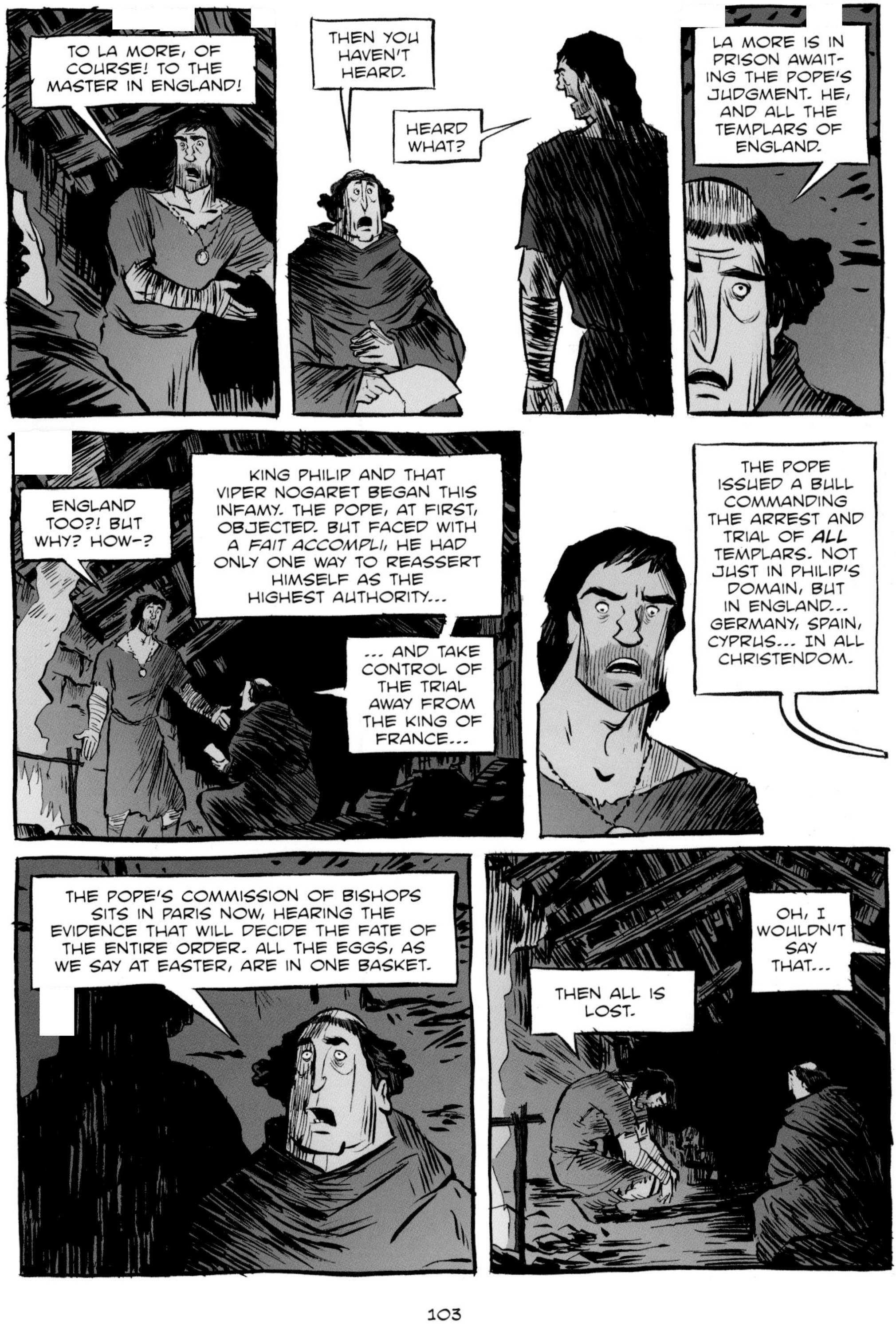
TO LA MORE, OF COURSE! TO THE MASTER IN ENGLAND!
THEN YOU HAVEN'T HEARD.
HEARD WHAT?
LA MORE IS IN PRISON AWAITING THE POPE'S JUDGMENT. HE, AND ALL THE TEMPLARS OF ENGLAND.
ENGLAND TOO?! BUT WHY? HOW-?
KING PHILIP AND THAT VIPER NOGARET BEGAN THIS INFAMY. THE POPE, AT FIRST, OBJECTED. BUT FACED WITH A *FAIT ACCOMPLI*, HE HAD ONLY ONE WAY TO REASSERT HIMSELF AS THE HIGHEST AUTHORITY...
... AND TAKE CONTROL OF THE TRIAL AWAY FROM THE KING OF FRANCE...
THE POPE ISSUED A BULL COMMANDING THE ARREST AND TRIAL OF **ALL** TEMPLARS. NOT JUST IN PHILIP'S DOMAIN, BUT IN ENGLAND... GERMANY, SPAIN, CYPRUS... IN ALL CHRISTENDOM.
THE POPE'S COMMISSION OF BISHOPS SITS IN PARIS NOW, HEARING THE EVIDENCE THAT WILL DECIDE THE FATE OF THE ENTIRE ORDER. ALL THE EGGS, AS WE SAY AT EASTER, ARE IN ONE BASKET.
THEN ALL IS LOST.
OH, I WOULDN'T SAY THAT...

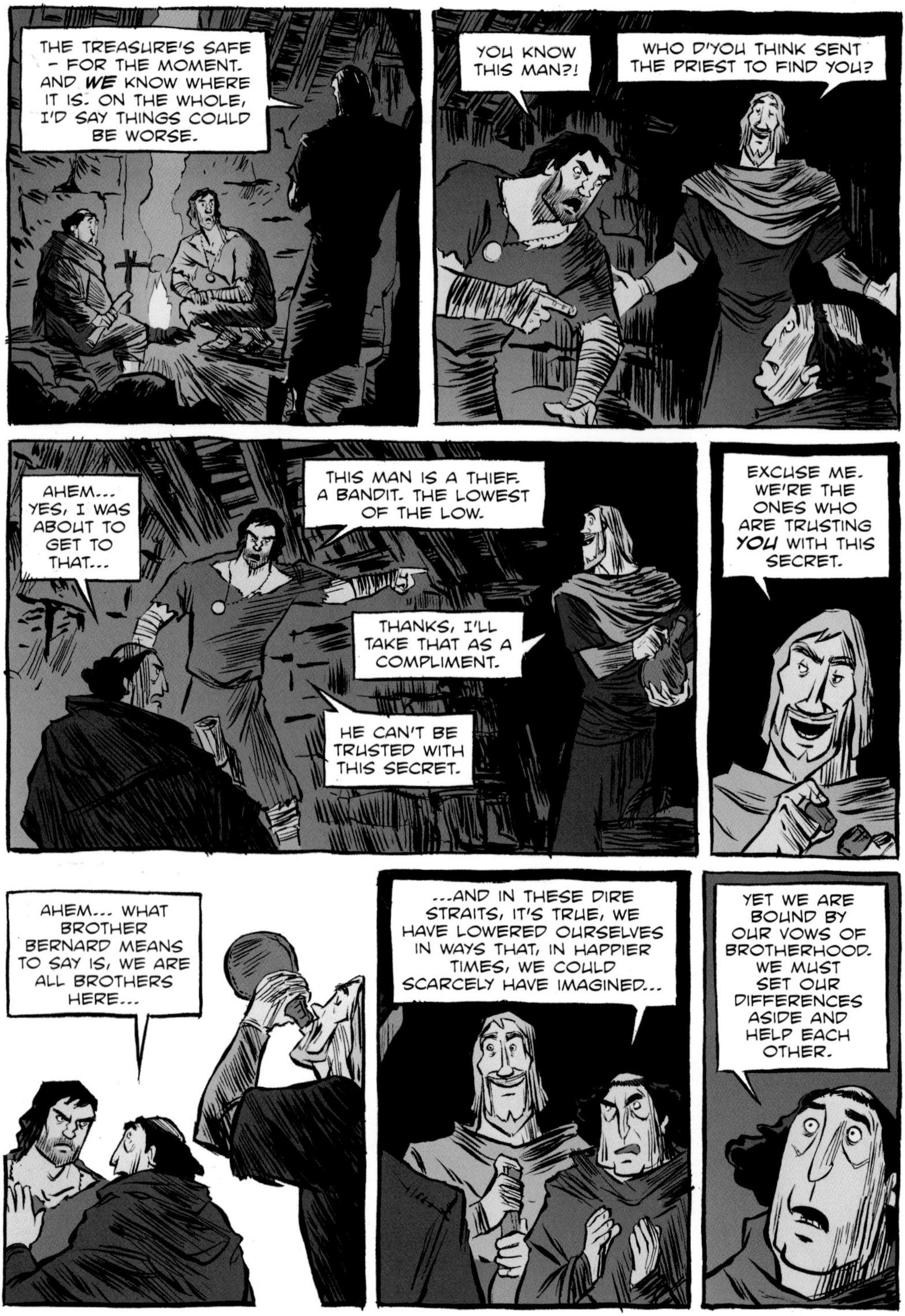
THE TREASURE'S SAFE – FOR THE MOMENT. AND WE KNOW WHERE IT IS. ON THE WHOLE, I'D SAY THINGS COULD BE WORSE.
YOU KNOW THIS MAN?!
WHO D'YOU THINK SENT THE PRIEST TO FIND YOU?
AHEM... YES, I WAS ABOUT TO GET TO THAT...
THIS MAN IS A THIEF. A BANDIT. THE LOWEST OF THE LOW.
THANKS, I'LL TAKE THAT AS A COMPLIMENT.
HE CAN'T BE TRUSTED WITH THIS SECRET.
EXCUSE ME. WE'RE THE ONES WHO ARE TRUSTING YOU WITH THIS SECRET.
AHEM... WHAT BROTHER BERNARD MEANS TO SAY IS, WE ARE ALL BROTHERS HERE...
...AND IN THESE DIRE STRAITS, IT'S TRUE, WE HAVE LOWERED OURSELVES IN WAYS THAT, IN HAPPIER TIMES, WE COULD SCARCELY HAVE IMAGINED...
YET WE ARE BOUND BY OUR VOWS OF BROTHERHOOD. WE MUST SET OUR DIFFERENCES ASIDE AND HELP EACH OTHER.

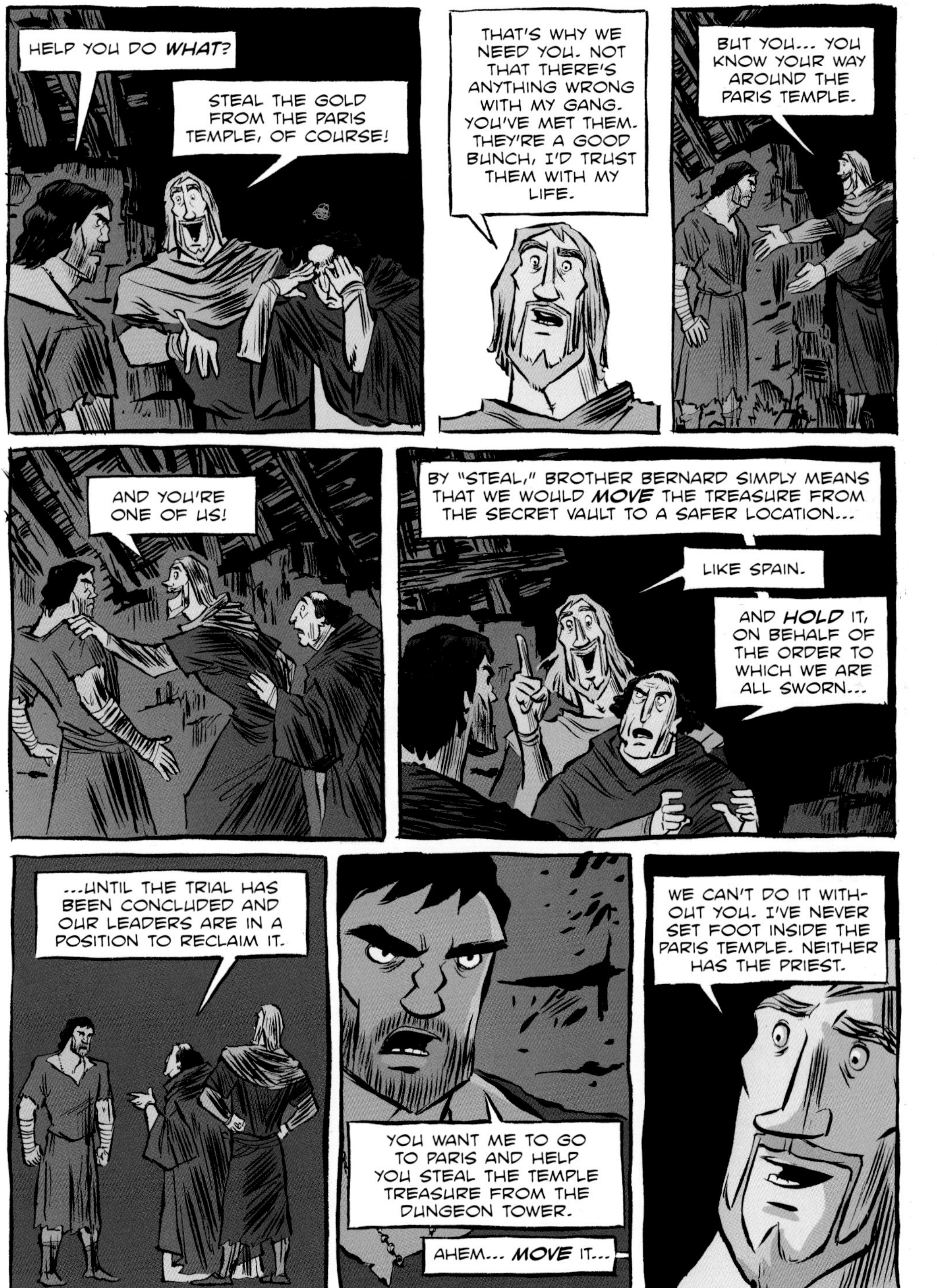

HELP YOU DO **WHAT**?
STEAL THE GOLD FROM THE PARIS TEMPLE, OF COURSE!
THAT'S WHY WE NEED YOU. NOT THAT THERE'S ANYTHING WRONG WITH MY GANG. YOU'VE MET THEM. THEY'RE A GOOD BUNCH, I'D TRUST THEM WITH MY LIFE.
BUT YOU... YOU KNOW YOUR WAY AROUND THE PARIS TEMPLE.
AND YOU'RE ONE OF US!
BY "STEAL," BROTHER BERNARD SIMPLY MEANS THAT WE WOULD **MOVE** THE TREASURE FROM THE SECRET VAULT TO A SAFER LOCATION...
LIKE SPAIN.
AND **HOLD** IT, ON BEHALF OF THE ORDER TO WHICH WE ARE ALL SWORN...
...UNTIL THE TRIAL HAS BEEN CONCLUDED AND OUR LEADERS ARE IN A POSITION TO RECLAIM IT.
YOU WANT ME TO GO TO PARIS AND HELP YOU STEAL THE TEMPLE TREASURE FROM THE DUNGEON TOWER.
AHEM... **MOVE** IT...
WE CAN'T DO IT WITHOUT YOU. I'VE NEVER SET FOOT INSIDE THE PARIS TEMPLE. NEITHER HAS THE PRIEST.

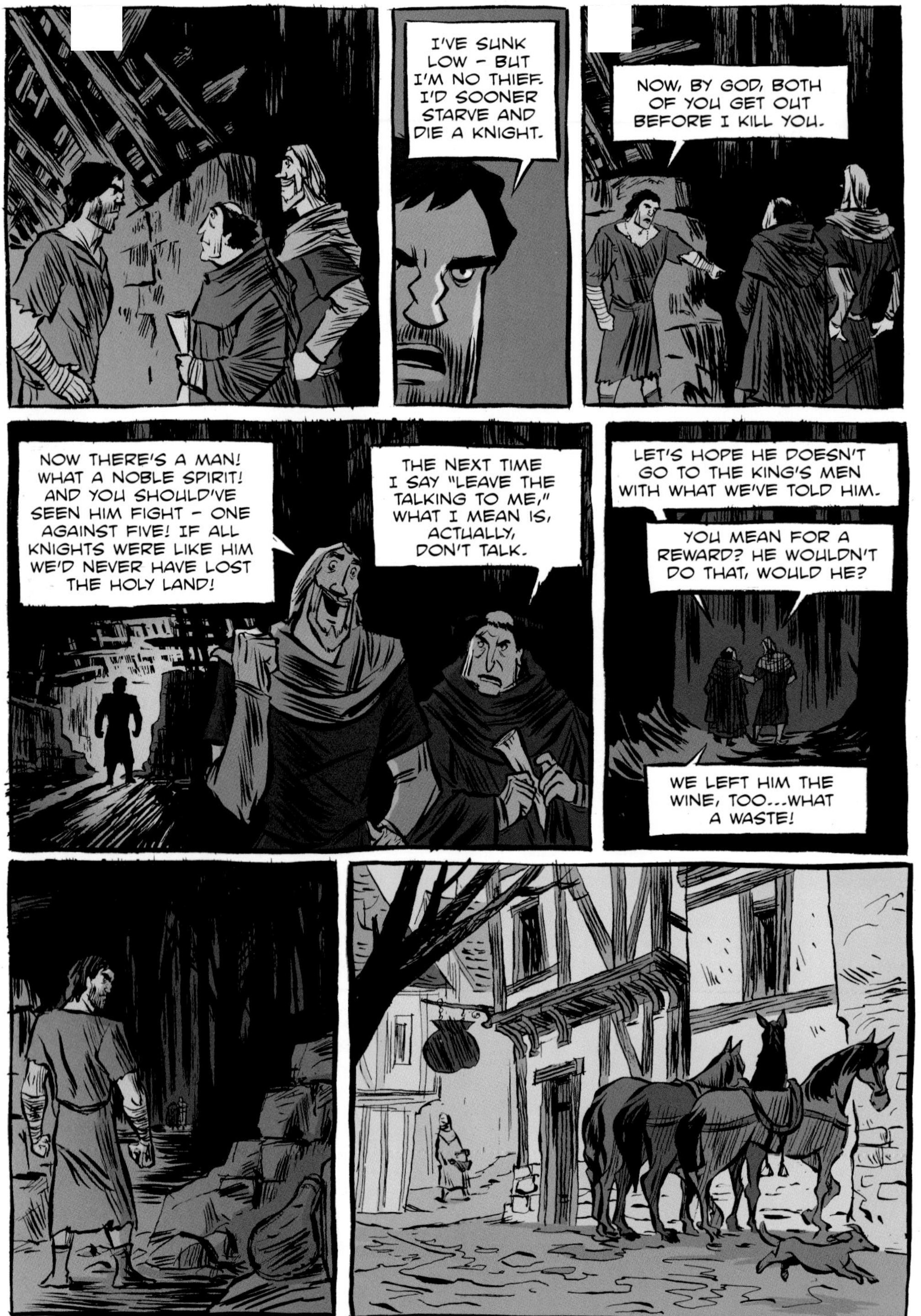
I'VE SUNK LOW – BUT I'M NO THIEF. I'D SOONER STARVE AND DIE A KNIGHT.
NOW, BY GOD, BOTH OF YOU GET OUT BEFORE I KILL YOU.
NOW THERE'S A MAN! WHAT A NOBLE SPIRIT! AND YOU SHOULD'VE SEEN HIM FIGHT – ONE AGAINST FIVE! IF ALL KNIGHTS WERE LIKE HIM WE'D NEVER HAVE LOST THE HOLY LAND!
THE NEXT TIME I SAY "LEAVE THE TALKING TO ME," WHAT I MEAN IS, ACTUALLY, DON'T TALK.
LET'S HOPE HE DOESN'T GO TO THE KING'S MEN WITH WHAT WE'VE TOLD HIM.
YOU MEAN FOR A REWARD? HE WOULDN'T DO THAT, WOULD HE?
WE LEFT HIM THE WINE, TOO...WHAT A WASTE!

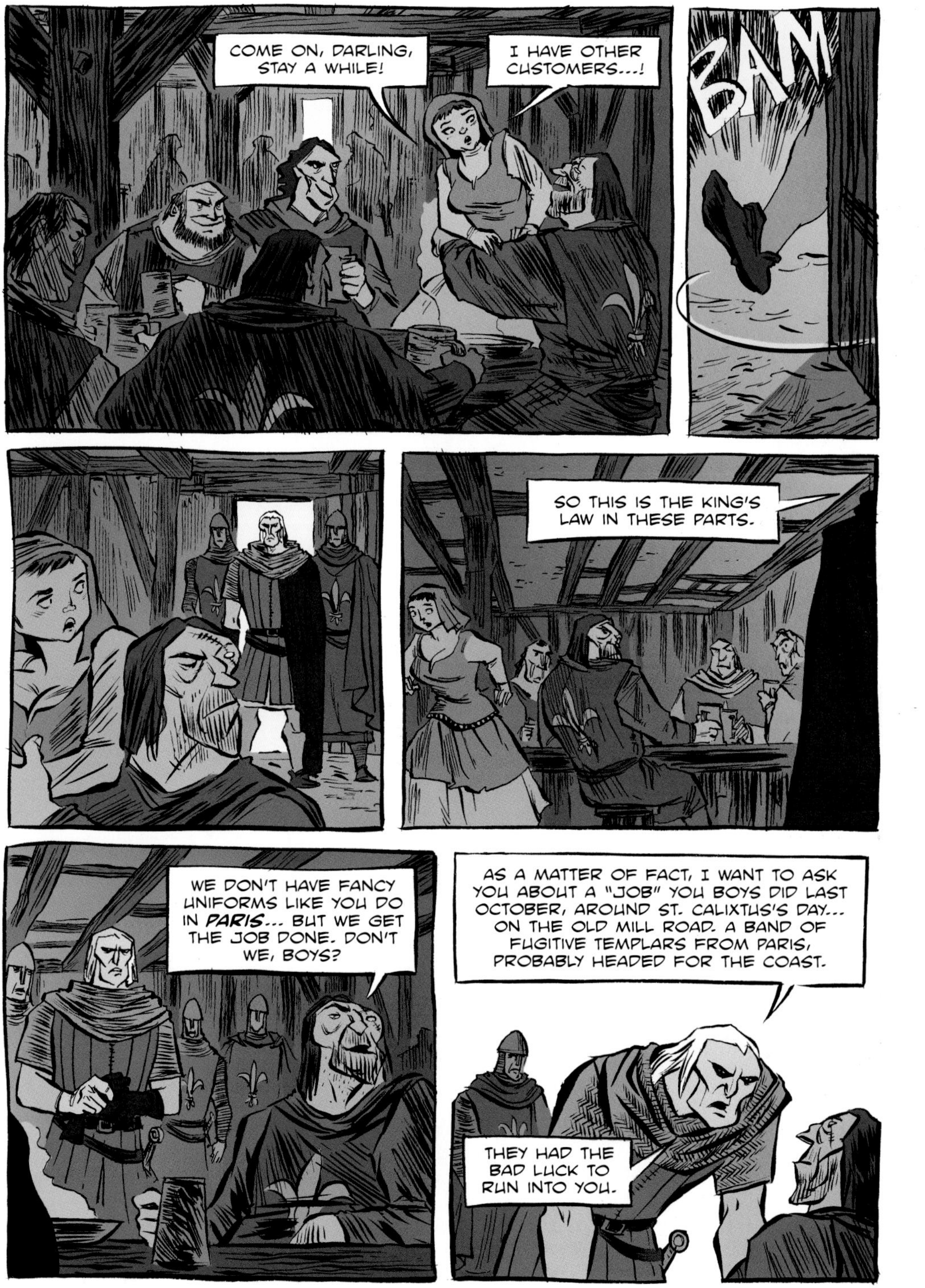
COME ON, DARLING, STAY A WHILE!
I HAVE OTHER CUSTOMERS...!
BAM
SO THIS IS THE KING'S LAW IN THESE PARTS.
WE DON'T HAVE FANCY UNIFORMS LIKE YOU DO IN PARIS... BUT WE GET THE JOB DONE. DON'T WE, BOYS?
AS A MATTER OF FACT, I WANT TO ASK YOU ABOUT A "JOB" YOU BOYS DID LAST OCTOBER, AROUND ST. CALIXTUS'S DAY... ON THE OLD MILL ROAD. A BAND OF FUGITIVE TEMPLARS FROM PARIS, PROBABLY HEADED FOR THE COAST.
THEY HAD THE BAD LUCK TO RUN INTO YOU.

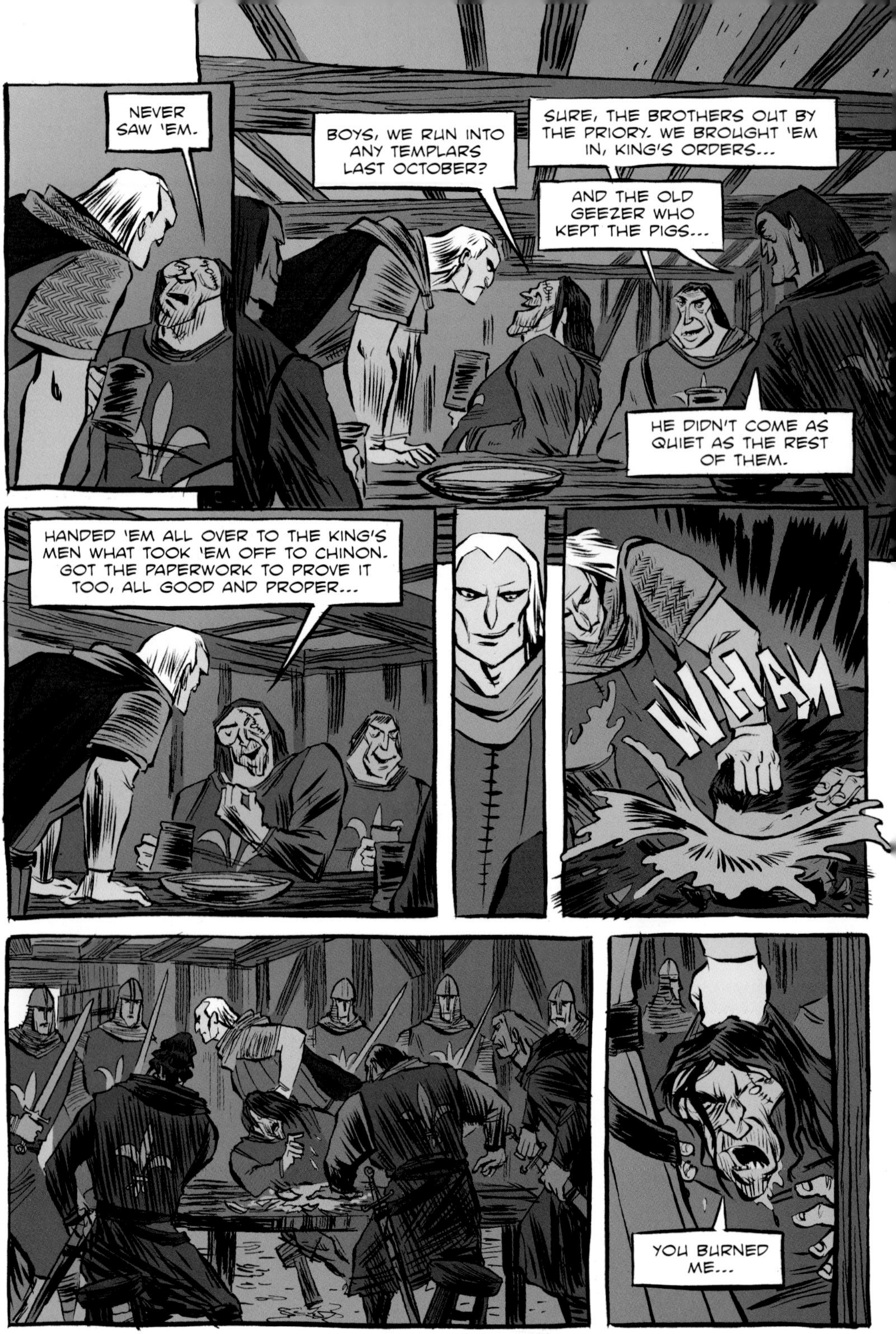
NEVER SAW 'EM.
BOYS, WE RUN INTO ANY TEMPLARS LAST OCTOBER?
SURE, THE BROTHERS OUT BY THE PRIORY. WE BROUGHT 'EM IN, KING'S ORDERS...
AND THE OLD GEEZER WHO KEPT THE PIGS...
HE DIDN'T COME AS QUIET AS THE REST OF THEM.
HANDED 'EM ALL OVER TO THE KING'S MEN WHAT TOOK 'EM OFF TO CHINON. GOT THE PAPERWORK TO PROVE IT TOO, ALL GOOD AND PROPER...
WHAM
YOU BURNED ME...

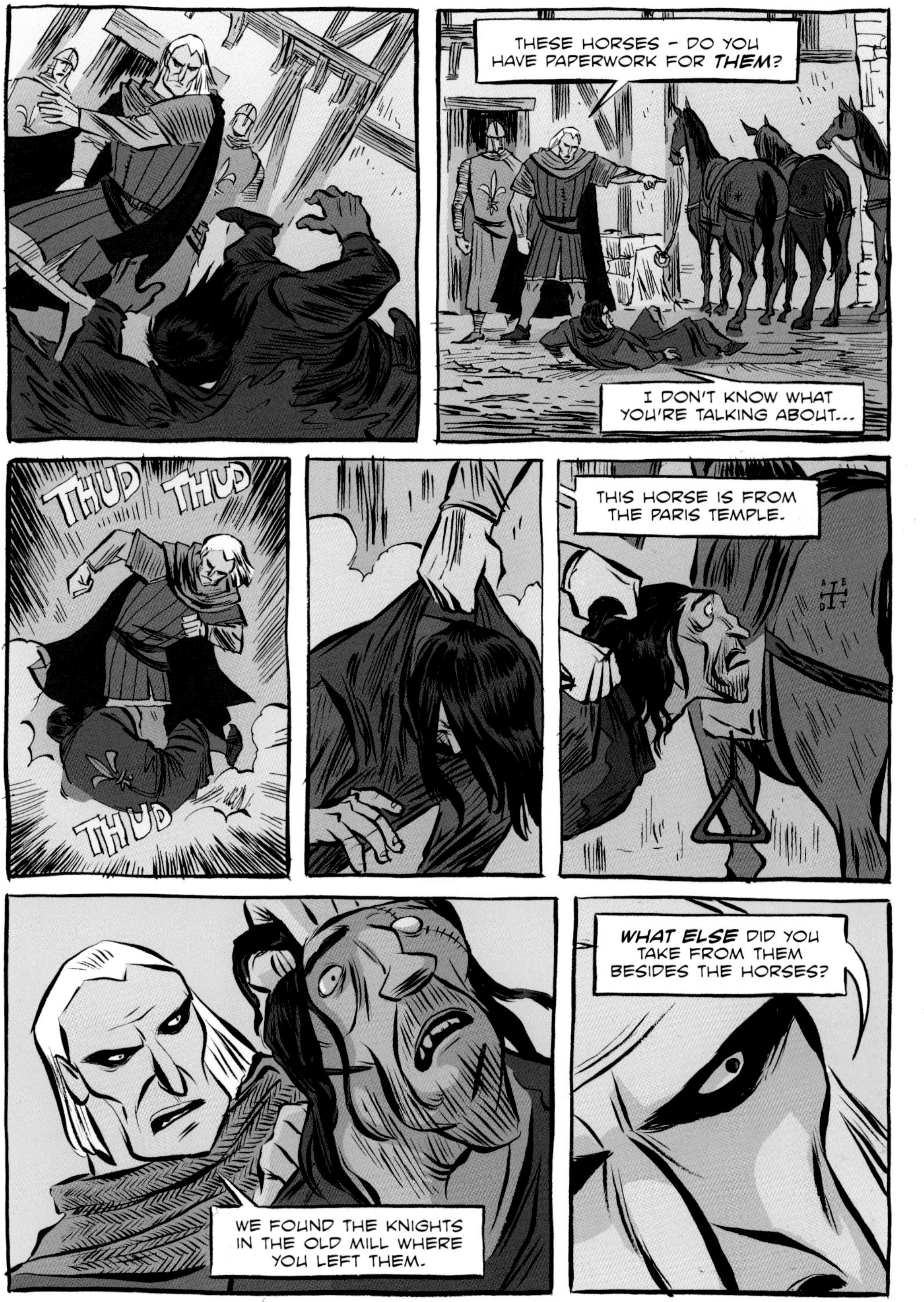
THESE HORSES - DO YOU HAVE PAPERWORK FOR *THEM*?
I DON'T KNOW WHAT YOU'RE TALKING ABOUT...
THUD THUD
THUD
THIS HORSE IS FROM THE PARIS TEMPLE.
WE FOUND THE KNIGHTS IN THE OLD MILL WHERE YOU LEFT THEM.
WHAT ELSE DID YOU TAKE FROM THEM BESIDES THE HORSES?

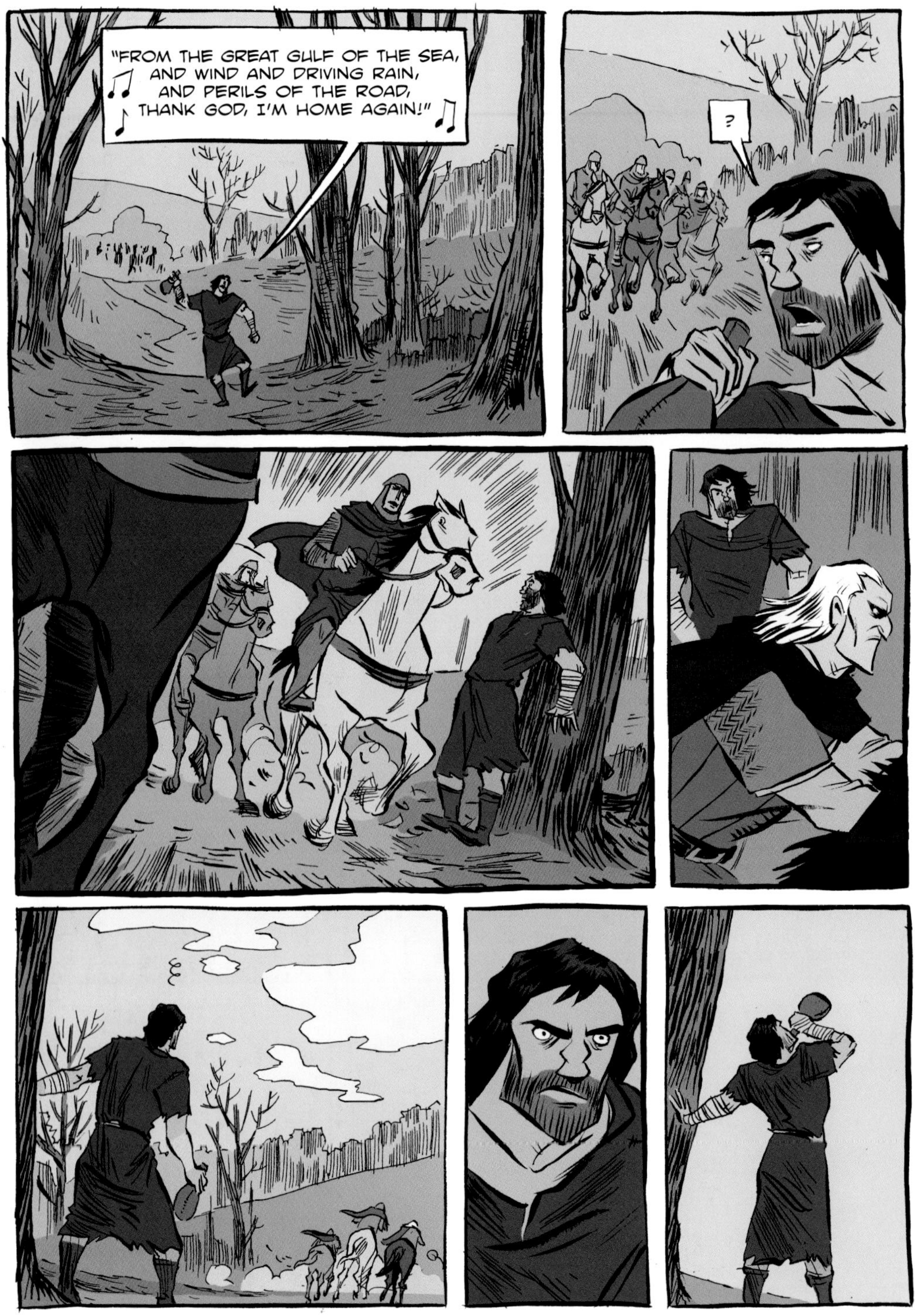
"FROM THE GREAT GULF OF THE SEA,
AND WIND AND DRIVING RAIN,
AND PERILS OF THE ROAD,
THANK GOD, I'M HOME AGAIN!"
?

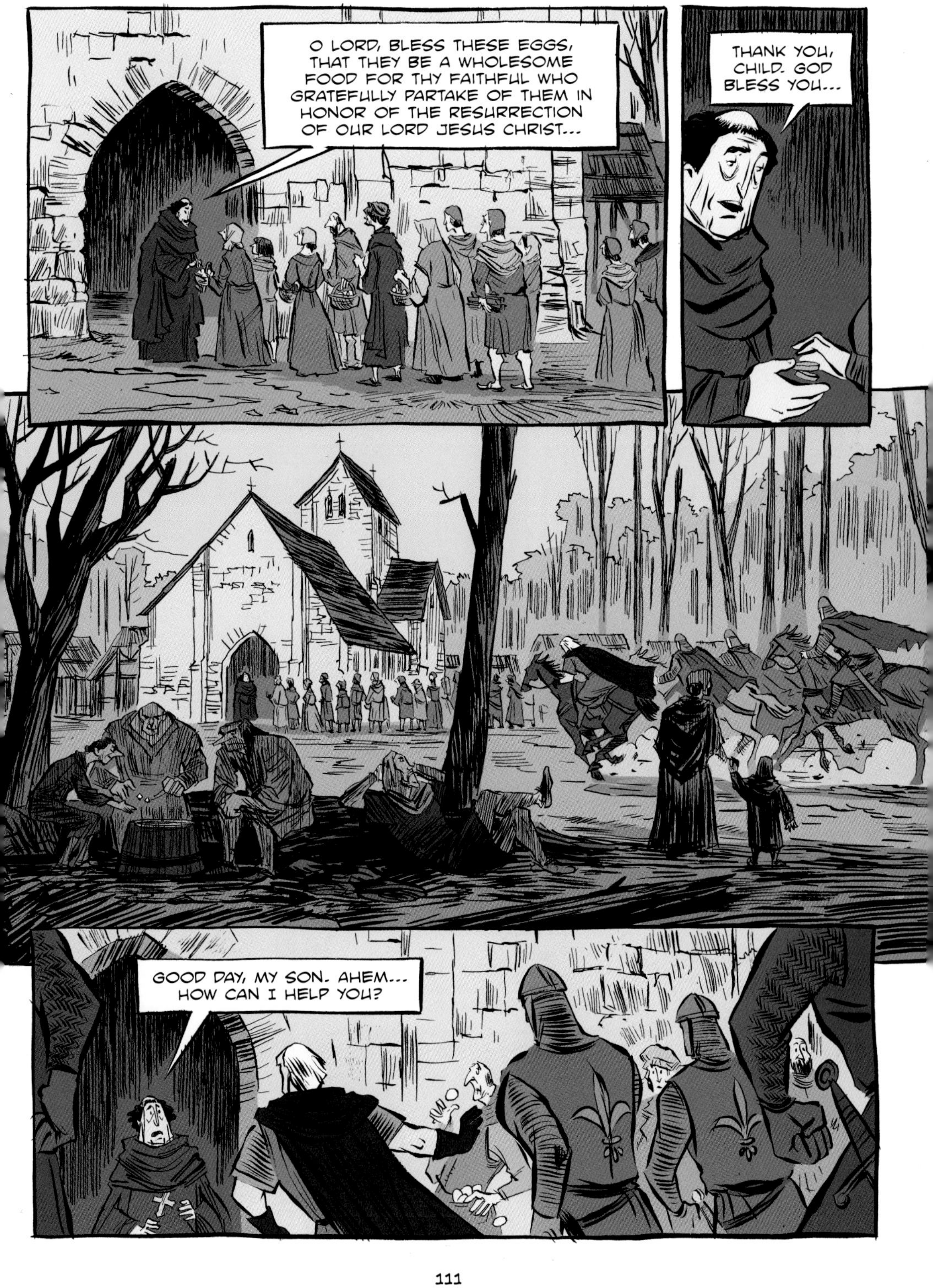
O LORD, BLESS THESE EGGS, THAT THEY BE A WHOLESOME FOOD FOR THY FAITHFUL WHO GRATEFULLY PARTAKE OF THEM IN HONOR OF THE RESURRECTION OF OUR LORD JESUS CHRIST...
THANK YOU, CHILD. GOD BLESS YOU...
GOOD DAY, MY SON. AHEM... HOW CAN I HELP YOU?

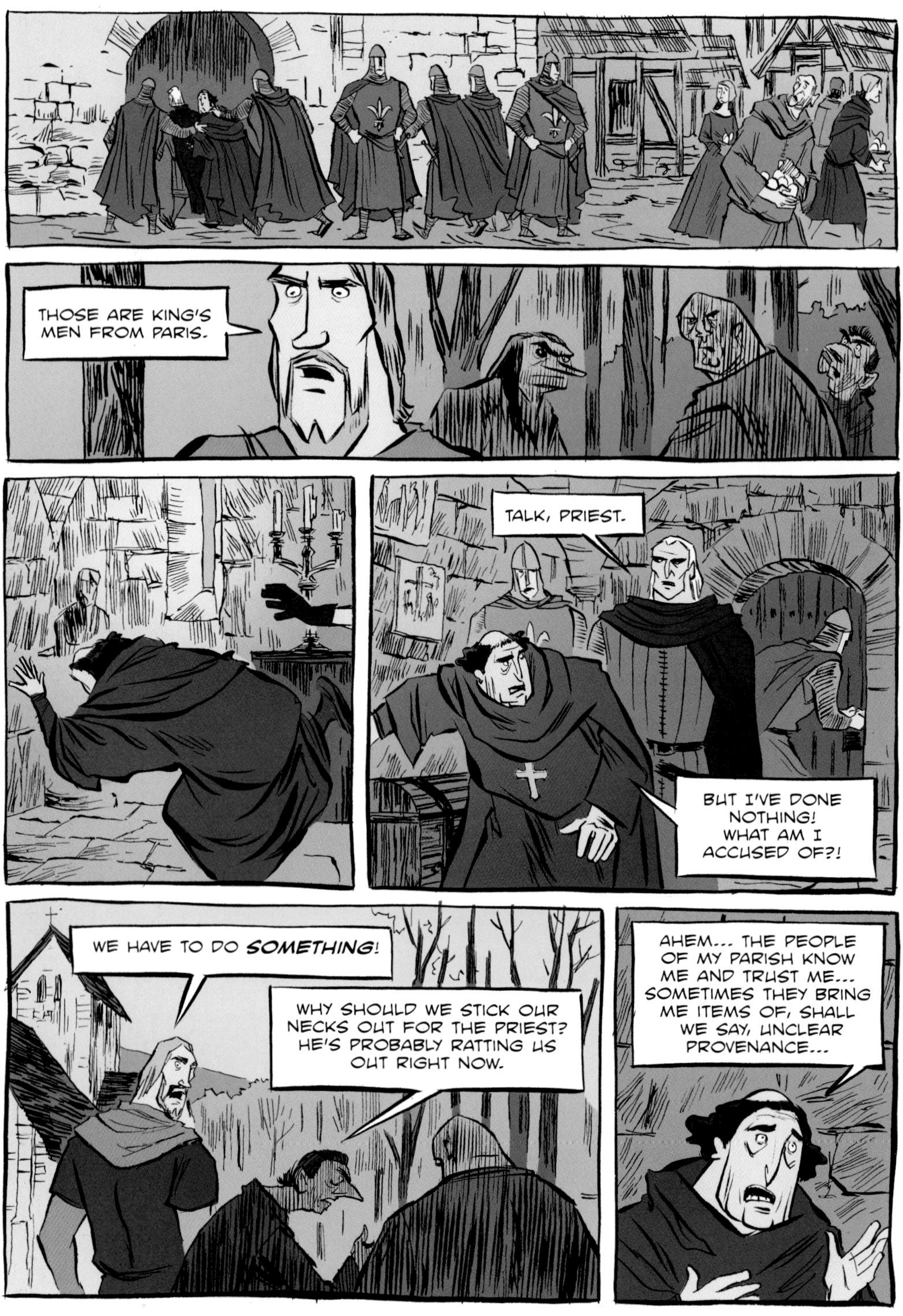
THOSE ARE KING'S MEN FROM PARIS.
TALK, PRIEST.
BUT I'VE DONE NOTHING! WHAT AM I ACCUSED OF?!
WE HAVE TO DO *SOMETHING*!
WHY SHOULD WE STICK OUR NECKS OUT FOR THE PRIEST? HE'S PROBABLY RATTING US OUT RIGHT NOW.
AHEM... THE PEOPLE OF MY PARISH KNOW ME AND TRUST ME... SOMETIMES THEY BRING ME ITEMS OF, SHALL WE SAY, UNCLEAR PROVENANCE...

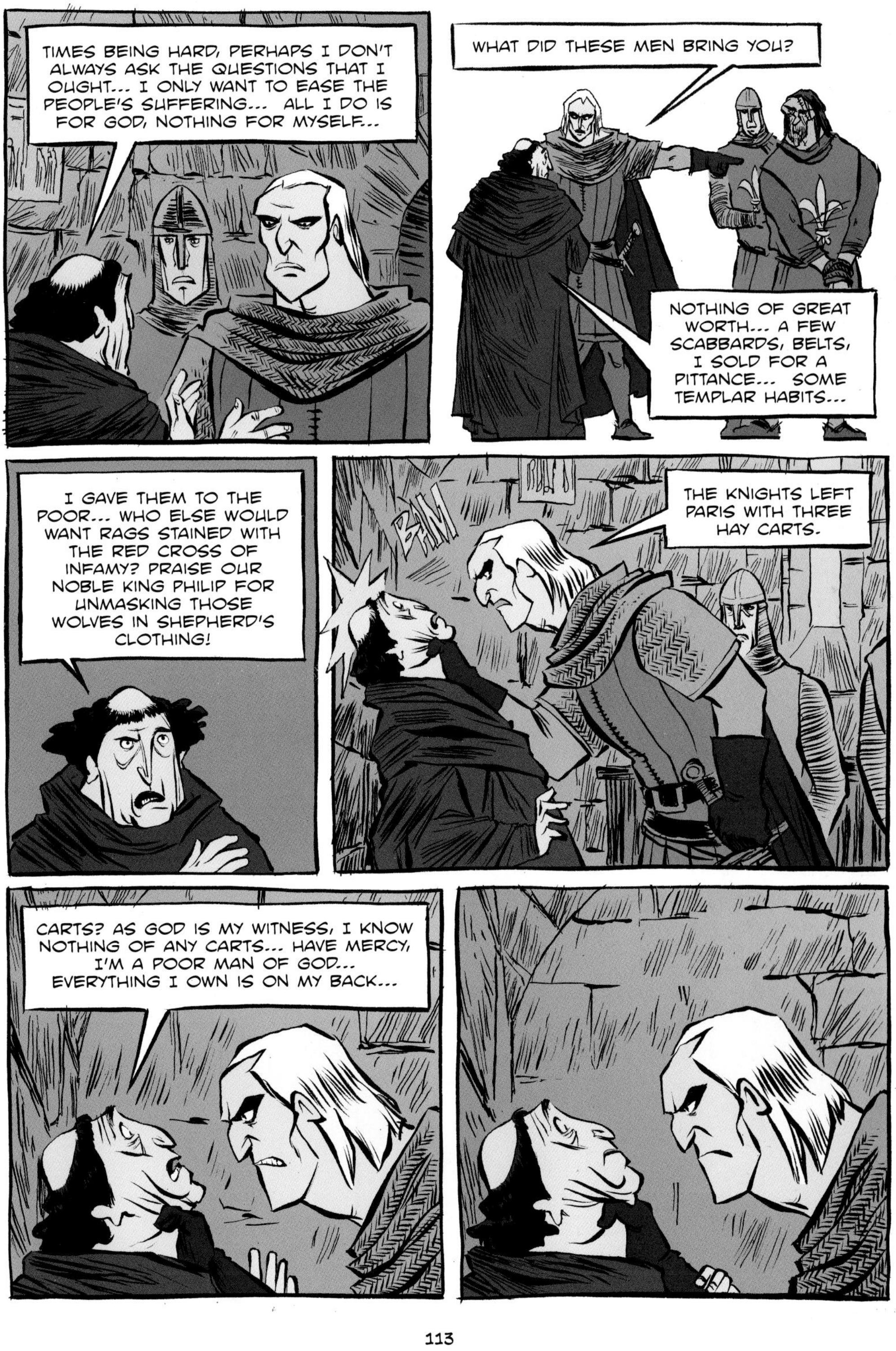

TIMES BEING HARD, PERHAPS I DON'T ALWAYS ASK THE QUESTIONS THAT I OUGHT... I ONLY WANT TO EASE THE PEOPLE'S SUFFERING... ALL I DO IS FOR GOD, NOTHING FOR MYSELF...
WHAT DID THESE MEN BRING YOU?
NOTHING OF GREAT WORTH... A FEW SCABBARDS, BELTS, I SOLD FOR A PITTANCE... SOME TEMPLAR HABITS...
I GAVE THEM TO THE POOR... WHO ELSE WOULD WANT RAGS STAINED WITH THE RED CROSS OF INFAMY? PRAISE OUR NOBLE KING PHILIP FOR UNMASKING THOSE WOLVES IN SHEPHERD'S CLOTHING!
BAM
THE KNIGHTS LEFT PARIS WITH THREE HAY CARTS.
CARTS? AS GOD IS MY WITNESS, I KNOW NOTHING OF ANY CARTS... HAVE MERCY, I'M A POOR MAN OF GOD... EVERYTHING I OWN IS ON MY BACK...

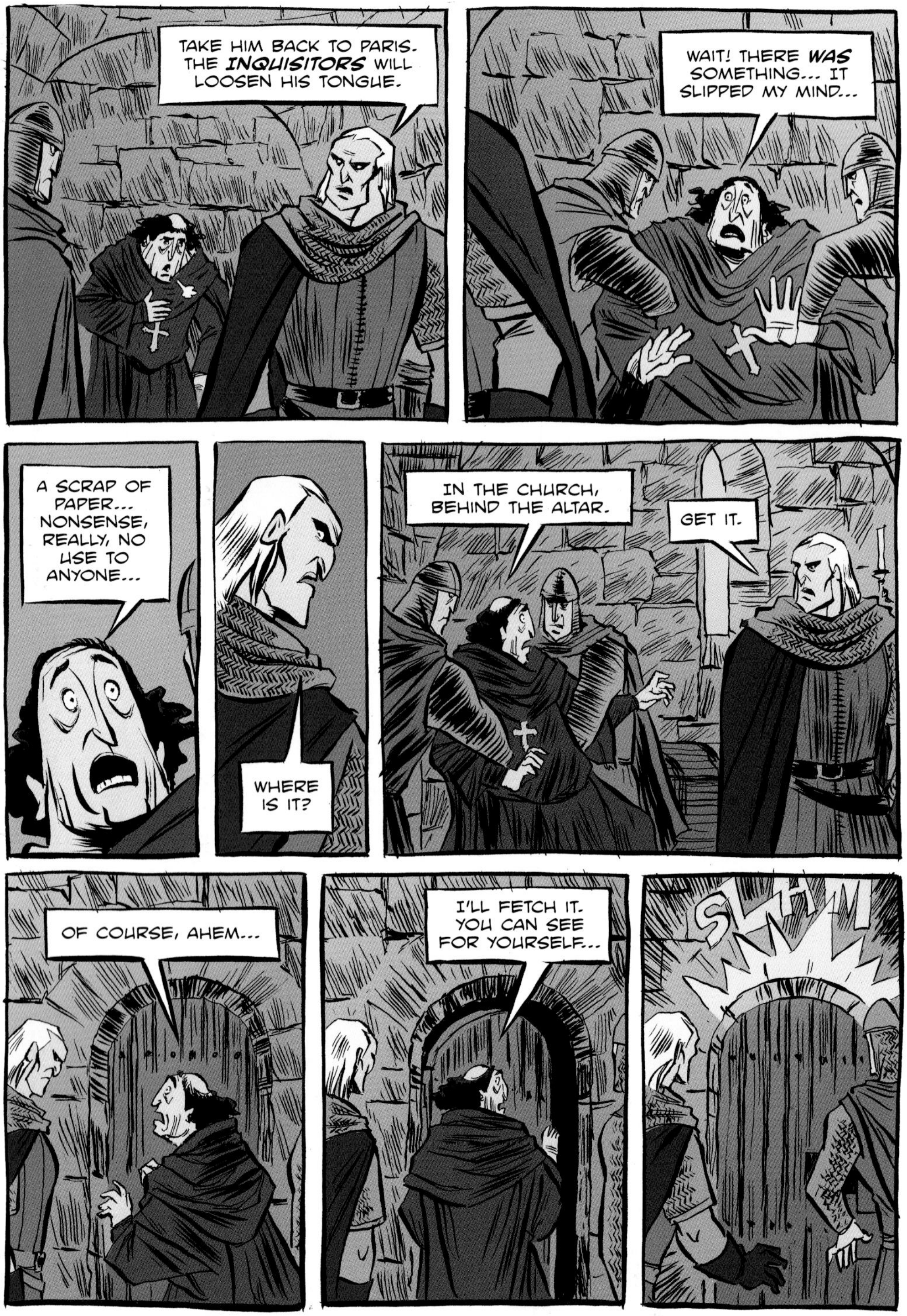
TAKE HIM BACK TO PARIS. THE INQUISITORS WILL LOOSEN HIS TONGUE.
WAIT! THERE WAS SOMETHING... IT SLIPPED MY MIND...
A SCRAP OF PAPER... NONSENSE, REALLY, NO USE TO ANYONE...
WHERE IS IT?
IN THE CHURCH, BEHIND THE ALTAR.
GET IT.
OF COURSE, AHEM...
I'LL FETCH IT. YOU CAN SEE FOR YOURSELF...
SLAM

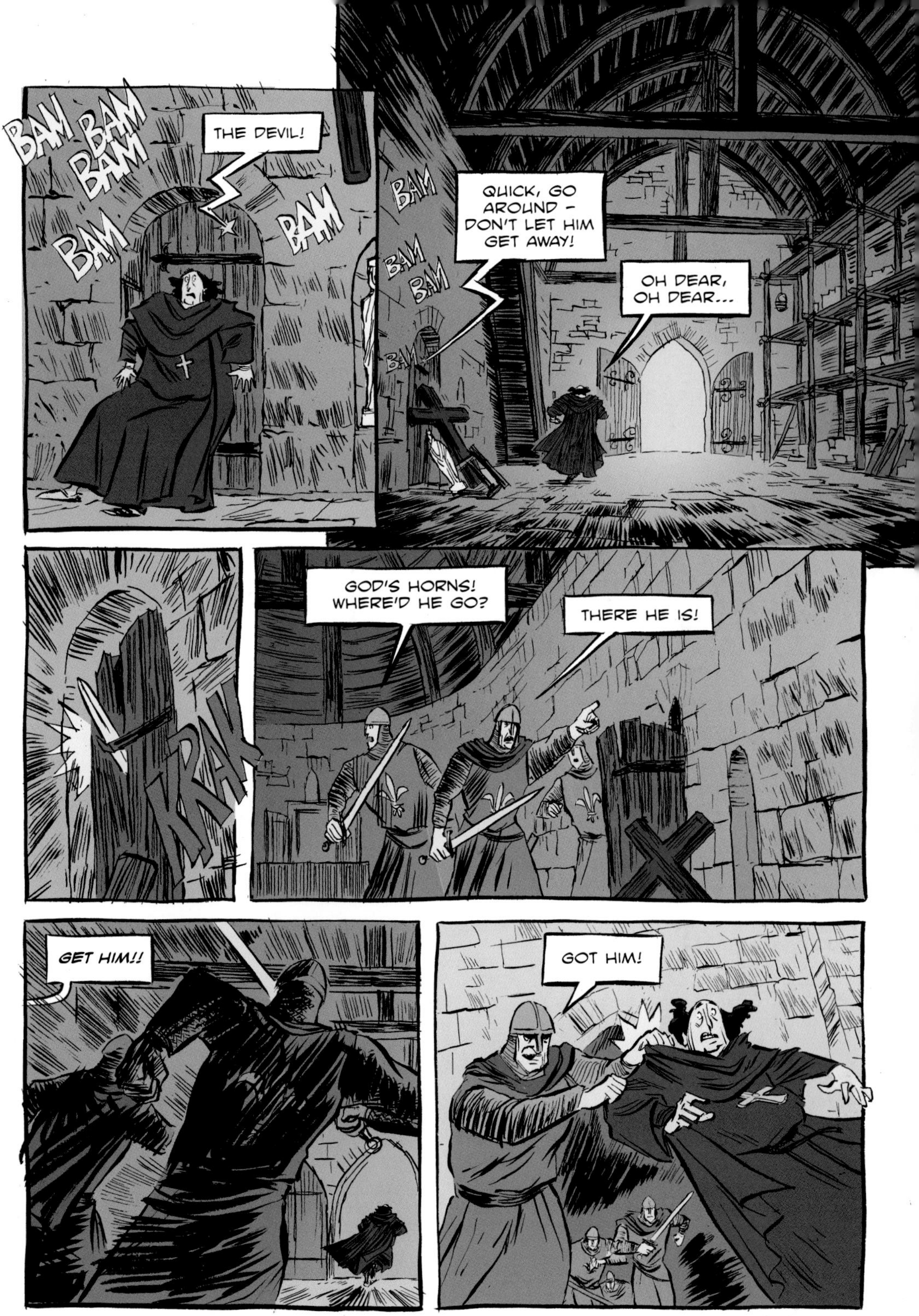
BAM BAM BAM BAM
THE DEVIL!
BAM
BAM
BAM BAM
QUICK, GO AROUND – DON'T LET HIM GET AWAY!
BAM
OH DEAR, OH DEAR...
KRAK
GOD'S HORNS! WHERE'D HE GO?
THERE HE IS!
GET HIM!!
GOT HIM!

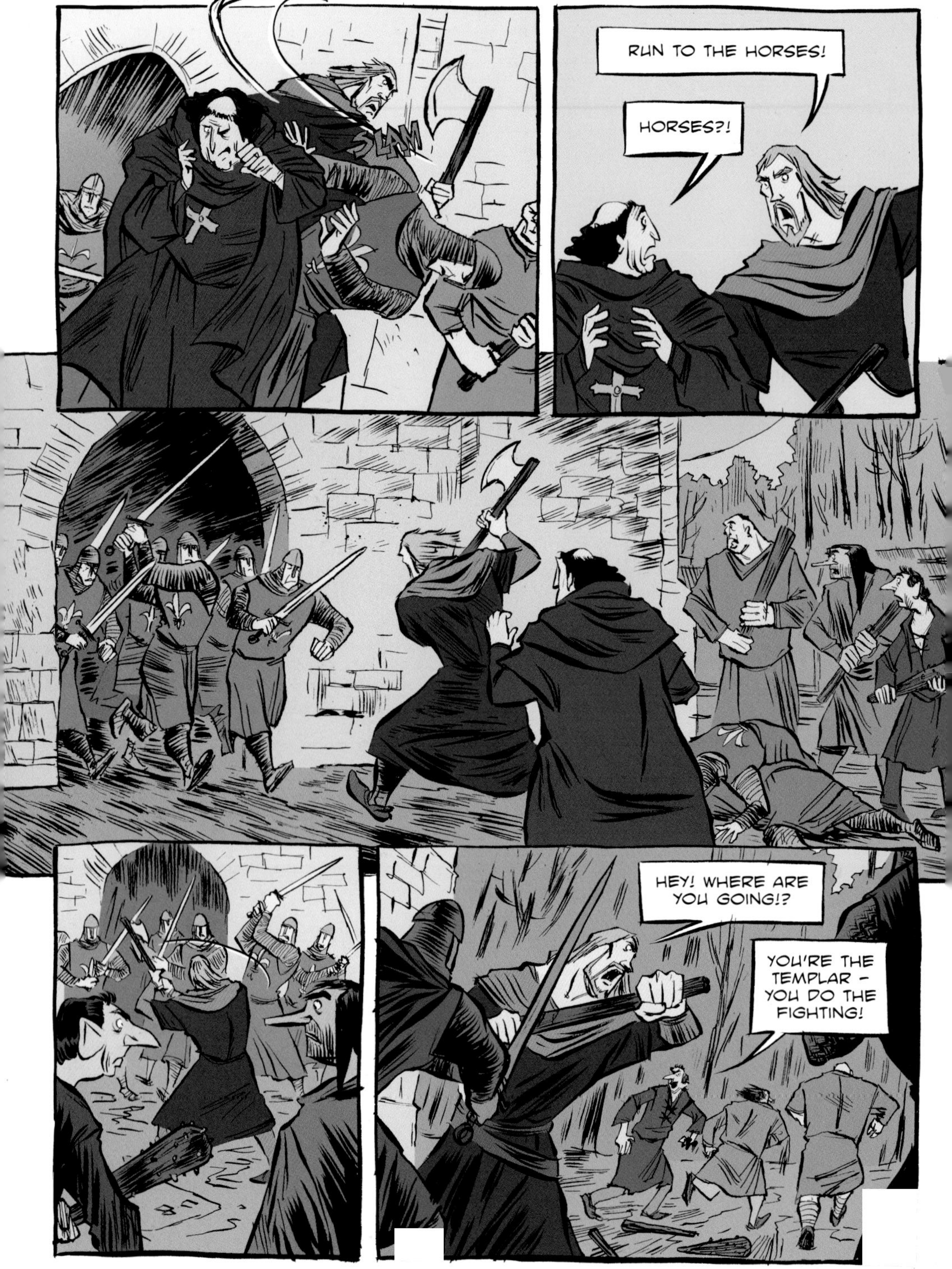
SLAM
RUN TO THE HORSES!
HORSES?!
HEY! WHERE ARE YOU GOING!?
YOU'RE THE TEMPLAR - YOU DO THE FIGHTING!

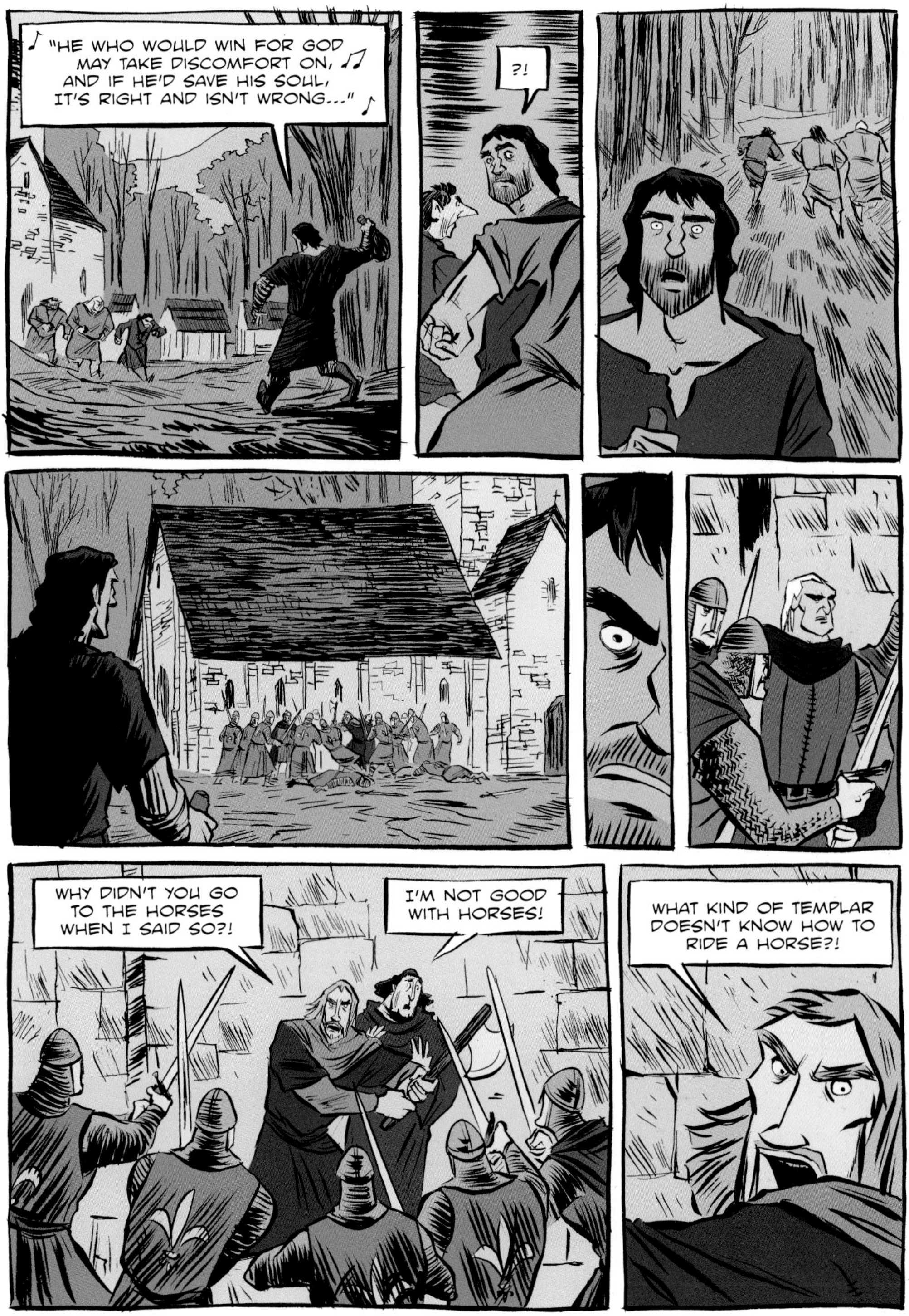
♪ "HE WHO WOULD WIN FOR GOD MAY TAKE DISCOMFORT ON, ♫ AND IF HE'D SAVE HIS SOUL, IT'S RIGHT AND ISN'T WRONG..." ♪
?!
WHY DIDN'T YOU GO TO THE HORSES WHEN I SAID SO?!
I'M NOT GOOD WITH HORSES!
WHAT KIND OF TEMPLAR DOESN'T KNOW HOW TO RIDE A HORSE?!

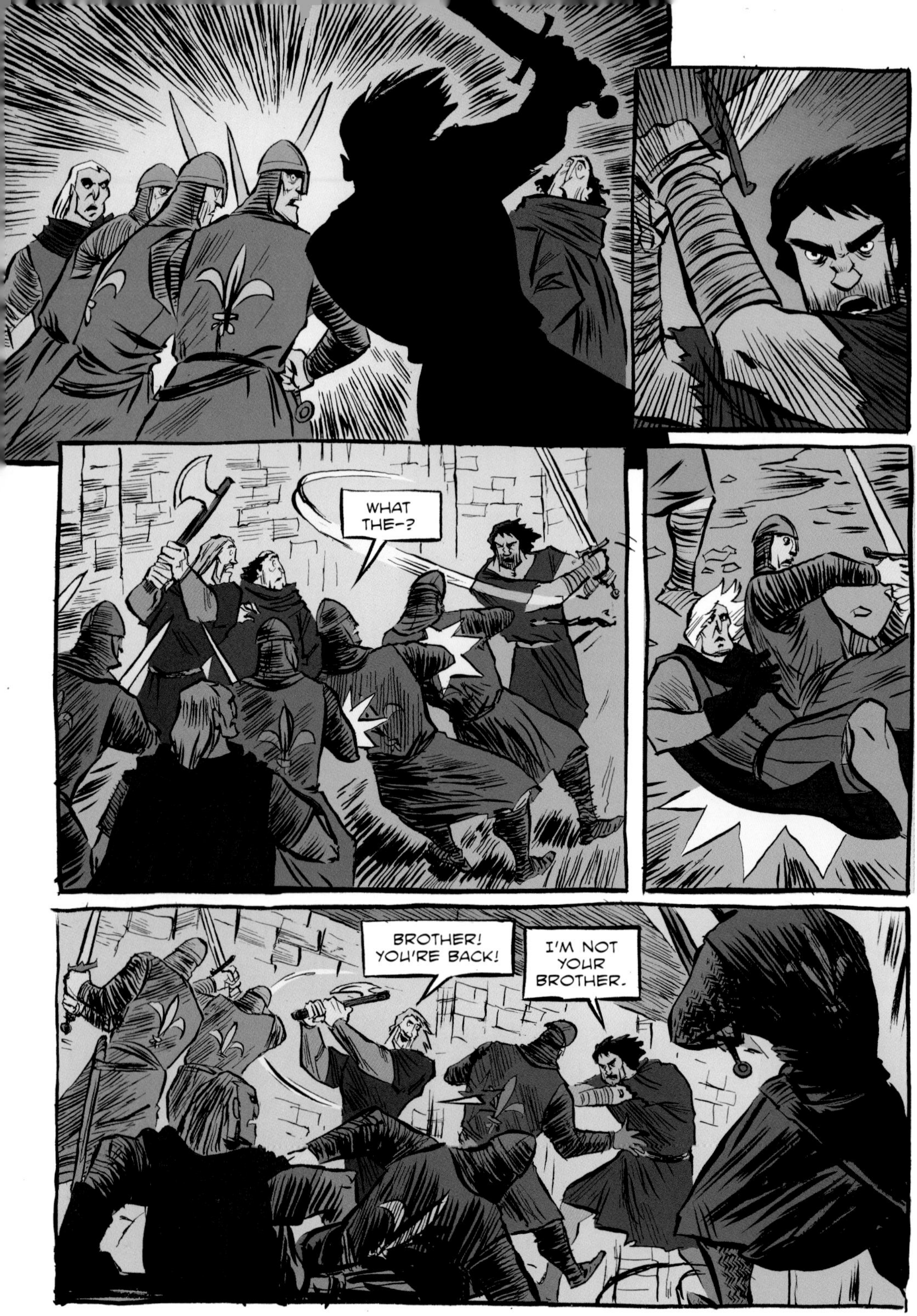
WHAT THE-?
BROTHER! YOU'RE BACK!
I'M NOT YOUR BROTHER.

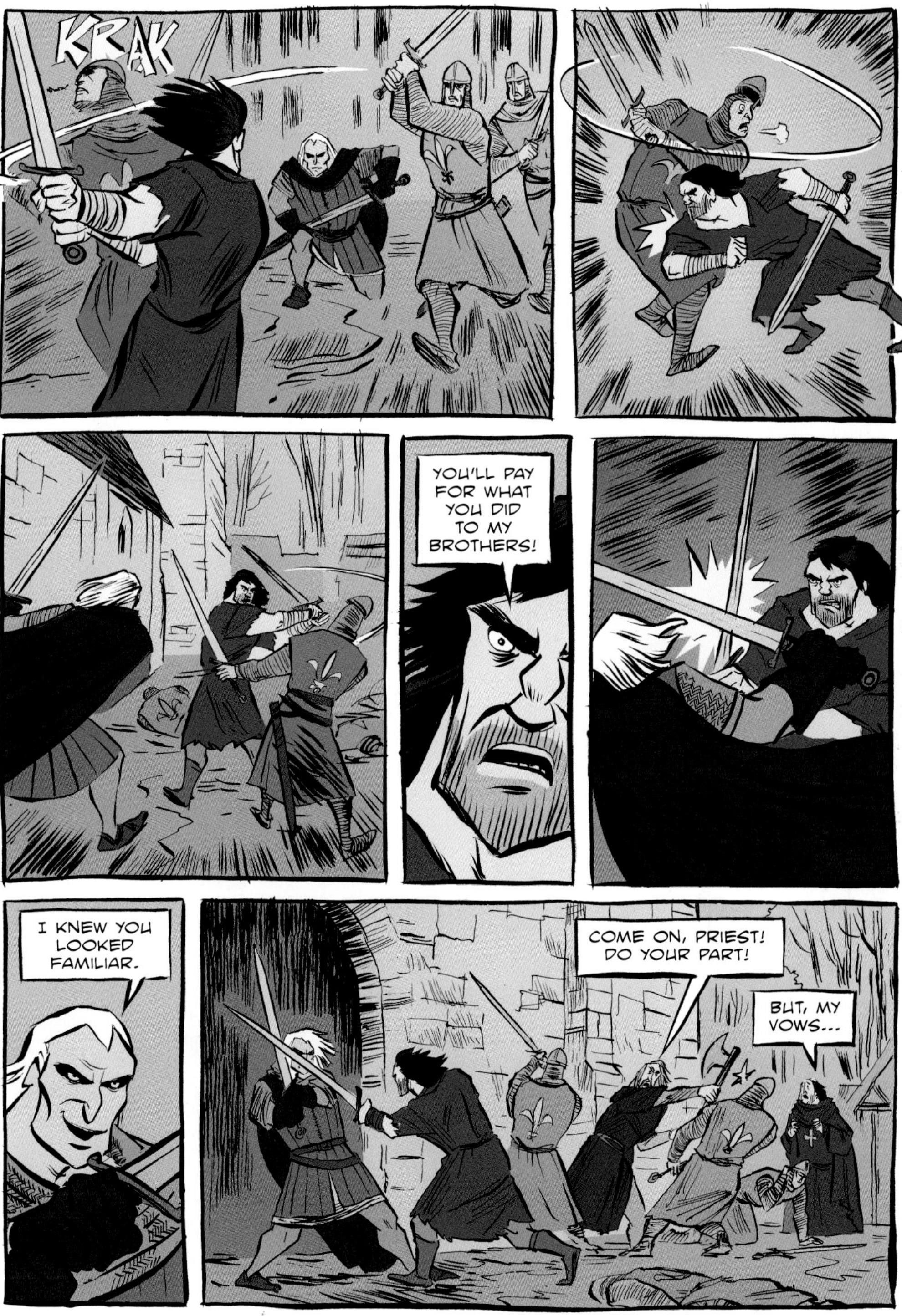
KRAK
YOU'LL PAY FOR WHAT YOU DID TO MY BROTHERS!
I KNEW YOU LOOKED FAMILIAR.
COME ON, PRIEST! DO YOUR PART!
BUT, MY VOWS...

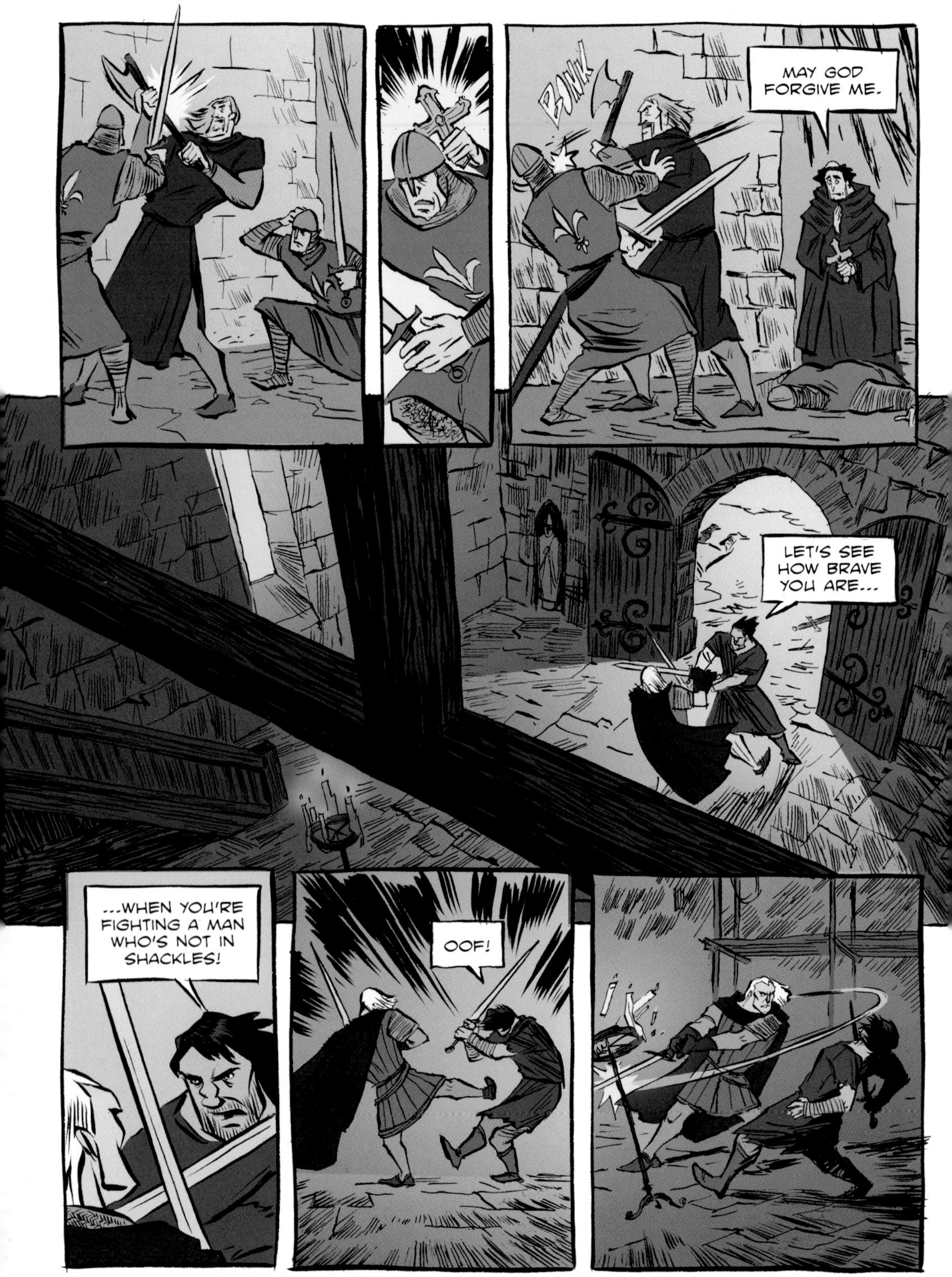
BONK
MAY GOD FORGIVE ME.
LET'S SEE HOW BRAVE YOU ARE...
...WHEN YOU'RE FIGHTING A MAN WHO'S NOT IN SHACKLES!
OOF!

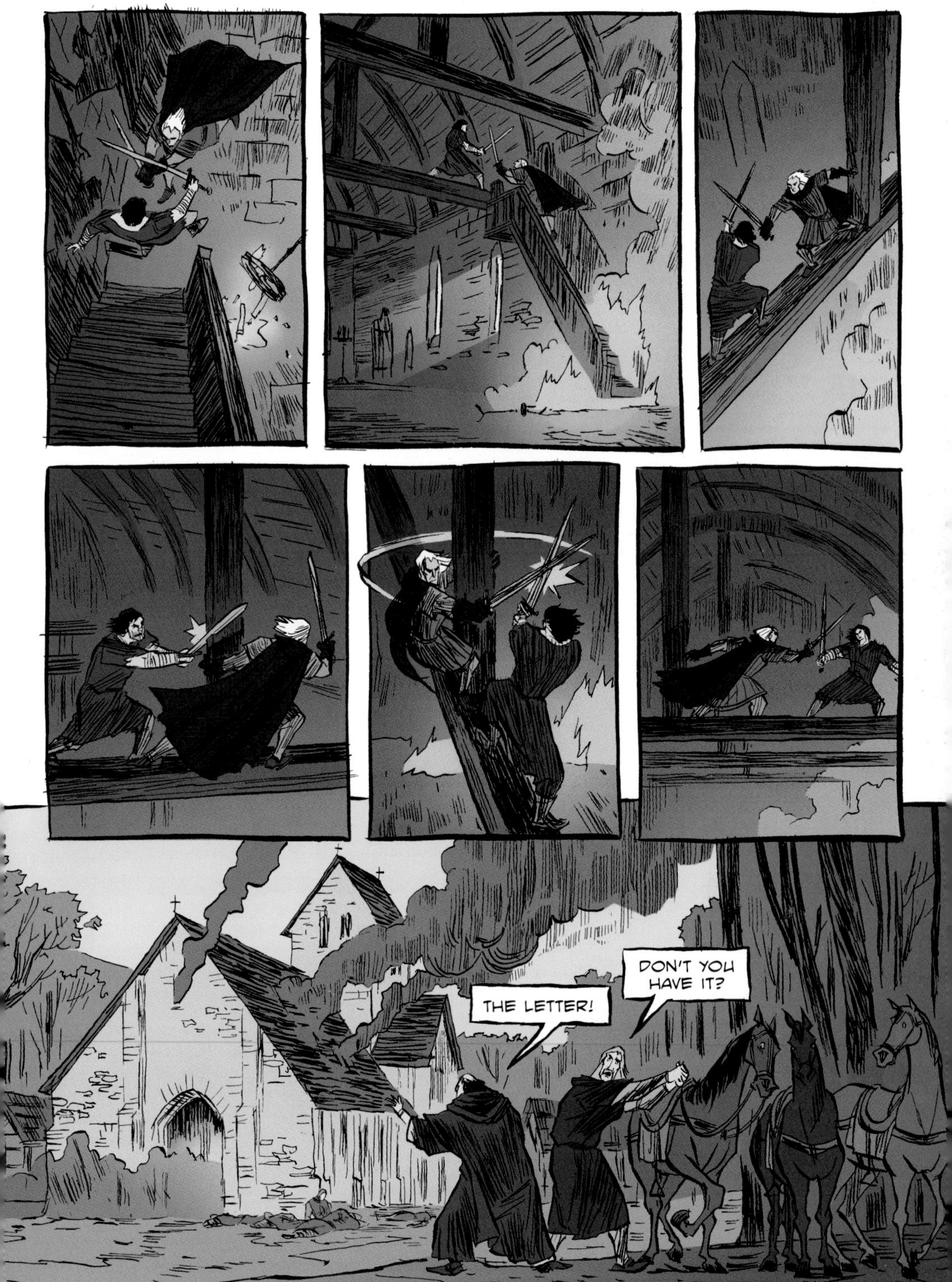
THE LETTER!
DON'T YOU HAVE IT?

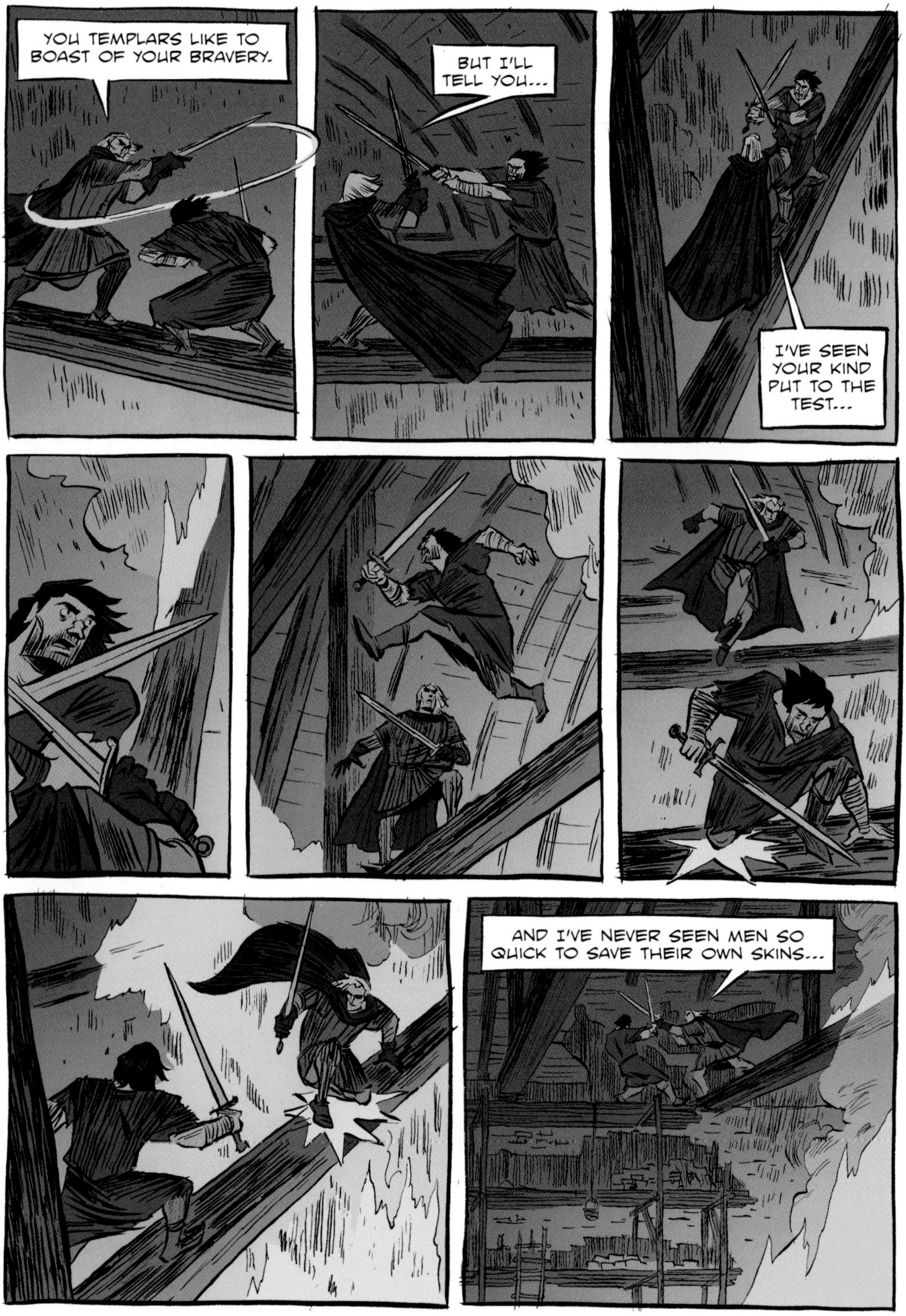
YOU TEMPLARS LIKE TO BOAST OF YOUR BRAVERY.
BUT I'LL TELL YOU...
I'VE SEEN YOUR KIND PUT TO THE TEST...
AND I'VE NEVER SEEN MEN SO QUICK TO SAVE THEIR OWN SKINS...

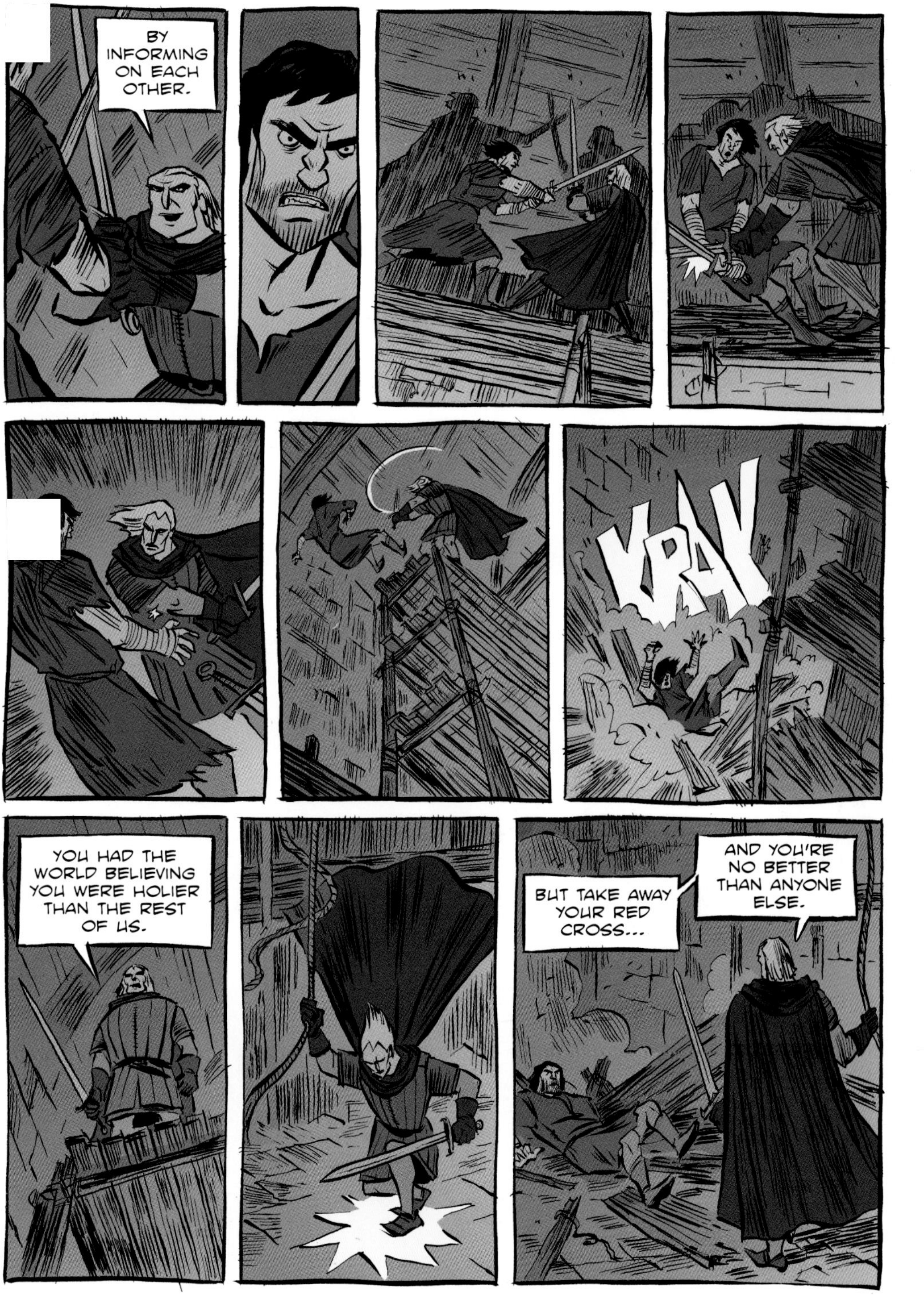
BY INFORMING ON EACH OTHER.
KRAK
YOU HAD THE WORLD BELIEVING YOU WERE HOLIER THAN THE REST OF US.
BUT TAKE AWAY YOUR RED CROSS...
AND YOU'RE NO BETTER THAN ANYONE ELSE.

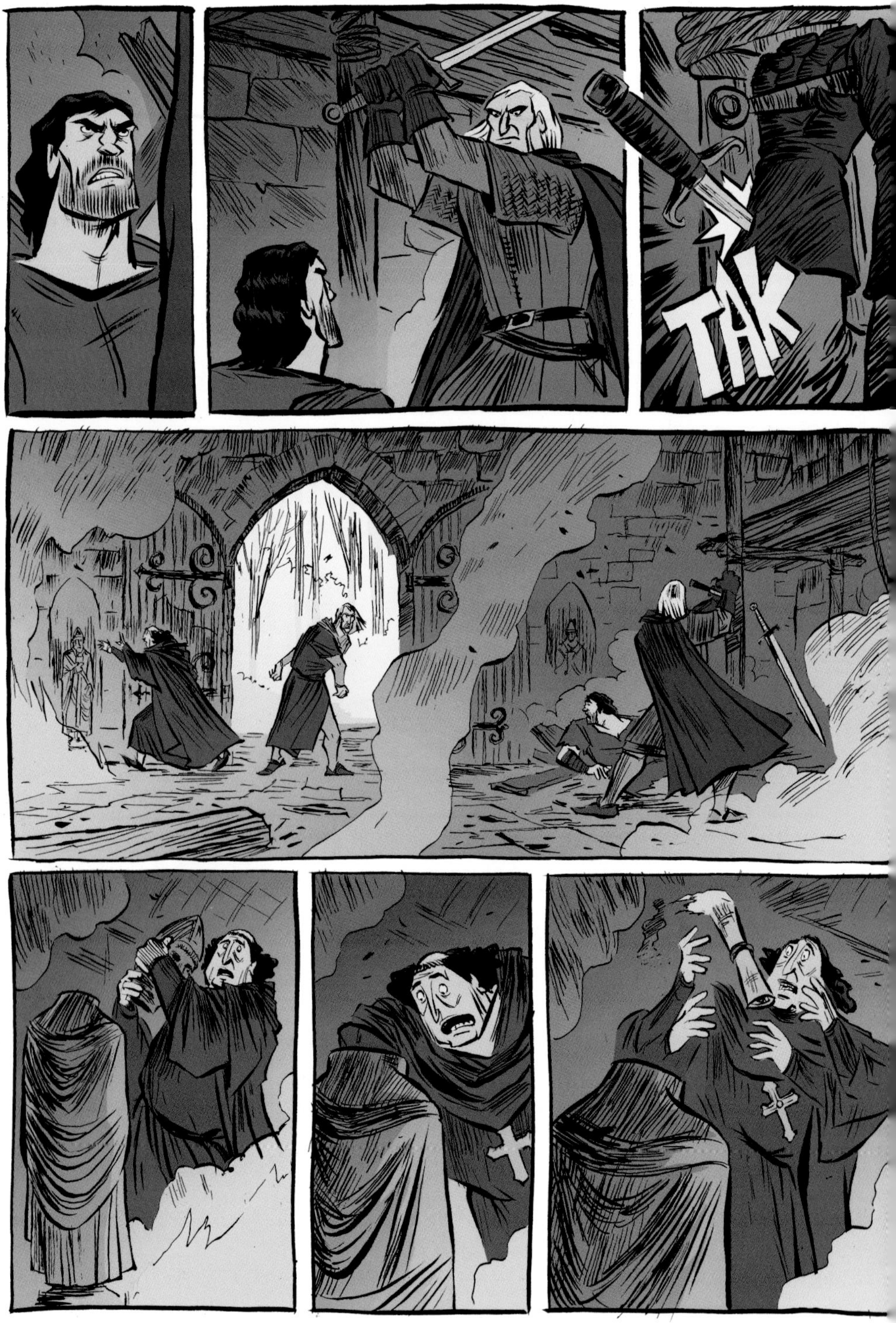
TAK

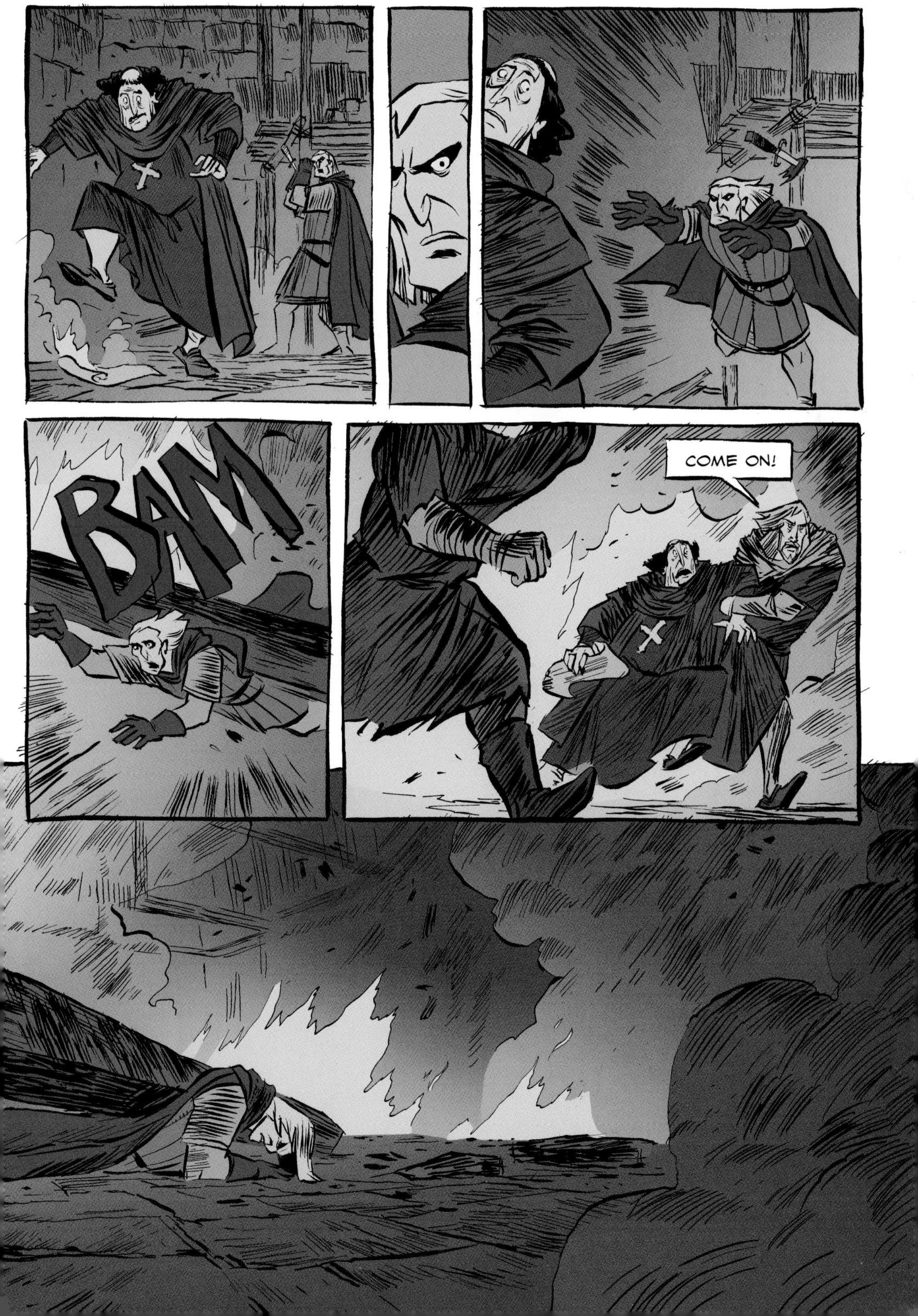
BAM
COME ON!

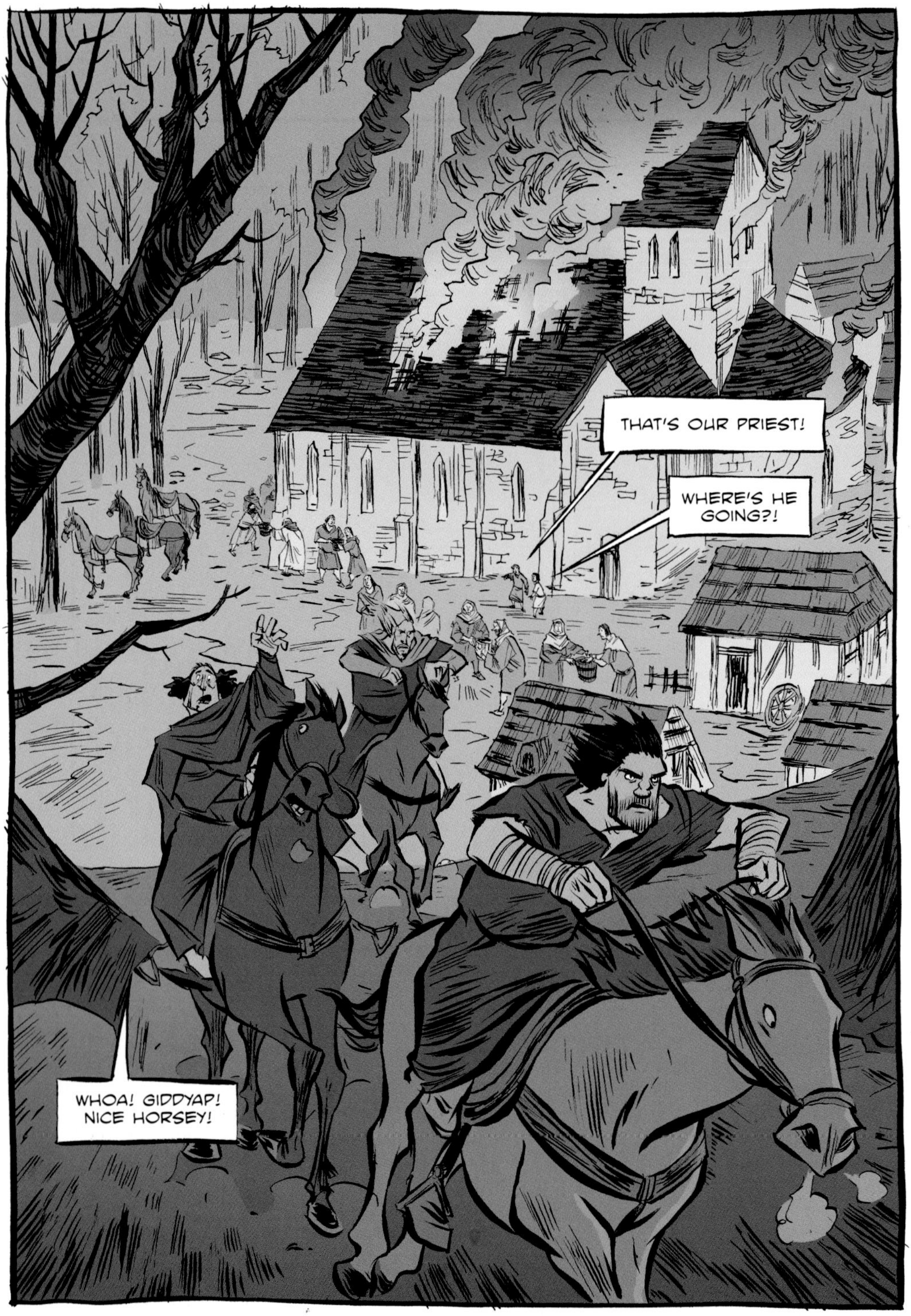
THAT'S OUR PRIEST!
WHERE'S HE GOING?!
WHOA! GIDDYAP! NICE HORSEY!

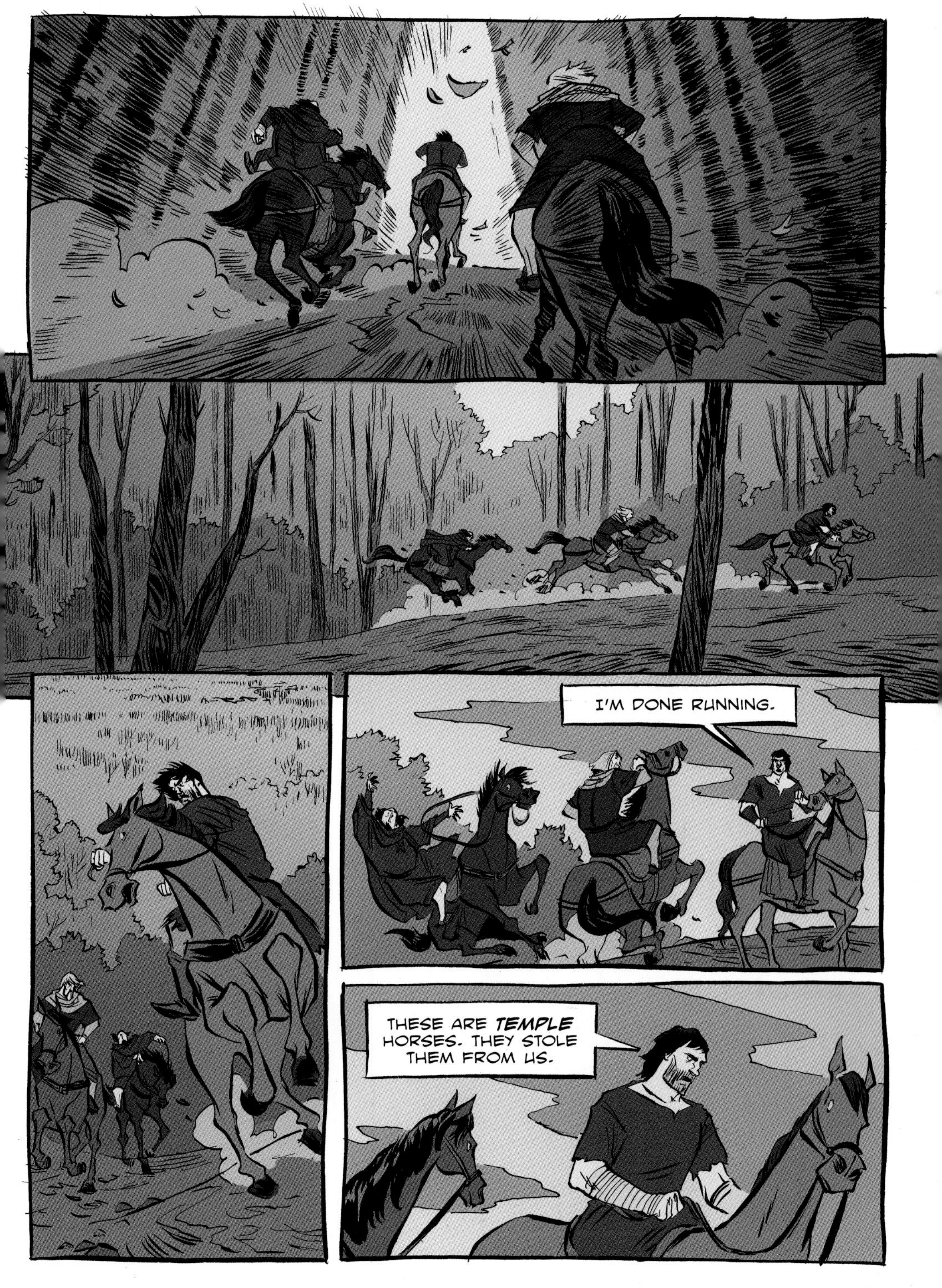
I'M DONE RUNNING.
THESE ARE *TEMPLE* HORSES. THEY STOLE THEM FROM US.

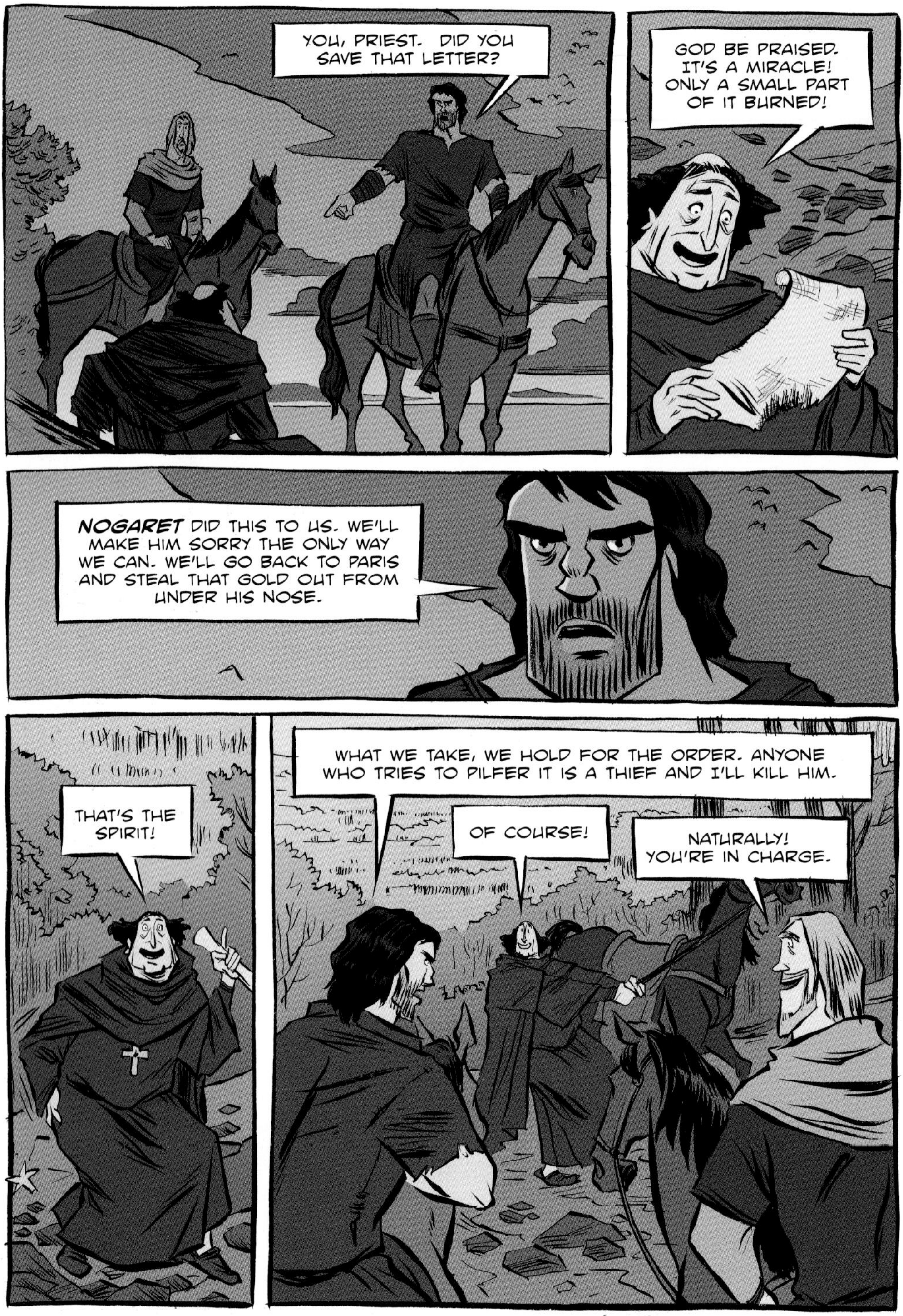
YOU, PRIEST. DID YOU SAVE THAT LETTER?
GOD BE PRAISED. IT'S A MIRACLE! ONLY A SMALL PART OF IT BURNED!
NOGARET DID THIS TO US. WE'LL MAKE HIM SORRY THE ONLY WAY WE CAN. WE'LL GO BACK TO PARIS AND STEAL THAT GOLD OUT FROM UNDER HIS NOSE.
THAT'S THE SPIRIT!
WHAT WE TAKE, WE HOLD FOR THE ORDER. ANYONE WHO TRIES TO PILFER IT IS A THIEF AND I'LL KILL HIM.
OF COURSE!
NATURALLY! YOU'RE IN CHARGE.

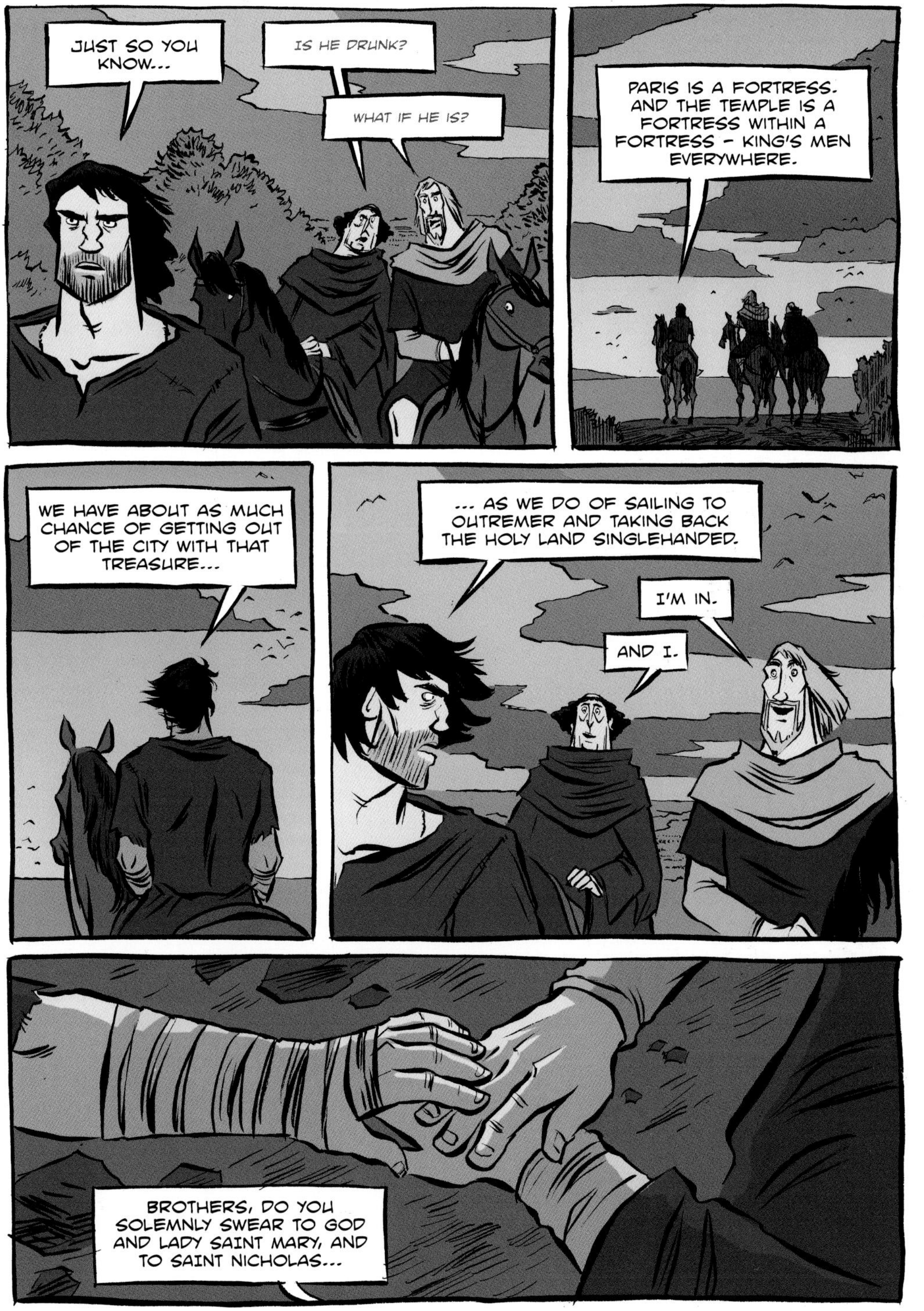

JUST SO YOU KNOW...
IS HE DRUNK?
WHAT IF HE IS?
PARIS IS A FORTRESS. AND THE TEMPLE IS A FORTRESS WITHIN A FORTRESS - KING'S MEN EVERYWHERE.
WE HAVE ABOUT AS MUCH CHANCE OF GETTING OUT OF THE CITY WITH THAT TREASURE...
... AS WE DO OF SAILING TO OUTREMER AND TAKING BACK THE HOLY LAND SINGLEHANDED.
I'M IN.
AND I.
BROTHERS, DO YOU SOLEMNLY SWEAR TO GOD AND LADY SAINT MARY, AND TO SAINT NICHOLAS...

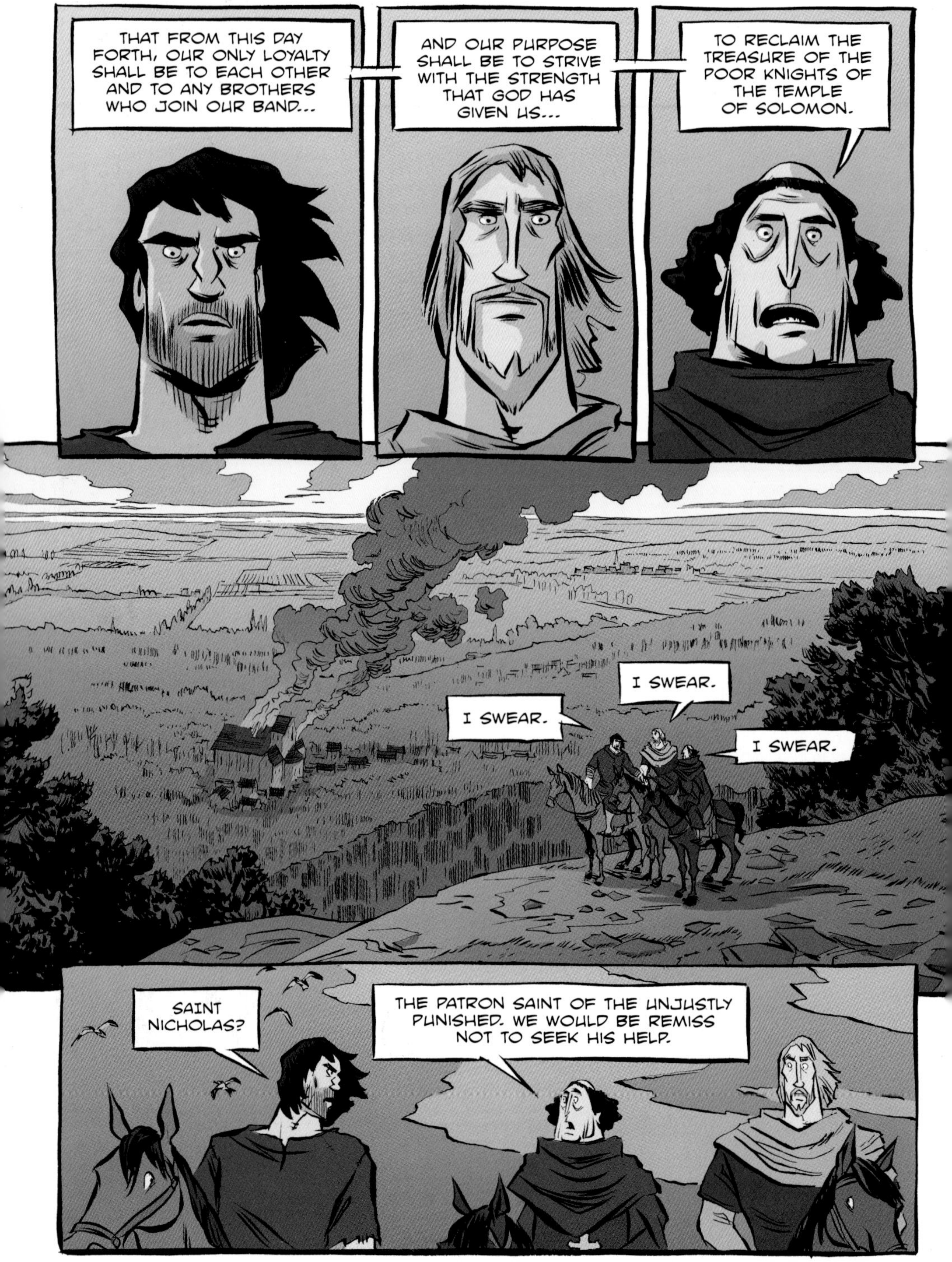
THAT FROM THIS DAY FORTH, OUR ONLY LOYALTY SHALL BE TO EACH OTHER AND TO ANY BROTHERS WHO JOIN OUR BAND...
AND OUR PURPOSE SHALL BE TO STRIVE WITH THE STRENGTH THAT GOD HAS GIVEN US...
TO RECLAIM THE TREASURE OF THE POOR KNIGHTS OF THE TEMPLE OF SOLOMON.
I SWEAR.
I SWEAR.
I SWEAR.
SAINT NICHOLAS?
THE PATRON SAINT OF THE UNJUSTLY PUNISHED. WE WOULD BE REMISS NOT TO SEEK HIS HELP.

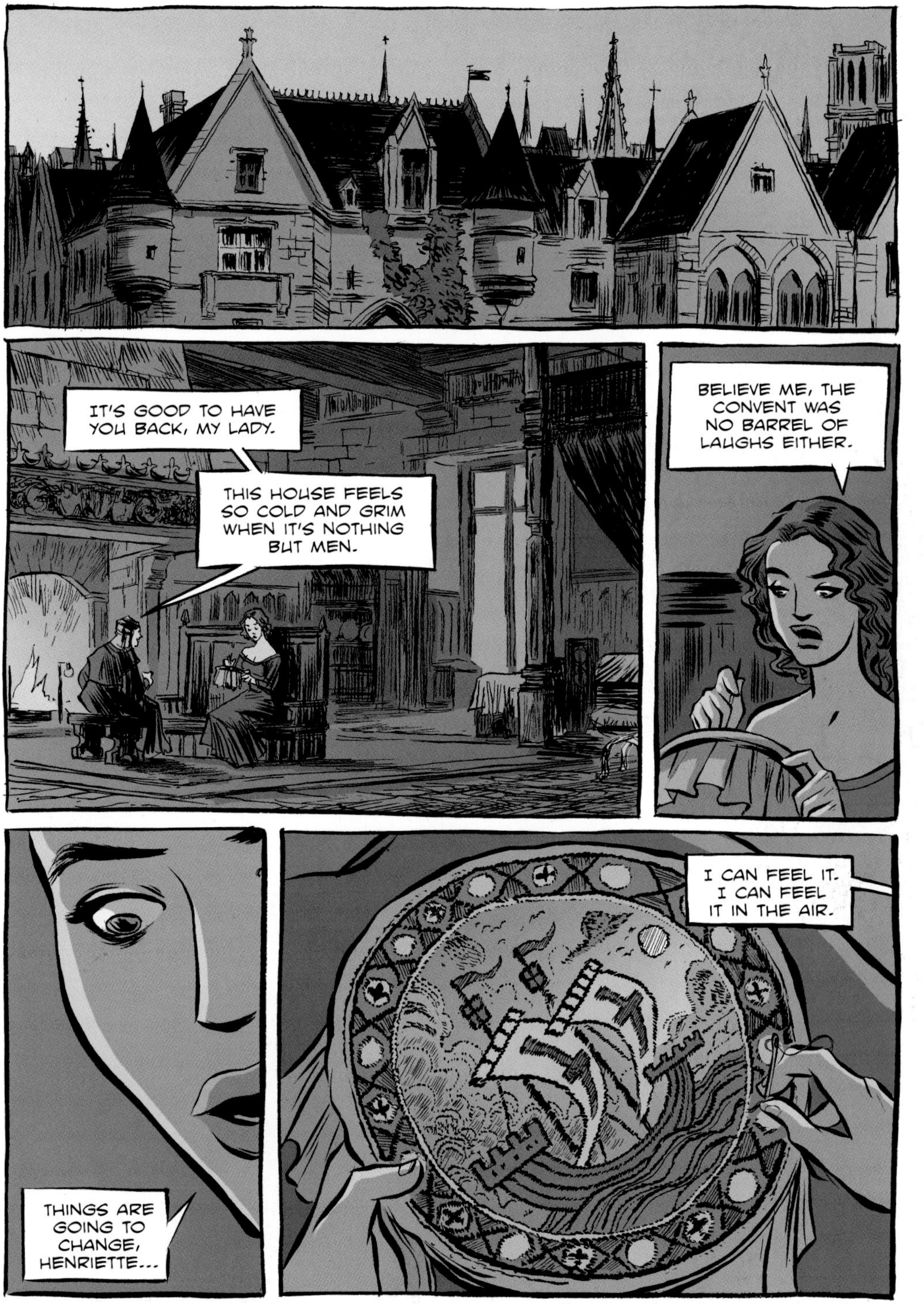
IT'S GOOD TO HAVE YOU BACK, MY LADY.
THIS HOUSE FEELS SO COLD AND GRIM WHEN IT'S NOTHING BUT MEN.
BELIEVE ME, THE CONVENT WAS NO BARREL OF LAUGHS EITHER.
THINGS ARE GOING TO CHANGE, HENRIETTE...
I CAN FEEL IT. I CAN FEEL IT IN THE AIR.

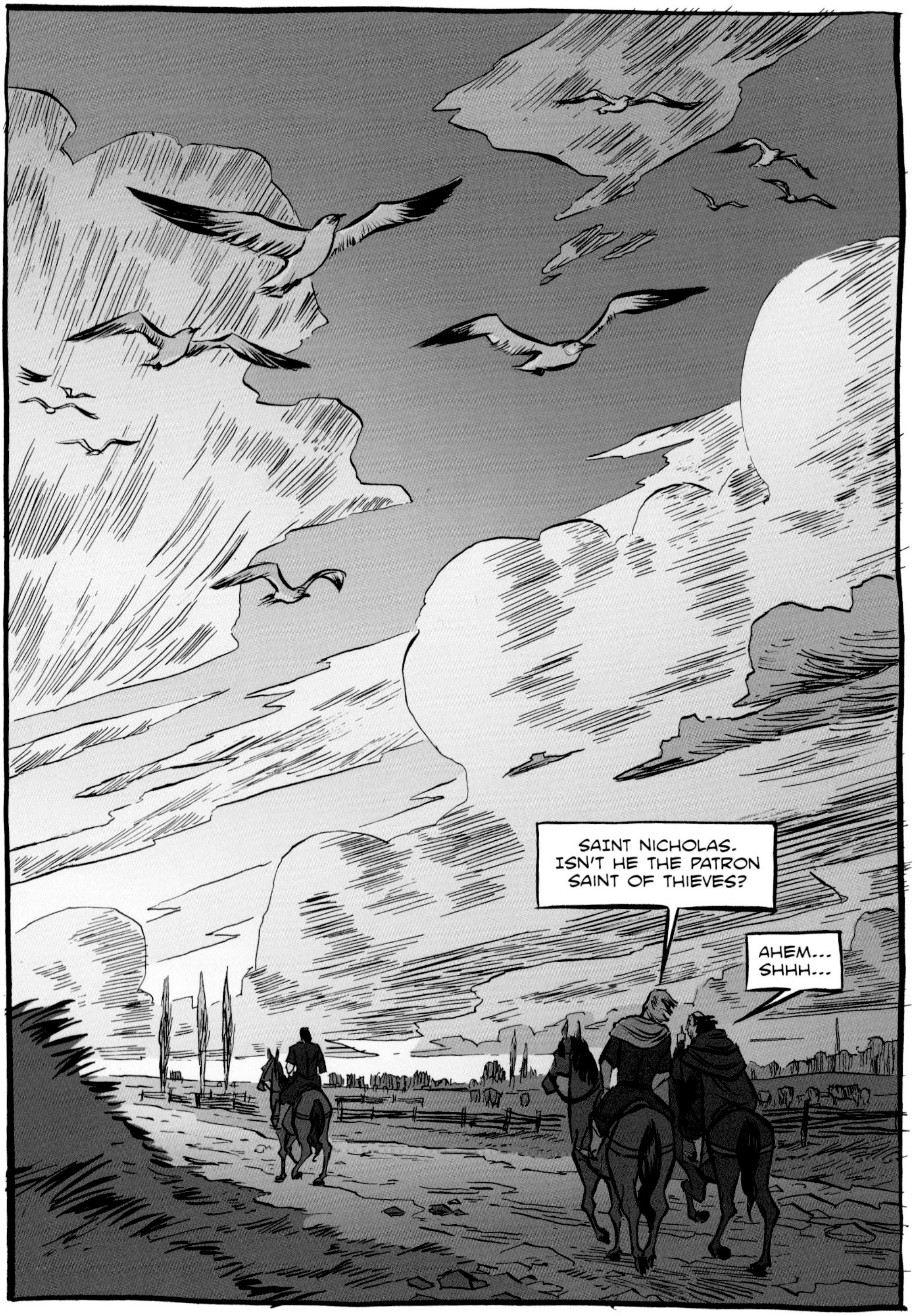
SAINT NICHOLAS. ISN'T HE THE PATRON SAINT OF THIEVES?
AHEM... SHHH...

END OF BOOK ONE

Afterword

by Jordan Mechner

A lunatic is easily recognized....
You can tell him by the liberties he takes
with common sense, by his flashes of
inspiration, and by the fact that sooner or
later he brings up the Templars.

— UMBERTO ECO,
FOUCAULT'S PENDULUM

ONE OF THE BEST THINGS ABOUT MAKING UP STORIES FOR A LIVING is that I get to read lots of cool books in the name of research. Sometimes the research turns up a story that's better than the one I'm writing.

I started reading up on the Knights Templar as background for a conspiracy-thriller screenplay it's probably just as well I never wrote. I lost heart after reading too many stories in which a clandestine society tracing its lineage back to the Templars guarded the Ark of the Covenant, Christ's bloodline, the Holy Grail, or other long-buried secret that would shake civilization to its foundations if, etc. I figured the world didn't need another one of those. (I was wrong, of course: The world still needed *The Da Vinci Code* and *National Treasure*.)

Out of all that historical and pseudo-historical research, what gripped my imagination more than any invented conspiracy theory was the real story of the spectacular rise and fall of the Knights of the Temple. Formed to protect pilgrims during the Crusades, the Templars gained fame as the noblest and bravest knights in Christendom. Like Western gunslingers or

Japanese samurai, their legend grew, and it attracted new recruits, donations, and privileges. By their peak in the thirteenth century, the Templars had grown into a religious, military, and banking organization whose assets, power, and reach rivaled any of the kings of Europe. They were the Jedi of their time. Their incredible downfall rocked the world. Its echoes reverberate to this day.

Here's what happened: Early one October dawn in 1307, the King of France ordered the simultaneous mass arrest of all Templars in his kingdom—15,000 of them, from the lowliest serving brother to the Grand Master himself. The Templars were hauled before the Inquisition and accused of witchcraft, heresy, sodomy— the most evil crimes in their world. It's as if the FBI were to raid the World Bank, confiscate its U.S. assets, and arrest every employee on charges of terrorism.

In the big picture, the arrests were a challenge by the King of France to the omnipotent Pope and Catholic Church, under whose protection the Templars had flourished. The king's chief minister, Nogaret, had shrewdly judged the tenor of the times. It was the first modern political show trial, prefiguring Stalin and McCarthy by more than six centuries. Prisoners who denied the charges were tortured, and those who didn't confess were burned at the stake. The Pope backed down, sacrificing his once-mighty Templars to ensure his own survival. The Order of the Temple was shattered, never to rise again.

The more I read about the trial, the more I sympathized with these Templars. Not so much the leaders like Jacques de Molay, but the rank and file—regular knights (and their support staff) who'd donated their worldly goods, taken vows of poverty and chastity, and gone off to the Crusades to fight for God. They'd spent years in a Middle Eastern war zone, risking their lives for what the Pope had told them was a just and holy cause, and came home to find themselves scapegoats—pawns in a political chess game their simple ideals of chivalry and brotherhood hadn't equipped them for.

I wanted to do a story about those guys—ordinary enlisted men who slipped through the cracks of history.

Passages like this one, in Malcolm Barber's *The Trial of the Templars*, intrigued me:

A small number of Templars did escape, twelve according to official sources, although there seem to have been at least twelve others; but only one of the escapees, Gerard de Villiers, Preceptor of France, was a figure of any importance... For some, like the knight Pierre de Boucle, the respite was only temporary; although he discarded the Order's mantle and shaved off his beard, he was still recognized and taken into custody. Two others, Jean de Chali and Pierre de Modies, who had made off together, were later apprehended in the striped clothes which they had adopted as a disguise.

I got the feeling it was the troublemakers, the ones with a slightly scoundrelly streak, who had a better chance of slipping through the net, while the morally blameless ones who followed the rules went dutifully like lambs to the slaughter.

Medieval society was particularly inhospitable to those on the fringes of society. Without a family, a trade, a legitimate means of support, you were by definition an outlaw. And here were guys who'd been out of civilian life for years, whose whole world was the monastery, the barracks, and the battlefield—thrown out into the cold, hunted by the kings' men. What would they do, how would they survive, in a city like Paris?

This speculation provided the spark for *Solomon's Thieves*. I wanted to weave an adventure yarn in the spirit of Alexandre Dumas, about a bunch of unlikely heroes whose main interests are fighting, gambling, drinking, and women (even though the last three are prohibited) and, caught in the backwash of history, have no one left to turn to but each other.

For readers curious to learn more about the Templars, here's a selected bibliography of books I found valuable in my research.

Pseudo-history and Fiction

I highly recommend Umberto Eco's novel *Foucault's Pendulum,* which not only precedes and supersedes *The Da Vinci Code, Holy Blood, Holy Grail,* and other Templar conspiracy-theory books, but brilliantly encompasses them. Aside from its sheer entertainment value as the conspiracy thriller to end all conspiracy thrillers, Foucault's *Pendulum* contains one of the best-written digests of the real Templar history to be found anywhere.

Templars

If you're looking for a pocket history, *The Knights Templar: The History and Myths of the Legendary Military Order,* by Sean Martin, is a quick read and packs a lot of good information.

For more in-depth, scholarly reading, these three general histories are excellent: *The New Knighthood: A History of the Order of the Temple,* by Malcolm Barber; *The Templars,* by Piers Paul Read; and *The Murdered Magicians: The Templars and their Myth,* by Peter Partner.

The dramatic saga of the Templar arrests and trial is well documented in *The Trial of the Templars,* by Malcolm Barber. Grounded in medieval legal documents and trial records, it's fascinating reading.

Knight Templar 1120–1312, by Helen Nicholson. Part of the Osprey Warrior series, this slim paperback is full of concrete details about the Templars' actual daily experience and mindset, both in the West and during military operations.

Knights and Crusades

The Templars were only one of many groups of Christian knights that went to the Middle East to fight in the Crusades—a series of wars and civil wars that lasted two centuries, and changed the medieval world (and ours) forever.

Of the many excellent books on the Crusades, one I especially like is *Chronicles of the Crusades,* edited by Elizabeth Hallam. It's vivid, epic, and beautifully illustrated, with excerpts from first-hand accounts on all sides.

Another is *The Crusades Through Arab Eyes,* by Amin Maalouf, a well-written, informative and gripping account of the crusades from start to finish, drawing from eyewitness accounts by Muslim chroniclers of the time.

Two very different books that reconstruct the life stories of individual knights: *William Marshal: The Flower of Chivalry,* by Georges Duby, and *The Last Duel,* by Eric Jager. Both provide fascinating insight into the chivalric mindset of the period, and are so well written that they read like novels.

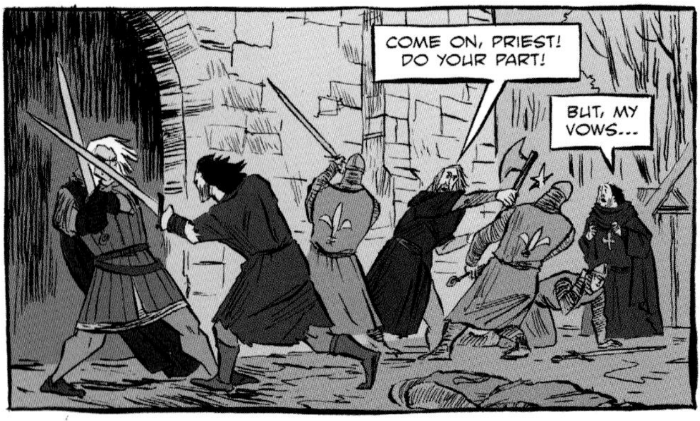
COME ON, PRIEST! DO YOUR PART!
BUT, MY VOWS...

Life in the Middle Ages

I found *Daily Life in Medieval Europe,* by Jeffrey Singman, to be an invaluable resource for writing a story set in medieval times.

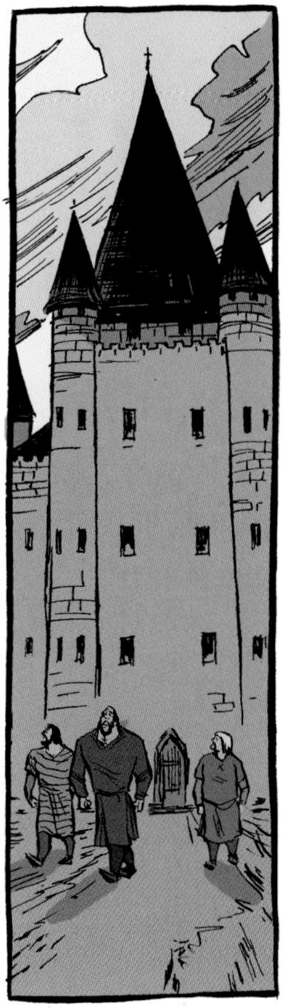

A Distant Mirror, by Barbara Tuchman, is all about the calamitous fourteenth century that was to come, right after the period of *Solomon's Thieves*. Wide-ranging, brilliant and highly readable, like all her books.

My very favorite medieval historian is Jacques Le Goff; he just "gets" the period, and manages to convey its essence, in a way all his own. His books explode a lot of clichés about the Middle Ages. If you read French, I especially recommend *A la recherche du Moyen Âge* and *Le Moyen Âge expliqué aux enfants*.

And if you ever need to find your way around medieval Paris, the indispensable book is *Atlas de Paris au Moyen Age* by Philippe Lorentz and Dany Sandron. Beautifully designed and printed, chock full of maps and architectural drawings, this is an extremely thorough and reliable resource that the artists and I went back to time and again.

Happy reading—and I hope you'll enjoy *Solomon's Thieves* as much as I've enjoyed these other books.

Los Angeles, April 2009

Bibliography

Barber, Malcolm. *The New Knighthood: A History of the Order of the Temple.* Cambridge and New York: Cambridge University Press, 1995.

____. *The Templars: Selected Sources.* Malcolm Barber, translator. Manchester (UK): University of Manchester Press, 2002.

____. *Trial of the Templars.* 2nd ed. Cambridge and New York: Cambridge University Press, 2006.

Duby, Georges. *William Marshal: The Flower of Chivalry.* New York: Pantheon, 1987.

Eco, Umberto, and William Weaver. *Foucault's Pendulum.* William Weaver, translator. Boston: Houghton Mifflin, 2007.

Hallam, Elizabeth M. *Chronicles of the Crusades.* New York: Weidenfeld and Nicolson, 1989.

Jager, Eric. *The Last Duel.* New York: Broadway Books, 2004.

Le Goff, Jacque. *À la recherché du Moyen-Âge.* Paris: Louis Audibert, 2003.

____. *Moyen Age explique aux enfants.*

Lorentz, Philippe, et al. *Atlas de Paris au Moyen-Âge.* Paris: Parigramme, 2006

Maalouf, Amin. *The Crusades Through Arab Eyes.* New York, Schocken Books, 1989.

Martin, Sean. *The Knights Templar: History and Myth of the Legendary Military Order.* New York: Thunder's Mouth Press, 2004.

Nicholson, Helen. *Knight Templar, 1120 - 1312.* Gloucestershire (UK): Sutton. 2004.

Partner, Peter. *Murdered Magicians: The Templars and Their Myth.* Oxford and New York: Oxford University Press, 1982.

Read, Piers Paul. *The Templars.* New York: Macmillan, 2000.

Singman, Jeffrey. *Daily Life in Medieval Europe.* Westport CT: Greenwood Publishers, 1999.

Tuchman, Barbara. *A Distant Mirror.* New York: Random House, 1979.

:01

First Second
New York & London

Text copyright © 2010 by Jordan Mechner
Illustrations copyright © 2010 by LeUyen Pham and Alex Puvilland
Published by First Second
First Second is an imprint of Roaring Brook Press,
a division of Holtzbrinck Publishing Holdings Limited Partnership
175 Fifth Avenue, New York, New York 10010

Distributed in Canada by H. B. Fenn and Company Ltd.
Distributed in the United Kingdom by Macmillan Children's Books,
a division of Pan Macmillan.

Cataloging-in-Publication Data is on file at the Library of Congress

ISBN: 978-1-59643-391-5

First Second books are available for special promotions and premiums.
For details, contact: Director of Special Markets, Holtzbrinck Publishers.

Book design by Danica Novgorodoff
Colored by Hilary Sycamore and Sky Blue Ink.

First Edition, May 2010
Printed in October 2009 in China by C&C Joint Printing Co., Shenzen, Guangdong Province
10 9 8 7 6 5 4 3 2 1